John Tana

John Tana

An Adventure Novel of Old Hawaii

BILL FERNANDEZ

Published by Makani Kai Media

ISBN-10: 1539315002
ISBN-13: 9781539315001
ISBN: 97899903262626

Library of Congress Control Number: 2016917720
CreateSpace Independent Publishing Platform
North Charleston, South Carolina

www.kauaibillfernandez.com

facebook: Bill Fernandez Hawaiian Author

A Kauai Made Approved Product

Read what reviewers say about Bill Fernandez:

Kirkus Reviews:

"Set in **19th-century Hawaii**, a historical novel stars a handsome young hero.

The story begins in **1867**, when **17-year-old** John Tana, an **orphan**, is thrown off his land by the **evil sugar baron Robert Grant**. John finds himself on the run, not only from Grant's henchmen, but also from the **vengeful Capt. Julius Shaw and the murderous crew of the whaler Jeremiah**. But friends and relatives abound, including his beautiful **cousin Leinani** (who in fact is not his cousin; it's complicated). He escapes to Maui with Shaw in hot but futile pursuit. When things get too dangerous, John and company eventually **flee to Honolulu (Oahu)**. Along the way, readers meet John's Aunt Malia, his cousin David, Ah Sam (John's close Chinese friend), and many, many others. This is all against a backdrop that has **Caucasians (**Americans**)** at the top of the heap, then the **native Hawaiians**, then the **Chinese**. (The Hawaiians themselves are divided between those of supposed royal blood and commoners like John.) The story **chronicles a hatefully racist time and place**, in which the Chinese, especially, live in fear of the next mob to bubble up. And don't forget **missionary Christianity** versus the native religion. John is adept at the **ancient Hawaiian martial art of lua**, which stands him in good stead as combat has become a crucial part of his daily survival. **Fernandez** (Cult of Ku, a Hawaiian Murder Mystery, 2016, etc.), a **native Hawaiian, is an authentic voice for John and the Pacific archipelago's turbulent history**. Plot twists come thick and fast, and there is always the seductive undercurrent of John's love for Leinani, a romance that at times seems doomed. The author expertly moves the plot along (through short chapters), and the **vivid and intriguing details of Hawaiian daily life** in the 19th century ring true. At times, John's virtue and especially his fighting prowess test the reader's credulity, but the striking ending is not tidy, a plus.

For the setting and era alone, this **ripping adventure yarn** offers sufficient rewards." (Emphasis added.)

***

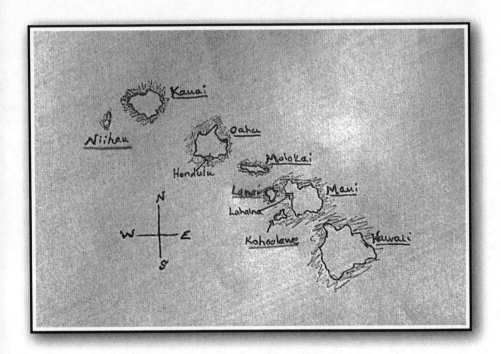

Dedication

I lovingly dedicate this book to

my wife,

Judith Fernandez

Acknowledgments

The Hawaiian ethic of family, *ohana*, means no one accomplishes alone. We are who we are today because of those who came before us and who are with us along our path of life. I particularly want to say *mahalo* (thank you) to my teachers, especially those at Kamehameha Schools who turned this barefoot boy into a serious student. Vernon Trimble, my sophomore class advisor, stands out in my memories as a strong influence on me, urging me to attend college.

My editor and friend, Bill Bernhardt, taught me about commas and tries to mold me into a good writer.

Many others have helped me in many ways, encouraging me to continue writing. Thanks to the Kauai Historical Society and Kauai Museum for honoring me by including my books in their publication sales and inviting me to give book talks. Bill Buley of the Garden Island Newspaper and his wife Marianne encourage me in many ways.

Without the support, encouragement, hard work of editing, publication, and promotion of my writings and book talks by my loving and devoted wife, Judith, I could not have written my books. All the credit for what I have written goes to her.

Note: Hawaiian words often have diacritical marks such as the okina (looks like an apostrophe) which affects the meaning and pronunciation. For ease of reading, I am not including the okina or other diacritical marks in the Hawaiian words.

One

Kahului, Maui 1867

John Tana heard the clashing of metal harness coming through the tall grass. He shivered as two horsemen burst from the shrubs and galloped to the edge of the stream bordering his land. The riders stood in their saddles, black silhouettes against the setting sun. John watched them cross his bamboo bridge, heard clopping feet on the wood like drums calling soldiers to war. With mounting anger he saw them stomp onto his tilled land, trampling his sweet potatoes.

One man seized a hoeing stick embedded in the ground near the destroyed plants. He leveled it like a lance and charged the naked orphan who stood by his grass shack. "Get out *kanaka*," he yelled. Both horsemen raced toward him. Alone, his family dead from the diseases destroying the Hawaiians, John resolved to be brave. He waited for the attackers to strike, his leg muscles tensed, ready to leap away.

With bull whips held high, the men reigned in twenty feet from the boy. The harsh grinding of metal and the tall animals rearing above him sent shafts of fear through John. The larger man thrust the long hoeing stick at him. "Didn't I tell you to get off this land, *kanaka-boy*? Your days here are over. Get out." The bully bent the digging tool until it cracked then flung the pieces at the brown-skinned youth.

John glared. His fists clenched. This is his home, the only one he had known for seventeen years of his life. But this supervisor from Grant Plantation is telling him to leave, walk away, as if the shack, the land, did not belong to him.

"I told you three days ago to get out. Didn't you hear me, you brown piece of shit. Get off this land!"

1

"I'm not leaving!" John shouted. An older man might have considered the fact that he was outnumbered and out-sized, but John was young, with no one to turn to for advice. What did he have to lose? "This land belongs to me. My family got it from King Kamehameha seventy-five years ago."

"Yeah, well the king's been dead for a long time." The supervisor sneered. "Grant and Company owns this land. That makes it private property. You go peacefully or we'll drag you out."

John remained silent. He did not understand the words: "private property." Land among his people had always been shared. He knew that the dead king's gift of land to his grandfather did not give him exclusive rights, but it did give him the authority to supervise and distribute what was grown on the land.

The man who came with the field supervisor slid from his horse, releasing the plaited lash that he held. He remained a good distance from John, and tapped the rawhide whip rhythmically against his palm. "*Kanaka-boy*, answer the man," he said, voice low.

John shifted his weight to his left foot. He saw the whip rise up. In one quick motion he unwound the braided sling from his forehead and inserted a stone into its pouch.

There came a menacing pause, a standoff between man and youth. John watched as the whip uncoiled, settling like a snake onto the ground. In the fading light, he kept his eyes on the man's legs, waiting for that moment just before power is unleashed, when the extremities tense. He saw it, the tightened muscles, the arm ready to strike.

John believed he could defend himself, unlike so many of the Chinese workers beaten by these men. He gripped his sling, prepared to hurl his rock when his enemy made his move.

The supervisor raised his hand. "Miguel, get back on your horse. We'll let the sheriff handle this." With that, he sat straighter in his saddle and flung a sheaf of papers at the boy. "You've been served. If you can't read them, ask the parson." The men chucked their horses and headed back toward Wailuku.

John watched them leave; saw their careless destruction of rows of his crops as they disappeared. He had a gnawing feeling in his stomach. With no family, who would advise him? He picked up the papers and read the top line: "Eviction Notice."

"Dad, why did you have to die?" he muttered, tears coming to his eyes. "Should I take these papers to the *kahuna*? Ask him what to do? Just like we did when I had a bad dream or got sick? Will prayers or poisons work against the white man's power?"

John shook his head. He studied the writing without understanding its words. He would decide in the morning where to seek help. Shivering with uncertainty he rolled himself into his blanket and fell into a troubled sleep.

Before the sun rose, John headed into Wailuku. He visited the shack of old Makula, but the kahuna shook his head. "Go see someone who understands the white man's words."

Frustrated, John went to the parsonage to see Reverend Zachariah, the man who had taught him to read and write. Zachariah was tall and gaunt, with worry lines etched into his high forehead. His mouth perpetually set into a tight, grim, line, but his eyes were kind. He sat behind his desk, and John took the chair facing him. When they were settled, there came an awkward pause. Finally, John blurted out a description of the visit and placed the papers on the desk.

Zachariah studied the documents for several minutes then removed his glasses. "These say that you're squatting on land owned by Grant and Company. They've demanded that you be evicted from the property. If you fail to leave," he added, punctuating each word with a flick of his glasses, "you'll be thrown in jail and charged with trespassing."

John stared at the man, eyes nearly round from fear. "Jail? What did I do?"

"It's not what you did, John, it's what your father failed to do." When John said nothing, the parson explained, "He was supposed to file a claim with the patent office in Honolulu."

These were words that meant nothing to him and he shook his head in confusion. "The king gave my family this land seventy-five years ago, it's mine."

Zachariah sighed and leaned back in his chair. "Times have changed. Now, we have law and order and the right to own private property. Our legislature passed a land division law providing a process to acquire a land patent. From what I see in these papers, your father failed to comply."

"But why didn't somebody tell him what to do?" John asked, his voice as much a plea as a demand.

"My dear boy," Zachariah said, "ignorance of the law has never been an excuse. The government doesn't have a duty to ask every citizen if he wants to make a claim. I'm sorry, but it was your father's responsibility. Judging from this eviction notice," he added, pressing the palm of his hand against the paper, "Grant and Company got the patent, instead of your father. John, they own the land."

Two

Minutes before sunrise, John heard the creak of wagons moving toward his farm. Oxen lowed in the cool air. Whips cracked and horses stomped the ground. John smiled. They would never get across the stream. A torch flared in his hand and he set the brand to the grass of his shack. He raced to the outer buildings and set them afire.

An angry voice yelled, "The bridge is busted. That damn kanaka destroyed our property. He is burning everything. Get him."

"Liar," John said. "My family built that bridge, these buildings. You bastards get nothing from me." He lit the last of his huts and stood in its flaming light for a moment. A shot slammed into the smoking wood. He dove for the ground then bent low and began a twisting run south toward the sand hills of Kahului. The flames reflected golden from his brown skin. Another bullet whined over his head.

As he entered a copse of coco trees, a fusillade of musket balls shredded bark. In the darkness behind him, John heard men cursing. Someone screamed, "When we catch that boy we will roast him in his own fire. Miguel, where the hell is that ford?"

Hidden by the small forest, John changed direction. He headed onto a path leading northeast to the sea. It was a trail he had used since childhood, and he ran on it unafraid. Behind him he heard horses thrashing through the water. He prayed that his ruse had deceived his enemies.

A pink glow spread over the horizon ending night's grip on the land. Many yards away a rider was outlined by the early light, his face turning from left to right searching the ground.

Fear gripped John. He bent low, dashing from cover to cover. At a gully, he sat on loose rocks, rolling with them to the bottom. With his fingers digging into dirt, he crawled up its other side.

John looked back and saw someone on a horse behind him. He dropped to the ground and lay still. Despair came over him. Had he been seen?

Brush rustled. A large animal snorted. The sound of hooves tramped the earth near John's hiding place. Panic made him tremble. His breath came fast. What to do? Run?

"Fear is the killer," his dead grandfather had said. "Control it when in trouble. Think of all you might do. Then choose what is best."

John's heart slowed its rapid pace. He would be caught if he rose. Remain still, and listen like a rabbit in the bush, he thought.

A whip flicked the shrubs. Its crack stabbed his ears making him shiver. He stifled his breath bringing his trembling body under control.

Again and again the rawhide struck the thickets nearby. With agonizing slowness the hissing sound moved away. With care he wormed his way through the ground cover until he heard the sea. His fingers dug into sand, and he chanced a glance behind him. Many yards away a man on a horse rode along the gully. The rider lashed his whip against the shrubs that grew near its edge as he moved beside it.

Prone, John pulled himself over the slope at the edge of the beach, and slid toward the ocean. The steep dip of the ground along which he plunged convinced him that he could not be seen. He stood and ran toward the crashing waves. A voice cried, "There goes that damn Hawaiian. Get him."

His lungs clamoring for air, John reached a canoe. He put his shoulder to its prow, pushed his feet deep into the sand, and shoved his eighteen-foot outrigger into the surf. A whip flicked on his shoulder, its iron tip scoring his flesh. Waves freed the boat from the clasp of the beach and pulled the craft into the sea.

A horse galloped at him, but shied away from the thundering surf. Its rider tried to control the rearing animal. John leaped into his vessel, seized a paddle, and pushed into the rising tide. A sting laced his back, the salt water burning his torn flesh.

"Damn you," the horseman yelled, urging his mount into the water. "I'll skin you alive."

With all his power, John paddled over a wave. A whiptail wrapped around his neck, drawing him back. John grabbed the braided leather. The momentum of the canoe, dipping into the back side of the cresting swell, jerked the whip from its master. John uncoiled the snaked rope, flinging it into the sea.

He plunged his paddle into the water and shoved his craft over another wave. As it rose onto its crest, John looked back. His attacker struggled in the surf. His horse wandered on the sand. With his clenched fist held high, the man yelled, "I'm going to get you kanaka-boy."

John's powerful strokes forced the canoe through the early morning swells. Waves swept past him into shallower water. They crashed onto the beach and flung their energy into a crest of bubbles that reached the shards of wood and debris fringing the shoreline like the jumbled pieces of an unstrung necklace. At this high water mark the enemy sat on his horse watching. Applying spurs to the animal, the Grant henchman rode along the shore.

John directed his canoe toward the deep blue slot between the islands of Molokai and Maui. The craft was common for its time, carved from a koa log with fore and aft sections made of tapered blocks of wood lashed to the center by fibers, sennits, strong enough to withstand the pounding surf. Today, it creaked with the stress of the tide, but John believed it would withstand the power of the ocean.

John glanced at the shore. The sand beach ended in a mound of stone. The morning light brushed away the darkness that mantled the fingers of hardened lava that flowed fan-like from Puu Kukui Mountain into the sea. The top of the dead volcano was hidden by a canopy of clouds painted golden by the rising sun. At the rocks the horseman had halted his shoreline pursuit. John prayed that the man would give up his stalking.

Pulling hard he sped alongside the wrinkles of basalt that plunged for miles into the sea. Once again he looked back. His adversary had disappeared.

A wave smashed into his canoe flinging him toward the hardened lava. He noticed the small Hawaiian flag at the top of his sail pole flapping wildly, its red, white, and blue stripes fluttering toward land. Gusts of wind roiled the ocean. Giant swells smashed into his craft, rolled past, and shattered in huge fountains of foam against the dark stones bordering the water.

John forced his paddle into the turbulence, angling his craft into the wind, and away from a shoreline engulfed by massive waves. An hour passed. His hands blistered. Bolts of pain shot through his arms and shoulders. He could not stop or else the waves would hurl his craft into the dead volcano. John despaired. He had made this trip around the north end of Maui before, but never alone. All who might have helped him were dead. Should he have left Kahului peacefully, giving his farm and all he possessed to Grant?

"No! I am not a dog who runs away when beaten. *Haoles* get nothing from me." But he knew his defiance had created his peril.

His small Hawaiian flag, a combination of the British and American colors, fluttered in a new direction. John raised his fiber sail. Gusts dashed his canoe over the swells and away from the rocks.

"Eeyah! Eeyah!" came the sharp cry of a Red-tailed Tropicbird soaring above the water. It roused John. "You are free, and I'm a prisoner of laws I don't understand," he called to it. The only response came from the waves crashing onto stones.

John's eighteen-foot craft sailed past the great volcano that had created the northern end of Maui, its massive cliffs hidden from the sun. They appeared to melt into a dark blue nothingness, as if great caves had been scooped out of the rock. The mountaintop had cleared of clouds. Only a few wisps of vapor lingered. Salt spray plumed upward from his prow, intermittently dousing John with brine. The ocean appeared particularly dark on this day, its texture almost molten.

Great danger existed as you rounded Maui. The southeast trade winds could sharpen, causing the ocean to rise up and fling your canoe far out into the Pacific.

Using all the tools of navigation he possessed, John cruised around the island's north end. The wind shifted and slammed into his sail, pushing his craft away from the land. John released his lanyard. His braided leaf mat flapped in the wind. He grabbed his paddle and pulled against the currents that thrust him out to sea.

His knuckles turned white. "Pull. Pull." he repeated, fighting the sweep of the ocean that threatened to swamp his vessel. With supreme effort, he forced his canoe back to Maui's northern shore. Waves caught his boat, pushing him.

Other wild swells crashed into his canoe, threatening to overturn it, but its out-rigger kept it steady. Propelled by his paddling he rounded the northwest end of the island

Dusk came. John approached Honolua Bay. He knew landing with the surf is more challenging than heading seaward. He watched the rhythm of the waves crashing onto the shore. When the pulse of the swells seemed optimal, he dug his paddle into the water and pulled. With the force of the Pacific behind him, he achieved wave speed, surfing past two rocks and into the quiet waters of the bay. John leaped into the shallows and dragged his canoe onto the sand.

He gathered dried wood, and started a fire. Retrieving a fish from his vessel, he scored it, added salt to the cut, and fried it on the hot coals. With raw limpets pried from the rocks, John sated his hunger.

He lay back onto a tapa cloth. Thousands of stars twinkled in the blue of a moonless night. In the darkness, he thought over his decision to burn and flee. What else could he do? Other than the kahuna and the minister he had no one to turn to in Wailuku.

John rolled himself into his blanket. "Tomorrow, Lahaina," he told the sky, then drifted into sleep.

Three

John woke with his back and neck flaming. He choked down water, munched a sweet potato, and headed south.

By late afternoon, he paddled into the roadstead of Lahaina, a town named by Hawaiians "blazing sun" for the heat that baked it most of the year. Huge wooden boats were anchored offshore, their mast posts sticking into the sky like dead fingers poking through spider webs.

John worked his way into the shallow anchorage, struggling to make sense of Reverend Zachariah's comments about private property. A malicious thought struck him, maybe he should have gotten a bundle of charms from Makula to bury in his land and poison the ground forever. John shrugged, it's too late now.

He pulled through the calm water. Its gentle surf made it a favorable resting place for whalers preparing to tackle the rigors of the Arctic Sea. In the growing darkness, he counted ten big ships anchored around him, with many canoes, longboats, and barges plying the waters.

Beyond the ships lay a two-story white house with groves of coconut trees growing to its side and behind it. In front were two women. "Aloha, come inside," they called. Their red garments billowed in the light breeze like flags on a mast. Leis surrounded their necks and flowers pushed out from behind their ears. Each had long hair flowing past well-rounded shoulders and down to tight-belted waistlines enhancing their breasts and hips.

John thought they were inviting him into their home and smiled. But they only laughed at him and instead embraced two sailors who walked into their arms. They entered the white house with the men. One of the women called back, "If you got money little boy come and try us."

"Money? For what?" John said.

His canoe bobbled in the wake of a longboat surging toward him. Its crew pulled hard at the oars, skimming the craft through the placid water.

"Make way," a man in a tricorn hat gestured for John to move.

"Prod that savage out of here," he yelled.

A sailor with a livid scar on his face flung a harpoon at John's canoe. The metal spear pierced a hole just below the upper rim of the wale, leaving John speechless with rage. Before he could muster a response, the sailor used his prod to heave the canoe aside. "Serves you right," the sailor said.

Water from the flashing oars showered John. The whalers laughed at his discomfort. With that, the vessel swept past, leaving the canoe rocking in its wake.

By the time John regained control the longboat slid onto the beach. The best he could do was thrust his paddle into the air and clench his fists, but doing so made him feel foolish. He wanted to go after them, but realized he would lose a fight with ten whalers.

These new experiences grated on him: the rudeness of the men, the demand for money by the women. John lay on his paddle bewildered by his welcome to Lahaina. His home land in Kahului was rural, friendly. Here in the big town things were different.

John decided not to make enemies. He came to find his aunt, the only living relative he knew of. Once with family he might be able to cope with this new world.

John paddled past grass shacks paralleling a long road fronting the water, its hole-pocked tributaries led up to dry hills. He steered nearer the shore, his canoe surged with each small wave. A shriek drew his eyes to a pathway. A small Asian with a long pigtail of hair sprouting from the center of his shaven head pulled a two-wheeled cart laden with goods. When the wheels struck potholes, metal rubbed together emitting a grinding sound.

"Do you know Malia Makanani?" John asked.

The man shook his head, his ponytail swinging like a metronome.

John asked again.

This time the man sang out, "No spik Inglis. China spik." And then pointed to the water and a canoe in which several Hawaiians paddled toward the shore.

John waited as the laughing crew drove their craft onto the beach, creating a sharp furrow in the sand.

"Aloha," John said, "Do you know Malia Makanani?

Four pair of dark eyes turned toward him. "Who wants to know?" the biggest of the men asked. "Why you want Makanani?"

"She's my aunt," John answered. "I came from Kahului to see her."

"Eh, you come from Kahului in that?" The man pointed at the canoe. "By yourself?"

John nodded.

"Eh, you some good sailor. What's your name?"

"John, John Tana."

As he grabbed his paddle, the man turned to the others. "I'll take our brother to Makanani." Three strides through the water and he wrestled himself into John's canoe. "My name's Kawika, Makanani family is my friend. Let's go."

The two men paddled along the shoreline. Throngs of sailors marched on the street. Honky-tonk saloons blared out raucous laughter and the occasional squeals of women.

"This place get lively since the American war ended," Kawika said.

"Sailors mean guys?" John asked.

"Yeah, in whaling times this is a rough town."

"How far to Malia's?"

"Maybe a mile, maybe less."

"Is it always noisy?"

"Nah, been quiet for long time. Big war in America over, lots of oil ships coming back."

"What about that white house at the end of the beach road?"

"The one with the red lantern?"

"I didn't see any lantern, but I saw two women taking sailors inside."

"That's a whorehouse."

"What's a whorehouse?"

Kawika smiled. "Where you been? Oh yeah, you from da sticks. Kid, you got a lot to learn. In this town, the loving is not free. You want it, you pay for it."

John pulled his paddle from the water, his mouth agape. "Pay money—for love?"

Kawika threw his head back and laughed. "Man, you don't know nothing. For those women, you pay."

"What about the whaler guys? They run around like they don't give a damn about anybody, like they own this town."

"When they got the numbers, my brother, they act like big shots." Kawika pushed his paddle deep into the water and pulled it backward with a violent heave. The force he generated caused John to correct their course by pushing his paddle just as hard. His muscles and bruised flesh cried out with the painful effort, but the sensation of keeping up with this powerful man exhilarated him. Once they were back on course, he told his companion about the man wearing the tricorn hat in the stern of the boat who acted as if he owned the sea. "Do you see the hole those bastards put in my canoe?"

Kawika glanced toward it and shrugged. "How many?"

"Ten, but I wasn't afraid of them. I would've taken them on, especially the guy with the harpoon. But in a new town my grandfather warned me to walk slow, know my enemy, and remember that there's always somebody tougher than me."

"Sounds like good advice. Let me tell you this: When there are as many sailors in town as there are today, don't mess with them. They can be mean."

John thought about this for a moment. "So how are the women in Lahaina?"

Kawika smiled. "You don't want women who wear red, so come with me and I'll fix you up with some nice girls, no charge." He directed the canoe toward the beach. Just beyond the shoreline, grass shacks and huts dotted the land. "Makanani family lives up ahead."

They pulled the canoe onto the sand. Satisfied that his craft was secure, John followed Kawika to a large shack set back several yards from the sea. In the darkness, his new friend called out, "Hey, David, Auntie Malia, I got your family here. John Tana's his name."

A voice from within the shack called back, "Come inside, no stand out there. Come eat, plenty food."

"No way, Auntie, I got to go home. But here's your cousin, or maybe your nephew, I don't know."

The big man said, "Good to meet you. Call any time you need help."

"Sure thing," John answered his face alight with friendship. "A big aloha to you."

Standing near the door of the shack, John heard a woman say, "Eh, Leinani, bring your cousin inside. Go, go right now."

When the girl came through the doorway, her youthful beauty made his body tingle. His nerves ablaze he followed her into the house.

Coconut oil lamps filled the shack with flickering light, the flames revealing ribs of hala logs and bamboo with pili grass overlaying the frame of the shelter. An older woman with stringy salt and pepper hair squatted on a floor mat. She offered her nose to John and they exchanged breath.

Malia held his hand, looking into his eyes, "John, last time I saw you was at my sister's funeral. You were only three years old. You are a big boy now. Why do you come here?"

John thought for a moment deciding to tell the truth, "I have no other place to go. Grant Plantation kicked me off my land. They said my father didn't get a land patent for the Kahului property we lived on and they did. So I have nothing, no home, no family."

"Ah, that is the way it is these days. The white folk take all the land saying it is theirs and push the Hawaiian out. And I know you lost your father just two months ago. You are welcome here. Go sit by David. Leinani, bring food, cousin must be hungry."

During the meal, John could not keep his eyes from the young girl. She was lovely, high cheekbones, sparkling hazel eyes, elegant nose, and heart-shaped lips.

As for her skin—oh, that skin—it had to be smooth to the touch, although he dared not touch it. A brown tapa cloth covered her shapely waist and hips, and the nipples on her rounded breasts peeked through her flowing hair.

John held his breath managing to conceal the tremor that ran through him. He thought of those many centuries when Hawaiian chiefs practiced mating with family members to keep their genealogy pure. Yet since the Christians had come to Hawaii he knew that it was forbidden to make love with family. Could the Makanani family be Christian?

As he munched on a banana, David said, "You say you have nothing. All you have is the loincloth around your waist?"

"There is the canoe of my grandfather, *lua* weapons, and a few personal things in it. The larger items and my animals are being brought here by Wong Sam."

"Lua? You mean you know lua, the outlawed fighting?"

"Grandfather and Father taught me."

David leaned close. "Can you teach me?"

John nodded. "But we must keep it a secret. I don't want trouble to come to our family."

With the meal finished, Malia said, "Go sleep, everybody. You boys outside, rest under the stars. John, tomorrow we get you some clothes. We are Christians in this house and we do not let people run around half naked and that includes you, Leinani."

The boys left the shack. Finding shelter under a lean-to John wrapped himself in his tapa blanket and contentment settled over him like a warm hand. He felt the pleasure that comes when one has been alone and then suddenly is not. Finally, he was with *ohana*, his family. Within minutes, John fell asleep.

Four

S unlight poked through the slats of the lean-to, and John turned from the glow of morning playing over his eyes. He heard David inside the shack prodding Leinani, "get some water."

He watched her leave the building throwing her brother a defiant look. "Since you got up so early, you get the water," she answered.

David yelled, "I have things to do before I go to work. Mama, make us something to eat."

John rose onto an elbow and tried not to stare at the young girl, an almost impossible task for a boy of seventeen. She was the most beautiful woman he had ever seen.

He called to David. "What are we doing today?"

Pulling a shirt over his shoulders David came from the shack saying, "Got to work for the white guy in town."

John stood. "I'll go with you and find Ah Sam."

The boys finished breakfast and set off for Lahaina. Dogs harassed them as they walked along a dirt pathway leading to a village filled with A-frames and lean-tos.

"Noisy curs," John said, watching that none came too close. "Not like my village, where everything's peaceful."

They passed through the village and came to a dirt road.

"Sacrifice Street," John said, "why is it called that?"

"It's because the sister of King Kamehameha III wouldn't marry him due to her Christian beliefs forbidding incest—the mating of blood relatives. She ran away, but loved him so much that her heart broke and she died. That is why they call the street 'Sacrifice.'"

They walked on a bit farther before John suddenly stopped. "Christian morality sure messes people up. Why can't the missionaries leave us alone? Our kings have been mating with their sisters for centuries, so what's wrong with making love to a relative?"

David thrust a finger into the young man's chest. "I'll tell you what's wrong. The children of the same family get sicker than other children and some are crazy. That's why Christians say 'no' to incest. That's why they condemn to hell anyone who does it."

John realized he must curb any feelings he had for Leinani. He feared that he might somehow betray this new family—and if he went the way of his ancestors, it would indeed be a betrayal. In several minutes, they entered the heart of Lahaina.

At Front Street David pointed. "Ah Sam's is ahead. If the door is locked, knock hard. He sleeps in back. See you after work, over there by that tree."

John watched his cousin enter a mercantile store and looked around him. He needed to pick up his belongings but he was not ready to seek out the man's shop. He found a rock wall, perched on it, and studied the ocean. Miles away he saw the grim shape of Lanai, shining red in the early sunlight. To the north Molokai loomed, shaped like a giant cleaver held fast by the ocean.

Low waves washed onto shore, sweeping the beach and scrubbing the sand a lustrous light yellow. John marveled at the transparency of seawater, clear as the early morning air. But as much as he willed his mind to be as clean as sand, sea, and air, it remained a jumble of words: private property, hired women, incest.

What's wrong with mating with a relative? Hawaiian religion permitted it. He had been with his father to the kahuna many times and the priest never discouraged free love. But Reverend Zachariah taught him Christianity and the evils of unmarried naked bodies pressed together.

Then there was this idea of private property. His father told him that land is a living thing, it could not be owned. Whatever it produced should be shared. But this ancient concept of sharing had been shattered by ruthless men and the law. What is this thing called law? John wondered if every seventeen-year-old took such a battering while growing up.

This internal battle he could not win alone. He needed help to learn more about this new world he found himself in. But where could he get the knowledge he needed to survive in a Christian dominated culture, to overcome the power of the sugar planter who had taken his home? With a sigh, John left the wall and searched for Ah Sam's store.

Golden light glimmered over the north Maui Mountains. No one walked on the roadway. The saloons stood shut. John spied a sign and rattled the door below it, but found it locked. He peered through the glass, searching for the shop-keeper. He recalled David's comment about the man living in back. He pounded on the wooden frame. An inner door opened and a Chinese shuffled toward him, fumbling with the buttons on a long silk garment.

"What you like?" the Asian grumbled from inside the shop.

"Are you Ah Sam?"

The man nodded,

"Your brother, Wong, has he come with my property? My name is John Tana."

"No come. No come. Go away," the Chinese said turning his back.

John knocked again. "Can I come in and buy something?"

Ah Sam paused, "You have Mexican gold, Yankee silver?"

"Plantation tokens."

"What one?"

"Grant Plantation."

"Come back one hour." Ah Sam snorted, then walked away.

Bright sunlight warmed John's face and flooded over the buildings on Front Street. What to do for an hour? Ugly thoughts that had troubled him earlier arrived in his mind. He decided to run along the street, the morning air still cool.

Shedding his garments he sprinted along the road. Within moments he came upon a snoring sailor lying in his vomit by the side of it. That's what Lahaina has become, John thought, a place for whoring and drunkenness. A wiry, dark-haired cur trotted up, sniffing at the recumbent man, his claws scratching around the body. He scolded the animal away. Striding towards them was an old heavily-bearded man who whistled at the dog.

"Good morning, grandfather. It is a beautiful day."

The old Hawaiian eyed John, then nodded, "It's a fine morning, but soon La will blaze full upon us and we will burn. Enjoy this place while it is still cool. Aloha."

John watched the man and his dog wend their way to the beach, then he ran towards the hills. He loped along, his work-toughened feet impervious to the sharp stones that lay loosely along his path. Soon he was into the high ground overlooking Lahaina. The land for miles was brown, covered over by tufts of scrubby weeds. Scattered outcroppings of dark rock poked through the flaxen growth, mute evidence of the great lava flows that built the island.

John paused, wiping sweat from his eyes. He gazed toward the distant mass of Molokai, looming sinister and forbidding in the mist of morning. He shivered as he recalled the whispers of frightened Hawaiians telling stories of those sick with the disease that melted flesh away. They were cast into the sea near an isolated peninsula on the far side of the island. Forced to swim ashore, the survivors lived as savages in a barren peninsula as their body parts slowly fell off.

South of the leper colony Lanai lay, a treeless hump of rock, the home of ghosts who "march in the night." Legends said that dead chiefs and kings inhabited the island. They would come in the darkness to walk the land seeking men's souls.

Though he could not see it, John visualized Kahoolawe, a pancake of hardened lava that could not sustain human life. The island was important to Hawaiian mariners. Its western end pointed the way to Tahiti. For centuries Polynesian sailors had come from the central Pacific navigating by the stars to Hawaii. When they wanted to return home they canoed to Kahoolawe, and followed its pointing tip to Tahiti, a journey of thirty days. Any other route would take months of ocean travel to their destination.

On his return, he found the business open. Bells tinkled when he entered, the store empty except for the owner, a slender, middle-aged man in flowing red pajamas. Ah Sam stood behind the counter reading a newspaper. He looked up, the dragon on the front of his gown staring fiercely. The beast's paws were outstretched, as if preparing to attack. "So you came back. What you like?"

"Have you heard from Wong Sam?"

"I told you before, he no come yet. Maybe tomorrow."

John felt suspicion building in his mind. "He's bringing my things from Kahului. You sure he hasn't come?"

Ah Sam placed the newspaper on the counter. "When my brother pick up your stuff?"

"I loaded his wagon three days ago."

"What's a matter you? You think Kahului around corner from Lahaina? Is long way, must pass big mountains. No worry, my brother be here soon. He not thief, I not thief. You think we steal from you?"

John chided himself for being abrupt. He fumbled for the right words and then thought of his grandfather's advice. "I'm sorry. Please excuse me for being rude."

The man's expression shifted from hostile to accepting. He pointed to the newspaper on the counter. "Nobody believes Chinese. Treat us like dirt. Look what paper says, we all bad. You never complain that Ah Sam not honest," he said, his voice more pleading than angry. "Honest is only thing I have that no one can take away."

John averted his gaze from the pain in the man's eyes. He shuffled his feet and felt ashamed of his insensitivity. "I will never doubt you again," he promised.

Ah Sam nodded. "It's okay, happen all time. Have some tea." The Chinese poured two cups of the steaming brew. Then he sighed, "Right now biggest trouble is, no business."

"There's a bunch of ships in the harbor."

"They no come my shop. Not like old days, when you have hundred, two hundred ships in bay, so many you walk from one boat to another, then to shore, without getting feet wet. Plenty business when I first open store."

"There can't be more than ten ships out there. What happened?"

Ah Sam drank slowly and appeared to relax, as if warming to the aroma, to the mildly narcotic taste of the caffeine. He poured another cup and drank most of it before speaking. "In America, a few years ago, they find oil in ground, then big war. Whaling ships stop coming. Big war over, maybe more ships come and business better."

John glanced out the window. "How about the other merchants, are they making money from those ships?"

"Don't know, but they blame Chinese if business is bad. White businessmen say we no good, sell too cheap. We live like rat. Spend no money, only sell cheap. Plantation people plenty angry with me. I come from China, five-year labor contract, but work too hard. After five years, I no sign new contract, so boss mad and want to cause big trouble. Look this paper!"

John turned the paper around and bent over to read.

COOLIES REFUSE TO WORK

The Hawaiian government and the Plantation owners have spent hundreds of thousands of dollars bringing Chinese workers to Hawaii. The plantation owners give them housing, food, water, medical care, and fair treatment. When labor contracts expire, Chinese workers refuse to re-sign labor contract. Instead they move into Honolulu or Lahaina, opening businesses that undercut other merchants. Worse, these Chinese merchants pursue Hawaiian women, thereby corrupting the morals of the Hawaiians. Robert Grant, prominent businessman in Honolulu said, "The government must pass new vagrancy laws compelling these wayward Chinese to return to plantation work for their own good."

"Newspaper all lies. Housing, food, recreation, fair treatment all lies. Hawaii law no protect Chinese. We work hard, long hours every week, every month, penalties and bad treatment. Five minutes late to work, penalty. No work fast, penalty."

"If you don't like plantation work, and you're having a hard time selling, why don't you go back to China?"

Ah Sam shook his head. "China more trouble for me. Plenty war. Foreign countries—Britain, France, Germany—send armies to beat up Chinese emperor because he won't let them sell opium. Millions of Chinese die from war, starvation. Many leave my province, Kwangtung, go all over world. I tell myself if I find good woman, I stay here, raise family." Having revealed this to a stranger, he smiled sheepishly.

The door swung open and loud voices interrupted by the pleasing overhead bells brought the conversation to a halt. Two sailors entered, one wearing a broad-brimmed black hat, a dark ribbon trailing from it, the other a tricorn, with a red cockade fixed above the upturned flap. Both men were in the basic sailor's garb of white blouse and dark pants. Tricorn stepped up to Ah Sam. "You run this place?"

When the shopkeeper nodded, the man announced, "I'm Shipmaster Jonathon Brown. I need supplies. I'm told you're the cheapest in town."

Ah Sam nodded again.

"Good, then give me hemp rope, fifty feet white, and 100 feet tarred. How about some ship's caulk, resin, mallets, and caulking irons? Also, a copper kettle, we sprang a leak on our last trip and dripped whale oil all over the deck." Having delivered his order, he cocked his head to one side and waited.

"I have what you need," Ah Sam said.

The man nodded again. "We could use some food, too. Do you have any pigs or cattle, maybe some limes or oranges?"

Before Ah Sam could speak, John jumped in. "Your brother's bringing some of my pigs in his wagon, and there's a cow tied behind it. They're for sale."

Master Brown looked at John Tana. "You work here, kanaka-boy? You're a pretty good-sized guy. Want to go to sea? Great work, lots of adventure."

Brown's companion guffawed, pressing his hand to his mouth as the shipmaster gave him a kick.

"Don't pay no 'tention to Swede, he's a little touched in the head. So how about it, young fellow?"

John stifled a hateful response. Yesterday it was the men in the long boat. Today it's this man calling him kanaka-boy. "No," John said, so firmly that he saw surprise in Brown's eyes. When the man called Swede squared his shoulders, John added, "No, thank you."

"Too bad, we could use a strapping fellow like you." Brown turned to Ah Sam. "When can you deliver the goods to my ship the *Thaddeus*?"

"I no have men to get goods to your ship."

Fearful that Ah Sam might lose a sale, John stepped in, "I got Hawaiian friends and we're meeting at lunch. We can haul the stuff over this afternoon, and then bring the animals as soon as they get here."

Brown grunted, turned to Ah Sam, and the two men were soon haggling over price. Meanwhile, Swede wandered about the store, fingering various items. John saw no reason to stay. "I'll see you later this afternoon."

For the first time since the two men met, Ah Sam smiled. "Maybe I give you good job."

John laughed. "I'll go for that, see you later."

Front Street was thronged with people baked by the midday sun. A few horses trotted past, their size and power forcing John off the road, their riders indifferent to his presence. Sailors walked the streets. From saloons came sounds of men playing cards or darts.

Kawika, the man who had brought John to Aunt Malia's, appeared from a glade of trees set in a grass-covered park. "Eh, Tana, come eat. Where you been? The poi almost gone."

He walked into the copse. Two other Hawaiian men sat by a mat covered with bowls of food. Kawika clapped John on the shoulder. "Good to see you, brother. This is Ian and Moki. Hey, you guys, meet John Tana from Kahului."

The men gave John appraising looks, but said nothing. Kawika held out a bowl. "Try this dried fish. Poi's over here, some yams. Caught an octopus, salted and boiled it. Whack, a meal."

John squatted at the mat. Moki refused to make room for him. He shifted to an open space. "I got us a job. It's hauling stuff from Ah Sam's store to a whaling ship."

"What's this?" Moki challenged. "You some big-shot guy from nowhere making jobs for us? You no care what we think?"

John looked at Moki in surprise, wondering if he had spoken without proper humility. "I'm sorry. I meant no offense. I'm just a small shot trying to learn." How many times had his grandfather warned him that youthful eagerness can sound arrogant. If he wanted something, show humility, make the other guy believe it's his idea. "Walk soft," the old man told him. "No make loud noise."

"You big body and no smarts, kid," Moki said, shooting John a harsh look.

John glanced sideways at Moki. He saw him sneering. This derision blew caution away. "Better than having no brains."

Moki clenched his fists. "You telling me I got no brains? Come on, let's go, I'll bust you up."

"Just eat," Ian said.

Kawika made a gesture for everyone to settle down. "Moki, cut it out. John came here for lunch as a friend, not to fight."

"What you think? I let some little kid push me around? No way! I bust him up real good." Moki lunged.

John lurched sideways. The older man grappled with air as he slid onto the mat, sending food in all directions.

Suddenly John felt alone. Two days in Lahaina and he created an enemy. He scolded himself. To make peace, he backed away, saying "No need to fight, It's no big deal."

"It's a big deal to me," Moki answered, swinging a wild punch.

John caught the man's fist and applied pressure to his wrist, forcing him to his knees. He saw pain and released his hold. "Let's stop before someone gets hurt."

Moki regained his footing and charged, sending John onto the beach.

"Look at them monkeys fighting among themselves," a sailor said. "Anyone got a banana for the monkeys?"

Other men on Front Street joined in, yelling, "Hey, you guys fight like babies, not like real men."

"Come on, you pansies, we'll show you how to fight," one of the whalers taunted. "Or are you kanakas too dumb to know how?"

John counted eight men.

"Let's get out of here," Kawika said. "Those guys are spoiling for trouble. You can bet they got a bunch of guys behind them, ready to beat up on Hawaiians."

"Don't want any trouble," Kawika called to the seamen. "We have to go to work, another time, maybe."

"Run, you damn Hawaiians," a whaler said. "Okay, guys, let's get the hell out of here."

Ian watched the men walk away. "Those swabbies were just waiting for us to make a move. They would've beat us, then blamed us for starting a fight."

Kawika put a hand on John's shoulder. He turned to Moki. "You guys make peace. Mo' better we stand together than fight each other."

John and Moki touched fists, but made no eye contact. John felt his grandfather's presence and said "Moki, I was stupid, I had no respect for you and my brothers. You keep my share of whatever we make today."

A sunlight of a smile filled with gleaming white teeth brightened Moki's face. "Eh, brother John, you one good guy, no big head."

Five

Robert Grant paced along his mahogany desk, his handsome face twisted into a scowl. He glanced out the office window at the carriage traffic clacking along Fort Street in Honolulu. He needed a moment to contain the anger rising within him. Not wise, he thought, to show an underling his emotions. But he could not contain his fury. He turned, clenched his fist, and pounded the leather covering of his work table.

"Would you mind explaining to me, Gonzalez, how a dozen men let a naked Hawaiian set fire to my property and then slip away?"

Opposite him, a burly Portuguese, his face crimson from too much sun or embarrassment, said, "Excuse me, sir, it's his buildings that he burned."

"Nonsense, that's only a technicality. The court hasn't ruled on our eviction complaint, but I know the judge will see it our way. That kid didn't file a claim to the property. I did. Whatever is on the land belongs to me. How could you let him burn everything?"

"We followed your instructions. Two days after I served him, we came in the dark to grab him."

"But he found a way to fool you. Maybe the kid's not so dumb. Maybe he might just show up in court. Maybe a judge might just buy into his claim that King Kamehameha gave the land to his family. You got to get rid of him. I need his land to build the biggest plantation on Maui. The American South is ruined by war. There's no competition from them in the sugar business. Where's that boy?"

"I had a fight with him on the beach. But the kid got away. He headed north around Maui. My guess, he's gone to Lahaina."

"How can you be sure of that? There are many places in the mountains to hide."

"Boss, I checked around in Wailuku. The kid has an aunt on the west side."

"Lahaina."

"Exactly."

Grant smiled. His hazel eyes widened. The stiffness in his body eased. He unclenched his fist, pointing a finger at Gonzalez's chest. "Then you take the next boat to Maui. Find that brat. Have the sheriff charge him with arson. See that he is put away in prison."

Grant looked at Gonzalez, his lips pursed in a straight line. He whispered, "Of course if he is killed avoiding apprehension, all the better."

"I'll do as you ask. Maybe to find him I need to post a reward for his capture."

"Five hundred dollars."

"I'd kill him for that kind of money."

"If you do the reward is yours. I want to teach these Hawaiians that they can't mess around with Grant Sugar Company."

Gonzalez took his newly bought Stetson hat from the table, folded it over his dark hair, the brim shadowing his face. Long sideburns flared down his cheeks. A handlebar moustache grew over his upper lip. With a nose flattened by one too many brawls, the barrel-chested cowboy looked like a man you did not want to meet in a narrow alley.

"Don't worry boss. Tana is a dead kid."

Grant watched his henchman leave. "I'm setting in motion a path to great wealth. Hawai'i is on the verge of riches. America is hungry for sugar and I will feed them."

He strode back to the window staring at the harbor a short distance away. Scores of ships filled the port of Honolulu. "Whaling will soon be dead. Pennsylvania oil will replace blubber. Fools who stick with fish will lose everything. It is sugar that will be king in these islands," he announced to the parade of people passing by.

Six

D avid and John exercised outside the family shack, rhythmically twisting and kicking. "Step to the side," John instructed. "Now turn, thrust one leg, and then the other." He stood back to watch his student. "Flare those arms, fists closed."

"Hey, Cousin, when are we going to knock each other down?" David complained, coming to a stop. "We've been going at this for a week and all we do is run, lift weights, dodge, side step, and block punches. I'm getting tired of this shit."

"I never told you lua training was easy. Babies learn to crawl before they walk, right?" He executed another twist-kick combination, his breath coming quickly, drops of perspiration flying off his hair, running down his neck. He knew that training in the fundamentals is essential to learning lua, a complicated martial art. "Patience, commitment, that's what you need. Once you know the basics, we'll do the hard stuff."

David squinted into the new day's light. "You do the basics, lua-man. Me, I need to eat and get to work." With a wave, he disappeared into the family shack.

John slowed his movements, allowing both his body and his frustration to cool down. He had promised to teach David, but he found it more difficult than enjoyable. His cousin wanted to learn how to break bones, not the spirituality of the art. John felt unwilling to train a bone breaker.

He used his shirt to dry his face and crawled into the home, where he found Leinani laying out yams, poi, dried fish, and breadfruit on a plate of ti leaves. She wore an ugly sack. It covered her from neck to toes. She often paused to scratch under the bag.

"What's a matter, you got fleas?" John laughed, reaching toward her with clawed fingers. "Let me help you."

Leinani rapped him across the hands with a switch of ti. "You want break-fast?" she challenged. When John backed away, still laughing, she added, "I don't need you to make my life any more miserable, Mr. Tana."

He enjoyed her snappish rejection, as if it were saved just for him. It excited him, but with his aunt in a corner watching, John knew better than to respond. Malia protected her daughter, demanding she cover her nudity. The girl complied, but whenever she could, Leinani pulled off the sack.

"Eat your food. Go to work," Malia scolded.

The verbal slap struck home. John stopped eying the girl, grabbed a handful of yams, and scooted out the door. David followed close behind.

He ran through the village, distancing himself from his cousin. Angry with him for his poor attitude toward lua training, but he was more annoyed with his aunt for her suspicions.

"Hey, wait. I want to tell you something," David yelled.

John stopped.

David came to his side gasping. It took him a moment to catch his breath. "I meant to tell you this sooner, but I forgot. I heard some men talking, and they're angry at Ah Sam for making those sales to the whalers. Someone even said something about running him out of town, so you better warn him that trouble's coming his way."

"Yeah, I expected it. Ah Sam is almost sold out. I don't know if that will make his competition happier."

David shook his head, "I don't think so. Yesterday my boss complained about 'that damn chink stealing his business, undercutting him left and right.' When I left, he swore he would throw Ah Sam in jail."

"He must've read the news article about the Chinese not extending their labor contracts with the sugar plantations. I've heard the talk about criminal charges if they don't go back."

"Yeah, there probably is a combination of reasons why my boss is upset. One thing is for sure, when somebody like Ah Sam makes a killing then the losers will want to get rid of him one way or another."

John mulled this over, unsure how to respond. He liked Ah Sam. He didn't want him harmed. But he knew that a lone Chinaman who competed with white merchants was asking for trouble.

In silence, the cousins continued into Lahaina. David took his leave at the general store where he worked. John went on to Ah Sam's. The usually taciturn Chinese smiled when John entered. "You have brought me good luck," he said.

John frowned, should he spoil the friendship that had developed between them? With a sigh he decided to relate what David had overheard. "I'm worried about your safety. My cousin says merchants are threatening to do bad things to you, especially because the whaling ships have returned."

Ah Sam looked away. "This on door when I open." He withdrew from a drawer a large piece of paper. Centered on the sheet was a skull with black eyes. Above the cartoon, someone had printed *Death to Chinks*. Under the skull a sword dripped blood.

John felt a frisson pass through him, as if he had been struck by an evil force.

"What do I do?" Ah Sam moaned. "I can't leave store, much work and money invested." He looked around the room, his eyes dulled by the fate that seemed inevitable. "Remember newspaper talk about Chinese doing bad things to Hawaiian women? I have Hawaiian woman, she having baby soon."

Ah Sam led John to a shack behind the store and introduced him to Lehua whose belly ballooned against her dress. John saw the love between them, how Ah Sam spoke to her and her responses. They exchanged a few words before the Chinese led John back to the store.

At the counter, John mustered his confidence. He might be young, but he knew danger when he saw it. "You can't stay here," he said, his voice taking on the timbre of an adult. "It's too risky, putting everyone in danger, including the baby."

After more discussion and soul-searching, Ah Sam agreed that it might be best to close and move in with a relative doing business in Honolulu. "But I can't go right away. Lehua's time is near." Then he added, "John, why don't you come to Honolulu? Plenty opportunity for Hawaiian. Learn many things."

While John helped Ah Sam pack he thought over what his friend said. Maybe Honolulu would be the place to go to learn about private property and the new culture brought to Hawai'i by Christians.

While the two men took a break, Kawika walked in. "John, on your way home check the bulletin board at the prison."

"What's there?"

"A wanted poster with a big reward."

"So?"

"I think your name's on it."

Worried, John finished his work, then rushed to the local maritime office to arrange shipment of goods. He booked space on the *Reuben*, a coastal schooner running freight services between the islands. He consigned the items to Ah Sam's uncle, in Honolulu. Finished with his tasks he headed home.

He changed his usual route from Sacrifice to Wainee Street a block to the north. John turned south heading for the massive lockup called Hale Paahao, house of criminals. His heart beat faster as he drew nearer. It had been built by convicts who used stones from an old fort at the harbor to construct the compound. When he first saw it with its massive iron entry gate and the windowless stone buildings inside, he vowed he would never be held in it.

As John approached the nine-foot-high rectangular walls surrounding the prison he speculated on what the poster might claim about him. Most people sent to the jail were guilty of adultery or had engaged in unmarried sex. Could his interest in Leinani be a cause for a complaint?

John ran his hands through his hair wondering what could be on the public poster board. As he strode along the long white wall, fear gripped him. He caught a glimpse of a familiar figure standing by the entry to the prison.

John slowed his pace. He watched the man. He recognized the broad shoulders, squared chest, and big hips. Should he challenge Grant's supervisor? The bully who had threatened him at his farm? No one else walked on the street. They were alone.

But what if his enemy had the law on his side? Indecision made John pause. The man at the poster reached to his side. He drew out a large knife. John saw him plunge the tip into the board, laugh, and say, "Grant must want you dead real bad."

Gonzalez admired his handiwork. Big red letters announced: "WANTED FOR ARSON". Below the words came the name, John Tana, followed by: "REWARD

$250 for information leading to his capture." A sketch of a face with his knife stuck into it completed the poster.

The Portuguese hadn't offered the five hundred dollars Grant promised. "Why give away all the money?" the supervisor muttered. "If I get help catching him, I'll pay the two-hundred-fifty dollars and keep the rest. If I nab him myself I earn the five hundred. Either way he's gone."

Gonzalez chuckled, thinking of how he had missed the kid three times when he shot at him in the firelight. Two weeks ago he cursed his bad aim. But today he felt good about his failure. Five hundred dollars is more pay than he would get in a year of work.

Grant's henchman looked at the poster. Satisfied, he turned toward Wainee Street.

Seven

John heard a voice calling, "Mr. Gonzalez, you wanted to talk to me?"

"Yes, I did sheriff."

He ducked behind some bushes by a side wall of the prison.

"You're offering a big reward for this man. What did he do?"

"He burnt barns, huts, and pens of my employer, Robert Grant."

"Where?"

"Kahului."

"Not in my jurisdiction. It's a problem for the sheriff in Wailuku."

"My employer, Mr. Grant, will pay you well if it becomes your problem."

"Your poster says arson, anyone injured or dead by the fire?"

"Yeah, one of my men."

"That's a major offense which I can handle. If you swear out an affidavit I'll make out a criminal complaint for his arrest."

"Much obliged sheriff. I'll do it. This Tana is a mighty mean fellow. He almost killed me trying to capture him. Take no chances. The reward is good, dead or alive."

"Well, we like to see justice done in Lahaina, but I'll keep what you say in mind."

The two men walked away. John pushed deeper into the bushes. What chance did he have to survive if he stayed in Lahaina? Maybe Ah Sam is right, move to Honolulu. Retreating further into the shelter of the shrubs, he waited. In a few minutes horse's hooves clopped on the pavement of Prison Street heading past its intersection with Wainee and moved into town.

He remained hidden until dark. When the stars came out he rushed to the poster, saw the wanted notice, and hastened home.

"You late," Malia complained on John's arrival.

"Sorry, I got held up at work. Ah Sam is packing to leave for Honolulu. He wants me to come with him."

"If you want to go, go."

"You should come too. I'm not too smart, but I can see that this place will die. The whaling business will be over soon. Fewer whales and oil is coming out of the ground in America. The family should think about moving to Honolulu. It's growing fast and there's plenty of work." Ashamed of what he had heard, John did not mention the reward poster.

The family sat quietly. John understood the pain of leaving one's home and said nothing while they considered his suggestion.

David spoke first. "John's right, Mama. In Honolulu, we can be with our family. Besides, I hear there are good schools, some just for girls."

John listened to his cousin and said nothing. He knew David and suspected that his interest in leaving had little to do with family or education. How many times had he pined for life in Waikiki, the little Honolulu enclave known for its nightlife and excitement? John felt tempted to point this out, but he knew that it would create a wedge between David and himself. He needed an ally to encourage the move.

Malia listened. When there was a lapse, she turned to her daughter. "How about you, Leinani, would you like to go?"

"Oh, Mama, no. All my friends are here, I couldn't leave."

With the issue unresolved, John left for Ah Sam's early the following day. He took a circuitous route avoiding the jail and the town. He arrived to find a front window broken and his friend shaking.

"What's up?" John asked.

Ah Sam jabbered wildly in Chinese, then said, "Look." In his hand he held a rock. A cord wound around the stone with a noose at one end strangling a yellow doll smeared red.

John stared at the warning. "You will die if you stay in Lahaina," he whispered.

He helped his friend board up the broken window and noticed how the man's hands trembled. With planks in place, they returned to the task of packing the store's merchandise, each item placed in a crate, everything breakable wrapped and protected.

In the afternoon they finished. The walls of the store bare of merchandise. When John prepared to leave, Ah Sam asked him to wait. "You do so much for me. I plead for one more favor. Lehua is afraid. Will you sleep in the store tonight?"

What a request John thought. He had serious trouble with the law, needed to convince Malia to leave or prepare to go without the family. But he saw his friend shaking. "I have to meet David. When we are done I'll be back."

He raced home by the way he had chosen in the morning. His cousin stood at the door of the shack. "Let's get packing."

They joined John's canoe to a second one that David had acquired, building a platform between them with a new red sail in the center. Leinani and Malia watched the boys working. John could see that while they understood that he and David wanted to leave, they were reluctant to go. "You're coming with us," he said, more as a question than a statement of fact.

"We'll tell you tomorrow," they promised, as if the next day would be better.

"If you don't," he threatened, "we'll leave without you."

It was almost midnight when John ran into town. He took an alley leading to the rear of the store. A terrified Ah Sam waited for him, wringing his hands. "Thank you for coming back."

He led John to a bed tucked away in a corner and bade him goodnight. John slept with an ear open for the subtle noises of entry, the whispers of evil men.

With first light, he dragged himself up and found Ah Sam in his home behind the store packing. At mid-morning, Wong Sam arrived from Wailuku with his wagon to help his brother. He said to John, "Big reward money for you, two-hundred-fifty dollah. Grant Company want you for arson. Posters all over Wailuku. No picture, but your name and description on it. Best thing, you should run away."

"Ayah," Ah Sam said. "You in trouble? You come with us to Honolulu."

John's heart sank. He knew he had to leave, the sooner the better. For the rest of the day he helped load Wong Sam's wagon and watched him travel to the beach where Kawika, Moki, and Joshua transferred the load out to the *Reuben*. By late afternoon, all that remained were items consigned to Wong Sam's store in Wailuku.

Worried, John said good-bye to Ah Sam and saw the man's eyes widen with fright. "I need to do some business at home. I'll be back later."

A great smile wreathed his friend's face.

He ran to the Makanani shack and found that David had fully rigged the sail of the double canoe and packed the center platform with goods. Malia stood nearby and watched her son work, something between displeasure and confusion on her face. "I'm still not sure," she told John.

"But Auntie, I have to leave Lahaina."

"Why must you go?" Leinani demanded. "Aren't you happy living with us?"

John choked, he did not want to say that he was a wanted criminal. "Let's eat," he answered.

Leinani moped, her expression sullen. She remained so throughout the evening meal. When she finished cleaning up, she left to visit a friend.

John felt anger for her unwillingness to recognize the danger that hovered over him. It's not her fault, he thought. She doesn't know.

He returned to Ah Sam's store, stumbling in the dark, arguing with himself. What would he do if Leinani and Malia refused to leave? Take them by force to Honolulu or leave them behind? The question tore at his young heart.

John helped Ah Sam with a few final chores then fell into bed. His sleep was troubled, filled with dreams of biblical characters Adam and Eve bringing sin into the world, the forbidden apple. He shook himself awake, thinking: could it be wrong to want Leinani? Drenched in sweat he willed his mind clear. He lay down, then the sound of splintering wood brought him upright. His lua training kicked in, and he rolled onto the floor, grabbing a club. A voice muttered, "It's too damn dark. Start over there, break up the place, then we'll get the Chinaman."

John slithered along the wood floor. In the dim glow of a half-moon, he made out a man wielding an axe. As he moved closer, he saw a second man with a sledgehammer. He pressed himself against the floorboards as the axe came down on the shelves. With the next blow of the blade, John rose with cat-like quickness and whipped his hand across the neck of the second man. A howl broke the air. The axe-wielder spun around. John sprang, driving a clenched fist full force into his stomach. The axe clattered to the floor as the man doubled over. He flailed his arms. John swung his club making contact with bone.

Moans filled the room. John saw a man stagger toward him. He knew that the chopping blow caused heavy pain in his attacker's neck and back. He pivoted on one foot, aiming the other directly at the knee cap. With a howl, his opponent dropped to the floor.

"Had enough?" John asked, looking from one trespasser to the other. "Or shall I finish you off?"

The men crawled toward the splintered door, one clutching his belly, the other his dislocated leg. John stood in the middle of the room, club in hand, and watched his assailants skulk away. Once out of sight his heart began to pound and his knees buckled. He rushed to the house behind the store, waking Ah Sam and his brother. Together, they assayed the damage. Little was said, but John felt certain they shared his thoughts: A tragedy had been averted. This family needed to flee or they would not survive.

Eight

Captain Julius Shaw paced his cabin on the *Jeremiah*. A year that started with a promise of good whaling had turned into a nightmare. What colossal losses he had suffered in the Arctic Sea. A sharp knock on the door forced him from his introspection. He settled in his chair and called, "Who is it?"

"Permission to enter, Captain."

"Enter."

A well-built seaman stepped into the cabin.

"What is it, Mattoon?" Shaw's voice rang surly, still gripped by his recent tragedy.

"I have to tell you, Sir, that the men are talking. I don't think they're ready for mutiny, but they are grousing about no lay."

The captain pounded his fist against his desk. "How can I give them lay when we have no prizes to sell? You know what happened in the Arctic Sea. The biggest whale I have ever seen destroyed our long boat, several men drowned in the freezing ocean, and we have two in hospital with frostbite."

"Sir, I know what happened, but our men have been gone from home for almost a year. Maybe a little money and shore leave will pacify them." The mate leered. "Women and whiskey always does some good."

Shaw waved him away with "A month's wages and shore leave for all, except for you and two men of your choosing. Return to me within an hour for an assignment."

"Yes, Sir," Mattoon replied with a laugh. "That's three dollars for all. Silver, Captain, or Hawaiian script?"

"Silver, now go."

Mattoon returned within the hour with Lazarus and Will, well-muscled, men. In Will's face, however, Shaw saw more delicate features with clear eyes that reflected someone of more than ordinary intelligence.

Lazarus had a disfigured nose and a scar along his right cheek, evidence of too many barroom brawls. With his large frame, Shaw had no doubts that he had won more than his share of fights.

Mattoon stepped up to his leader. "Captain, I gave the news to the men and they are drawing straws to see who goes first. Two will stay on board to secure the ship; eighteen will go ashore. I'll have one of the men check on Roberto and Allard and see how they are coming along with their gangrene."

That revelation caused a sense of dread to run through Shaw. He had lost four men at sea to the whale. Roberto and Allard were lucky to be alive, but their digits and limbs, too long in the icy water, might be lost.

Shaw studied the three before him. When he spoke, he drew out his words to emphasize them. "We are two men short, with two others disabled. Though we can work this ship with twenty-five, it's not enough. Heavy whaling is ahead of us 'til the end of the year and I want some kanakas."

"But, Sir," Mattoon protested. "We don't have silver to put up the return bond for kanakas. That's four hundred dollars. Do you have that much silver?"

Reaching into a drawer, Shaw retrieved a small bottle. "Here is my four hundred in silver. A drop or two in whiskey and—"

Mattoon let out a coarse laugh. "Out like a light and the pigeon is in our hands."

"A double share of lay for each of you, if you get the men I need. How it's done is up to you: mickey, belaying pins, just get me two kanakas."

The three men saluted and walked out.

Nine

John finished cleaning the mess made by the nighttime intruders. He had helped install a double lock on the front door and also the one into Ah Sam's small home in back, and reinforced the windows out front with extra slats. Satisfied with his cleanup, he said to Ah Sam, "David's coming here to meet me. There is work we have to finish on our canoe before it is ready to sail. I think whoever is trying to hurt you has learned a lesson and won't trouble you again."

David walked in. John said, "Malia and Leinani ready to leave?"

"I convinced Mom, but Leinani, I don't know."

"A decision must be made tonight. We can't wait any longer."

"You didn't tell us about the wanted poster," David said in an accusatorial tone.

"I didn't want to tell you my troubles, besides Ah Sam must escape this place."

"Two-hundred-fifty dollars is more money than I'll see in a lifetime," David said a smile on his face.

"You give away your family for money?" Ah Sam interrupted.

"Nah, just wanted to say how valuable my cousin is."

"Time to go, we will head out the back way."

"I want to go down Front Street, maybe have one last drink before we leave town."

"Somebody might recognize me."

"Wear this hat. Pull it low around your ears," Ah Sam said.

Evening had come with cool breezes defeating the heat left by the sun that had descended beyond the red earth of Lanai. John hugged the sides of the stores on Front Street, David behind him. Ahead there were three whalers leaning against the entrance of the *Seaman's Bar*. One asked: "Did you have a good time?" A second man with a scar on his face yelled, "Hell no, Mattoon. Maybe Will had a good time, but mine was just a kid, must've been her first time. She kept yelling 'hurt, hurt.' I slapped her around to get her to do it. But all she did was yell 'hurt, hurt.' I whacked the broad real hard and left without paying."

John paused for a moment wondering whether he should continue or find an alley to duck into. He heard the man called Mattoon say, "Maybe you shouldn't a done that, beating the whore and all that. Malama might get pissed off for your bruising one of her girls and not paying. She is one hefty madam. Could probably roll right over you and never feel a bump!"

Then John saw one of the men pointing toward Ah Sam's store. The man named Mattoon said, "Let's go make friends with those guys." He eased himself away from the doorway.

David passed John. One of the three men stuck out his hand, "Hello, young fellow, my name is Mattoon. Us'ns, we been talking about how we wanted to meet some Hawaiians. We're new to Lahaina and want to learn about the town and its people. Can we buy you a drink?"

David grinned, "Sure would like to. Can my cousin have one too?"

The three sailors exchanged quick glances. "Yes," the men said in a unified chorus.

"John, come and meet these guys."

He didn't like the look of these men. Why were they so anxious to be friendly, especially to Hawaiians? John moved out of the shadows and approached David and the strangers.

"Hey," David burst out. "These nice guys want to buy us some drinks."

The first mate moved aggressively toward John, extending his huge paw of a hand. "Name's Mattoon, young fella. This here is Will and the other man is Lazarus. Just met your good-looking friend here. We're new to this port and would like to learn more about the place. Buy you some whiskey inside?"

John ran his fingers through his hair. The man standing behind Mattoon looked like the sailor who had speared his boat. "Don't want to put you guys out," he replied.

"You're not putting us out," Mattoon said.

"Yeah, come and join us inside," Will chimed in, his pleasant features and attitude marred by thin, pursed lips.

David nodded toward the bar. "Come on, Cousin, let's go inside." Without waiting for John's response, he marched into the *Seaman's Bar*, Lazarus's hairy arm draped over his shoulder.

John followed them in, but he felt like an animal being lured into a trap. Were these men after the reward money? The jovial look on Mattoon's face caused him to be suspicious.

From the second story of the Pioneer Inn, Gonzalez watched the five men on Front Street. His search for John Tana had not paid off. But what he saw beyond him stirred memories of events that occurred weeks before. A broad-brimmed hat concealed the features of one of the men, but his physique appeared similar to the boy he pursued.

He watched the group enter the *Seaman's Bar*. "Maybe I should get ready," Gonzalez muttered. He reached for his long knife, took out a hone, sliding it across the blade. While he worked he wondered what to do? If his quarry drank in the bar with friends he couldn't go in and grab him.

"Best to be ready," he said. He sheathed his knife, took his whip, and headed downstairs to saddle his horse. He decided to keep a watch on the saloon and see what the night might bring.

Ten

Mattoon rushed past Will and Lazarus, directing the men to a corner table. He indicated two chairs for David and John, leaving both men seated with their back to the wall. Will, Lazarus, and Mattoon sat facing them. John's sense of entrapment increased as he saw the semi-circle of sailors hemming him in.

"I'll get us some drinks," Mattoon offered. "Whiskey?" He looked at David first.

"Yes," David said and turned to John. "Seems like a swell guy."

"Never drank alcohol."

"Always a first time," Mattoon answered.

"Grog for us," Will and Lazarus said. They knew rum and water is the cheapest drink in the saloon.

John watched Mattoon sidle to the bar, while at the same time aware of how the others were engaging them in small talk. When David mentioned something about land, the sailors turned to John.

"So you lost your land?" Will asked. "That's too bad. Why don't you try whaling?" Without waiting for an answer, he continued, "Whaling is great. Lots of good food, adventure, an easy life on board ship, and the sleeping quarters are first rate." Had he been honest, he would have mentioned the hot, stale, and putrid air below decks, how the hammocks swung to a never-ending beat of waves. How the timber creaked during the night, mixing with the noise of rats chasing cockroaches and the insects making scratchy sounds as they scuttled away.

John watched the bartender pour the grog and whiskey. He saw Mattoon sheltering the amber filled glasses and with his left hand pouring something into them.

"The places you go, the people you meet, the ports you visit, nothing like it," Will summed up his sales pitch.

Mattoon carried the whiskey to the table, a toothy grin on his face. The bartender followed with three pints of grog.

"Damn Frisco's the best," Lazarus swore. "Finest cat houses in the world. And the women, long blond hair, lush red lips, gorgeous bodies." He cupped both hands around his breasts, leering at David.

Mattoon placed the amber glasses before the two young men. "Sam, give my men the grog." With his rum and water in his hand he said, "Drink up."

David downed his whiskey in one gulp, asking for more. John sipped his, choked, spat it out, and stood.

With a crash the swinging doors of the bar blew open and a buxom Hawaiian woman rushed in, her bare feet slapping the floor. The flowers in her hair behind her ears and circling her neck flew around the room like sparklers on a New Year's Eve. She rushed to Lazarus shrieking, "Why you no pay Pua? Why you beat her up?"

"That lousy piece of—"

"Okay, okay," Mattoon soothed. "He's sorry Malama. I'll come tomorrow to pay."

Her anger cooling, the dusky woman said, "Okay, you come tomorrow, pay for his fun, pay for doctor."

Malama looked at John. "You are the boy in the canoe. I have been watching you. Come see me. Maybe free?" She embraced him. Her lips brushed his cheek, nibbled his ear. She whispered, "Come outside."

With a laugh, Malama pushed John away. "See you tomorrow."

She said to a smirking Matoon, "Bring the boy with you." With her breasts pushing out from her tight blouse she swiped them by Mattoon's face and walked out.

"That's a hot one," Mattoon said, watching the woman leave.

"I must go to the bathroom," John groaned holding his stomach.

"What's a matter, can't take a little drink?" Lazarus sneered.

Rubbing his belly as his answer, John grabbed his whiskey and walked to the bartender. He squatted, pointing at his buttocks.

"That way," Sam gestured with his thumb.

John exited the rear door of the bar. On his right was the outhouse. On his left grew a banana grove. Just beyond them, a white fence and house. He recalled an alley to Front Street. He placed his whiskey glass on the ground and shoved his way into the trees, their broad leaves dripping sticky milk on his hands and body. Dead tubers clutched at his feet. He slipped on one of them. After struggling for a few moments with a rubbery jungle, he found the alley and took it to Front Street. He spied Malama waiting for him.

"Eh, you the guy who yelled 'damn it' a few days ago. I recognize you when I see you in bar. Eh, no talk loud, just whisper," Malama cautioned.

John moved closer.

"Pua tell me the ugly guy beat her and brag 'We goin' drug some kanakas, take 'em on our ship, they never coming back.' So you watch out, you're with some bad men."

"Thank you," John said. "Why are you helping us?"

"These sailors are evil, they hurt Pua real bad. If they get you tonight, they leave tomorrow. Besides," she added, eyes shining, "you some good-looking guy. Come see me."

John looked into her eyes and saw a wicked hunger.

The two separated and he returned to the back door of the bar, dumped the contents of his glass, and entered the saloon. He saw David sprawled over the table. The three whalers huddled in conversation. John knew they didn't stand a chance of escaping while inside the saloon. Get outside, he told himself. On the beach, there would be opportunities.

Mattoon turned. John cupped the empty glass, raised it to his lips, made gulping sounds, banged it on the bar, walked back to the table, and fell into his chair.

"You okay, big fella?" Mattoon asked.

"I don't know. That's my first drink. I feel unsteady."

"You'll get over it, breathe deep."

"I'm trying, but the room is rocking."

"You finished that shot real good. Just like a pro. Maybe a little too fast."

John swayed, seeing the three men smile. He didn't want to roll over too soon. He let his arms drop, his face bent to the side. He slid off the chair and under the table.

"We got 'em," Mattoon laughed. "I'll grab the small one, you two pick up the big guy and we'll head for the boat."

No one in the saloon paid attention to three sailors holding onto two limp men. Nor would anyone come to the aid of drunks being dragged from a saloon. Whaler's law ruled the town.

When the group reached the sea, Mattoon flung David against a beached long boat. Will and Lazarus struggled with John, as they dragged him through the sand.

"Drop that kanaka and help me with this one," Mattoon ordered. Lazarus obeyed instantly, releasing John and striding towards the boat. Will was slow in letting John fall. A delay that proved fatal.

John pulled Will to his chest with his right bicep crooked around the sailor's neck. He thrust an open palm into Will's face, crushing his nose with a cracking sound. John restrained the force of his blow, understanding that such an impact could push bone into the brain. He wanted to escape, not be charged with murder. With a head butt, he released Will from his arm lock.

Feebly the sailor swung a fist at John's face. He ducked and slammed a left hook into his opponent's stomach followed by a knee into his groin. Staggered by the blows, Will fell to the sand blood flowing from his nose.

Lazarus turned, yelling, "You dirty kanaka. Get ready to visit hell." He aimed a vicious punch forgetting that he wasn't facing an opponent befuddled by booze.

John's head was clear. His body and mind well trained, thanks to combat skills refreshed from practice with David.

Moving inside his opponent, John blocked the onrushing punch. With the fingers of his hand pointing tight, he jabbed a powerful openhanded blow into Lazarus's abdomen, driving his arm deep into the belly.

Lazarus's gasped as air gushed from his mouth. John head-butted the grizzled seaman who went to the ground, struggling to breathe.

Mattoon dropped David against the gunwale. The unconscious boy rolled from it onto the beach. Two men lay on the sand, one trying to stem blood gushing from his nose, the other kicking his legs as he fought to fill his lungs.

John stood silent. He stared at Mattoon, his eyes saying he wanted this man's soul for the evil he had done. Mattoon trembled. He reached into the long boat and retrieved a belaying pin. He faced John. Through clenched teeth he said, "You filthy bastard. You sucked us in by playing possum. You're gonna wish you'd never been born, kanaka-boy."

John's body relaxed, his fists unclenched. "If you're smart, you'll get in your boat and go."

"I don't walk away from a fight," Mattoon announced, now armed with both a knife and club. "You have nothing, so who's giving the orders?"

When John didn't respond, he added, "Kanaka-boy, you're about to get a whipping that'll turn your body into raw flesh. The ocean will become red with your blood." Mattoon began to circle, raising his weapons into fighting positions.

John watched the whaler move. He thought of his grandfather, who always counseled patience. "Let the opponent come to you. Use his own energy to defeat him." In the lua temple, John had spent hours in meditative thought, gaining *mana*, cleansing himself of anger, hostility, and emotions. John trusted himself, knew that his body and mind were at peace. Being relaxed would be his best weapon.

"Scared, brown boy? Your mother's a whore; your father's a queer just like you." Mattoon taunted, waving the club and knife.

John watched the man's face, watched his feet.

As if tiring of this unproductive baiting, Mattoon made his move. With a roar, the whaler stepped forward. He feinted to the head with the belaying pin. And then, in a blur of practiced movement stemming from years of experience, he lunged at John's belly with the knife.

John recognized how his attacker's foot movements betrayed his intent. He knew the man's cry was intended to frighten him. Make him run. With a deft sidestep, he blocked the thrusting knife with one hand and used the other to aim an uppercut to Mattoon's neck, landing it directly between his chin and Adam's apple.

Mattoon staggered back, choking. He dropped the belaying pin. He reached for his throat. The hand holding the knife wavered like a leaf in the wind.

Nearby, heaving great gasps, Lazarus attempted to regain his footing. John clasped his hands together and smashed them into the back of the man's neck. The seaman sprawled to the sand, unconscious.

A huge coughing spell rumbled in Mattoon's throat. He moved his head back and forth, as if searching for his opponent.

John moved low. He snatched up the belaying pin, and swung it into the knife hand of his enemy.

Shaking from the pain of the blow, Mattoon tried to plunge the sharp iron into John's body. But the Hawaiian grasped the slow moving arm of his enemy, twisted it, forcing the struggling sailor to the sand. He slammed the pin against the side of the seaman's head followed by a crushing blow to his neck.

Mattoon attempted to stand. John swung a punch with all the force his body could muster into the seaman's belly. He watched with satisfaction as the bully draped onto the sand. The knife slipped from his hand. John grabbed it and thrust it into his belt.

Will stumbled toward John making a clumsy attempt to tackle him. Side-stepping, John tripped the injured sailor and flung him into Mattoon. Both men flattened out with neither attempting to rise.

With the kidnappers immobilized, John rushed to David. "Get up. We have to get out of here before someone comes!" David did not answer.

John lifted his cousin onto his shoulders. He ran along the beach, over the embankment, and across Front Street, heading upland into the hills. Satisfied that there was no one in pursuit, he headed for home.

Eleven

Concealed within a coconut grove, Gonzalez watched the entrance to the *Seaman's Bar*. Oil lamps flickered casting weak light through the windows of the saloon. But their blubber-fueled energy was too dim to make out the faces of the men inside. This is stupid, he thought, sitting in the dark pursuing a hunch. But his gut told him to stay with the surveillance.

A large Hawaiian woman in a filmy red outfit burst through the swinging doors of the saloon. He heard her, but couldn't make out the words. After a time the lady came out, walked a few steps, then slipped into the shadows.

A dark shape joined her. Gonzalez's pulse quickened. The weak light from the saloon lit the face of a man. "That's John Tana," he whispered. He rose from his seat, loosening his whip.

But as he strode toward the pair, Tana disappeared and the woman walked away. Hurrying past the saloon, Gonzalez searched the darkness, but saw nothing. He peeped through a window just as his quarry came from a back door into the bar.

"Damn it. The kid's slipping out of my hands." Gonzalez considered bursting into the saloon and confronting the boy, but he felt uncertain about the attitude of the whalers. He had a knife and whip, maybe not enough to cow tough seamen. He decided to wait, slipping into the darkness of the alley.

Within minutes the swinging doors blew open and three men, carrying John and another Hawaiian came through. "We got our prizes," one of the whalers said. "We can sail tomorrow," another answered.

Make your move, he thought. But caution held him back. They were too near the bar to start a fight. From his hiding place he watched the men march to the beach. "Once those guys get Tana on that ship I'll never get him back," Gonzalez muttered, weighing his next move. Should he rush to the seamen and demand the kid? Maybe he could promise them some of the reward. As he stood in indecision a fight erupted.

Within minutes, three whalers lay on the beach and John Tana carried an inert man toward the street. "This is my chance," Gonzalez said. He hurried to his horse, already bridled and saddled. He leaped onto it and trotted along the road in the direction he last saw his quarry.

John's feet slid on loose rocks in the darkness. With an unconscious David on his back, a moon hidden by clouds, and weak starlight, it proved difficult to keep his balance on an uneven path. "Please God, let there be no pursuit," John prayed. Silence surrounded him. Maybe God is answering my prayers, he thought.

As he hiked up the low hill a sound made John pause in his shuffling walk. A cool ocean breeze swept his face. It brought with it the crash of waves striking the shore, the rustle of leaves in the trees, but nothing else.

But while he waited, John sensed something in the air different from the clean smell of the sea. He inhaled. "Damn, that's a horse."

He breathed slowly, controlled the rasp in his throat, the heave of his chest. Maybe if he laid David down he could learn what might be coming. He found grass at the side of the path and placed his cousin there. He squatted beside the still body, held his breath, and listened.

Mixed with the noise of the wind and sea there came a metal clopping of hooves drumming on the stone. He heard a faint jingle of harness clashing together.

John's eyes darted about looking for a place to hide. He saw low shrubs growing near the path. He shoved David against the plants. He felt around for something he could use as a weapon. His hand grasped a round stick. Stones lay within his reach. He built a small cairn of rocks, stopping in his work when the wind brought the unmistakable smell of a horse. He faced the sea, waiting to confront this nocturnal traveler.

Clouds drifted past the moon silhouetting a rider on horseback. "I know you're here, Tana." A crisp crack of a whip switched into the shrubs beside John. Another lashing caught him on his side. The horseman laughed, flailing his weapon once again. The rawhide crackled like thunder as it scored John's back. He grasped his small supply of stones and darted away from the next strike of the leather rope.

The horse loomed gigantic in front of him. John flung a rock into its side. The animal reared, unsettling the rider whose whip fell lazily onto John's arm. Gripping the rawhide, John severed it with Mattoon's knife. He loosened the cut piece, flinging it at his attacker.

The man pulled his mount away, raising the stump of his whip for another strike. John took a sharp rock from his pocket and smashed it into the horse. The animal screamed, leaped up, its forelegs pawed the air. John grasped a boot. He pulled. The rider tumbled from the saddle and sprawled on the ground.

John searched the darkness. There could be others. He thought to run, but knew that meant abandoning David. He could not do this. He must stay and fight whatever evils confronted him. His attacker staggered to his feet.

"You're hard to catch you damn kanaka-boy, but I don't think you will run away and leave your friend. Give it up."

"You're the guy called Tony. You came charging at me when I stood by my shack. You whipped me on the beach. Why are you doing this?"

"Mr. Grant wants you real bad. He'll pay five hundred dollars to see you dead. I aim to collect," Gonzalez said, dropping his severed whip, unhooking a baton at his side, and drawing out his knife.

"How...how did you find me?" John stuttered buying time as he fought to control his trembling. The endless threats of the evening took a toll on his emotions. He needed to return to a feeling of peace where he could react from wisdom and not stress.

"I've been searching the streets from my hotel room. Saw you tonight with the sailors. I thought I'd lost you to the shanghai they were pulling off, but you finished them real good. I watched you running away with your friend on your back. I came after you to collect the reward which will be mine when you're dead."

"Why kill me?" John asked, seeking more time to gain control of his body.

"To silence you forever."

"If you let me go, I promise not to return or make trouble for Mr. Grant."

"Hah." Gonzalez sneered. "My boss wants you eliminated. Besides, how can I collect the reward if I have no body to show for the money?"

John's breathing slowed as his emotions came under control. His mind assumed a state of peace as fear disappeared. His body relaxed, relieved of tension and fatigue. He assessed his chances against the big man. Gonzalez held a knife, a club, and had an incentive to kill. But darkness, the uneven ground, the horse, and Tony's cowardice were his allies.

As if he sensed weakness, Gonzalez brandished his knife. "This is a weapon designed for Jim Bowie. With it he killed more than a dozen men. Never has it been defeated. Give up and I'll promise a quick death. Otherwise I will slice you into ribbons and let your blood flow down this street to the ocean."

John remained silent listening for his enemy's movements. Behind Gonzalez his horse became restive, chains around his neck jingling in the night. The moon disappeared into a cloud.

"I offered Mattoon a chance to leave unharmed," John said. "He didn't listen. You must have seen what happened. I offer you the chance to go and live. Get on your horse and ride away. No one but you and I will know."

Booted feet stumbled on loose stones. A knife blade caught faint light as it thrust into the dark. Rocks rolled downhill dislodged by rapid movement. A bludgeon whipped the air, left, right, and around in a circle. "Where are you Tana? Show yourself." Gonzalez screamed.

A smack of wood against hide raised a frightened whinny from the horse. It dug its legs into the path, leaped forward, and knocked its master to the ground. John heard a cry of pain and threw a rock at the sound.

"Damn you. You're dead."

More rocks cascaded on the Portuguese as John followed the sound of his heavy breathing as Gonzalez struggled to get up. Ill fortune came when the clouds passed the moon revealing John a few feet from his enemy.

Grant's henchman swung his baton smashing it into the left side of the boy's body. He followed with a wild swing of the knife that sliced through the cloth of John's shirt, leaving a slight cut along his chest. John answered the attacks with a crushing right hook to the jaw bringing the plantation bully to the ground.

Finding his stick in the half-light John smashed it onto the hand with the dagger, followed by a sweep of his leg into the face of the Portuguese. His enemy howled, rearing from the blows. John smashed his foot into his opponent's kidneys and Gonzalez crumpled to the ground. Stepping into him, he whacked his ears with his palms.

Gonzalez screamed, writhing on the path. His wails turned into moans. John backed off. Rushed over to David, lifted him, and left.

After midnight, an exhausted John Tana shoved his unconscious cousin through the entrance of the Makanani shack.

Aunt Malia rose, startled awake by the noises made by the entry of the two men. "Eh, who dat?" she demanded.

"Just David and me," John answered.

Malia focused on her snoring son, saw John's ripped shirt. "You boys drink too much. You bad John, how come you no take care of David? What's wrong with him? Drunk?"

John struggled for breath, unable to speak.

"That's what I thought. You drunk like your cousin."

"Auntie, I'm not drunk," John said as his gasping slowed. "David got drugged by sailors who wanted to take us away. I had a big fight."

Malia stared at John unsure what to believe. "Eh, go sleep," she finally said. "We talk about it tomorrow." She rolled into her tapa ending the conversation.

With a shrug, John placed David onto the mat. He dragged himself outside, shivering as the early morning breeze dried the sweat from his body. John threw himself to the ground, closed his eyes, and dreamed.

He lay in a cell. White-gowned, hooded men charged in to seize him. He struggled to resist, but his arms were like mush and his legs would not let him stand. Dragged before a man robed in black and sitting high above him, a hammer thumped on a Bible. "You are evil. You have broken the law. You are condemned to burn in hell for your crimes."

John tried to explain but he could not move, nor speak. The judge waved his hands and a pit opened in the floor. John fell into it, screaming. His cries mixed with the grinding noises of chains and the crackling of fierce-burning fires. The horrid sounds faded as the pit closed above him. Utter blackness ended John's nightmare.

Twelve

Sunshine flooded into the cabin of the whaling ship, illuminating Captain Shaw sipping claret while he brooded over his losses: several crew dead in the Arctic Sea, three of his best injured, done in by a damned kanaka, and two men in a Lahaina hospital. What of the whale that would have made his fortune? It had disappeared into the northern ocean.

A hail from topside accompanied by the bump of wood on wood interrupted his thoughts. A boatswain's whistle announced the arrival of the first of the captains summoned to a council of war. Shaw left his cabin and headed on deck where he greeted Cartwright as he heaved himself onto the deck. Other ships' tenders bumped against the *Jeremiah* and two more men in dark coats and white pants hoisted themselves onto the vessel.

Within minutes, the four men were assembled around a table in the aft cabin: Shaw, Cartwright, Rustin, and Jensen.

"Gentlemen," Shaw saluted. "I make a toast to your health and to good fortune in the coming whaling season."

As the ship's cook filled the crystal glasses with more claret, Rustin spoke. "It's too bad about your boys being jumped by kanakas. You say those brown thieves robbed them?"

"As God is my witness, that is so," Shaw declared. "Six cowards ambushed my men as they returned to the *Jeremiah* after a little fun on shore."

"You can't trust these barbarians," Jensen said. "Give them an opening and they will steal, rob, and take anything they can get their hands on. Those Hawaiians need to be taught a lesson."

"Wait," Cartwright said. "Let the law settle this. Send word to the sheriff in town and let him punish these men."

Pounding on the table to emphasize his point, Shaw declared, "The sheriff has gone to Wailuku. We are the law in Lahaina and I say we give my injured boys justice!"

"Justice, justice," the others echoed.

"I vote we set up a sailor's court, find these bastards, try 'em, and hang 'em," Shaw proposed.

"Stringing up kanakas is a pretty risky thing to do," Cartwright said. "Reverend Parson would have just cause to condemn us all and set the law against us. I say we turn our boys loose, find them, and beat them good."

"That's the right thinking," Jensen agreed. "Let's get our men liquored up and start the hunt."

Shaw smiled. The lies that he had spread among the fleet had galvanized whalers into action. Soon, more than two hundred sailors would be on shore spoiling for a fight. With enough alcohol to raise their courage and more false talk to incite them, Shaw would not only get the two Hawaiians who hurt his men, but also kidnap enough kanakas to fill out his crew.

Morning's light washed away the shadows of night. Daylight pestered John awake. He woke unready to deal with the violence of the night, though he knew he had much to explain. As he rubbed his eyes, he heard a rhythmic tapping, the familiar sound of Auntie Malia smashing a purple taro root into a grey paste.

John found David still asleep in a corner of the Makanani shack. There was no sign of Leinani. "Where's your daughter?" he asked.

"She's with her friend Monapua," Malia said, pausing in her pounding just long enough to fix John with a stare that demanded answers. "What you do to get David drunk last night?"

"I didn't get him drunk. David was drugged!"

"You trying to tell me you didn't go into a bar and drink whiskey?"

John weighed how much he wanted to reveal. "Well, we did go to a bar, but I—"

"Don't you lie to Auntie. Tell me the story what happened."

As best he could, while being constantly interrupted by Malia, John described the events at the *Seamen's Bar* and the battle that followed.

"You telling me that this big Hawaiian woman came into the bar and helped you? Why would she do such a thing?"

John explained how the lady had seen him on his first day in Lahaina. "Maybe she liked me or maybe she just hates the whalers. I don't know, but I'm sure she didn't want Hawaiians forced into slavery on some whaling ship."

Malia lowered her head for a few moments studying her graying paste. When she looked at John, her eyes were filled with concern. "You had a big fight on the beach, beat them up, and rescued David. Our family got big trouble. Those sailors will come looking for you boys." Malia wiped sweat from her forehead with the back of her hand and moaned. "Big trouble we got. What we going do?"

John felt his stomach tighten and anger rise within him. It was bad enough to be kidnapped, but to make this woman afraid was too much. "Auntie, I told you that we must leave Lahaina. With this new trouble, we have no choice. We must go now. The canoe is packed and ready." John decided not to tell of his fight with Gonzalez. He did not wish to add his personal problems to the growing calamity.

Malia looked earnestly at John, a tear trickling down her cheek. "I don't know, maybe we have no choice, but I can't answer right now. Wait until David gets up."

John stuck his finger into the poi, whirling it around like a stick twirled into the hardening mud of a drying pond.

"Stop that." Malia slapped his hand. "Not ready yet. Still got big pieces inside, not broken up."

John escaped Malia with his wad of goop intact. He licked the grey paste from his fingers as he busied himself with preparations to leave.

A tormenting sun stood level in the sky, boiling the Makanani compound. Flies buzzed in tight circles within the hut. One of them flew by David's ear and forced him awake. "Water," he croaked. "Get me water."

"Here, take this," John said, handing his cousin a gourd.

David drank greedily. Sated, he placed the vessel on the floor and poured water into his hands, which he pressed against his aching head. "What happened last night?" he asked.

John described the attack and explained the sailors' plans. "Once we got to the beach," he added, "I was able to get us away from them."

"Are you telling me that those guys were going to take us—?"

"John Tana," a voice called, interrupting David. "Where are you?"

Ah Sam came running to the shack, his chest heaving in great gasps. "John," he shouted.

John crawled out, David close behind. Auntie Malia, who had been bundling items into ti leaves, appeared. "Ah Sam," she said. "What's up?"

"Boys must go away quick," Ah Sam answered. "Sailor men plenty angry. They drink plenty, they want find you, beat you up. Maybe kill you boys. Look my face." He turned to reveal a swollen cheek. "Sailor men try learn who you are, want to know where you live. I say 'don't know.' They hit me in stomach, I tell them nothing. Hit me in face. They say 'going hunt for Hawaiians, maybe come back, burn store down.' You no come Lahaina, maybe betta you leave."

Malia released a wild cry. "Woe is us. God have mercy."

"Mama," David said, "stop that loud noise, you're making my head split." He turned to John. "I can't believe those nice men who gave us such aloha would do something evil."

John nearly laughed for the absurdity of his cousin's naiveté. "David, I'm telling you that they drugged you and wanted to drug me, too. If I hadn't stopped them, we'd both be sitting in chains in some dark hold of their ship. If you don't believe me, ask Malama."

"I talk with Malama," Ah Sam interrupted. "She tell me what she know. John did right thing, save boys from big trouble. Better you leave Lahaina."

"Sorry cousin for being hard headed," David said, and then turned to Malia. "Mama, we have to leave Lahaina."

The old woman fell silent and began bustling about the compound, mumbling to herself and packing.

John put his hand on the shopkeeper's shoulder. "Ah Sam, you and your wife must come with us. It's dangerous for you to stay and wait for the next passenger boat. When Leinani returns, I'll send her into town to help you. Neither David nor I dare show up in Lahaina. Some of those men in the bar last night might recognize us and there would be trouble."

Ah Sam nodded. "I will go home and get ready. Send Leinani right away."

In mid-afternoon, the young girl walked into the compound with her friend Monapua. She stared in surprise as John, David, and Malia loaded her family's possessions onto the platform of the double canoe. "What's going on?" Leinani demanded.

It took an hour of explanation and begging before the girl consented to leave. Once she had agreed to go, John asked, "I need a favor. David and I can't show up in town and my friend Ah Sam needs help. His wife, Lehua, is going to have her baby soon and they're coming with us to Honolulu. I hate to ask you to do this, since it could be dangerous, but we need someone to go into town and bring them here."

A hint of irritation crossed Leinani's face. "Mr. Tana, you seem to be worried that a woman can't handle such a job. Monapua and I will go." Without another word, she seized her friend's hand and they set off at a brisk run for Lahaina.

Thirteen

When Leinani and Monapua slowed to a stop at the intersection of Sacrifice and Prison Streets, the sun had descended past the western horizon. They heard wild yells. "Bad things in town," Leinani whispered. "We must be careful."

The girls bent low, taking advantage of any cover they could find as they fled along Sacrifice Street. They would run, stop, listen, then move again. The closer they came to Ah Sam's store the louder the noise became. The heat from the sun drenched Leinani's face and body with sweat, adding to her misery. She vowed to rid herself of her hot sack once she reached Ah Sam's home.

At his door the girls pounded it saying, "Ah Sam, it's Leinani and Monapua. Let us in."

Sounds from Front Street a long block away increased in volume.

Spurred by the shattering of glass, Leinani kicked the door.

"Who is it?" A voice asked.

"It's Leinani," she answered. "John Tana's cousin, here with my friend. Please open. Men are breaking into your store."

Iron squealed against iron as bolts slid apart. The door came ajar a notch, held in place by a chain. A frightened Ah Sam studied Leinani. "John's relative?"

"Yes".

"Who is with you? Anybody else outside?"

"She's my friend, Monapua. There's no one else. If you don't hurry, angry people will be here soon."

Splintered wood from Front Street signaled that the barricaded front door of the Sam store was breached.

"Okay, we ready," the shopkeeper said. "Cart behind shack. Come Lehua." A woman emerged from the hut, her belly swollen.

Monapua said, "Real big baby, dis one."

Lehua smiled as she waddled into the alley.

"You have anything I could wear?" Leinani asked. "This bag is heavy with sweat."

Lehua laughed. She rubbed her large belly, "Plenty inside. No need anymore."

Ah Sam darted to the shed and pulled out a two-wheeled handcart already filled with sacks of possessions. Lehua moved into the small wagon and nestled her large body among the bundles. From the nearby store glass broke and wood splintered.

Ah Sam harnessed himself to the family cart. He said, "Come, we go quick. Bad sailors be here soon."

Monapua seized the left side of the yoke and helped Ah Sam pull the cart away from the shed. Leinani wound a pareu around her body. She paused for a moment to grasp a javelin that rested against the wall.

The fugitives hauled the cart and a pregnant Lehua north along an alleyway to Sacrifice Street. Within moments after they left, the back door of the store blew away.

Leinani saw debris flying everywhere. Several sailors emerged from the destroyed side of the building. They pushed their way through the wreckage.

"Yahoo, there they are. Get 'em," whalers hollered.

"Go, go, go!" Leinani yelled. She grabbed the yoke and helped to pull the cart through the alley. Impelled by the threat at their backs, Ah Sam and Monapua ran faster. They ignored the affect the bumps and pits had on Lehua.

They swerved the cart right and southeast onto Sacrifice Street, the left wheel of the vehicle lifted high. "Lean," Leinani yelled.

The pregnant woman threw her weight against the side of the cart. Her effort forced the elevated wheel down onto the roadway.

In this manner, the human powered two-wheeler raced towards the safety of the Hawaiian village. Ah Sam continually implored: "Baby no come, baby no come."

"There are a dozen sailors after us. Faster." Leinani said.

"We can't pull any faster," Moanapua answered.

"Throw out bags, throw out bags," Ah Sam yelled.

"Oh no," Lehua pleaded.

"Save baby, throw out bags," Ah Sam cried again.

Lehua reluctantly jettisoned family possessions. Like an air balloon lightened of ballast, the wagon shot forward like a frisky colt.

Leilani looked behind her. "They're walking fast, but not fast enough to catch us."

"That's because we are being herded into a trap," Monapua said. "Men are on Dickenson Street planning to block us from getting to the village."

Lehua screamed. "I think my baby coming."

Ah Sam, Monapua, and Leinani searched the area around the intersection of Dickenson and Sacrifice Streets. They heard a cheer akin to the cry of men on long boats chasing a whale, sailors appeared on Dickenson, headed for the cart.

"Angle left, run faster," Leinani shouted.

"I can't run any faster," Monapua gasped.

Ah Sam pulled the cart to the left, the wheel of the vehicle struck a pothole and tossed Lehua upwards. She plummeted down, landed hard, screamed in anguish.

Ah Sam yelled, "Baby no die!"

Galvanized by Ah Sam's words, Leinani released her hold on the cart, and faced the seamen. She brandished the javelin above her head. For a moment, the horde slowed.

Leinani stood tall, a slim arm raised high. Her javelin held back a mob of angry men.

After a moment's hesitation, someone in the fore of the group yelled, "It's only a woman, after them. Don't let 'em get away." He charged. While in mid-stride a javelin speared his thigh.

Ugly is the roar of a mob when blocked from its prize. Hostile eyes turned toward the half-naked Leinani, who spun and raced toward the hills. The leaders surged after her with a few laggards in the rear, pursuing the cart. Leinani's heroism gained time for Ah Sam and his family as the wagon sped through the intersection toward the Hawaiian village.

Exhausted, the human power that had been pulling the cart limped into the Makanani compound. Ah Sam collapsed onto the ground while Monapua kneeled, her chest bellowing with a rapid intake and exhaling of air.

Lehua screamed, "Help my baby."

Shadows of men crowded behind the wagon. John and David, alerted by the sounds of entry into the compound, quit their preparations to leave and prepared to fight.

"Peace, brothers," a familiar voice said. Kawika stepped into the low light shed by a coconut lamp that flamed at the entranceway of the shack. John and David relaxed as they greeted him, and several other men from the village.

A few women rushed into the compound, alerted by Lehua's cries. Auntie Malia directed them to place her on some clothing piled on the ground near the shed. "Go away," she said. "We take care of this woman."

Some distance from the delivery place Ah Sam explained their escape and Leinani's selfless act in drawing the angry sailors into the hills. "Very brave woman," he added. "If she no run away, the sailors catch us for sure. But we lucky, we not have far to go before Kawika and his friends come to help us. If they no come, then sailors get us."

"We heard all this noise from Lahaina," Kawika explained. He flexed his biceps. "So the guys and me got together, got some weapons, and went to the edge of the village. We saw this cart and heard a woman scream." He went on to describe the whalers chasing them. "Us guys didn't think it was fair, so we jumped 'em. They were chicken. There were more of them than us, but they couldn't stand our pounding. Before you know it, they ran back to Lahaina."

"Did you see Leinani?" John asked.

A quiet fell over the group. They all looked around. Concern grew to fear for the safety of this woman warrior.

"Sorry, none of us saw her," Kawika said. "There were loud noises in the hills and some torchlight, but it was too dark to see what was going on."

John leaned against Ah Sam's cart, fear seared through him. Despite his desperation, he felt a tinge of pride for the courageous woman who had saved his friends.

Fourteen

Shaw whirled his glass. He watched the amber liquid slosh against the sides of the tumbler. Seated in the *Seamen's Bar*, with his riding crop against a chair, he thought over the events of the day.

Early in the morning, Shaw questioned Mattoon, Lazarus, and Will, but they were too injured to provide useful information. From the little that he learned, he surmised that the kanakas who beat them were on Front Street when they met. He sent men ashore to question shopkeepers. What they learned caused Shaw to suspect Ah Sam. Beaten by his men, the merchant refused to talk.

Shaw questioned his injured men again. Two of them were unable to help. Mattoon couldn't speak. Lazarus did little more than groan and hold onto his stomach, as if this might stop his innards from spilling across the planks in the ship's hold.

Will, despite a broken nose, revealed that the Hawaiians had emerged from the vicinity of Ah Sam's store. Armed with this news, Shaw came ashore to make the *Seamen's Bar* his command center.

Not all of the ten ship captains had agreed with the scheme for revenge, but there was enough support that, by evening, around a hundred and fifty whalers had landed in Lahaina, prepared to render every Hawaiian bruised, senseless, or worse.

At the *Seamen's Bar*, Shaw and his cohorts prepared whalers for battle with rum and whiskey. Liquored up, courage stoked, the men were soon ready for serious action.

Shaw sent sailors back to Ah Sam's store with orders to torture the truth out of him. One of them returned to report that the merchant was fleeing into the hills.

"Rufus take three dozen men from the bar and head up Dickenson Street. Capture that Chinaman and bring back whoever's with him." Shaw ordered.

The second mate of the *Jeremiah* released a whistle and the bar fell silent. "Follow me, swabs. We got a Chinaman to catch, and maybe some women."

Drunken sailors ran to Dickenson Street to intercept the fugitives. Only a handful remained with Shaw.

Within fifteen minutes, Rufus returned. "Our boys almost got the Chinaman. But this near naked woman—Captain, she was g-g-gorgeous...I swear, you'd give your ship for her..."

"Rufus, just tell me what happened,"

"The boys and I ran up Dickenson Street when this two-wheel cart came along pulled by a Chinaman and two women. Our boys hollered. Oh Christ, I thought we sounded like hunters after a fox."

Shaw leaned forward, his eyes narrowed. "Rufus, where are the prisoners?"

The second mate shifted his feet, kept his eyes from his captain. "There aren't any prisoners."

Shaw leaned closer, anger in his voice, "You're telling me that thirty men couldn't catch an unarmed Chinese and some women?" Before Rufus could respond, Shaw struck him with his riding crop.

Rufus drew back. He rubbed his forearm. "No cause to do that, Captain. Wasn't my fault they got away."

"Just tell me how you let those people slip through your fingers."

Rufus moved back. He kept a table and chairs between them. "This woman rushed us from the cart, a spear in her hand. I tell you Captain, the boys were shocked."

Shaw balanced his crop in his hands and then whacked it against the table, "An army of men frightened by a woman. Go and find me some torches."

Rufus left. The Captain played with his switch, idly hit the handle against his palm. Should he take what remained of his whalers and go after Ah Sam? But that meant entering the Hawaiian village. It was pitch black outside and with so many Hawaiians south-east of Lahaina, they could be stepping into a hornet's nest.

But, Rufus's account of the woman's beauty intrigued him. She was alone in the hills, away from all settlements, making her an easy quarry to hunt down. A nighttime chase of a defenseless female could prove exciting. Once caught, she would tell him where those kanakas lived.

Shaw stepped outside. He called for Runyon. "Did you find me a horse?" he asked.

"A fine brown gelding," Runyon said. "Name's Thunder and he's tied in the alley. I'll bring him straightaway." The man disappeared, and returned with a frisky colt on the lead.

Shaw mounted, yanked the reins, chucked a few times, and horse and rider trotted off. Before he could ride up Dickenson Street, Rufus and another sailor came toward him, arms laden with torches.

"Light one," Shaw ordered. Rufus struck a match. Carbon and orange flame flumed from the fire stick, its smoky light flooded the street. "Follow me," the captain said. He took the beacon in one hand and canted northeast. The flames soon lit groups of unhappy whalers. Spying a familiar face among the disconsolate men, Shaw yelled, "Lucas, get me three others and follow me," and then rode to a level area beyond Sacrifice Street to await his men. As each arrived, he handed out a torch.

When five men assembled, Shaw pulled his horse around to face them. "We are going hunting, boys. Anyone see where the woman disappeared to?"

"I think she went there," a sailor said. He pointed into the hills.

"Spread out. Rufus, you take the far left flank, I'll take the right. The rest of you form a line between Rufus and me. Together, we will find this devil woman."

Like beaters preparing to flush birds from thickets, the men formed a ragged line, torches held high. Slowly, they marched forward searching the rock-strewn ground.

Soon a whaler yelled, "I see something." Someone on the left flank raised his torch higher. Visible in the flickering light and partially hidden by a boulder, crouched a figure. Shaw urged his horse closer. Leinani jumped from behind the rock hurling a stone.

One man howled, "I'll fix you good, you damned vixen."

Shaw and his men converged on the battle between Leinani and the whaler.

"Don't hurt her too much, boys," Shaw ordered, dismounting. He stood by his horse and watched Leinani kick and punch sailors trying to wrestle her into submission. Two of them finally pinned her arms and Shaw, stepping forward, gripped her face. He forced her head back and, retrieving a vial from his waistcoat, pushed a few drops of liquid between her lips. When he wrapped his arms around her, Shaw felt an arousal that comes from too many months at sea. "Tonight, she's mine," he told his men. "Tomorrow, she's yours."

Fifteen

John could not keep David calm. His cousin was frantic, talking about Leinani in the hills with men after her. "We must get to my sister before the whalers find her," David pleaded. "Kawika, will you help us?"

The Hawaiian nodded, the three other men with him murmured their agreement. "You no need ask, brother. We all *ohana*."

Monapua stepped forward. "Eh, you guys, Leinani my best friend. You are not leaving me out of this fight."

John started to say "no" but stopped. He remembered how men and women supported each other in battle in ancient times. "Come," he said.

John took charge. "Kawika, you and David lead the ohana to the grass glade at the edge of Lahaina. Gather weapons as you go and wait for me there."

The group submitted to John's control. They also understood that a warrior needed time alone, to prepare for battle. Knowledge of his victories over the men on the beach was fresh in their minds. His self-assurance acted as another reason to trust the leadership of this country boy from Kahului.

The ohana left the Makanani compound and rushed into the darkness. At the same time, John crawled into the shack, where he retrieved a sack and withdrew his *maa*. He wrapped the sling around his forehead and then twisted the strangling cord, called *kaane*, around his waist. Finally, he thrust the solid *piikoi* into a fold of his clothing, feeling the heft of the wooden club. He took a handful of coconut oil and rubbed it on his body. At the threshold of the shack, he scooped up some pebbles and hurried to the meeting place.

A brisk wind sang through leaves of coconut trees, causing a racket like a thousand crickets rubbing their legs together. Oil lamps lit the saloons on Front

Street, their light stabbed out of windows while the breeze caused doors to swing onto the beach.

John ran into the grove that grew in the park near Front Street. His warriors huddled with a middle-aged Hawaiian.

"John, this is Moses," Kawika said. "He's been on watch, in case the whalers attacked the village. He has some interesting news."

"Eh, I saw this white guy ride up Dickenson Street," Moses whispered. "He held a torch and headed to the mountains. Pretty soon, I see other torches. They string in a line and move into the hills." Suddenly, the old man pointed. "That's the guy coming back. He holds somebody."

John peered through the coconut trees and saw a horse. On it sat Shaw, with Leinani cradled in one arm, her head limp against his chest. John's impulse was to charge out of the copse and seize her, but the captain moved fast and his ohana was outnumbered. One shout from Shaw and whalers would arrive in droves.

"What we going do?" David demanded, panic in his voice. "Just sit here?"

"Wait," John cautioned. Lua had taught him patience, seek knowledge, and plan. There would be a right time to act.

He watched Shaw fling an unconscious Leinani into a long boat pulled onto the sand. With the help of two seamen, Shaw shoved it into the water, the men leaped into the vessel and rowed away. John watched. He said nothing. Once sure where the sailors headed, John asked Kawika. "Is there a canoe nearby?"

The big man nodded and gestured for him to follow.

They came to a cluster of boats resting on the sand. John selected one and, with David, Kawika, Monapua, and two others shoved it into the sea, climbed inside, and paddled toward the ships at anchor in the roadstead.

The moon hid below the horizon. Feeble oil lamplight in grog shops struggled against the dark, their uncertain light served as a guide to the anchored boats. Heavy clouds shrouded Lahaina. They blocked any light from distant stars and hid the fleet offshore in a mantle of black.

"No sound, paddle slow," John cautioned as he steered the canoe along the ocean side of the anchored boats. Most of them faced the beach, except the ship Shaw had oared to. The *Jeremiah,* lay parallel to the shore.

Hidden by darkness, the canoe slid to the starboard side of the vessel. Beneath the main wale of the ship, John gestured for the ohana to remain silent and pulled himself from the canoe onto the wale. He grasped a handhold on the main channel and lifted his oil-sleeked body over the starboard rail. When his bare feet touched the wooden deck, he squatted, watched, and listened.

A faint light came from the ship's prow. It flickered and died, flickered and died. John figured it was a lookout smoking, but where could the other man be? There had been two rowing the long boat with Shaw. Could the second sailor have returned to shore? Were there other seamen on board?

John heard a muffled sound, a bump that was not from his canoe. He reasoned that it must be a long boat on the port side. His heart beat faster, anxiety and concern for Leinani's safety ate at his patience. He decided to make his move but, in mid-stride stopped. "Control, control," he told himself.

His grandfather's voice came to him. "You young people are impulsive, impatient, you cannot wait. Calm your emotions. Do not let anger or fear possess you. Control yourself."

John returned to his crouch, peered into the darkness that protected his enemies. He needed to find all sailors on the deck before he made his move. A rhythmic tapping followed by humming came from the bow of the ship. He knew where the two men were.

For a minute, John listened and searched, but heard no other sounds, saw no other lights. Satisfied, he padded toward the front of the ship. Near the prow, he smelled pungent smoke. Mounting stairs, he took the *kaane* from his waist and grasped its knob in one hand, wrapped its three-foot cord around the other.

He caught a whaler by surprise, twisting his choking cord around the man's neck. The sailor tried to fight with hands and feet, but John lifted him above the deck and away from the rail. A gurgle rose from the man's throat and his pipe dropped from his teeth, bounced against the rail, and plunged into the sea with a sizzle. When his body fell limp, John released the cord and lowered the man to the deck.

"Hey Abel, what's that noise?" a voice called from the back of the ship.

John unwound the *maa* from his forehead, inserting a large pebble into its coconut fiber pouch. He heard footsteps approach. He saw a figure move toward him. He rose, whirled the sling, and flung the stone. The whaler came to an abrupt stop and dropped to his knees. John rushed in and clubbed the man who fell to his back with a groan.

John paused and listened. Silence. He returned to the starboard side, motioning his ohana to come on board. He pointed to the entranceways to the innards of the ship, assigned his team to guard them, then crept into the main hallway to the captain's quarters.

Shaw debated whether to restrain the woman, but experience with Leinani taught him that she needed to be controlled. He tied her to his bed by wrists and ankles. He spread her out in the shape of an 'X'. He stroked her tan body as he did his work. It aroused him, but his captive remained unconscious. He wanted her awake for questions. He planned to torture her to make her talk. The thought of it aroused him again.

He removed his coat and shirt, washed himself over a basin of water. On a whim, he doused himself with an aromatic powder, white wisps rising in puffs from his chest. He splashed cologne over his face and neck. A little sweetness in the air would be good, since the cabin would soon be fouled by the carnal tortures he planned to administer. His toilet completed, he put on a clean blouse and sat down to study Leinani.

He thought her complexion was lighter than most Hawaiian women, her features aristocratic. Her hair, although long and brown, lacked the coarse texture of most native women. Shaw wondered if she might have white blood in her veins. Turning to his desk he entered notations into the ship's log. When his work was done, he returned his attention to his captive. Impatience took hold and he strode to the bed. "Wake up, you bitch," he demanded, He prodded the girl. When she did not respond, he slapped her and ripped the tip of her pareu. Her breasts spilled out. They taunted him. Excited, he tore the garment away. The cabin door burst inward, its lock exploded into the room.

Sixteen

John muscled his way through the door. The sight of Shaw ripping Leinani's clothes enraged him. Patience, control, evaporated. Anger drove him across the room.

Shaw sidestepped the charge, tripped John, and sent him over the bed with its naked captive. Before the fallen youth could gather himself, Shaw released his sword from its scabbard, his face contorted with rage. "You will pay for this interruption of my pleasure."

John realized he had been foolish, ill-prepared. Hadn't his grandfather cautioned him that combat is unpredictable, that body and mind must be prepared for any event? In battle, strength is not decisive, quickness and agility can overcome mistakes. With these admonitions in mind, John dropped to the floor, rolled onto his back, and pulled himself to his feet. He leapt to the door, turned, and assumed a fighting stance, his short-handled piikoi unsheathed and looped around his wrist.

Shaw stared at the youth. "You are the kanaka who hurt my men. You are a sneaky, dirty Hawaiian, you are rubbish. It will be a pleasure to kill you." He lifted his sword in a mock salute and flourished it in a whirling pattern. "But the true pleasure will be in your slow death."

John stood near the door and faced the man. He kept his weight evenly balanced between both feet, ready to slide to either side. He ignored the taunts, the movement of the captain's blade. He focused on his posture and the tension of his feet, arms, and shoulders that would signal an attack. He knew that he could not defeat a trained swordsman by being still, but would need to depend on agility to escape a cutting blow.

He retrieved stones from his pouch. John saw the tension in the captain's leg and shoulders. As Shaw lunged John hurled his small rocks into his face. Distracted, the captain missed his target, his blade slicing into his opponent's loincloth. John pivoted and swung his club. The captain howled when the heavy wooden knob struck his eye. John re-gripped the handle of the weapon and smashed it into the captain's side.

Shaw grunted, staggered backward. He blinked and wiped a sleeve over his injured face. John checked the wound at his side. The cut was shallow with little blood. He tightened his grip on the piikoi, bouncing rhythmically from side to side.

"Damn you. So you're going to play with me with that knobbed stick. I'm going to chop you in half." Partially blinded Shaw raised his sword, stepped forward, and swung down in a body-severing blow.

John slid away. He whirled his piikoi by its cord attached to his wrist and flung the knob around his opponent's neck. With his sideways momentum he yanked Shaw into the cabin wall. The captain dropped his sword. He fumbled to unwind the string around his throat. John pulled harder forcing Shaw to the floor. Choking, he reached for his sword. John stomped his foot into the captain who fell away from his weapon.

Leinani's moans distracted him. John rushed to where she lay, worried that she might have been hurt. A chamber pot struck him, its ugly contents spilled over his body, blinding him for a moment. Leinani's torn pareu lay close to his hand and he pulled it free from her body using it to clear his sight. He saw the captain pull himself up against a wash basin and seize a straight razor with one hand and reach for a poniard sheathed at his waist with the other. The sword lay near the broken door, and Shaw glanced at it as he drew out the long thin knife.

"Help me," the captain croaked, his voice hoarse, the cord marks burning red around his throat. "Help," he said his word just above a whisper. Coughing, the knife wavered in his hand. John stepped into him, grasped the captain's arms and smashed his forehead into his face. Shaw went down. Blood ran from his broken nose and onto his fine-laced blouse. He waved his razor and John kicked him in the crotch. The captain shrieked, reaching down with his hands. John smashed him across the jaw. Shaw collapsed onto the floor unconscious.

John took the sword and cut Leinani's bonds. He cradled her in his arms, their breath mixed. The sweet dampness of her smooth skin mingled with his sweat overwhelmed him. Stirred by the fusion of blood and smell, desire rose inside him like a serpent. As if he needed to be reminded, John heard Malia condemn him for the lust that consumed his body. But there came a hardness that he could not control.

Shaken, John let Leinani slide onto the bed. Her nude body invited him to take what he had saved. Moans awakened him to reality. He could not shame his family by violating a helpless woman. He stepped to where the captain's coat hung, took it and draped it around the nude girl's shoulders. Her eyes fluttered as she struggled to come awake. John lifted her from the bed, held her close, and helped her to the deck of the ship.

Monapua rushed to Leinani, eyes filled with tears. She folded her arms about her friend and together the two women crossed the quarterdeck and climbed into the canoe.

The trip home was without incident. A tired ohana trudged into the Makanani compound. John and Leinani moved slowly behind the others. They were greeted by Ah Sam and Auntie Malia, whose faces glowed with the pleasure of their safety. "Come see, come see," they chorused in unison, Malia pulled Leinani into the shelter.

Lehua lay there on soft covers. Nestled against her breast, eyes closed as he suckled, was her son. His face was wrinkled and wizened from the rigors of birth, but his hair shined in the circle of thin light glowing from a coconut lamp suspended above mother and child.

Lehua smiled at her friends. "Thank you, without your help, this treasure would not be here."

Leinani kneeled on the covers and kissed the baby's forehead, and then touched noses with Lehua. Their ha blended and flowed over the feeding infant.

"Eh, I don't want to break this up," David said. "But, for what we did tonight, those whalers going come get us tomorrow." His eyes took in John, Leinani, Ah Sam, Lehua, and his mother. "We better leave now."

"Eh, bra, no way," Kawika said. "You not going without us." The others nodded their agreement.

"But you will be leaving your homes? We can't ask you to do that," John said.

"Eh, no worry," Kawika answered. "In a few days, sailors go, all cool down, then we come home. Right now, you need help to make it to Honolulu. You got baby to take care of, rough sea to cross. We come with you, so let's get going."

In minutes, the double canoe was ready to sail. Lehua and her son nestled safely on the platform between the two vessels. Everything was strapped down to withstand the sea's tumult.

The ohana pushed the craft into the water, women worked alongside the men. When they reached the waves, they leaped inside the boat and began to paddle.

Once underway, John left his steersman position, stepped the mast, and raised the red sail. He returned to his task of guiding the vessel. He glanced around, satisfied that his friends and family were safe.

Kawika began a chant which asked for divine help in their journey to Oahu.

E makua oka lani; malama palekana; alakai e ohana e Oahu nei.

As they paddled, the others repeated the words.

John leaned against the bow of the canoe and gazed up at the wind-filled sail. Contentment washed over him as he recalled that for months he had been alone, then lost his land, and came to Lahaina bewildered by the great changes that occurred around him. A psalm Reverend Zachariah taught him came to mind:

Yea though I walk through the valley of the shadow of death, I will fear no evil,
for the lord is with me.
My cup runneth over.

With his newfound family John knew his cup was full. Although he was happy, the desire he had developed for Leinani plagued him.

Seventeen

Shaw heard shuffling in his cabin. Fear gripped him. He rose with a start, his sudden movement bringing on a world of pain. The agony blinded him. "Who's there?" he croaked, the effort to speak creating an unbearable hurt in his chest.

"Rufus."

"Why didn't you knock and announce yourself?"

"No door." The second mate gestured to pieces of splintered wood clinging to metal hinges.

Shaw lay back, "Bring me a damp cloth."

Marching to a pitcher, Rufus soaked a cloth in it and returned to the bed.

"Put it on my head." Shaw squirmed as the cloth cooled his hot brow. "Why are you here?"

"Have you forgotten? Last night when we came back and found you beaten your orders were to 'find that kanaka '"

"Did you?" Shaw whispered, his eagerness overpowering the pain of talking.

"No, but I got a pretty good idea where he's going. Talked to some Hawaiians who said he left for Honolulu with friends in a canoe with a red sail."

Despite the agony of speaking, Shaw asked, "What's the report on our men?"

"Well, sir, we still got three in sick bay, the Frenchman and Portuguese are mending and ready to come back on board, the two taken down last night by the kanaka are doing okay."

"Good, get everyone back on the ship. We will make sail."

"Captain, even with Roberto and Allard back at work we will be short-handed. Not enough men to go whaling."

"Rufus, who said anything about going whaling—" Shaw choked with the effort of speaking, his innards flamed with pain. "We are going to hunt kanakas."

Their sail lay useless against the center post of the canoe as the breezes that had carried the ohana from Lahaina died as the day wore on. David, John, Kawika, and Moana pushed the double canoe through the calm blue water into the slot between Lanai and Molokai. After hours of paddling the black rock coastline of the 'Island of the Ghosts' loomed above them.

"Everybody tired, maybe we make a stop around that jutting point of rock," Kawika said. "Small beach beyond it. Protected from the wind. We can find water there. Rest and then go on tomorrow."

John knew the family had little sleep since fleeing Lahaina. Though it was midday he said, "Yes, stop and rest."

Weary fugitives landed on rock-strewn dark sand. The ground sloped from the beach in undulating waves of stone and shrubs toward a central plateau on the top of the island. Lanai was drab, without flowers or tall, green-leafed coco palms.

"Hey, you boys go fishing, get some food, "Auntie Malia ordered, adding "Monapua, Leinani, set up camp. Take care of Lehua and the baby."

By nightfall a cooking fire had been started, and fish sizzled over hot coals. Kawika advised Leinani of a small waterfall around a corner of the bay. She headed in that direction.

John watched her leave. They had not spoken since the escape from Shaw's boat. Despite this John sensed that she might not reject him if he pursued her.

He glanced around the camp. Malia fussed with Lehua's baby and David mended the sail of the canoe. This might be his only opportunity on this voyage to speak with her privately.

Indecision held him back. Did he dare risk her rejection, and the possible condemnation of his new family? But the aroma of her nude body, the smoothness of her skin still lingered with him. John slipped away.

From a high point, he watched the young woman step around rocks at the edge of the bay then disappear. John found a path uphill from the beach and climbed it heading toward a low ridge. He judged that it would overlook the gully where Leinani intended to bathe.

Rocks, disturbed by his climb, fell in a small avalanche down the side of the ridge. His conscience tugged at him. Go on and find the nude girl a part of him urged, but on the other hand, he knew that this was not the right thing to do.

John faltered. His pace slackened. He shrugged as he turned and hiked back to camp.

Eighteen

"Glad to see you topside, Captain," Rufus said as Shaw pulled himself up the stairs from his quarters onto the main deck of the *Jeremiah*.

"Who's got the con?" Shaw groused.

"'Tis Mr. Mattoon. He groans and complains, but he says 'he's going to get that damn kanaka.'"

"Good. Looks like he thinks that poltroon's heading for Oahu?"

"Yes sir, that's where Mattoon believes that fellow and his bunch are going."

"Then we got a chance to catch them. Who's aloft in the boson's chair searching for that dirty bugger?"

"Frenchy, sir."

"Tell him to keep a sharp eye out for a double canoe with a red sail. I'm going back to my cabin to make entries in the log."

"Are you going to make entry that we are pursuing a blooming kanaka and a beautiful Hawaiian girl?"

"Nothing of the sort. Make sail and find me that scallywag."

In the morning, Auntie Malia came to John as the double canoe readied for departure. "Nephew, the old ways are gone. No more is there a belief in the kahuna. No more is there mating between blood relatives. No more are women to be easily taken by men. We are Christians."

"But Auntie—"

"No buts. That word is for those who refuse to listen. You are a good man John Tana. You know what the right thing to do is. The Christian way of doing things, you hear what I say?"

"Yes."

"Good. You sit on the left and steer the boat, and Leinani and I will sit on the right."

Once loaded, the family pushed out to sea. The water lay calm. A mild wind blew over Molokai. John steered the vessel for blue water, the ohana paddling the craft with easy strokes up, over, and down the swells. Like the waves, John felt that his life rocked up and down. Why did Malia question his intentions? Didn't Christians make love too? It wasn't a kahuna that brought a boy and girl together; it was love for each other. John was puzzled until he remembered that Christians taught the importance of marriage and the demand that the woman be virginal until then.

How disgusting. He must wait until marriage, to love Leinani. But Malia wouldn't let him marry her, she was a blood relative. Maybe he should just take her and run away. But what if the fourteen-year-old said no to his plan?

John scowled, wiggling his paddle to add his energy to the movement of the double canoe. He had no choice but to do the Christian thing,

The morning wore on as the travelers sailed alongside Lanai heading to Molokai. A few boats plied the sea between the two islands. Most were canoes, but at least one was a sailing vessel. Maybe a whaler, John thought.

Kawika called to John, "We sail to Molokai, take advantage of its protection from the heavy winds, once past the island, shoot for Waikiki."

John nodded in agreement. He had never made this voyage so he trusted Kawika's judgment. But the closer they came to Molokai, the more troubled John became. Their escape from Lahaina had been too easy.

By afternoon the double canoe lay in the shadow of the island, the mountainous central spine blocked the wind. The sail became useless so the ohana relied on paddling to make headway.

John looked back. He spied a whaling ship, its sails spanking in the wind. He called to Kawika, "What do you think about that boat?"

"It's from Maui for sure. Maybe headed for Honolulu. If it's a whaler it should be going north not west."

"It could be going north around the island then shoot for the Arctic Sea."

"Maybe. But the shorter route from Lahaina is the east side of Molokai, not the west."

"Keep an eye on that ship. Paddle harder," John said.

"We can't beat a fully rigged sailing ship," Kawika answered, a worried frown on his face.

"We're making good time Captain, even if we didn't get underway until morning," Rufus said.

Shaw, sitting in a chair on the upper deck, nodded his agreement. "How are Lazarus and Will?

"Getting along well —"

"Captain," a sailor yelled from his perch near the top of the main sail. "I see a double canoe about a mile ahead. Looks like ten Hawaiians in it."

"Does it have a red sail?"

"Can't rightly tell. A sail post, no sail. Everyone is paddling."

"Rufus," Shaw yelled. "Add a jib to our canvas. Let's investigate that boat."

"Don't know if any extra sails will help Captain. Wind's dying. We are in the sheltered area of Molokai.'

"Do as I order," Shaw said. He moved to the starboard side of his ship pulling out his glass. "Don't know," he muttered. "Big guy in the back could be the one that waylaid me and stole the woman."

Imperceptibly, the distance between vessels narrowed. Shaw noted the men in the canoe glanced back several times. Their nervous looks roused his suspicions. "Faster," he yelled, gripping the rail of the ship.

The wind moderated to a light breeze, but still the *Jeremiah* gained on the double canoe. Ahead of it Shaw saw the western tip of Molokai coming into view. The setting sun shone full into his eyes. It blinded him for some moments. He shaded his eyes with his hands to get a better view of his quarry and felt his ship wallow for a moment, the musical sounds from the rigging dying away as the wind faded. The swell of the sea lifted the *Jeremiah* for a moment, pushed it gently forward, and then pulled her back as the wave slid under it.

"Damn it. We are losing way. Rufus more canvases."

"Sir, it has all the sail it can take, see, the sheets are slack, the wind is no longer with us."

Pounding the rail in frustration, Shaw yelled, "Load the forward cannon. We will give them a taste of iron."

"Cannon's loaded," Mattoon said. "I took that precaution as soon as we left the harbor."

"Good, give them a shot."

"Mighty long range," Rufus said, "A little over half a mile."

"Close enough. Fire."

"The ship behind, I think it's the *Jeremiah*," Kawika said.

John looked back. "Everyone paddle faster, you too, Lehua. Pull as hard as you can."

Despite their efforts the gap between the boats narrowed. John saw ahead the western tip of Molokai, and beyond it the sun bursting with multi-colored light as it dipped below the horizon. Moving south across the island flowed banks of clouds dark with moisture.

A cannon boomed, its shot whistled through the air. A geyser of water blew high, twenty yards behind the canoe. Lehua screamed, "My baby," and abandoned her paddle. She crawled to the center platform and clutched her child. The canoe slowed.

"We can't beat cannon," Monapua cried.

"I won't surrender to that evil man," Leinani said.

Another shot screamed at them, the ball plunged into the water. "If we can make it around the point before they hit us we have a chance to raise sail, catch the wind, and maybe get away in the dark," John said.

Rain pelted down as moisture-filled clouds swooped over the mountain peak of Mauna Loa. "Maybe this water will dampen their gunpowder," John said.

"Mattoon, two shots and you missed on both," Shaw complained. "Now we have to deal with this blasted rain."

"The good news Captain is that we slowed them down a tad," Rufus said. "The gap is narrowed."

"Get some sharpshooters up top. When the rain slackens we will put some lead into their bodies. What's up with the wind Rufus?"

"Rain is killing it, but when it's over, the big gusts will push the clouds and fill our sails, and we will catch them, Captain—unless night comes before we get them."

Shaw glanced at the sky. The heavens darkened. The rock cliffs of the island next to the ship were in deep shadow. Ahead he saw the double canoe with its red sail slack against the mast. The prey was close.

"We're losing way," Shaw bellowed, seeing sails droop. "Get men in the long-boat and oar us ahead."

A line was fixed to the *Jeremiah* and the longboat. Eight sailors bent to the oars of the smaller vessel pulling the big whaler forward. The gap between ships did not change. Shaw lifted his head to the sky and prayed, "God give us wind,"

Rain slackened. "Sharpshooters, on my command be ready to fire," Shaw ordered. The ocean swells gained size and began to push the *Jeremiah* forward, then back, then forward again in ever greater tempo. The gap narrowed.

"Mattoon, can you load the cannon?" Shaw yelled.

"Too wet to try, but I'll be ready once it lightens up."

Darkness mantled the ocean, yet in the dimness, Shaw saw the outline of a mast two-hundred yards ahead. "Prepare to fire," Shaw screamed.

"I'm steering hard left into the squall," John said. His paddlers followed his instruction and moved into the darkness of the rainstorm. Gunfire furrowed the sea with spouts of water.

John jumped to the platform and lowered the mast. He cautioned the ohana to be silent and asked them to bend low as they paddled. A hundred yards away, he saw the sails of the *Jeremiah* fill with wind. The ship slipped through the ink of night, the rainfall shrouded the ocean in mist. John held his breath, would the low profile of the canoe escape detection? He suspected that the lookouts on the *Jeremiah* searched toward Waikiki.

John watched a glow of light coming from a lantern in the Captain's cabin recede into the night. From a distance he could hear men run and yell on the deck of the ship. He knew that Shaw had lost the ohana in the night.

"Where we going?" Kawika asked.

"While Shaw searches toward Waikiki we head for Waianae," John answered.

"I dunno if that's a good idea. Some mighty mean guys in Waianae. Maybe mo' betta we just go to Honolulu."

"That's what Shaw will expect, that we will land somewhere between Honolulu and Waikiki. It's the logical destination from Molokai. If we can make landfall in Waianae before he finds where we are, we will have a good chance to escape him."

"I might have some friends in Waianae," Kawika said.

"We going to need all the friends we can get," Monapua said, her voice filled with terror. "I hear they still make sacrifices to Ku in the temple in Makaha Valley."

John shrugged. "Human gifts to the ancient war god are over since the missionaries brought Christianity to the islands. I will take my chances with Hawaiians anytime."

"These are not your ordinary Hawaiians," Moanapua said. "They eat the heart, liver, and kidneys of those they capture."

"Maybe we shouldn't go there," Lehua said. "It's too dangerous for the baby."

"I don't think we have a choice. It's either Shaw or the people of Waianae," John answered.

"I'm not going to let that filthy man get his hands on me again," Leinani said with a vehemence that silenced all dissent.

John bent to the task of forcing the double canoe over the swells. He worried whether he had made the right decision. Ten people had placed their lives in his hands. Fear mounted within him. He dared not show indecision. Calling out a slow, rhythmic cadence, he urged his ohana to push the canoe through the night, aiming their boat toward sparse light from the fires on the far west shore of Oahu.

Nineteen

Low clouds scudded across the sky. The double canoe wallowed in the waves two miles off the Waianae coast. John stepped the mast post and unfurled the red sail. The wind caught it, flinging the vessel through the water. Exhausted, the paddlers rested while John steered their craft toward shore.

Kawika scanned the sea. He studied the coastline near Waikiki. Other eyes searched the waters to the east. There were boats in the distance with two or three masts, their white sails filled by the early morning wind.

"Damn," Kawika swore. "I see a ship coming. It's our red sail."

"Everyone is bone tired," John answered. "The wind is our best chance to reach Waianae before our enemy gets us."

"Maybe yes or maybe no, boat long way off, but wind good for us is better for him," Kawika answered.

John steered toward a rock-studded shore. He searched for a bay of sand that they could safely land in. He watched the white sails of a black ship grow larger. "Paddle! Paddle!" he shouted. "Shaw is coming."

Though the gap between vessels was huge, the wind favored the *Jeremiah*. The whaling ship raced through the ocean, its sails puffed outward. John measured the distance to the Waianae shore. He judged that the ohana would make it to a beach before the *Jeremiah* could intercept them. He smiled, confident that he had bested Captain Shaw.

As the double canoe neared land a group of Hawaiians waited on the shore. "That's all we need is a welcoming committee," John said, seeing the array of men standing on the sand several armed with spears or clubs. A mile away, the *Jeremiah*'s prow cleaved the water flinging waves of foam out from both sides of the ship. A voice rang over the water. "Go away. You are not wanted here."

"We need to come ashore," Kawika pointed toward the *Jeremiah*. "Those whalers intend to kill us."

"Do you come in peace or war?"

"Peace, peace," John said, suddenly realizing they were caught up in a landing ritual.

"I am Iolani, the Hawk," a man on shore said. "You must seek permission to land in the ancient tongue."

"Who speaks in the old language?" John whispered. "Someone do something Shaw's boat is coming fast."

"I am Kawika of Lahaina. This is my family. I have friends in Waianae, let us enter your land."

"No," the Hawk answered, "maybe you come to steal—"

A cannon ball plowed into the sea showering the canoe with salt water. Malia stepped forward. "Everybody stand up. Show you have no weapons." She began chanting in the language of the ancients asking that the ohana be allowed ashore and be permitted to enter the tribal territory of Waianae.

Another ball landed just short of the canoe. The resulting wave pushed the vessel ahead. Iolani stroked his chin. "Maybe you coming to steal our women?"

A third cannon ball smashed into an outrigger, flinging shards of splinters into the air. Lehua, joined by Monapua, screamed, their shrieks having an effect on the hostile party on the shore.

"We're coming in," Kawika said.

A fourth shot plowed into the sand, scattering the men on the beach. "Land, land," Iolani yelled. He ran up the shore to escape the attack.

"Load with grape shot," someone yelled on Shaw's ship.

Whatever this armament was, John knew it could not be good. "Paddle," he said. The canoe lifted on the crest of an incoming wave and surfed toward land. Multiple tiny iron balls shredded the mast, some of the hot metal sliced the scalp and shoulder of Kawika.

The wave pushed the fugitive's vessel onto the sand. "Run!" John yelled. "Get off the beach."

A buzz filled the air like the sound of angry hornets whose nest has been attacked. John felt stings over his body, a sharp pain in his side. He struggled through the soft sand, Lehua clutched her baby, Leinani helped them. John plodded next to them, put his arm around Lehua's waist, and pulled her up the beach.

Anchor chains slowed the *Jerimiah* to a stop. Muskets popped. David fell. Blood spread over his face trickling onto the sand. Kawika reached down, picked him up, and carried his wounded friend over the edge of the beach.

"Down," John yelled as he pulled Lehua onto the grass that bordered the shore line. The baby whimpered. He saw that the child was okay. He searched for Leinani, and found her prone staring at the sea.

By a low sand hill, John spied Kawika huddled with Iolani. He crawled to them. He heard the Hawk say, "Oh yeah, I know you. We cousin's on my mother's side."

John pressed himself into the sand. Besides him were a dozen men armed with rocks and spears. Another low hill had a group of men defending it. John studied the *Jeremiah* at anchor off the beach. A longboat swung out from the ship and dropped into the water.

"Rufus get your men into that boat," Shaw ordered. "Mattoon stay on board. You're in charge. Roberto, Allard, help me."

His voice raspy, Mattoon said, "Captain what are your orders?"

"Stand by the cannon. When we get ashore, I'll signal you where to fire it."

"We don't have much shot left, only enough for two rounds of fire."

"That will have to do. Boys lower me into the long boat. I want that kanaka."

Ten whalers landed on the beach. Shaw remained in the longboat directing the attack. In diamond formation, with three men at the point, the whalers climbed up the sand. When the men in front reached the grass line, stones showered them. Two men fell, the third running back to the base of the formation.

Shaw watched injured sailors crawl back, stones pelting them as they fled. Rufus came saying, "Captain, I told you these folks in Waianae are mean. They live and fight like the old days. No quarter given and they eat what they kill."

"Damn savages," Shaw answered.

Another hail of stones plummeted onto the sand. Whalers ran to the long-boat, one of them pointed upland. "Them rocks will kill us, Captain."

Shaw remembered the stories of the death of Captain Cook and some of his crew, brought down by stones thrown by angry Hawaiians. He shook his fist in the air. "I'll get you someday, you damned kanaka."

He ordered his men to push the longboat into the surf and row back to the *Jeremiah*. Once the whalers were on board, sails were unfurled and the ship stood out to sea.

Book Two

Twenty

At the deep water port of Honolulu, the small band split. Kawika and his friends returned to Lahaina. Ah Sam and Lehua moved in with uncle, Muk Fat. Malia and her family canoed to Waikiki and found Makanani relatives farming taro in the marshlands near Diamond Head. Four of them lived in a small compound by an immense wet field of green-leafed plants, Uncle Edward, Aunt Emma, and Cousins Sara and Mary. Edward's deceased brother had married Malia.

The combined families set to work adding housing to the compound. A shack for the three unmarried females, John and David shared a new hut, Malia moved into a vacated shanty, and Edward and Emma remained in their home.

Once settled, John and David worked with other Hawaiian sharecroppers in the wetlands cultivating the purple tuber that, once full grown, they pounded into poi and sold at market. Aunt Malia focused on making cloth, but refused to let Leinani work in the fields, insisting that she complete her education.

Each day John walked Leinani to school. They both enjoyed this time alone and the opportunity to discuss what she had learned the previous day. On many occasions he attended classes with her, and there were evenings when they read together by candlelight. These were special times for both of them, moments of innocent affection between two members of a family.

Malia insisted that they go to church each Sunday. When John asked what is so good about Christianity, she answered: "They believe in one God. Teach the difference between right and wrong. They don't believe in black magic like the kahuna and forbid human sacrifice."

Malia went on to explain that before the Christians came, the chiefs would make male gifts to a god for all kinds of reasons, success in war, or to end a calamity, or even to cure sickness in a ruler's household. "But you know what I think," Malia said. "They wanted the person's land, or wife, or something else." Then she laughed, pushing her finger into John. "I lucky, they only sacrifice guys like you. Not the women, we unclean." Malia smiled and added, "You know me John, I take bath every day. Sometimes three or four. This unclean talk all rubbish, but thank God those olden time chiefs believe that. If they didn't, I am dead long ago, bleeding on an altar before some pagan god."

For several months the families lived in peace, but David chafed at the monotony of work. One evening he announced that he was going to Honolulu with friends. Soon he spent every night away from home, and when he returned early in the morning he was drunk. It was not long before he suggested that the females join him in an evening on the town. "Plenty wild hula and lots of good looking guys," he said.

But Emma and Malia were adamant, "The girls are fourteen and fifteen they cannot go."

Their answer angered David, and he kicked the side of a shack. "They got to grow up sometime. What you saving them for? I got friends who'd like to meet the girls, give them a good time."

John interrupted, "You've been asking me to come with you. Let me join you tonight, see what it's like."

David looked at him, "I been thinking you're a prude. Asked you to come with me couple times, but always no. Yeah, come tonight, see what it's like then you can tell those old women they have nothing to worry about." David turned on his heel, calling back, "We go in an hour."

Disapproval flared in Malia's eyes, "John, no matter what you see. No matter what you say, those girls are not going to go with David, or meet his friends."

"I don't want to go, but I am trying to keep peace in the family. Once I'm there maybe I can convince David to be reasonable. I don't know, but I'll try."

Malia spat out her answer. "Don't become like David. Drunk all time. Alcohol bad for Hawaiians."

As soon as he walked through the door of the large shack, John knew he shouldn't have come. Light from kukui torches barely penetrated the gloom.

Their smoke spiraled up and disappeared. John did not know if the building had a roof. He thought it might since he saw no stars.

Crates with detached doors laid on top joining them together served as a bar. Wooden benches and stools provided seating. Big beer barrels acted as tables. With the floor made of sand John had the uncomfortable feeling that fleas swarmed in the ground. Noise came from a guitar, flute, and calabash drum. Two fat women danced on a floor of mats their hips gyrating in time to the beat of the music.

A dozen men sat or leaned onto the makeshift bar with a pair of females loaded with flowers in their hair and around their necks. They reminded him of Malama. He wondered whether the madam still did business in Lahaina. David pulled him over to a wooden crate, and ordered beers.

One of the women came, ran her fingers through John's hair, and rubbed her thigh against him. "Hello handsome, buy me some whiskey?"

Before John could answer, David chimed in, "Sure thing. I'll buy you a whole bottle."

One of the thugs at the bar hollered, "David, where are those young girls you promised us? We're tired of this old stuff."

The floozy by John's side flung a raised middle finger at the man, yelling, "Yeah, your dick's so limp you can't even wet a knot hole let alone frighten a fourteen-year old with it."

The thug moved away from the bar scowling, his fists clenched.

"Hold it." John interceded, his voice rising with anger, "None of David's family is for sale."

"Who's talking about buying, you dumb shit, whatever I want I take, free."

The woman by John stepped away muttering, "don't want any trouble."

David piped up, "Hey brother, don't listen to cousin. I'll fix you up. No worry. Besides this guy," pointing, "he big time lua man. Wipe out three whalers by himself. Don't mess with him."

"Yeah," the thug said, splintering two beer bottles into jagged pieces, "Let's see how tough the lua man is."

"Stop it you two," the bartender yelled, whacking a club on the bar. "I don't want any trouble in my saloon. You," he pointed at John, "you're not a regular here, get out." At that moment, two big Hawaiians appeared and positioned themselves between the angry men.

John raised his hands palms open, "Hey, okay, I'm going. Don't want trouble." He backed out the front door, one of the bouncers following him. As he left, John kept an eye on the thug who had challenged him. The man dropped his broken beer bottles, picked up a drink, and gulped it with one swallow.

Once out the door, John hiked for home. He sensed the bouncer coming fast behind him and he turned, assuming a lua stance, arms thrust to the side, hands cupped, legs spread out, knees bent.

His pursuer slowed. "*Mokomoko* position," he said. "You are trained in lua. Listen, there are very few of us left. Come to our *pa lua*, our school in the valley. You know the entry chant?"

"Yes, *E hea i ke kanaka*."

"That is so. You know the rituals."

The bouncer gave John detailed instructions as to where the school was hidden. "Come when you can, someone is always there." They touched fists and parted.

The next day, John confronted an inebriated David. "You will not take your sister or your cousins to that place."

"What's a matta' you?" David slurred his words, belligerence evident in his voice. "I can do what I want."

"Not while I'm living here," John answered.

"Yeah, big shot, maybe you won't be here for long," David said, turned and shuffled back to town.

Weeks went by of work and school. The two men fell into an uneasy truce, each one avoiding confrontation. John was surprised when one evening, a month after the near battle in the saloon, David asked him, "Why don't you join us tonight? We have good fun, lots of hula and alcohol. Remember the woman that wanted whiskey? I think she likes you. She keeps asking for you."

John knew that he was being set up, but for what? "I love hula," John replied, hoping to keep the conversation relaxed. "As for the woman…." His voice trailed off. "You must know that they spread disease. Some of them can kill you."

David threw John a scornful look. "You talk like a minister. I bet you're still a virgin. Get with it man, live a little. Come with me. I'll pay for everything."

Alarm bells went off, David had no money. Someone else was paying for the evening's fun, but why? John answered in a neutral tone, "Look David, I'm not a minister, just being careful. Go on and enjoy yourself. I'm going to visit Leinani and her cousins in their shack."

"Oh ho, fooling around with the women instead of coming with me. Remember, you're a baptized Christian and can't seduce relatives."

"Shut up and get out of here," John scowled, and left for the quarters of the three young women. He spent the evening swapping gossip with them, then after ten o'clock returned to his hut to sleep.

Twenty-One

Dogs barked. One yelped, its whine piercing the night. Leilani heard a voice. The words slurred, "You make noise. Wake everyone."

"You said there were juicy women. Show us."

"Yeah, I could use a little fun."

"Me too, the ones at the party were trash. I want young stuff."

"Three good ones inside," David's voice answered.

Leinani rose, whispering to the girls who slept near her, "Get up. Get up right now."

At the threshold, a body covered the entryway. The man lunged in. Leinani screamed. The figure pressed a rough hand against her mouth. She fought for air, beat him with her fists. He smashed her across the face, reached for her neck, and tore at her sleeping dress.

Leinani twisted and the attacker's palm slipped from her lips. "Help me!" she screamed. Next to her shrill cries of her cousins erupted. Other men had entered the shack.

Leinani's assailant came at her again, breathing fast. "Shut up. You're going to like what I give you." With his open palm, he cuffed her across the face.

Tears, pain, fear came. She struck again. Her clothing ripped away. Hands palmed her skin.

"Fight me. It's good when a woman fights."

A mouth smothered her breast. Hands forced her legs apart. Terror gripped her. A scream died in her throat.

Roused awake, John sped to Leinani's shack. David snored in the dirt near the building. He pushed in. A man straddled a girl. He grabbed his feet and dragged him from his prey. He twisted a leg, hearing the sound of cracking bone, followed by a howl of pain. "You're lucky I don't break your back." He delivered a hard kick to the man's kidneys. The rapist screamed. John bashed his head against the side of the shack.

Another figure rose unsteadily. He lunged. John hit him in the jaw followed by a chopping blow to the neck. The man went to his knees and rolled onto his back. John's sideways kick into the chin put him to sleep.

Leinani crawled to aid her sobbing cousin. A third thug straddled her, moaning with the pleasure of rape. John seized the ecstatic man and pulled him off the girl. Despite the rapist's attempts to fight, John shook him like a rag doll, his hands squeezing his throat. He butted the attacker's forehead with his, heard a sharp gasp, and threw the stunned man through the opening of the shack. Within moments the air filled with the cries of men and the sobs of assaulted girls. It was then that David stumbled into the grass building.

"What are you doing to my friends?"

"What am I doing? You dare ask that, after you brought these drunks here?"

The two men squared off just as members of the Makanani family arrived. Malia, Emma, and Edward came into the hut. Malia restrained her son while Emma turned her attention to the girls.

"Why you hit my friends?" David demanded. "They meant no harm, only having fun." He made a feeble attempt to strike John, who easily fended off the blow. David's belligerence continued, as he repeated, "How come you beat up my friends?"

John knew if he hit his cousin, it would be with damaging force. Hoping to avoid this, he exited the shack and retreated to the edge of the taro field. David rushed at him, his arms outstretched, his hands shaped into fists. John stepped to the side and the drunk tumbled face-first into the mud.

Afraid his cousin would drown, John pulled him up and deposited him on the bank, where he sloshed fresh water over him. Wet and dirty, a sullen David staggered to his feet and made his way to his hovel. He fell through its door, onto the floor, and went to sleep.

John returned to the three girls. One cousin wept in the arms of Malia, relieved to have been spared a rape. But another cried hysterically, Emma stroked her hair, spoke soothing words, while at the same time washing away the fluids of her attacker. Leinani stood alone, her hands clasped to her face. John took a garment, handed it to her, and looked away. "Thanks for saving me," she said.

In the confusion, the three men escaped. Nearby, David snored, unaware of the damage he had caused.

Malia and Emma comforted the distressed girls as best they could. They covered them with clean clothes, hugged and kissed them. But the intermittent cries of hysteria from the raped girl forced Emma to take her into her home.

John could not leave Leinani alone. When she complained of the redness on the side of her face, John smiled saying, "I will paint your other cheek red and you will look like a precious ruby." They laughed.

When morning came, Malia suggested that they go to church to give thanks to God. The family trooped into town. At noon, they were back in the compound with David still asleep.

Leinani came to John and asked, "Will you hike with me to the top of Mount Leahi?"

Happy to be alone with her, he accepted.

They tiptoed on the berms of the taro ponds, walking carefully not to slide into the muddy field. The early afternoon sun glistened from Leinani's hair as it swung across her shoulders. John smelled the sweetness of her body, his senses arousing him.

When they came to a hedge, Leinani asked, "Please look away."

He nodded and turned his back. He knew she intended to remove the ugly sack that Malia forced upon her.

"You can turn around." Leinani finished straightening the pareu that wrapped around her body.

"You look great." John said, admiring how the garment accentuated the natural curves of the young girl's figure.

Leinani smiled and reached for his hand. They climbed upward. John felt her trembling. He thought she was still frightened, traumatized, by what occurred a few hours ago. He said nothing, believing she would speak of it when she was ready.

"It was horrid," she said, her voice barely above a whisper. "I have never felt such despair, that feeling of being trapped and unable to save myself. If you hadn't come, if he had..." Her voice trailed off and tears filled her eyes.

"I would have killed the bastard!" John said with a vehemence that caused Leinani's eyes to widen. The girl touched his shoulder and they stood together. "There is still fear from the brutality, but I feel safe that you are with me."

With a rueful smile, John looked at her, shrugged and mumbled, "Yes, cousin, you are safe with me." What he wanted to do was pull her close, hold her, kiss her.

They worked their way beyond the fields and marshes of Moiliili-Waikiki, hiking all the way into the crater of Mount Leahi, known to foreign sailors as Diamond Head. Lore had it that seamen who explored the dead volcano scooped up thousands of bright crystals, mistaking the worthless stones for diamonds.

When they reached the top, Leinani looked across Waikiki. "Isn't this stunningly beautiful?"

John followed her gaze. Far beyond them were the Waianae Mountains, the western sun's glancing rays adding specks of gold to the spectacular colors of the earth and foliage on the hills. Greenery spread like a great mantle over the mountains of Waianae and Koolau, and into the valley of Nuuanu, where many warriors died in the last battle of conquest. Up and over what was called Punchbowl Volcano the vast green cloak spread, spilling down into the valley of Manoa. The land was colored by clumps of bright flowers and leaves, and then wet fields filled with waving stalks of taro and rice.

Cumulus clouds towered overhead, their shapes dark with moisture as they drifted across the sky. Great blue rifts of the heavens slashed into the clouds, letting columns of sunlight shine onto a vast and restless sea, where caps of white bobbed endlessly above the dark waters. The salt of the sea threw out a refracting prism of colors, from deep purple, to blue, to a light blue-green. Sweeping waves topped with flecks of foam rushed onto the sand shores of Waikiki.

Their bodies touched as the two were blown together by the wind sweeping up the steep sides of the volcano. Gusts twisted Leinani's hair into strands that whipped against John's face. "Nani," the enraptured young woman sighed.

"Yes, you are beautiful," John agreed, as his arm went about her waist and he pulled her close. As he bent, she drew away. He saw a flush of emotions wash over her.

What he wanted was forbidden. But he disregarded his conscience, bending into her. Leinani's tension weakened as her body melded into his.

"Hui," a voice called. Up the hill came Aunt Emma and Cousin Sara. They soon stood with John and Leinani.

After several minutes, Emma announced that it was time to return to the compound. "I need your help going down, John," she added, indicating the steep descent.

The two young girls trooped ahead while John helped Emma. When they reached the base of the mountain, Leinani returned to John. With a smile, she took his hand, "You are a very special man," she said.

Though he flamed with desire the cool softness of her flesh calmed him. They let Emma and Sara hurry on while they ambled toward home.

Rays from a vanishing sun lit on a pleasant scene of happy people picking their way along the earth barrier that separated two wet fields of taro. The bridge ended at the compound of the Makanani family. Emma and Sara entered it. Leinani held John's hand, leaning against his shoulder as they walked.

David rushed to them. "What you doing with my sister?" he demanded. "Get away from her." His harsh words blasted across the compound. When he neared John, he said, "Why you throw me in the taro patch?"

A wide-eyed Leinani separated herself, flustered by David's screams. A crimson sheen of red colored her face.

"I didn't throw you in the taro patch," John answered. "You charged me and fell into it because you were too drunk to stop." Before David could respond, John added, "And why did you help your drunken friends attack the women of your family?"

"What friends?" David said. "And what you mean *drunken friends who attacked my family*? What you mean I helped somebody? You attacked me and now, look at you, fooling around with my sister." Saliva formed in the corners of his mouth and his face became contorted with rage.

Malia and Uncle Edward rushed to the two young men. "Hold it! Hold it!" Edward yelled, stepping between them. He turned to David. "You've been asleep all day. Don't you remember what happened early this morning?" When there was no answer, he said, "You don't recall that three men attacked your sister and your cousins? Weren't these men your friends, and didn't you bring them here?"

David shook his head. "I don't remember anything. Maybe somebody follow me from the party, but they not my friends."

"The truth is, you were too drunk to remember who you brought here and what you did to help them," John said.

David stood taller, shoulders thrown back. "Eh, brah. Don't you call me a liar. Maybe you are the one who attacked my sister. I see you play around with her."

"Stop," Malia said. "David, go back to your house." She turned to Leinani. "You, Sara, and Aunt Emma come with me. John, you must leave."

He wandered from the compound, disheartened that the possibility for healing had turned ugly. John kicked the dirt as he walked, emotions threatened to overcome him. Maybe he should just go back, take Leinani, beat David and anyone who stood in his way. Tears brimmed in his eyes. The inner conflicts tore at his heart. He knew he was suffocating. He needed to bring peace to his soul. Escape this torment of forbidden desire that consumed him. It is best to go away, he thought. Maybe escape to the lua school in the valley?

Twenty-Two

Leinani's hand shook as she washed the massive entry door into Saint Sebastian's School for Women. The memory of the assault still terrorized her. She felt ashamed, unclean, especially since her mother had hid her in this awful school. Thrust away from John and the family.

A pretty young girl working at her side jostled her arm. "I can't believe that just a few months ago you were a coarse little savage planting taro and beating tapa cloth," Maria Francois teased, as she polished the brass doorknobs of the front door.

"And it wasn't too long ago that you slunk like a guttersnipe through the sewers of Paris," Leinani shot back. She threw a wadded wet cloth at her tormentor. The missile missed its target, but managed to leave drops of dirty moisture on Maria's dress.

"Ladies, what is going on out there?" Headmistress Seldon demanded, her face peering through an open casement window.

"Nothing, Mistress Seldon," the girls chorused.

The woman, director of Saint Sebastian School, drew closer to her students. "I heard the word *savage*, Miss Francois. Our Miss Makanani is Hawaiian, but she is not a savage." The girls exchanged glances. If Headmistress Seldon noticed, she did not let on. "I daresay it is unfortunate that these native people fell into the hands of the horrid Calvinists. They are hypocritical New England missionaries bent on teaching Christianity. And what do they do?"

Leinani nearly answered, but thought better of it.

"Ingratiate themselves with the Hawaiian royalty and take control of the government. Although, I must say, I approve of their doctrines regarding the female body being covered, head to foot."

Leinani felt her ire rise. "The Calvinists you seem to like made women cover themselves, forcing us to wear those horrible sacks. Nudity, the minister told us, is evil. But that isn't all. We weren't allowed to practice our culture. Whether it was displaying love for each other, dancing the hula, surf riding, swimming, wrestling, and even speaking our language. It was like being in prison," she declared with youthful indignation.

"This is exactly why King Kamehameha IV and Queen Emma invited us of the Anglican Church to show Hawaiian commoners how to regain their culture, as well as educate everyone, men and women alike." She lifted her chin proudly, as if she, herself, had been responsible for these good works. "Our church practices tolerance of the natives, not suppression, and we are especially proud of Saint Sebastian.

"Enough of this, since both of you are intent on silliness, it's best to split you up. Marie, continue your work on the door. Leinani, come with me to the kitchen."

The rectory pots, pans, windows, and floors looked fine to the girl, but she expected the headmistress to deem them otherwise. "Polish all of them. I'll check on you in one hour," Seldon said, then turned and left the kitchen.

Leinani set to work, performing her tasks. With vigorous rubbing, she wiped away a dirty spot that had glued itself to a frying pan. It had been several months since the attack at the Makanani compound that resulted in her placement in the school. Malia had made the arrangements. In exchange for labor and a small monthly amount, the girl would receive room, board, and an education. David's drunk thoughtlessness had condemned her to what amounted to a prison sentence in this cloistered school.

Leinani moved to the next chore and began polishing the teapot. It had been painful enough to be sent away, but the fact that it had been done in such an underhanded fashion still pricked at her skin. In secret, her mother had spirited her to the school, telling no one in the family where she would be. To make it even more difficult, she was not permitted to return to the family compound.

Leinani sighed, "Where is John?" She missed him very much.

Twenty-Three

Trees arched up, their topmost branches blending into each other creating a leaf roof for the small clearing within the valley. Braziers set in each corner flamed high, their light reflecting from the oiled body of John Tana. He squatted on the smoothed earth floor of the natural amphitheater purging his mind of emotions.

"*Ka hana*," the teacher ordered.

John stood and picked up a long rod. Ten feet away the bouncer from the saloon rose and retrieved a similar rod.

"Attack!"

The two men came together, their staves clashing. For minutes they fought until the bouncer scored a hit. Then they squared off to punch, block, jab, and kick, blows that never fully landed. The teacher constantly interrupted the sham battle, to correct a movement or demonstrate a strike. After an hour of mock combat, more hours of exercises followed until the exhausted students were permitted to sleep.

John was happy to be in the lua school. It was a dying art, outlawed by a Hawaiian government influenced by missionaries determined to stamp out the culture and its heathen practices. Including the teacher there were six who practiced the ancient martial techniques made famous by Kamehameha the Great in his wars of conquest.

For a year John lived in the secluded valley working in the school's farm during the day. In the late afternoon and evening, he exercised and practiced lua moves with the other students employed at daytime jobs.

John was exhilarated by the periods of physical activity, his toil in the mud, and the mental healing he found in early morning meditations. His infatuation for Leinani and the pain of being forced from her were cleansed from his thoughts.

A flaw existed in this idyllic existence, the still. His teacher insisted on brewing alcohol for sale. "We need the money," he said.

"Selling homemade booze is illegal," John argued. "And Hawaiians go crazy when they drink it."

"You're talking like a preacher man, demon rum and all that. We have to sell something. The few potatoes and taro we raise is just enough to sustain the students and their families. You tend to the fields; I'll take care of the still."

"There will be trouble," John muttered as he gave up his protests. He was proved to be right.

The revenuers came in the early morning while John mediated above the valley waiting for sunlight. Angry shouts, the smashing of wood, the breaking of glass penetrated his mind with a cacophony of sound. He rose from his squat to study what lay below. He could make out lantern light. He heard the voice of his teacher, the sounds of combat.

John picked his way down the mountainside trail he climbed the night before. He heard a voice yell, "Shoot the bastard before he kills us all." John smiled. His instructor was proving too much for his attackers.

A shot, then a scream, resounded through the hillside. John's heart beat faster, his recently cleansed mind filled with new emotions. Am I too late to help my master? As he stepped onto the valley floor his teacher staggered toward him. "Run. Warn the others."

John hesitated.

"Go!" the man ordered as he fell into the leaves and twigs littering the valley. Discipline kicked in. John turned and re-climbed the mountain trail.

A voice yelled, "Halt!"

A bullet smashed into rocks near his hand. Tiny stones splattered against his body. He did not stop, leaping from foothold to foothold up the mountain, worrying when the next shot would come.

Someone screamed, "Shoot him." A bullet slammed into the mountainside wide of its mark.

"Damn the bugger."

John risked a look below and saw his *olohe,* white garment drenched red, grasping a uniformed man. The constable pistol whipped the teacher who collapsed. For an instant John thought to go back, but realized that his master had sacrificed himself to allow him to escape and warn the others. He accelerated his climb. More shots chased him until the brightness of a new day burst around him and he realized that he was above the trees. Their leafy branches blocked out the men below.

John scrambled over the ridge, found a dry stream bed choked with rocks, and followed it toward toward the sea. Except for the clothes he wore, all of his possessions were in the lua school.

Twenty-Four

Honolulu, August 1870

John supervised a team of oxen pulling on a drag rope of a heavy iron bucket that scooped through the limestone at the bottom of Fair Haven harbor. The power of the animals lifted the container from the ocean through a pulley and guy arrangement and dumped the dredged stone on a wooden pier at the Port of Honolulu.

John sectioned the rocks and placed the rough-hewn blocks onto a wagon adjacent to the wharf. He shoveled broken pieces of limestone and deposited them into a box in the vehicle. The ground was soon cleared and the next limestone load was ready to be dumped, shaped, and lifted onto the wagon. John worked for hours in the sun, his job made more difficult by the lack of help. Very few men were willing to handle the sharp, heavy pieces of dead reef.

John needed this job and preferred work on the waterfront to cutting sugar cane stalks then loading them onto carts for transport to the sugar mills. He especially disliked the plantation supervisors who loved to ride about like lords with their black whips flicking on the backs of the field laborers to make them work harder.

Using his palaka handkerchief to wipe sweat from his face, John saw a group of Hawaiian stevedores lounging against a shed erected a hundred yards away. One of them stared in his direction.

John shifted his attention back to the coral, but he sensed the man's intense gaze. He dared not return the stare, understanding that this would be a challenge and he did not want trouble on the docks. He also understood that, as the new man, he would soon be tested.

With the setting of the sun, the bell sounded, and men packed up for home. John washed his hands in a trough and trudged along the busy streets to Ah Sam's restaurant. Entering, he smelled the sweet aroma of cooking food and saw Lehua holding baby Leinani in her arms and yelling at her young son.

"Hey you, Choi, come here right now," an exasperated Lehua said as the little boy scrambled under a dining table, upsetting several chairs in his dash to escape. She took a menacing step toward her son and demanded, "Choi Waihoku, come out now or big angry." The boy dashed by John and out the open door of the restaurant.

Lehua thrust the baby into his arms. "Hold her while I catch that humbug."

John cradled little Leinani and watched as her frustrated mother pursued Choi. He knew the boy would hide and torment Lehua only as long as it took her to get really angry, then he would give himself up to a spanking, the price the toddler paid to win his mother's attention.

As he rocked Leinani, his mind moved back over the events of the previous three years. He thought of how the ohana had escaped from Waianae and reached Honolulu safely. And how, on this journey, Ah Sam had christened his new son, Choi, in honor of his grandfather. Lehua had not argued with this choice, since it was the Chinese way, but she insisted on giving Choi a Hawaiian middle name, calling him Waihoku.

"Why that?" Ah Sam asked.

"Our son is born under stars and at the water," Lehua replied.

When their daughter had come the parents decided to name her Leinani in honor of the woman who had rescued them from the angry whalers. Though Leinani's birth was a blessing, her arrival forced Lehua and Ah Sam to leave the home of Uncle Muk Fat and open the restaurant.

Ah Sam had confided to John that the trouble came when Muk Fat arranged to acquire a wife from China, her name was Sui Chan. The woman proved to be a high-class witch. She demanded that the two daughters of Muk Fat, born to him from a common law relationship with a Hawaiian woman, have their feet bound. "Daughters of rich men in China have lotus feet, small and tiny," Sui Chan said. "Husband, you will show your wealth with daughters having small feet."

"Yet," Ah Sam confided, "It's impossible live with two girls with bound feet. They cry all the time. Feet stink from pus. No can work. Must carry them everywhere."

John remembered Ah Sam explaining, "Our joint families broke up when Sui Chan demanded that Leinani have bound feet. I say to her, 'Golden Lotus woman worthless. No can walk. Feet stink. No way bind Leinani. If you want that, we leave.'"

The baby stirred and gurgled in John's arms, rousing him from his reverie. He hugged her close and gently patted her back. She gave a loud burp and then stared into her godfather's eyes. John hardly noticed, his thoughts locked into the past, the turmoil of the Makanani ohana, and the distressing series of events that forced him to leave, the lua school, his escape, and his taking up residence with Ah Sam.

"Aytah, Aytah," Choi screamed. Tears streamed down his cheeks as Lehua, with a firm grasp on his arm, pulled him into the restaurant.

John glanced around him. Kerosene lanterns lit the interior, their inexpensive glow signaling the end of the whaling era. Ah Sam cooked, mixing sweet and sour sauce with spareribs in a large black pan. There was a perfume of savory steam from the meat and vegetables, a pungently sweet smell that drifted through the restaurant and then billowed out into the darkness.

Several men ate, their chewing rhythm undisturbed by Choi's cries. The baby began to fuss, and John scanned the room for Lehua. She bustled over to him and scooped Leinani from his arms.

A tall Hawaiian, dressed in a dark suit, white shirt, and trim string tie knotted at his throat walked in. Ah Sam hurried to the entrance, "Joshua, you came. Please, come meet my friend."

John stood, apprising the man who strode toward him. Slim, with a dark beard circling his chin, Joshua came with an air of confidence unusual in a native man. His face, like John's, was unmarked by the pox that had disfigured many Hawaiians fortunate enough to survive the dreaded disease brought by the foreigners.

"Mr. Kanakoa, this Mr. Tana, the man I tell you," Ah Sam said adding, "John, this is Hawaiian lawyer. I tell him about your land. Sit, I bring food."

Ah Sam hurried away leaving the two men. John pointed to an empty chair. Joshua reached out and took his hand in the Western fashion and shook it saying, "Mr. Sam has told me about you. How you aided his family and lost your property."

John liked the firmness in the man's handshake, not flabby like those who are insincere. He looked into a pair of brown eyes and saw confidence etched there. Despite his inexperience he knew that this is a wise man, older by ten than his twenty-one years. He felt he could trust him as they released hands and sat.

An awkward pause existed for some moments. John too awed to speak to an attorney. Joshua broke the silence, "I'm told you originally came from Kahalui, Maui."

John nodded.

"You had some trouble there, lost your property."

Ah Sam placed steaming plates of rice, ribs, chicken, and vegetables in front of the two men. "Eat. Enjoy." He sat in an empty chair and said, "I tell Joshua, a good customer, he only come for lunch when you working, about your troubles. Maybe he help you. What you think?"

"I need to know more about his Kahalui land and what happened," Joshua answered. "Tell me your story and even draw a map of your place."

Heartened by the lawyer's interest, John related his family's history, the gift from Kamehameha, their farming and sharing of the land with others that had occurred for seventy-five years. He drew a crude map using the stream that flowed by his fields as a reference point. He finished saying, "Grant and Company stole it all. Is there anything I can do?"

Kanakoa had listened patiently to the tale, eating sparingly of the food. He finished a rib, wiped his hands, thought some moments before answering. "All land was divided in 1848 by a law called the 'Great Mahele.' It allowed commoners like your family to file claims to property that they had historically farmed. Many Hawaiians did not understand the process and failed to act. Men like this Mr. Grant took advantage of ignorance, filed land patents and stole the land."

"Is there any hope to regain what I lost?"

"I will look into the matter at the patent office. Part of my practice is land claims."

"I don't have money."

"I will pay," Ah Sam interrupted.

"Good, then it is settled. I will start research tomorrow. I can find you here when I have something to report?"

John nodded, too excited to speak. The men parted. John went to his room in back of the restaurant. He prayed that he might recover what he had lost and went to sleep.

Twenty-Five

"**T**his Sharps carbine is a good weapon. It's a decent breach loader but limited to a single shot," Robert Grant said as he fired the gun at a gourd bobbing in the sea at Honolulu Harbor.

"You missed," Jones, a business associate, said. "Not a very accurate weapon."

"It's better than a muzzle loader. Can you image the Union and Confederate infantry marching against each other in long lines and then stopping, firing, and trying to reload a musket while bullets whizzed into them? At least this gun allowed you to insert a paper cartridge at the breech and fire more rapidly."

"Didn't the Union folk have Henry repeaters? Those could fire up to sixteen rounds a minute," Jones remarked.

"Yes. The Confederates hated the weapon. Said it could be loaded on Sunday and fired all week. But the Union Commissaries wouldn't buy the rifle for their soldiers. They claimed it wasted ammunition."

"How foolish, a gun like that could have won the war in a year. Talking to our French minister he says that Europeans are giving up on muzzle loaders. Several countries are arming their soldiers with breach loading weapons."

"That's the trend in warfare. I just bought a beauty from a whaling captain who needed money. Look at this gun," Grant said, opening a case and removing a glistening brown-stocked weapon. The brass at its center shone in the afternoon sun like minted gold. "This is a Winchester repeating rifle. They call it 'Yellowboy.' It holds fifteen rounds of .44 caliber ammunition. It has a lever action which ejects a bullet, loads another, cocks the rifle and has it ready to fire in seconds. It outranges a musket by more than three times and is much more accurate."

"That's a weapon for the ages."

"Yes, and if we could get enough of these guns we could topple this decrepit monarchy in a day."

"That's seditious talk. Many of our brethren support the kingdom."

"I know, but this Lot Kamehameha will not help our enterprises grow. He won't make deals with America. The sugar industry in the southern states is reviving. With the high tariffs and shipping costs we can barely compete with them."

"Didn't you make money during the war and after?"

"Yes, but now it's harder. We need annexation to the United States."

"It won't happen under Lot."

"That is true, but if we had enough Winchesters and determined men we might convince him to be more sensible."

"Robert, best you keep these thoughts to yourself. There is not enough support for a revolution. How are your Maui holdings progressing?"

"Our new fields in Kahului are producing large amounts of sugar per acre. I think it's the best cane land in the world."

"Then it's the smartest investment you ever made."

"Yes, and I stole the land right out of the hands of a dumb kanaka. He didn't know what he had, growing sweet potatoes and taro, and sharing it with a bunch of poor people. Maui land and sugar can make us all rich. But we need annexation or an end to tariffs."

"I'm with you," Jones said. "But only if you can figure out how to get what we want without a revolution. See you at dinner."

Grant watched his friend ride away. He placed his new Winchester into a shiny leather holster on the side of his horse, hung the Sharp on the pommel of the saddle, mounted his gelding, and rode into town.

At his office Grant discovered a crony from the Honolulu Patent Office waiting for him. "Need to see you," the man said.

"Come into my private chambers," Grant answered, perturbed by the presence of the man at his place of business. They usually did their transactions in secret.

Grant's inner office was sumptuous. Its highly polished koa walls glowed in the midday light. An intricately woven deep red Persian rug covered the floor.

The four chairs and couch in the room were bound in red leather. Pictures of seascapes and sailing vessels on the walls were framed in gold. The entire aspect of the room exuded wealth.

"Sit and tell me why you are here," Grant said barely masking his irritation at this intrusion into his sanctuary by an underling.

"I would not have come if I didn't think what I have to say is of the utmost importance to you."

Grant raised an eyebrow, withdrew a cheroot from a gold case, lit it, and blew smoke. He knew the man wanted money. Whatever the information he imparted could prove costly. He decided not to appear too eager. "Nothing could be that important to take you away from your work."

"It involves your Kahului property."

Grant fought to maintain his composure. The fields of sugar cane he planted in that Maui land had been harvested. 'Highest yield in the world' he had told his associate. Gonzalez had assured him the kanaka was gone, finished. He had his land patent in his safe. What could this news be? "What of it?" he asked, blowing smoke into his companion.

The man waved his hands clearing away the dense cloud that intruded between them. He made eye contact with Grant. "The inquiries concerned your title to the property."

"I have the patent papers here in my office. You signed them."

The Bureau of Conveyance man shifted his eyes, looking down, up, and away from Grant's stare. He squirmed in his seat and swallowed. "Maybe you should know what was asked?"

"Well?"

"A little something for my time would be appreciated."

Grant looked away, gazing beyond the intricately woven curtains that bordered the window opening onto the street. The bargaining had begun. What must he pay? "How much?"

"Ten silver."

"Whatever you have to say can't be that valuable. Five silver."

"Eight."

"Seven."

"Done. An attorney came to the office and searched the records on your Kahului property. He asked if you had recorded a court order terminating allodial rights."

Grant leaned forward onto his desk. He chewed on the small cigar. "Allodial, what's that?"

"Go see an attorney," the man said, covering a smirk with a hand, his eyes bright.

Grant realized he had been caught in a cat and mouse game but, unusual for him, he was the one trapped in the claws. "How much more?"

"Three silver."

When Grant nodded, the Bureau man continued, "Allodial rights are the residual entitlements that a former owner of government property has in the land he once occupied."

"What are they?"

"Easements, the power to take water, timber, even some produce from the land."

"Doesn't a patent erase all that?"

"The law is not clear. That is why the attorney was asking if you had a court order quieting title."

"Damn!" Grant swore, no longer able to control his anger. He should have followed through with the legal process instead of doing everything himself, as he always did. His methods of bribery and force had worked in the past, but today he faced a problem that might not be solvable by his usual methods.

"If there is an attorney there must be a claimant?" Grant asked.

"That's logical."

"But if there is no claimant then there are no allodial rights?"

"Yes."

"Who is this attorney and where do I find him?"

"Five more silver and I'll give you what you want."

Grant paid and ushered the man out. At the front door he turned to a reception clerk, "Send word to Maui. Have Gonzalez report to me immediately."

Returning to his inner office, Grant grasped 'Yellowboy.' He shook the rifle saying, "I will have work for you."

Twenty-Six

John loved smashing the sharp coral into blocks for transport. He felt the muscles of his body strain with the effort of swinging the sledge into the limestone and then lifting the shaped blocks onto a wagon. The sweat that dripped from him attested to the work, but also bore witness to the physical strength that he had developed.

"It's end of work time," Mike, his boss, said. "That's enough for today. You do the work of three men. But I can only pay for one."

"Just so you pay," John answered with a smile.

He walked two blocks from Honolulu Harbor into Ah Sam's restaurant. Little Choi played on the floor with wooden blocks John had made. "Uncle, uncle," the child shrieked and ran to John. He scooped the two-year old up and lifted him high, shaking the boy until he laughed. "Come play with me."

Hand in hand they went to a corner of the room. John squatted and built wooden blocks into a tower which Choi swatted down with a hand. They both laughed at the mass of squares that were strewn on the floor.

Lehua came. "Time for bed."

"Want play with Uncle."

"*Moi, moi* right now. Say bye, bye."

Choi gave John a kiss saying, "Play tomorrow?"

"Yes."

Mother and child trotted off, little Choi holding onto Lehua's sack dress. She called back, "Hot water for your bath outside."

John smiled, happy to be with this family. He went behind the restaurant, bathed, changed, and walked back in. It was past nine o'clock. Only two patrons

116

were in the room sipping tea. Ah Sam came to John with a plate of food. "Kept this for you."

John mushed his chopstick into the rice wondering what news Joshua might have. Several days had passed since the attorney had taken the case. No report yet. Hopelessness swept over him.

Something thudded against the entryway. A man staggered inside. His head and upper body bent low, as if he were stooping under an overhang. From John's viewpoint, he seemed to be in terrible pain. The intruder made it to John's table and collapsed into a chair.

The tea drinkers looked up from their brew for a moment then dropped their eyes.

"*Poho, poho*," the stranger moaned.

"Why out of luck?" John asked, placing a friendly hand on the man's back.

"Aytah!" he cried, writhing away from the touch.

"I'm sorry. Let me get you something warm to drink." John stood and walked over to where Ah Sam still cooked and asked for a tumbler of rice gin. He returned with a full glass, and offered it to the injured Chinese, who accepted it, downing the gift in a gulp.

"Hungry?" John asked, and saw his answer in the man's face.

When he approached Ah Sam for pork hash with salt egg and rice, the chef was annoyed.

"What's a matta you," he grumbled. "You always give stray dogs food." Despite his grousing, Ah Sam produced a pot of hash with a duck's egg on top.

John watched the stranger wolf the succulent mouthfuls down, lubricating each bite with a swig of gin. When he was finally sated, he told John his story. "My name is Chin Sing. I come from Kwantung province six years ago to work in *Tan Hueng Shan*, the Land of the Fragrant Sandalwood Hills."

Chin Sing related that after landing in Honolulu, he had endured the lengthy quarantine period, and finally went to work in the cane fields of Oahu.

"My life was bad, whippings and penalties. If I late to work, that a *poho*. I work too slow, another *poho*. Too many *poho*," Chin Sing cried. "Every time boss say I'm out of luck, he fine me fifty cents. My contract pay is only five dollah a month, but many months I get nothing because of penalties."

When his five-year labor contract was up, Chin refused to sign a new agreement. There were threats of prosecution for vagrancy, so he fled the labor camp and disappeared into the back streets of Honolulu. After performing odd jobs for several months, he learned from a friend that a houseboy was needed for a white family on Nuuanu Street.

"When I go work for Mr. Charles two months ago, seem like good job. Pay good, eight dollah a month, I am happy. But if work for sugar man bad, work for Mr. Charles like having one thousand Chinese devils as your master."

"Is the man crazy?"

"Crazy with alcohol. Mr. Charles go work in morning, come home at night drunk. He beat me and then his wife. He drink and make demands until fall asleep."

Chin went on to explain that Mr. Charles had two daughters, both afraid of their father. They got married in order to get away from the house. "I have to always be around, take care of what Mr. Charles wants. Sometimes I cannot do what he wants, or he asks me to do bad things. If I no do it, he beats me with bamboo stick, he say 'poho' and I lose pay." The man took another sip of his drink before going on. "Tonight he come home drunk. He beat me. Hit me until fall asleep. I run away and come here."

John leaned forward, his brow creased with concern. "Chin Sing, you must quit this job. If you stay, he will beat you until you are dead."

"You right, Mr. Tana. I think tomorrow I get my property, ask for pay. I leave and go to my friend. He has duck farm in Waikiki where big reeds are. You know place?"

John nodded. This was where three waters came together to form Waikiki. He had planted taro near the duck place for many months.

By the time Chin Sing had finished his story, all the customers of the restaurant had left and Ah Sam was dousing the fires in the wood stove.

"Come," John said. "There are soft mats and blankets here," motioning toward a corner of the room. "Don't go back to Nuuanu tonight. Go in the morning."

Chin rolled onto the bed and was instantly asleep.

"You too kind to stray dogs and Chinamen," Ah Sam said. "That why you have no money." He smiled. Who could fault the young man for having a heart?

Ah Sam doused the kerosene lanterns, plunging the restaurant into darkness. As the men walked out, a few embers from the stove cast a dying light onto the corner where Chin Sing slept.

Twenty-Seven

When John woke, Chin had disappeared. He left for the harbor thinking of what the Chinese had said. Asians came to Hawaii believing life would be better; instead, they faced long work days and exploitation by unscrupulous men. "If I ever get land and power, I'll make life better for them," he thought. John looked at his calloused hands, "How do I do that as a dock laborer?"

John was relieved when the end of work bell rang. His meeting with the whipped Chinese man had dominated his thoughts during the day. He felt powerless to correct injustices.

Lost in gloomy thoughts, John trudged along the busy streets to Ah Sam's restaurant. When he entered, John heard the musical sounds of Chinese voices. Muk Fat, along with other merchants doing business at the waterfront, huddled in a corner. Vapor clouds of sweet, wet smoke soared from their hookahs and filled the room. "What's going on?" John asked, interrupting the conversation. Ah Sam waved in dismissal and continued speaking.

John made his way to the back of the restaurant and found Lehua feeding Leinani, and Choi setting up blocks and then knocking them down with a round rock.

"Alo Uncle," Choi called, his ball leveling a stack sending the wood in all directions.

"Stop that before you hurt somebody," his mother demanded.

John squatted to help the child pick up the square pieces of wood, giving the boy a conspiratorial wink. "Why are all these Chinese here?" he asked Lehua.

"I'm not sure. Something big happen on Nuuanu Street. White folk all mad. Better we wait 'til tomorrow when newspaper come, then we find out."

John accepted this with a shrug. He secured a pail of water and some cloth and walked to the back of the building. He exercised for more than an hour and danced around the compound in a precise pattern of foot movements. After his workout, he washed himself from the pail.

In the house, John found the children asleep and a dinner of poi and fish on the kitchen table. He ate alone and then retired to his little room where, by the light of a kerosene lantern, he searched through the Bible for passages that Reverend Zachariah had preached many years ago. He found what he sought in Proverbs: "Who can find a virtuous woman? For her price is far above rubies." John repeated these words several times and then turned to another passage, the one listing the Seven Evils abhorred by the Lord. The three that moved him were: *A heart that deviseth wicked imaginations. Feet that be swift in running to mischief. He that soweth discord among brethren.*

John had been able to cleanse his mind of evil thoughts while at the lua school, but the death of his teacher, his return to Honolulu, his living with Ah Sam and baby Leinani brought back all the memories that he had erased. He closed the book and rolled into his tapa cloth, hoping to sleep. He knew that, once the dreams came, they would be tumultuous. Perhaps tomorrow he would see a *kahuna moe'uhane* to have his dreams interpreted.

Before the sun rose, John awoke. He retrieved the family cart and trudged into the hills. Once inside the forest, he cut wood and stacked the pieces in bundles on the small wagon. By sunrise, he had returned to Merchant Street with the firewood.

Life stirred in the restaurant: Lehua poured tea and took orders. John dropped his cart at the entrance and carried bundles of sticks inside, loading them into a bin next to the stove that Ah Sam stoked. When he finished, he turned to his friend. "What's going on?"

Ah Sam continued to poke the fire, his eyes never meeting John's. "White man killed yesterday afternoon. Somebody kill him, maybe Chinese houseboy. Don't know. We wait for paper."

At that moment, shouting erupted on the street and John rushed to the door. Despite the cacophony of voices, he made out three chilling words: "Chinaman kills Charles."

Ah Sam and Lehua were soon beside him, moans came from both of them. Before anyone could act, an Asian boy ran into the restaurant, a stack of newspapers under his arm. The headline read: *Chinese Houseboy Murders Charles.*

"Oh Lord," John said. "It must be Chin Sing. What terrible thing caused him to take his boss's life?" No one spoke, but John knew what they thought: This could only mean trouble for the Chinese community in Honolulu.

John took a steaming bowl of stir-fry and rice from the kitchen and wolfed it down. He left for work deciding to return during the lunch break to get the latest news. When he arrived at the docks, he heard Mike Johnson, the J&J supervisor, ranting, "Those damn no good chinks, they cause nothing but trouble. We pay to bring 'em here from China, give 'em good jobs in the fields, and what do they do? Complain and refuse to work. They won't obey orders, they're slower than molasses, and most of them mark time until their contracts are up and then refuse to sign up again."

John listened as the supervisor continued his tirade about the Chinese having sex with Hawaiian women, smoking opium, and murdering white men. "We should run all those chinks into the sea and make 'em swim back to China," the man fumed. Like steam exploding from a boiling kettle, Mike hissed at John, "Hey, Tana, why don't you and some of your big Hawaiian boys get together and run these coolies out of Honolulu?"

John pretended not to hear, which was made easier by the din created by men and oxen preparing for the day's dredging. Out of the corner of his eye, he saw Mike Johnson walk over to a group of Hawaiian stevedores unloading goods from a ship and yell at them as well. They, too, ignored him and continued their work.

On his lunch break, John raced to the restaurant and found several Chinese men seated at a large table engaged in a boisterous meeting. Muk Fat was speaking and the others nodded. Ah Sam cooked with abandon, sweet aromas filled the air. John sidled over and inquired about news.

While ladling broth onto noodles, Ah Sam said, "Newspaper say that Missy Charles say Chin Sing come to house yesterday morning, but Mr. Charles not home. Sing tell her he going leave his job, want his pay. She tell him wait until

Mr. Charles come home. She goes out come back mid-afternoon. She find Mr. Charles on kitchen floor, blood all over, and she call for help. Mr. Charles dead. Somebody say they see Chin run up Nuuanu Mountain and men search hill, but no find. Today, more men go look for Chin. Much bad talk. When they find him, he hang. White men say Chinese evil people. Ayee" he added, shaking his head. "Big trouble coming for Chinese in Honolulu. Big trouble."

John frowned and tried to push away worried thoughts about the safety of Ah Sam and his family. He knew how much hatred resulted when the Chinese workers did not renew their labor contracts, choosing instead to open businesses in competition with the white merchants.

John's attention was diverted by a loud noise. Muk Fat hit his fist against the table. "A solution," he declared. "Chinese merchants will condemn the evil crime of Chin Sing and offer a reward of $500 for his capture, dead or alive. We will promise not to give him any aid or comfort and we will seek the cooperation of all citizens in capturing this criminal and hanging him."

John became angry, how could these men assume that Chin Sing was guilty? Then he reminded himself that, among his Chinese friends, there was an assumption of guilt. The accused could only soften the punishment by admitting he was wrong. This was not different from the system of *kapu* in ancient times. There was only one punishment for breaking *kapu,* death.

It took an English sea captain to end the deadly cycle of this automatic guilt-and-death punishment. In 1825, he introduced to Hawaii the concept of every citizen having the right to a jury trial and being considered innocent until proven guilty. John thought about this and decided that, in this clash of cultures, the white men had it right. It was better to presume innocence, hear both sides of a criminal charge, and then judge a person fairly. But now, it seemed that they were calling for blood.

With a renewed sense of foreboding, John returned to his work, unsure what he could do to protect his friend. At mid-afternoon, the foreman came to John and ordered him to move to the next pier. "The passenger ship *Hermes* has just arrived. There's a bunch of Catholics that need to be taken to the Church of the Sacred Heart. You know where it is?" When John nodded, his boss informed him that after accompanying these people, his work would be finished for the day.

John grabbed a handcart and hurried to the arrival pier. The visitors were easy to spot, three nuns dressed in the traditional habit and a smallish man wearing a broad-brimmed hat, black clothes, and a chain of beads adorned with a large cross.

"*Bonjour monsieur*," the priest said. "*Savez-vous la direction d l'église de Sacre Coeur?*" When John shook his head, the stranger said, "Pardon, monsieur, do you speak English?"

John nodded. "I've been sent to take you to the church."

"That is good," smiled the young priest. When John asked for their bags, he was directed to the ship.

"Show me where and I'll load them onto the cart."

Minutes later, John and the priest were stacking luggage. As the priest lifted one of the lighter pieces, he said, "I'm Father DeVeuster, and the three nuns are Sister Anne, Sister Catherine, and Sister Helen. And your name is—"

"John Tana."

The cart was large enough for all of the bags but one, which Father DeVeuster insisted on carrying. From the moment they met, John liked the priest. He smiled often, was helpful, spoke in a straightforward manner, and did not criticize. By contrast, the three nuns studiously avoided eye contact and said nothing.

It took nearly an hour to convey the visitors and their luggage to the church. Despite John's steady refusal, Father DeVeuster helped by taking a turn pulling the handcart along the streets. They arrived at the church and were met by a priest and several Hawaiians. Everyone worked together to unload the luggage, and then DeVeuster and the three women were herded into a building next to the chapel. Before leaving, the young priest insisted that John join them in the sanctuary's kitchen. John declined all offers of food and wine, accepting only a glass of water and a bite of bread.

As he busied himself about the kitchen, Father DeVeuster asked, "What is your religion, Mr. Tana?"

"My father believed in the old kahuna system," John answered. Then he began to laugh. "But he also tried Christianity. He wasn't taking any chances. He had one foot firmly planted in black magic and the other in the teachings of the Lord God Jehovah. I recall there were times when we would make the long trip to Wailuku and listen to the minister. But come a bad dream or a howling wind swirling about the house and he dragged me to the kahuna."

"What would the kahuna do?" the priest inquired.

"If it was a dream, the kahuna would force me to recite it. Then she would suck in and blow out her breath, rear up and shake her head, as if receiving a revelation from the gods, and then whisper her interpretation of the dream to my father." John smiled to himself, recalling many of their meetings. "There was no end to it, these strange practices, and they often ran my family's life."

The priest nodded. "When I was on the island of Hawaii, I saw much evidence that pagan beliefs are still in existence."

"Recently, I chose to be a Christian. I gave up all belief in the kahuna." He swallowed the last of the water, thanked the priest, and bade him goodbye.

DeVeuster accompanied John to the street. "Remember. There is only one God and he cannot be reached by the kahuna. Believe in the Lord thy God, for His is the kingdom of Heaven." Before turning away, he added, "And John, you are always welcome at our church. If you need help, or a home, come here first and we will care for you."

John thanked him and walked away, marveling at the man's kindness and his failure to convert him to Catholicism. It brought to mind the passage: *By his good works ye shall know him.*

Twenty-Eight

On his return to the restaurant, John noted several posters announcing the reward, dead or alive, for Chin Sing. The offer was made by a group calling itself: "The Chinese Community of Honolulu".

John entered the restaurant and found it empty, except for its proprietor. "Hello, Sam," he said. "What's the news?"

Ah Sam stopped what he was doing and carried a tray of Chinese cookies and a pot of tea with two cups to John. Sam proceeded to pour the herbal brew. "Big manhunt going on in Nuuanu hills," he revealed. "Plenty people search for Chin Sing, they no find him. Now white people say he hide in Chinatown. There is talk they will search every Chinese house, very bad for us."

Muk Fat, bustled into the restaurant, breaking through a cluster of flies. "You should close the front of this place," he complained, waving the pests away. "Too many bad things come through this opening."

"You are right, cousin," Sam nodded, exchanging a humorous glance with John. "When I get enough money, John and I will board up the front, keep the pests out."

Muk Fat poured a cup of tea and seized a cookie. As he sipped and munched, he related the events of his day. "I went to see Governor Dominis. He made me wait a long time, but finally he talked to me. He says, 'You are here to speak about this Chinese murderer,' so I told him, 'Yes and no.' I told him I came because of bad words being said about Chinese, that we know the whites are angry because of the labor contracts, and that we are seen as deserters when we start our own business."

John bit into a cookie, wondering when this issue would be resolved. The word that popped into his head was: never.

Muk Fat finished off his tea and poured a second cup. "I told him we are not hiding Chin Sing, but we are in danger of those who believe we are. The governor said he understood and would speak to someone close to the King, Colonel David Kalakaua who has formed a company of military to guard the Kingdom."

Ah Sam stood to refill the teapot, and then turned back. "What can we do?"

His uncle leaned back in the chair and pursed his lips. "We must call a meeting of the committee," he suggested. "If they don't catch Chin Sing soon, we will all be in danger."

John stood, his eyes glowed. "I think I know where Chin Sing is." He turned to Ah Sam. "Choose someone who is loyal to us and station him at the Waikiki Road from this moment until midnight. Tell him to watch for my return." With that, he ran from the restaurant, followed King Street to Waikiki Road, and then turned toward an area of ponds obscured by heavy reed and kiawe growth. It bordered on the taro and rice fields of Moiliili and Waikiki, a favorite nesting place for ducks. The Chinese tended these duck farms, collected eggs, soaked them in brine, and then harvested the fowl for food. What greater delicacy than sweet roast duck and month-old salted eggs?

John picked his way through the fields, emotion racing through him. His friends, the Makanani family, lived nearby and he wondered if he should stop and visit. It had been months since he had seen David and Auntie Malia. The setting sun was the decider. He needed all the daylight remaining if he was to find Chin Sing.

Ducks were everywhere, paddling, and searching the mud for food, some led families of yellow brown fuzz balls through the water. The reeds grew tall along the banks of the ponds, their green clumps creating hidden recesses. Just beyond the pools were the bushy kiawe trees, roots haphazardly anchored in the rocky soil at the base of Diamond Head. John headed for the densest growth and passed a Chinese farmer hoeing a rice field. He wore the standard broad-brimmed straw hat, its cord tied around his chin, a light smock that covered his chest, and a scrap of cloth to hide his loins. The man's wiry body was supported by spindly legs that disappeared into the muddy water of the field.

"Hey," John called. The farmer ignored him, continuing with his work.

John moved closer. "Do you know where Chin Sing is?" he asked.

The man shook his head, but John detected a momentary glance from the farmer toward the thick reeds and he moved in that direction. Pausing at the bank, John saw ducks paddle in and out of the tall grass and guessed that flat ground had to be near. That's where ducks would build their nests and hatch their eggs. It could also be where a man could hide and find food.

John skirted the edge of the spiky reed clumps and arrived at a forest of thick grass. A combination of dried shrubs and trees gave the appearance of an impenetrable wall. He searched for an opening, found it, and forced his body through it. Inside, he found a low tunnel carved into the thicket. On his stomach, he wormed his way along, an occasional thorn grabbed at his shirt, dried grass irritated his hands and feet. Errant strands of straw caught his hair and brushed against his face. Puffs of powdery substance floated away from the disturbed grass, forcing John to blink to wipe away the irritation.

The late afternoon sun filtered hot rays into the tunnel, turning it into a golden, pitiless oven. Sweat covering John's body mixed with the fetid air of the grass cave. It produced a noxious odor that made him gag. His skin itched, yet he could not scratch.

John continued forward, inch by inch, fighting the tough grass. With each small advance, the wiry straw sprang back on him like an expanding rubber ball, until he was forced to navigate by pushing with his feet and pulling grass with his hands. Finally, just ahead, there appeared level ground and a shed. To the right were clumps of green reeds; to the left, kiawe trees. Just beyond the small building, the ground sloped slowly upward towards Diamond Head. As he studied the terrain, he noted how the brush barrier created a natural amphitheater around one side of the extinct volcano.

John pushed through the dried grass and rose to his feet, brushing away shards that clung to his clothes. In the twilight, he saw a pale orange glow within the hut and realized that a pot was suspended over flames. He walked to the threshold and peered inside. Before he could react, warm water and raw eggs struck him. Yellow yolk dripped from his face and down his body. Then he heard a rustle of bending grass and whipped around just in time to see the farmer charge, a bestial grimace on his face, a hoe held above his head, like the cudgel of a barbarian warrior. With a wild yell, the farmer whipped his hoe like a lumber-jack driving an axe through a tree. John dove from the blow, and the farm tool struck the earth, causing dirt and debris to explode over the narrow entrance-way to the shed.

John and the farmer appeared equally surprised, but John proved to be quicker. He seized the hoe and struck the farmer. Like a bird hit by a spread of buckshot, the man fell to the ground unconscious.

"Ayah, ayah," a voice cried from inside the shed.

John tensed, preparing for what might charge across the threshold. After a moment, there was nothing but a repeat of "Ayah, Ayah."

By now, darkness blanketed the area, the last rays of the sun blotted out by the nearby mountains. Within the shed, reddish coals of a cooking fire burned low, they fought a dying battle to dispel the gloom. Beyond the ebbing firelight, a man squatted, a knife clutched in his hand aimed at the open doorway. John took a few steps toward the entrance. "Chin Sing, put down the knife and I will come in and speak with you."

Chin waved his knife, but only half-menacingly. "No come in, no come in. I cut you."

John inched closer. "Chin Sing, I'm here to talk. It's your friend from the restaurant, remember? I gave you drink, food, a warm bed."

The fugitive lowered his knife wailing, "Woe is Chin Sing. Woe is Chin Sing."

John crawled in and sat opposite the frightened man. He took pieces of wood and placed them on the embers, causing the fire to flare up. The sudden light cast away the darkness. As the Chinese wept, John wondered if he relived months, if not a lifetime, of abuse from others.

As if suddenly aware of John's presence, Chin Sing shook himself from his nightmares and looked directly at him. "All lies. Labor man tells lies."

"Who is this labor man, Chin Sing? What were his lies?"

"I fourth son of poor farmer in Cheng Shen village, Kwangtung province near Canton. Fourth son get no land from father. Labor man come to tell of work in Golden Mountain Country, so I and my friends go listen to labor man. We ask many questions and he say here is best place, California no like Chinese.

Here, miles of land to farm, good climate, many women who love Chinese, work easy in the sugar factories."

"I can see that this guy was a salesman. He told you what you wanted to hear."

"Labor man he say, 'If we want good job and adventure, we go to Canton, sign labor contract.' We go Canton sign contract. After that, we come to Hawaii. All he said, lies."

John frowned, he did not want to take Chin Sing by force, but hoped the man would surrender peacefully. The sky was dark and John needed to act before the vigilantes discovered the shed. "Chin, what happened at the Charles residence?"

The question caused Chin to flinch. An almost catatonic gaze came into his eyes. When he finally spoke, it was in a monotone. "I come in morning to house and I see Mrs. Charles, ask for pay. She says Mr. Charles gone, I wait for him. She leave and I work in kitchen. Mr. Charles come home in afternoon, smell plenty alcohol. I ask for pay, he angry, grab stick, hit me. I hurt plenty. I grab knife to stop him, he swing stick at me and walk into knife as he hit me. He so drunk he no see good. Big spurt blood. I scared and run away."

"Why did you take the knife?"

"I afraid, so I keep knife."

"You can trust me, give me the knife."

Chin Sing hesitated. He looked at John, tears in his eyes. "I don't know maybe I kill myself."

"Chin Sing, you must come back with me to Honolulu and surrender."

"I'm afraid of white men."

"I promise you, that you will have a fair trial where you can tell your story. If you do not come back with me, many Chinese will be killed while the friends of Mr. Charles search for you."

Chin Sing thought about this as his body heaved with emotion. "Ayah, I trust you. I no like other Chinese pay for my trouble. I come with you." Chin Sing took the tip of the knife and handed it to John.

The two men left the hut, squirmed through the grass tunnel, and picked their way in the darkness back to town. It was nearly midnight when the weary pair reached the top of Waikiki Road and headed west toward King Street. John heard noises behind a group of trees and saw Ah Sam and Muk Fat emerge. "Over here, come over here," they gestured.

When the four men were together, Ah Sam whispered, "Be careful, John. The sailors have torches, and they beat any Chinese they see."

"They're everywhere," Muk Fat added. "Beretania, Nuuanu, Merchant, King Streets, everywhere."

John ran his palm across his hair. "We'll stay on King Street as long as we can, then cut over near the stone church and head for the beach. After that, we'll try getting to the Government House. Chin Sing is exhausted, so we'll have to go slow. Can you two get to the Government House and find some help? Tell the soldiers the route we'll be taking."

Muk Fat and Ah Sam agreed and headed down the road, holding fast to the shelter of the trees.

With a subdued Chin following him, John set off. They walked in silence, their path illuminated by moonlight.

As they approached Merchant Street, torches flared in jerky undulations. John motioned for Chin Sing to wait behind a nearby building and then scanned the street. A few saloons cast weak light onto the roadway, the only brightness coming from torches held by a half dozen sailors zigzagging along the pavement.

John urged his friend to crouch low and run through the intersection. Chin hurried across, stumbled, and fell, emitting a low shriek.

The sailors heard the cry. One raised his torch and yelled, "Lookee at them pigtails, it's a Chinaman!"

John stood, raising a hand to ward off the sailors careening toward him. "Stop. This is my prisoner and I'm taking him to jail."

"You aren't taking him anywhere," the biggest of the drunken men snarled. "We're going to get that China boy and fix him real good." The burly sailor emphasized his intentions by breaking a liquor bottle against the side of a building. With the jagged weapon in one hand, a torch in the other he advanced on John. Behind him, his cronies waved their torches and made ugly sounds.

Faking fear, John stepped back and wailed, "Please, I don't want any trouble. All I want is to give this man justice."

The big man smiled, as if seeing his opportunity against this cowardly native. He rushed forward, aiming a wicked blow with the razor-sharp bottle. John sidestepped and, with skilled quickness, pushed away the bottle while delivering a powerful kick to the sailor's scrotum. The man dropped onto the dirt road. For a long moment he was silent, and then he released a painful howl. John seized the man's torch and squared himself to meet the other sailors. There were five, and they paused in their singing, the flames from six oil-soaked torches cast grotesque shadows on the walls. Except for the moans of the big man an eerie quiet descended on the roadway.

John watched, waited without emotion. The sailors seemed uncertain, their leader in the dirt. They looked at each other. One of them finally stepped forward. "We're five against one. Let's get him!"

Just as the men moved ahead, they came face to face with a tall Hawaiian, a handsome figure in a military uniform. Behind him were eight soldiers, each with a musket and fixed bayonet. "What's going on here?" the officer demanded, as his detachment came to a halt.

"This damned kanaka…I mean gentleman…attacked our friend," piped up one of the sailors.

"You're saying that this man," the officer pointed to John, "attacked this man, on the ground holding a jagged bottle. And all five of you did nothing?"

Without waiting for an answer, the officer turned to John. "What do you have to say about this?"

"I am John Tana. This is the houseboy accused of killing Mr. Charles. I found him in Waikiki and promised him that if he surrendered, he would get a fair trial. We were on our way to the Government House when these sailors attacked us."

The officer studied the scene for a few moments. "Yes, I heard you were on your way. The two of you, come with me. As for you," he said, pointing to the sailors, "if you have a complaint with Mr. Tana, file it with the Governor." He signaled his soldiers to form up and placed Chin Sing within the formation. With that, he ordered his troops to march with the prisoner to the Government House. When the procession was on its way, he turned to John. "I am Colonel

David Kalakaua. So tell me, Mr. Tana, how you managed to capture the Chinese without a big fight?"

As John recounted his search, the two men strolled toward the Government House. Their conversation eventually strayed from the capture of Chin Sing to other topics, such as the hula and the art of lua. By the time they reached the House, a friendship had been forged.

Twenty-Nine

"Wake up, Uncle," Choi tugged at John's arm. "Mama say get up, go work." John rolled from his blanket and stumbled to the bedroom door. Choi ran screaming from the room, "Mama, Uncle John up."

Hearing his son's cries, Ah Sam came into the room, a smile on his face. "Hey John, sun is up, come eat."

"Sorry I slept so long, Sam. I'll wash and head out for some wood right away." Bleary-eyed, John staggered outside to a trough, where he dashed cool water over his face and body.

"No worry," Sam said, close behind. "We have plenty wood. All Chinatown happy. You save us from big trouble. Eat, then go to work."

At the job, big Mike yelled at his crew in his usual surly way. "Get the lead out. Hustle, hustle, hustle." When John arrived at the docks, Mike gave him a long stare.

At lunchtime, John could see that Mike was in high spirits. To all who would listen, he went on about "that murdering chink was caught last night by public-minded seamen. The Chinaman was vicious; he put up a big fight with his knife, slashing and cutting like all those damn heathens. He got one sailor, kicked him in the balls, that sneaky bastard. But the other guys got him." He looked around to see that everyone listened. "Hanging is too good for the Chinaman," he announced. "I say castrate him, then draw and quarter him. That'll teach them coolies not to kill white men."

When Mike was finished with his tirade, John turned away, praying that his boss would not find out the truth. His wishes were short-lived.

"Do you know a John Tana?" a well-dressed gentleman asked a dockhand. The worker pointed toward the dredging area. "Over there."

With a brief "Thank you," the gentleman drew a notebook from his coat pocket and hurried over to where several men were working. Close behind the reporter came another man, this one toting a wooden box camera on a tripod. They stepped over chunks of limestone strewn about the dock and the reporter asked again, this time it was Mike, chiseling dead coral.

Startled by the sound of his name, John turned and saw two men speaking to his supervisor.

"Yeah, I know him. What do you want him for?"

The reporter smiled, "He's a hero, didn't you know? John Tana single-handedly captured the murderer, Chin Sing. I'm from the *Island Gazette* and my paper wants to do a feature article on Mr. Tana."

Mike nearly dropped his chisel. "Holy shit. I don't believe it. He never said a word to me. Hey Tana, you're a celebrity. These guys want to talk to you." Before John could respond, Mike added, "Take the rest of the day off, and give 'em a good story about how wonderful the docks are to work at."

The next morning, a feature article appeared on the front page of the *Gazette*, accompanied by a large photograph of John. The story detailed the murder of Charles, as well as John's role in taking Chin Sing into custody. In the interview, John's remarks were modest. Nevertheless, the reporter wrote the story with a flair for mystery and adventure. The article concluded by saying that John was a rich man, having received five-hundred dollars in reward money offered for the dead-or-alive capture of Chin Sing.

Thirty

At Saint Sebastian School, Maria held up the newspaper. "Look at this handsome man on the front page. How brave he is. He risked his life in the swamps to capture a killer. Oh, is he rich."

"Maria," Leinani said. "What are you talking about?"

"Don't you read the papers, you ninny?" Before Leinani could reply, the French girl laughed, "You always have your nose in a book. You are never interested in what is happening in Honolulu. Look at this." She thrust the newspaper in Leinani's face.

The young girl glanced at it, and then looked once again. The image caught her so by surprise that she felt faint. "John," she gasped.

The photo showed him to be handsome, with hair closely cropped fitting his head like a warrior's helmet. A light beard curved around his face, framing thick eyebrows, piercing eyes, a slender nose, and sensuous lips.

"You know this guy?" Maria asked, more than a casual interest in her voice.

Leinani ignored her friend and continued to read. When she finished with the article, she read it yet again. At the end of her third reading, she looked up at her schoolmate. "Yes, I know him, he's my cousin."

Maria clapped her hands and giggled. "Oh, that is great! You can introduce me to him. He's rich with the reward money. Let's go to the docks right now before someone else catches him."

"Who do you think is the ninny?" Leinani said. "You can't believe for one moment that I'll introduce you to my cousin just so you can get your hands on the reward money."

Contrition crossed Maria's face. "I didn't mean it to sound like that. But just look," she added, pointing to the image. "He is very handsome and the newspaper calls him a very brave, honest man. Since he's your cousin, you can't have a romance with him, right? But I can. Other girls will pursue him for all kinds of reasons, but I have the very best of reasons: I like him for what he is, a good man."

Leinani studied Maria, wondering if she was a gold digger or sincere. "I'm happy you say this," she finally remarked, "because I do not want my cousin to be taken advantage of by scheming women. He's family to me. There's a blood tie between us and I will protect him from anyone with evil intentions." Having spoken, she fixed Maria with a piercing stare.

Without blinking, Maria shot back, "I already like him for what he is, not for what he has. So don't worry, I'm not after the reward money."

Leinani nodded, as if satisfied with Maria's answer. She said, "All right, let's go, I'm dying to see him. We can visit the docks after school and I'll introduce you."

When John arrived at work, several people were standing at the harbor. Some ogled him, others shook his hand to thank him or asked for money. By midday, people had filled the walkways to seek the hero. He glanced toward Mike and smiled. Earlier the supervisor had been annoyed, now he reveled in the attention being paid to him. "I am the teacher of that great Hawaiian, John Tana," he told anyone who would listen. "I trained him to be a good fighter, made him strong by showing him how to lift and chop tons of coral dredged from the harbor. He owes all that he knows to me."

During the day, several Hawaiian women flirted with John as he worked. "The camera lied," one buxom lady said. "You are much more handsome than your picture. Meet me after work," she added, "I'll be waiting."

Another woman flattered him, "You are the best looking man in all Hawaii. Don't fool around with these worthless creatures. Visit me tonight. I promise you, happiness will be yours."

By early afternoon, more reporters and photographers showed up, pencils ready and cameras clicking. They interviewed John, Mike, and anyone else who would speak to them. As the day wore on, the docks became packed with people. John noted that they were all Caucasian or Hawaiian, with not an Asian among them.

Before the day ended, Leinani and Maria headed to the docks, their long, white, school dresses and light-colored straw hats singling them out from the work clothes-clad folk scurrying about. Carriages filled with well-dressed people lined the street. Scores of horses picked their way among the crowd of Hawaiian men in white *malos* and women in colorful sacks, with garlands of flowers around their neck and in their hair.

Maria stamped her foot on the pavement. "Leinani, look at the crowds going to the harbor. It's like when the packet ship arrives from San Francisco. We'll never get to see my John," she moaned.

Leinani was nettled by Maria's use of the possessive and darted onto Nuuanu Street.

"Wait for me," Maria called, doing her best to follow close behind.

The girls traveled along the roadway which slanted toward the ocean. As they neared the docks, they saw a number of people moving in the same direction, others leaving. "That must be where John is." Leinani pointed to the flashes of light emanating from the middle of the crowd.

"Why do you think they're all here?" Maria asked.

"It isn't every day that an Oriental kills a white man. Usually, it's the other way around." She went on to explain how many people feared that the large Chinese population would one day mutiny and go on a rampage in Honolulu, as it has happened in China. "And there are the curious, and all those others who want to see the hero who captured the murderer."

John was in the middle of another interview when the two slender figures in white approached the docks. Distracted, he glanced their way and then shook off the idea that one of them was Leinani. When he looked again, he realized that the delicate beauty heading his way was his cousin. "Excuse me," he said, abandoning the journalists and working his way through the crowd. "Excuse me, sorry, thanks," he replied as hands reached out to touch or grasp him. He rushed to Leinani, seized her by the waist, and lifted her from the ground.

"Put me down, put me down."

John gave her a little toss, then caught her against his chest. For just a moment he cradled her close, feeling her warmth.

"John, you're crushing me, so put me down this second!"

Reluctantly, John lowered his cousin until she stood on the street.

People on the docks heard the laughter, and gaped at this exuberant greeting. Even Maria pressed her hand to her mouth, as if uncertain whether to gasp or laugh with delight at this handsome hero's welcome. Somewhere in the shadows of the surrounding warehouses, hostile eyes stared at the happy scene.

"John Tana, let me introduce my school mate, Maria Francois. Maria is the daughter of the King's Minister of Foreign Affairs."

As if being presented to royalty, Maria grasped the hem of her dress, bent at the knees, and declined her head. "I am so pleased to meet you, Mr. Tana. I've read so much of your accomplishments; it's an honor to be introduced."

John took a step back, uncertain as to what he should do.

Leinani laughed and guided him through his embarrassment. "Please stand erect. Place your left hand behind your back and step toward Maria. Not too close. Reach with your right hand and take hers. Not like a handshake, but hold it delicately, not intimately, and with the lightest of pressure. Next, take the fingers on her right hand and guide her toward you. A true gentleman will kiss the back of her hand without slurping."

As John completed these instructions, a murmur ran through the crowd, followed by applause. Someone yelled, "Now there's a true Hawaiian gentleman." This was followed by another man making a sound, reminding John of an excited pig, and then he heard from the darkness of the warehouse, "That 'ladies' man is going to get his ass kicked tonight."

Embarrassed by the applause, and ignoring the threat, John let Maria's hand drop. She held it to her breast, her face crimson, her eyes fixed on him.

In this brief lapse of conversation, a reporter came to conduct an interview with the trio. He posed a battery of questions, which the girls seemed unwilling to answer.

"I don't want any publicity from this," Leinani whispered. Maria nodded her agreement. They made a quick decision to leave and turned to go.

John called out his thanks to the crowd at the docks and then took each girl by the elbow. "Come."

He guided them free of the sightseers, and hustled the girls to Ah Sam's. When Lehua spied Leinani, she rushed over, towing a reluctant Choi by the hand. Before anyone could speak, she thrust him into her, announcing, "Choi, this is your auntie."

Choi resisted. Lehua picked him up and pushed him closer. "Give Auntie big kiss. She is your savior."

The little boy made a slurping sound and then wriggled free from his mother's grasp. He hid behind her.

Ah Sam came up to them, his face one large smile. "You must see your godchild." He took Leinani's hand leading her to the back of the restaurant.

Nearly an hour passed in the back room with the Ah Sam family. When Leinani returned to the restaurant, Maria snuggled against John's chest. Her fingers twined in his hand.

"I'm surprised at you. We must get back to school before evening bells sound." She leaned into John, as if to pull Maria away.

John placed his hand on Leinani's waist and she flinched from his touch. Her nearness disturbed him, yet all he could think to say was, "Do you have to go?"

"Oh, let's not go," Maria begged.

"We can't stay. We must leave or suffer detention." She turned to John. "Will you join us at church this Sunday?" When he nodded, Leinani said, "Maria, we can visit with my cousin all day Sunday." Without waiting for a response, she grabbed her friend's arm and pulled her into the street, calling over her shoulder, "Meet us at the Anglican Church on upper Nuuanu Street before nine."

Having said that, she turned, "And John, can you do me a great favor? I broke the chain to my father's scrimshaw medallion. Can you fix it for me? If so," she added, proffering the jewelry, "please bring it on Sunday."

John took the chain and watched the two young women march toward Nuuanu Street. Before they were out of sight, Maria turned and waved, only to be dragged away by Leinani.

On a whim, John raced after them. "I'll walk you to school," he announced, when he came abreast of the girls.

Leinani shook her head. "We could get into trouble if you walk with us; it'll be better if we are seen together at church."

"Dear John," Maria sighed, puckering her lips into a kiss. "I can't wait until Sunday."

Contented with the meeting set for the Sabbath, John turned to the harbor. Any time he could spend with Leinani pleased him. As for Maria, he thought her interesting and pretty. This is a great day, he thought.

"I can't wait until Sunday, dear John. Here's a kiss for you. Oh, you are a true gentleman." A falsetto voice came from the dark.

Animosity and sarcasm tainted that voice. John saw the big Hawaiian who had been staring at him for days detach himself from a wall. He had avoided eye contact with him. Tonight, he knew, his courage would be tested.

Thirty-One

Robert Grant exulted over the reports he examined lying on his desk. His profits from sugar were huge. A clerk knocked on the door to his inner office, entered, and announced, "Mister Anthony Gonzalez to see you, sir."

His jubilant mood evaporated. Gonzalez's presence brought Grant back to the reality of his situation. Kahului is my most successful operation, he thought, but the claim of a Hawaiian boy threatens my ownership. Could this kid drive a wedge into my growing empire?

"Invite him inside," Grant said.

When Gonzalez entered his sanctuary, Grant assumed an air of conciliation. "You have done a great job on Maui. Our sugar production is off the charts. Your efforts in Kahalui have been extraordinary. I trust you feel well rewarded?"

Gonzalez stammered, "Thank you sir. You have been generous."

Grant followed with more praise. "You have kept our costs down. You have prevented those damn coolies from leaving. Bravo."

Gonzalez mumbled, "Much of the praise goes to you for the poho system."

"But this 'out of luck' idea came from you. The coolies can't argue to the court that they aren't being paid when we show the judge they are late to work or failed to do their job."

"Yeah, and a little whipping keeps them in line."

"Yes, it helps when you lie about their work. Like you lied to me about that boy?"

"Sir, I thought he was lost at sea."

"That's what you told me, three years ago. 'The sailors got him.'"

Gonzalez shuffled his feet.

"Don't dirty my rug," Grant snapped. "Somewhere in this city that boy still lives." Grant pounded his desk to emphasize his anger.

"I'll find him for you. Give me a chance."

"Yes, you'll find him for me or you're out of a job. I want him eliminated. Not just a beating, but a termination so his persecution of me is ended."

"I'll do it. I have a grudge to settle with him. Any leads?"

"Here is the name of an attorney. He's been asking questions about my Kahalui property. Find out who his client is."

"Any way I can?"

"Yes, even if you must beat it out of him. Don't kill him. I wouldn't want his death hung around my neck. If he represents Tana, find the boy and make him disappear. If you need firepower, come and use this gun." Grant walked over to the Winchester sitting in a rack in an office corner. "It's a superb sniper rifle. Range over five hundred yards." Grant fondled the weapon like a favorite child.

"How about money? I may need some help to find him."

"A hundred silver." Grant threw a purse onto his desk. "There will be more if you deliver."

"It wouldn't trouble you if I tortured him a bit before he died?"

"Exact your revenge as you desire, but make certain he does not bother me again. Go."

Gonzalez left. Grant drew out a cigar, lit it, inhaled, and blew three smoke rings into the room. He picked up a newspaper from his desk and threw it into the trash can. On its inside page, it had a picture of John Tana.

Thirty-Two

Three Hawaiians came from the shadows following a giant of a man. Their faces reflected the pleasure they would have in beating this young punk who had garnered so much publicity. John watched them come. He could outrun them and escape, but then he could not return to the docks to work.

"I am Aaloa," the giant said. "Some men call me the 'bone breaker.'" Before John could respond, the big man added, "You are no hero, you are a sissy, dear John. So tell us how you would like your beating: quick and easy, or long and dragged out. You can always try running away, but if we catch you…" Aaloa flexed a huge bicep, causing the jaws of the shark tattoo on it to open wide.

John fixed his eyes upon Aaloa. "Tell me, are you tough enough to beat me by yourself, or do you need those three to get the job done?"

"What you think? Bone Breaker needs nobody to beat up a sissy."

John understood this warrior mentality, going back to ancient times. Aaloa would try to defeat him with insults and then, having won the psychological battle, he would go in for the kill. On the other hand, Aaloa might have heard about John's success a few nights earlier and was actually bolstering his own courage.

John waited for the giant to make his move. He noted a repeated opening and clenching of the man's fingers. Suddenly, the aggressor leaped toward him, fingers splayed and reaching for his throat. A split second before he was gripped, John grasped Aaloa's fingers, sidestepped, and drove his palm into the giant's jaw. Before the man could respond, John tripped him, sending Aaloa sprawling onto the street.

The bully was at a disadvantage. John knew he could break the man's bones. With the others so near, he dared not. Besides, his purpose was not to win, but to survive.

The big man struggled to his knees, bleeding from coral cuts. It took some time for him to become fully erect.

John felt his arms grabbed from behind. Pain shot through both shoulders as two men tightened their hold around his biceps.

"Hey, Aaloa," hollered one of the goons. "Punch this guy out, we'll hold him."

John remained still, his body loose. The two that held his arms relaxed their grip. He dug his feet into the coral of the street, searching for the firm dirt base beneath the limestone.

A perplexed look spread over Aaloa's face, as if he wondered why this man wasn't struggling. Finally, he lurched forward and aimed a punch at John's midsection.

Body still relaxed, John timed the moment with as much precision as he could. He squatted, sprang upright, and twisted with all the force he could muster. The power of his sudden movements caused those that held him to release their grip. With everyone off balance, Aaloa smashed a fist into the ribs of one of his friends.

The man gasped and sagged to the ground.

John stepped back. Standing at a distance, he pleaded, "Hawaiians should not be fighting Hawaiians. We should be friends. I ask for *lokahi*, that we make peace."

"You know," one of the bullies said, "I think he's right. We should lokahi, get along. What you say, brother Aaloa?"

His breath coming in gasps, Aaloa scrutinized John, as if seeing him for the first time. "Eh, Keoki, maybe you right. Yeah, let's lokahi John Tana. But," he continued, "to be friends, you got to split the reward with us."

John shot back, "No way, I won't do that."

"Then you want the money for your girlfriend, eh?" When he got no response, he added salaciously, "Okay, I get it, you want have good time with Leinani?"

The way he emphasized her name caused John's jaw muscles to tense, but he restrained himself. His face impassive he said, "That's not the reason."

"Okay, bra, no hard feelings between us?" Aaloa said, managing a crooked smile.

John smiled back, stepped toward the large man, and they grasped each other by the biceps.

With his forehead against John's and his eyes boring into those of his new friend, Aaloa said, "You pretty tough guy, but I know I can beat you at arm wrestling. We go party."

Later, with sweat pouring from his face and a blue vein forming an angry ridge above the head and body of the tattooed shark on his bicep, Aaloa gripped John's hand and the two men fought to keep elbows on the table and forearms upright.

Despite John's strength, he struggled to keep his arm vertical. Slowly, inch-by- inch, Aaloa forced it horizontal. With a supreme effort, a sweating Aaloa pushed John's forearm onto the table. The minute flesh made contact with wood, he leaped to his feet shouting "I win." At that moment a chanter sang:

O ke aloha o ku ipo,
He wela ia no ku kino,
O ku wahine wale no
Ka'u makemake

The love of my sweetheart is
Like a hot fire within my body.
My desire is for my woman
I desire no other.

Open palms slapped the sides of large hollow gourds in a slow rhythmic tap—tap-tap-tap pattern, while six lei-adorned women began to hula. Their feet repeated the drums' rhythms as they swayed their hips, stepping to the left with a thrust of the left hand and face, then turning and stepping to the right with a thrust of the right hand and face. As their ti leaf skirts swayed, they chanted: *O ke aloha o kuuipo.*

John jumped into the group of dancers and joined in as they moved and chanted. His body writhed and turned vigorously, accompanied by forceful movements of his head and hands. He stepped sideways, forward, backward, placing hands on his hips gyrating with emphasis. The dance continued and his movements became more pronounced and stylized. As the calabash drums increased their booming, as the cadence of the chant became more frenzied, John substituted one word in his song: he used *Leinani* for *wahine.*

Thirty-Three

Robert Grant rolled his cigar between his fingers. The green felt table upon which he rested his hands was covered with ashes. He eyed Jones and Thomas Boynton, two Honolulu businessmen seated opposite him. The smoke from their cigars billowed in ever-widening circles of fume up to the ceiling of the private room in the Downtown Club.

"Gentlemen," Grant said, "we have problems making money in sugar. Too many Chinese are leaving after their work contracts are over, we can't control the Hawaiians because the law protects them, and the southern states of America are producing sugar again."

"We can make the laws tougher on the Chinese," Jones said

"We do well enough with the charges of vagrancy," Grant answered, "but still many find refuge in Honolulu after their work contracts are up and escape the law."

"Well, maybe Judge Andrews can fix that," Boynton said. "He's the one presiding over the trial of that Chinaman who killed Charles. The coolie is as good as dead. We'll string him up on the docks once the trial is over. That'll scare the Chinamen back to work in the sugar fields."

"Tom, setting an example like that is a good start," Grant answered. "But we still have to deal with competition. Our sugar is taxed when it enters the United States. We have to get rid of the tariff that raises the price when it is sold in America. We need either a Reciprocity Treaty or annexation."

"You've harped on those ideas before, but you and I know the present King won't go along with annexation. He becomes crazy when the idea is mentioned," Jones said.

"I don't think he has long to live; fat, sick, and drinks a lot. When he dies we could get United States Marines to land and take over the government," Tom suggested.

"We aren't ready for that, but we can get prepared. We can put together a body of soldiers, call them the Honolulu Rifles and use them when needed," Grant said.

"Good, I've already been working on the idea. Got some men lined up to do it. We have guns and can get more," Jones answered.

"Muzzle loaders? Winchesters, that's the ticket," Grant said.

"We can't afford them, besides they are impossible to get," Jones answered. "In the meantime we should be working on reciprocity with the United States. As soon as the present King is dead, we can get a new one elected by the legislature and have him promote such a treaty."

"Capital idea, without tariffs we can make millions in sugar," Tom said.

"Get all the land you can buy or steal, gentlemen. It won't be long before we can act. Then sugar will be king in Hawaii." Grant pounded the felt table. "I'm having a party tonight at my home to raise money for the Anglican School. You are coming, of course. Let's throw out some of our ideas to the gentlemen who will be there. It's time to go to church," he added.

Grant left the meeting believing he had started a sedition ball rolling. It would be difficult to convince others of the missionary families to topple the Hawaiian government. They had ridden to power by being cozy with the native elite. But there was nothing wrong in planning for closer ties with America. This was an avenue for change which would not be rejected. Most of his brethren had roots in New England.

John sat in the Anglican Church, listening with half an ear to Leinani's prattle. "In the front row is the King," she whispered, nodding toward a corpulent man whose face and neck disappeared into fleshy shoulders. "He's a bachelor. Lot Kamehameha believes that he can do no wrong. As the supreme power in Hawaii, he once called for a constitutional convention. He didn't like what the delegates came up with, so he disbanded them and made up his own constitution."

Leinani moved closer. "Next to him is Queen Emma, widow of Kamehameha IV, Liholiho. Isn't she beautiful? Her maiden name is Emma Rooke, and she is the granddaughter of John Young, the sailor who helped Kamehameha the First win his battles through the use of gunpowder. Of course, she could never have become queen consort without the right genealogy." Before John could ask, she explained. "It turns out that her grandmother was the half-sister of a half-brother of Kamehameha." When she noticed John's furrowed brow, she smiled. "That means she had the right lineage, so she could marry Kamehameha the Fourth. You must know that if you do not have a royal genealogy you are nothing, just a commoner."

When a mixed choir of young Chinese, Hawaiians, and Caucasian men began to sing the *Te Deum*, Leinani sat back in silence, giving John some relief from the ceaseless flow of words that she had thrown at him since they met at the church.

As John sat, he thought about how much Leinani had changed. She was no longer the sweet cousin with whom he could openly speak. Her education had elevated her, and John felt the chasm. His common school upbringing, while enhanced by the teachings of Reverend Zachariah, did not give him the command of language required for success in the cultured society of the new Hawai'i. John's grammar and speech made him ashamed to express himself in a setting where he could be ridiculed.

The choir came to the end of the *Te Deum* and they filed out from the altar. Bishop Stewart read from the gospels. As he droned on, Leinani nudged John and whispered, "I know that he's boring, but we need him to break the stranglehold the missionaries have on us." She went on to explain how Liholiho and Emma had brought the Reformed Church of England to Hawaii, primarily to relax the grip that Calvinists had on the islanders. Stewart was giving them another chance for religious and economic freedom, which included practicing many of the ancient ways: hula, chanting in Hawaiian, and performing with the musical instruments of olden times.

When the Bishop ended his reading, the organist played and the congregation rose singing a hymn.

"Look over there, see that man?"

John glanced in the direction Leinani pointed. "That is the Honorable David Kalakaua, the King's aide de camp, Colonel in the Hawaiian army, former Attorney General of Hawaii, and a fine lawyer."

Peering beyond a raised hymnal book, John felt a jolt of surprise as he recognized the Colonel who had saved him and Chin Sing several nights ago.

"Many people say that after Lot dies, he should be the next king. Yet he may not be royalty. Rumor has it that he is not the son of High Chief Kapaakea as he claims, but of John Blossom, a black boxer. I don't believe a word of it."

Leinani lapsed into silence as Reverend Robertson launched into his sermon. With a feeling of relief at being spared the tedium of gossip, John concentrated on the words of the preacher.

"Recently, we have borne witness to the evils that are visited upon the Kingdom by the failure of the Chinese to renew their labor contracts. They leave the plantations and come to live among us. While living in the heart of our community they receive kindness and friendship. Yet what is the reward for such generosity? It is the murder of one of our brethren. Murder is 'a deed most foul' and deserves the severest of punishments. That is not the only evil visited upon us by the Oriental. They corrupt the morals of our Hawaiian people. They sleep with the Hawaiian women without marrying them. Worse still, they are bigamists. Yes, my friends, they have wives living in China to whom they will return someday leaving their Hawaiian women and children behind to be cared for by you!"

John stopped listening. The words preached were false. Chin Sing killed a man by accident during a beating. Ah Sam would never abandon Lehua, Choi, and baby Leinani.

With John trapped in his thoughts, the sermon ended and, on cue, the Choir bellowed *Gloria in Excelsis Deo. Et in tona pax hominbus bonae voluntatis.* At the end of the *Gloria* came the benediction.

The service concluded, members of the congregation waited as the dignitaries filed out. When Colonel Kalakaua passed by in a handsome, well-fitting, dove gray suit, he nodded to John, a signal to meet after the service.

A tall, slender man with a cadaverous face walked rigidly along the aisle. "That's Minister of Finance Charles Harris," Leinani whispered. "He's a great supporter of the Anglican Church and the school I go to, and he's going to be a guest speaker at a special dinner tonight at the home of Robert Grant."

John winced at the sound of the man's name. "Is that the same Robert Grant who owns a sugar plantation on Maui?"

Leinani nodded enthusiastically. "He owns plantations on Oahu, too. He's very rich and I will be a servant at the dinner."

"Do you have to work for the man who took away my land?"

"The headmistress selected the best students to work at the dinner. I'm sorry, but we need the money that might be raised at that party."

John paid no further attention to the passing parade of dignitaries, upset by Leinani's decision. Soon it became their turn to depart and he left the church in haste, ignoring the blessing and proffered handshake of Reverend Robertson.

Within moments of his exit, Maria accosted John with an embrace. She touched his white vest, gushing, "You look so handsome, so splendid in your dark suit." And then she kissed his cheek.

"Naughty, naughty," Leinani chided. "You shouldn't make such public displays of affection."

"Why can't I?" Maria said. "You're the one who insisted that John kiss my hand in public, so why can't I embrace him in public?"

The banter silenced when Colonel Kalakaua, accompanied by a stately woman, walked up to the trio. "We meet again, John Tana. Permit me to introduce my wife, Kapiolani."

John remembered to give her a short bow, saying "I am pleased to meet you." He introduced Maria and Leinani.

"Ah, Maria, I believe I know your father. Isn't he Monsieur Edward Francois, the Foreign Minister?" Kapiolani asked.

Before Maria could respond, Kapiolani continued, "How very pretty you are."

Maria blushed and tucked her hands behind her back. She gave John a sidelong look, as if hoping that he had heard the compliment.

John noted that Kapiolani refused to look at Leinani. That's because she is a commoner, he thought.

"Ladies, if you'll excuse me, I'd like to borrow John for a moment." Without awaiting a reply, Kalakaua took John by the arm and led him a short distance away. "I have something I'd like to propose to you. Will you meet me at the barracks on Palace Walk at five o'clock?" John nodded and the men returned to the group. They found Maria and Leinani in a heated discussion. Maria rushed to John's side and took his arm. "Please, come with me and meet my father."

John glanced at Leinani, but she turned away.

Maria urged John over to where several people were conversing. "Father, I would like to present Mr. John Tana."

John found himself before an aristocratic gentleman dressed in a dark suit. He had graying hair, long sideburns, and a thin moustache. When he turned toward them, the man's face beamed at the sight of his daughter. "*Bon jour ma cherie.*"

With a curtsy Maria said, "*Mon pere*, Edward Francois Foreign Minister of the Kingdom of Hawaii, I am pleased to introduce to you Mister John Tana, a hero of the kingdom."

Edward Francois motioned Maria closer and then embraced her. It was only after he detached himself from his daughter that he extended a hand to John. "You must forgive my child, Monsieur Tana, she is very excitable." As Francois shook John's hand, he drew him closer into his group. "Mr. Tana, allow me to present you to His Excellency, John Dominis, Governor of Oahu, and his wife, Princess Lydia Liliuokalani Dominis. This is Mr. John Tana, our Hawaiian hero."

The princess smiled. "I have heard of you, Mr. Tana. My brother David speaks highly of you, praising your bravery, strength, and skill when faced with overwhelming odds."

The Governor added his own congratulations and shook John's hand, while saying, "Ah, the man who captured the notorious murderer, Chin Sing."

"*Mahalo nui loa kakou*," John answered.

"That is a magnificent thank you," a man said. "Your Hawaiian is excellent," he added. "Allow me to introduce myself. I am Bill Ragsdale."

"Ah, yes, Mr. Tana," Governor Dominis said. "Mr. Ragsdale should know good Hawaiian, since he is the official translator for the Legislature."

With a tone of deprecation, Ragsdale said, "Thank you, Governor, but all I do is smooth things out, thereby keeping internal arguments to a minimum. But you, Mr. Tana, tell me: who was your father, mother, grandfather, grandmother?"

John stammered, "My father was Isaac Tana and my mother was Konia. Didn't know my grandmother, but my grandfather was Kalani Moku Tana."

"That name, Kalani Moku Tana, has an unfamiliar ring to it. I can't recall if I ever heard it, but I'm guessing that your family is *makaainana*." Having identified John as the descendent of commoners, Ragsdale dismissed him from further consideration.

Maria quickly guided John away, her face having shifted into a scowl. They joined up with Leinani and left the church grounds, proceeding north on Nuuanu Street. Over eons of time, streams had cut Nuuanu Valley into one of the finest areas in all Hawaii. A vast green sheet covered its jagged heights, descending into uneven greenery at its flat bottom. Within its sweep were trees of koa, kiawe, and kukui, while profuse growths of flowers and tropical ferns, added a rainbow of color to the landscape.

Winds flowing southward over the *Pali* brought clouds of rain, feeding the land and making it fertile. Cooler temperatures from the winds and surrounding mountains and its proximity to Honolulu harbor made Nuuanu ideal for the homes of the island's rich and powerful. Still, there were members of the royal family who preferred the mangrove swamps, lily ponds, and sun-drenched beaches of Waikiki.

As the trio walked along the street, the opulence and grandeur of the homes astonished John. He saw two-and three-story structures with large verandas sweeping around the houses, some with porticos uplifted by Grecian columns. Most of the homes were painted white, with green or light brown coral-colored shutters. The roofs were dark, some bordered by low, delicate wrought iron fencing. Wide stone steps descended elegantly from the mansions onto black rock or coral-covered pathways.

Around the residences were mint-green lawns with borders of flowers and low bushes. Wrought iron or white picket fences, stonewalls, or hedges of hau wood created privacy. Coconut, kiawe, spiny leafed lauhala, and kukui trees planted in orderly fashion provided shade, shelter, and often a touch of elegance to the homes.

Compared to the shacks, simple wood shelters, or lean-tos where John and most of the common people lived, every home that he saw on his walk seemed like a palace. He asked himself why should so few need so much when there are thousands of Hawaiians and Orientals who had nothing.

As they strolled, the young women played poetry games. One would toss out a famous first line and the other needed to complete the couplet and supply the name of the poet. "In Xanadu did Kubla Khan a stately pleasure dome decree," Maria said.

Clapping her hands Leinani patterned Maria's rhythm, "'Where Alph, the sacred river, ran through caverns measureless to man down to a sunless sea.' Samuel Coleridge. Now it's my turn, and I'll bet you won't get this one. 'She walks in beauty like the night of cloudless climes and starry skies.'"

Maria pondered the words for a moment, and then took John's hand and pressed it to her face. Looking into his eyes, she recited, "And all that's best of dark and bright meet in her aspect and her eyes; with these she offers to thee alone her heart, and prays she will not be denied."

Leinani appeared vexed. "You got the first part right, but where did you come up with that second line?" She suddenly clamped a hand over her mouth. "You can't say—" Her voice trailed off.

Silence engulfed the trio. Finally, Maria took John's hand and pressed it to her chest. John did not resist her movement, yet it was clear by his expression that he was unsure how to respond. He was grateful to Maria for rescuing him from embarrassment only minutes earlier, but he also understood that she was in a class far above his and was therefore a woman he could never have. Gently, he took Maria's hand, kissed her palm, and then touched her nose and breathed her *ha*. "Thank you, Maria, but this cannot be."

Maria's eyes widened and she replied, her voice almost pleading, "It can, John."

He released her hand and took one step back. "Your father, his friends would not permit it." He reached into his pocket, turned to Leinani, and handed her a necklace. "The medallion you asked me to fix." Without another word, John left the two young women, and walked toward Honolulu harbor.

At five o'clock he arrived at the barracks on Palace Walk. Other than a disinterested soldier, no one was in the building. When John asked if Colonel Kalakaua had arrived, the soldier shrugged. When John checked various doors and found them locked, he resigned himself to wait for the Colonel outside. These minutes allowed him to think about what had transpired that day. It was like swimming in treacherous waters, meeting the source of Hawaii's political power, and John realized that power came to those who were born well. It had nothing to do with accomplishments.

The moment this thought crossed his mind, he remembered all those rich merchants and sugar plantation owners who had built so many of the homes he had seen during his walk. Surely they had succeeded not because of their birthright, but because they knew how to make money. They knew the importance of land. They knew how to acquire land. John needed to find out how to do it.

"Please forgive my delay," Kalakaua said, rousing John from his thoughts. "Come in and we can talk."

The colonel unlocked a door. They entered a spare room containing a desk and four chairs. The only light came from two closed windows. "Stuffy in here," Kalakaua said while opening them. He motioned John to sit and then took a chair facing him. "I'll get to the point. The kingdom needs help from Hawaiian men. Many vessels are sailing the Pacific and using Honolulu harbor as a way station for loading supplies, or for transferring cargo being shipped to other ports. Even though we have laws regulating sales of alcohol, drugs, and the services of women, these laws are often broken. As you know, Honolulu has had riots, brawls, civil disobedience, and murders. Being the capitol and the seat of government, foreign countries believe that anyone who controls Honolulu controls all of Hawaii. France has done that, Britain as well, and the Americans are threatening us. We need a Hawaiian militia of several hundred men who will assist our nation when it is needed. Can I count on you to help me raise a company of men willing to serve?"

Surprised by the proposal, John paused.

"You don't have to rush into a decision. Think it over and get back to me."

"What's the pay?" John asked, thinking of the men he knew and how desperate they were to earn a decent wage.

"I can't say for certain. But it would be at least twenty-five cents a day for military drilling, plus fifty cents for hazardous duties."

John thought this over for a moment. "Do we get uniforms and weapons?"

"Not right away, but in time I believe the answer is yes."

John nodded, and then a thought struck him. "If I do this, will I be able to keep my job?"

"We'll schedule training so it doesn't interfere with your work. In emergencies, we may have to take you away, but I'm sure employers will understand the nation's need."

John thought this through as well and then nodded. "Fine, I'll do it. What next?"

"Get some of your friends to meet with me and we'll discuss the militia. If they go with my plan, we'll form the company."

After Kalakaua finished, he stood as if to leave. But John had questions that were burning within him and needed to be asked. In his mind, there was no better time. "Tell me, why does Hawai'i need sugar? Sugar takes land from us. Sugar people are mean to the Asians and they don't like Hawaiians. Also, sugar plantation owners are rich. We are poor."

The colonel said nothing for a long beat, his eyes wide, as if taken aback by this unexpected vehemence. Finally, he said, "Why do you think Hawai'i needs sugar?"

John didn't like his question being answered with a question, but he trusted this man. "Because the missionaries came, saw our land, and knew it would make them rich. It was easy to convince the king to give them private ownership."

"Hawaiians could have acquired land for themselves by following a legal process."

John did not need to be reminded and felt himself becoming increasingly agitated. His hands clenched into fists and he pressed them into his thighs. "Nobody told me how to do it. I learned too late that you must pay to survey the boundaries of your land, file your claim with the government, and then pay a fee to make your claim. My father didn't have the money in 1848, and I don't have it today. But Grant and Company, they have lots of money and claimed that my land belongs to them."

The colonel inhaled and then let his breath out slowly, as if giving himself a moment to organize his thoughts. "I'm truly sorry about what happened. But why don't you use your reward money to buy land, set yourself up in business? Five hundred dollars will go a long way toward giving you a good start in life."

"I can't—"

"John, I have to leave for another engagement. Just remember my request for militia help, will you?"

John would have been angry at this dismissal, but he could see that the Colonel was thinking about what he had asked, moving the questions about in his mind. He liked the man and hoped there could be a friendship between them. "Will you come to a hula party? Lots of Hawaiians will be there. You can tell them about your militia plan."

Kalakaua accepted, and left.

It was twilight and great clouds heavy with moisture filled the sky, swallowing the faint light still glowing behind the mountains. John walked along Fort Street mulling over what Kalakaua had suggested about the reward. "Damn, I could buy land and a business with that money. Maybe become as rich as those people living on Nuuanu Street."

A cold feeling came into the pit of his stomach. Chin Sing was alone in a jail cell, facing death by hanging. He had made a promise to the man that he would receive a fair trial. The reward money had been kept from everyone else so it could be used to pay for his legal defense. On the other hand, if he used it for himself to buy land, he could become rich and maybe marry Leinani. Rich people found a way to get anything they wanted.

For more than an hour, John walked and fumed over his dilemma. A light rain fell, but he sought no shelter, welcoming instead the way the moisture cooled him. His thoughts returned to Leinani and a new heat built in him as he conjured up her image, a woman more beautiful than any other. He made a sudden decision to go to the Grant mansion, seek her out, and speak to her.

Thirty-Four

Robert Grant studied the dining room contemplating which guests could he best use to advance his schemes. Colonel David Kalakaua was a man of interest, intelligent, well-educated, impeccable manners, and related to Kamehameha the Great. He scoffed at rumors of his black father, scurrilous comments by those who sought power, knowing that Lot did not have long to live, and Kalakaua could be chosen to succeed him. Next to Miss Seldon was that rich bachelor, James Kingsley. He had heard that the man was making lots of money in merchandizing and finance. Good fellow to know especially if you wanted to expand your sugar operations.

He began to spoon in his soup, when his wife, Sheila, nudged him under the table. The two had met during Robert's student years at Yale University. Sheila had lived and attended college in New Haven, Connecticut. Her family traced its pedigree to a time before the American War of Independence. Women of the family claimed to be "Daughters of the American Revolution." Although Sheila's family had objected to her marrying someone who lived in Hawaii, they had relented when they learned that the Grants were wealthy. Despite thirteen years of marriage, they had no children.

Without looking up from his soup, Grant asked, "What is it, Sheila?"

"Robert, will you look at the lovely creature serving the salad. She looks like you."

Awakened from his speculation of how to use his dinner guests to make money, Grant lifted his eyes from his plate. His hazel eyes were caught and held by the hazel eyes of a serving woman holding an empty dish of soup in one hand, while placing a dish of salad onto the plate of Minister Harris.

Burning table candles brightening the room with their yellowish light, glinted from two pairs of matched eyes. For moments, the man and young woman stared at each other. Grant searched in the hidden recesses of his mind for some reason why there was a tantalizing filial familiarity about her.

Eye contact was broken when the girl finished serving Harris. She patted her hair, then rushed toward the kitchen. When she passed him, Grant caught a glimpse of something ivory held close to her chest by a golden chain.

"Robert, you're as white as a sheet. Do you know this woman? Have you been withholding something from me?" Sheila whispered.

"I don't know her, yet there is something about this young girl that is familiar to me."

Grant focused his eyes on the kitchen door until the servant wearing the golden chain bustled back into the dining room. He watched her clearing empty soup bowls and tried to make eye contact with her, but she avoided it. Finally, when she glanced toward him, Robert motioned her to come over, tapping his wine glass.

Grant watched the girl take a decanter from the sideboard, and approach him. His wife stared at the servant's face. Robert fastened his eyes onto the object dangling between her breasts. Pointing to the medallion he asked, "Where did you get this?"

"It came from my father," the girl said, covering the medallion with her hand.

"Tell me what your name is," Grant asked.

"Leinani."

"Your last name."

"Makanani."

"That pendant looks like something that once belonged to me. Where did you get it?"

Leinani ceased her wine pouring, turned, and rushed into the kitchen.

Robert Grant left the dining table in pursuit. Sheila Grant and Mistress Seldon followed him.

Inside the kitchen, Grant paused when he saw Leinani leaning against a kitchen counter, her eyes brimming with tears. A young girl stood beside her. Seldon rushed over to Leinani, dabbing the drops dripping down her cheeks.

"What has happened? Mr. Grant, did Leinani do something wrong?" Seldon asked.

Robert Grant came to the three women saying, "My apologies. I must have frightened this lovely child, but she has a keepsake that I believe was once mine. I need to find out how she acquired it."

Staunching her tears and regaining her composure, Leinani fixed Grant with a look of disbelief, "I said to you that it belonged to my father. My mother Malia gave it to me many years ago. She said that it came from someone special. It was a gift from my father."

"Do you know who your father is?"

"No, my mother never told anyone who my father is. To this day it remains a mystery."

"How old are you?"

"Seventeen."

"Please, may I examine your pendant?"

Perplexed, Leinani removed the scrimshaw medallion and handed it to Grant. He peered at the carved writing around the heart, rubbed his thumb over it, and gasped. "It's the same. There cannot be another like this one!"

Grant staggered into a kitchen chair, his hands covering his eyes. Sheila rushed to comfort him, but he waved her away. Suppressing a sob, he said, "Leinani, I would like to speak to your mother tonight."

Sheila said, "You can't just leave your dinner guests and go traipsing off into the night."

"I understand that we can't leave at this moment, but after the dinner guests depart I would request that Leinani accompany me on a visit to her mother, Malia."

"This is highly unusual," Seldon complained.

"I will make a generous contribution to the school fund."

"Hmm, well if Leinani is properly chaperoned, we could make an exception to the rules. Besides, she would be visiting with her family."

"It is settled then. After the guests depart we will accompany this young lady to her family's home wherever it may be."

The Grants and Seldon returned to the dining room, Excuses were made of a kitchen emergency that is presently under control. The dinner rushed to its finish. Grant announced that tea would be served to the women in the sitting room. He invited the gentlemen to retire with him to his salon for a cigar and some absinthe.

Grant's opulent salon exuded wealth with its walls of rich mahogany and its furniture of glowing koa wood. Within the room a half dozen gleaming red leather chairs were set in a half circle facing a large red leather sofa. Covering the floor lay a magnificent rug. The far wall of the spacious room held a recessed fireplace of stone, its long mantelpiece painted white with yellow curlicues and supported by two stylish Grecian columns.

From a side bar, Grant dispensed brandy and absinthe. Passing out a box of cigars to the assembled gentlemen, he draped his arm on the mantelpiece. Despite his inner turmoil, Grant calmly smoked his cigar. He noted James Kingsley moving to the fireplace.

"I am given to understand by Miss Seldon that you may be off this evening on a late night venture to Waikiki. It is a hazardous trip with many nasty holes in the road, as well as flowing streams, taro patches, rice fields, and unsavory characters," Kingsley said in a low voice. "May I be of help to you and the ladies who accompany you?"

"Oh, it is not such a bad journey. We can manage."

"But think of the women traveling at night in dangerous country. Do you have a lighted carriage for them?"

"Sad to say, since my wife and I are childless, all we have is a two wheeler. I do the majority of traveling on horseback."

"Then I can be of assistance. I have a four-wheeled phaeton and, like the Greek sun god for whom it is named, it has lanterns fore and aft. I will order it from my man straight away. We shall accompany your party and give you protection, illumination, and guidance. My Hawaiian servant is well acquainted with Waikiki."

Robert started to protest, Kingsley interrupted him. "My dear sir, we will have none of that. Your women need the conveyance and protection that I can provide. I am off to make arrangements." Before Grant could protest again, Kingsley left the den.

Although Minister Harris seemed bent upon making a long harangue over the needs of the Anglican Church and the schools that it wanted to create, Robert Grant cut to the chase at an opportune moment. He proposed a contribution of $1,000 and suggested that his colleagues do likewise. In a matter of minutes $8,000 was raised. Relieved that he had been able to navigate around the long-winded speech of the Finance Minister, Grant ushered his guests from the salon.

Thirty-Five

By the time John arrived at the mansion, the rain had slowed and the storm clouds were gone. Stars threw a luster across the heavens, casting light against the high wrought iron fence that guarded the opulent Grant residence. John found the entry gate locked, shook the spear-topped bars like a prisoner seeking escape, and then stood there, dejected. Finally, he turned and began to walk away. Before he reached the end of the property, the front door opened, throwing bright light onto the entrance, and three young girls exited the house. Behind them a woman called, "Wait for me by the gate. I'll be with you shortly."

One of the girls said, "What an evening. Did you see the way Mr. Grant looked at Leinani? He stared at her like she was a ghost."

As their steps made crunching sounds on the pebbles of the driveway, John slid into a darkened corner. He got into position just as one young woman said, "Not a ghost, but an image of himself."

After quiet murmurs that John could not make out, he heard, "Didn't you notice the resemblance between them? Just look at their hazel eyes. And did you see his fascination with Leinani's medallion?"

"Mr. Grant wasn't the only gentleman interested in Leinani," another voice added. "That handsome Mr. Kingsley couldn't keep his eyes off of her. When I waited on him, he kept asking me questions about her. The man is a bachelor and very rich." These words pierced John's heart, but he was at a loss as to what to do.

"Maria, about that medallion, you were in the kitchen when the Grants rushed in, what happened?"

"Leinani showed it to me before dinner. It was round and ivory, with whale-bone, and there was a heart in the center pierced by an arrow. Around the heart were the words *Rob me ke aloha Lei kuu ipo.*"

"What's that mean?" one of the girls asked.

"*Rob gives his love to his sweetheart Lei.*"

There was silence. John wondered what the girls must be thinking.

"What happened next?"

"Mr. Grant believes that the necklace once belonged to him. He wants to see Leinani's mother tonight and unravel the mystery."

The front door opened and an older woman stood at the threshold. John didn't recognize her, but he saw that she held herself with some authority.

"Headmistress Seldon, you will accompany Leinani and Mr. Grant on this evening sojourn to Waikiki," she said.

John heard whispering and moved closer to the girls.

"Darn, it's Miss Staley, who will take us back to school. I am dying to know what's going on," Maria said.

Staley, accompanied by two servants, came to the gate. It was opened and she passed through, followed by the students. One of the servants trotted beyond the gate and headed down Nuuanu Street. John decided to uncover the mystery of the necklace so he found a place in the shadows where he could watch the mansion.

Several minutes went by and a black four-wheeler, harnessed to two chestnuts, dashed up Nuuanu Street and rolled onto the driveway stopping near the entrance to the mansion. The front door opened and guests spilled out, each one bidding farewell. Soon, only the open carriage, its driver, two horses, and a horseman remained.

It was not long before the door opened again, and Leinani and several others exited the mansion and occupied the carriage. A Hawaiian and Caucasian mounted horses and followed the carriage as it sped out the driveway heading toward Waikiki.

Puzzled, John stepped from the bushes turning over in his mind what he had heard. Some connection existed between the medallion, Leilani, and his enemy. What could it be?

He watched the light of the phaeton disappear. A burning rose inside him. Should he follow them?

"It's too dark, I'll never catch them," he thought. He decided to head home.

Thirty-Six

G rant watched Miss Staley and the serving girls from Saint Sebastian leave the party. He said perfunctory goodbyes to the guests and waited until they left before urging Leinani, Seldon, and Sheila to make haste and depart.

In the close-packed cinder and coral driveway of the Grant mansion, a smart black four-wheeler harnessed to two frisky chestnut-bay horses waited. Lanterns fore and aft of the conveyance burnt into the darkness, illuminating beige coral steps bordered by white railings of stone that swept up to the elevated veranda of the mansion.

A grandfather clock in the front hallway of the residence chimed, as the Grants, Seldon, Leinani, and Kingsley exited through the mahogany brown front doors. Kingsley assisted the women into the carriage. As the bell of the grandfather clock struck ten, he offered his hand to Leinani. Grant saw that the bachelor held onto her overlong while his eyes searched for hers. She kept her face cast onto the steps of the carriage. He watched a chagrined young man direct her to the front seat next to the Hawaiian coachman. Somehow this infatuation with the serving girl could prove useful to him in the future.

Grant sat next to the coachman, saying, "Leinani, show us the way to your mother's home." With a clucking and slight whipping of the reins, the coachman urged the horses into action. Out of the long driveway the vehicle sped, the women and Grant in the phaeton, with Kingsley and a Hawaiian servant following behind. Except for the pounding of hooves, the creek of springs, and the crunch of four iron-shod wheels on hard-packed dirt, the trip was conducted in silence.

At the Makanani compound, a dog barked as the riders and carriage came to a stop. The animal trotted about them growling his displeasure at their presence.

Grant signaled to Leinani that she should lead him to her mother and asked the others to wait by the carriage so as not to disturb the families in the compound. The noise of the arrival and the yapping of the dog had alerted the occupants, and four women and two men emerged from their homes.

"My mother Malia, where is she?" Leinani asked.

One of the women pointed to a shack.

Leinani rushed to the threshold, calling "Momma."

"Hui, I'm in here. Wait, I come out." Malia emerged and embraced Leinani. "Eh! How come you folks make so much noise? Wake whole place up. Make everybody angry." Malia laughed.

"It is my fault for disturbing people," Robert Grant apologized, studying the woman's face, and realizing that she was not the person he thought she might be. "But I needed to see you and get important information. Is there somewhere we could talk privately?"

Malia scratched her head, rubbed her tummy, spat on the ground and said, "No."

Kingsley interrupted "I own a cottage and storehouse nearby we can go there and talk."

Thanking him, Grant asked, "Malia, will you come with us and explain your daughter's scrimshaw pendant?"

Malia's face sagged. Her eyes darted about. "Where we going?"

"My men will guide you to my cottage. I will get things ready," Kingsley said and galloped into the darkness.

Within a mile, Grant and the women were taken to a dark green, plantation style home raised on blocks of wooden stilts and surrounded by a white picket fence. Kingsley stood at its door and ushered the group into the cottage. The only furniture in the main room was a plain wood table with two sets of benches and some chairs drawn up around it. Flaming kerosene lanterns, smoky and smelly, illuminated the rectangular interior.

Kingsley directed Malia to the head of the table. Leinani moved next to her, and the host slid into a seat by her side. Amused by his clumsy flirtation, Robert Grant settled with Sheila and Seldon on the bench opposite them. He cleared his throat, drummed his fingers on the table, and said, "I understand that you are Leinani's mother?"

Malia blinked. Tears formed in her eyes. She clutched and un-clutched her hands and whispered, "I am not her mother."

Leinani gasped, "You are not my mother?"

Grant fumbled in a coat pocket searching for a cigar. He needed to relax, calm a rising anxiety. He asked, "Jim, do you have any whiskey?"

Kingsley called to a manservant, "In the kitchen. There's bourbon in a cabinet. Bring it with glasses for our guests."

Malia breathed hard several times and fixed her eyes on Leinani, sadness marring the wrinkled beauty of her face. "You are not of my blood. I met your mother when she came to Lahaina with her friend, Malama."

"For the love of heaven," Grant said startled by the name. "How long ago did you meet the mother and Malama?"

Before Malia could answer, Leinani said, "Why didn't you tell me that you are not my mother. Who is my mother?"

Malia rocked in her seat, looked down at her hands that she continued to fold and unfold. "Malama and I decided to hide the truth to save you from your grandfather, Eliza Grant, that man's father." Malia pointed to Robert. "We were afraid that if he found out that you are his granddaughter he would kill you."

Sheila gasped. Miss Seldon rose from her seat saying, "I need air."

Grant groaned, shaking his head. "My father was a hard man but I can't believe he would do that."

"From what I saw, I believed he would have killed the mother and her baby."

"What did you see that makes you accuse my dead father of intent to murder?" Grant snapped, rising from the bench, anger replacing his curiosity.

"Here, have a drink," Kingsley said, breaking the tension in the room. He poured whiskey into a glass and offered it to Grant who took it, downing the amber liquid in a gulp, and asked for a refill. He needed to calm himself, to still the gnawing suspicion that there might be truth in Malia's accusation.

The old woman studied him for many moments, a look of disgust whipping over her face. "Maybe eighteen years ago, Malama, my dead husband's cousin, came to Lahaina with a beaten fifteen year-old girl. Malama told me she was housekeeper for a man named Grant. He owned a ranch house near Wailuku."

One day she went shopping and met this young orphan. Her name was Leinani. The girl was without a home or family."

Grant became agitated, spilling his drink. Sheila pulled him down to the bench. She took the cigar from his nervous fingers, clipped the end, lit it, and returned it. Grant puffed several times on the dry weed, blowing curtains of smoke into the room. Gruffly he said, "Continue."

Malia made a wry face, waving away the smoke swirling around her, and said, "Knowing Mr. Grant would be away for a long time, Malama offered the girl a bed and work. Everything is fine for a few days because nobody else lives in the house. But one day, a young man shows up and say he is the owner's son."

Grant stood. Finished his drink and slid it to Kingsley, nodding for more. The young financier released his grip on Leinani's hand, poured another shot, and then returned his attention to the tearful young woman.

Malia continued her story, "On their first meeting, Malama saw that the two young people took an immediate interest in each other. Leinani was pretty and Robert tall and nice looking."

Grant's hand shook, spilling his drink. "Oh my God," he said. "I remember that first meeting. She was shy but in her shyness, absolutely beautiful." He paced the floor then stopped his frenetic walking as Malia fell silent.

"Please go on," Grant said and resumed his seat. Sheila reached her hand to him and gave a squeeze.

"As days passed, Malama saw Robert stay close to the house and not ride off to the sugar fields until mid-morning. She saw that Leinani always had some early task to perform near the barn and stable behind the home. In the evenings, it was her habit to retire early and she would leave the two young people deep in conversation. A sound sleeper she never noticed anything unusual occurring at night."

Grant sighed. He leaned back closing his eyes, remembering moments of exquisite love. Sheila stood and began pacing the room. Leinani rocked, and Kingsley put an arm around her shoulders.

"Everything was peaceful until late in the afternoon one day. Without warning, Eliza Grant came to the house. He asked for his son, and Malama told him that she thought he was in the stable outside. The master asked Malama to call him in. Within a few minutes Robert entered the living room of the residence through the kitchen, leaving its door open. Father and son greeted, held each other, and began talking.

"Through the kitchen door Leinani sneaked in. As she closed it, rusty hinges squeaked. The old man saw her, and say, 'Who is that?'"

"Malama say, 'A Hawaiian orphan girl who is here helping me.'"

"Old man Grant say, 'she can't stay in this house or on this property. Leave right now young lady.'"

"Robert got excited. He say, 'Father, she has nowhere to go. You can't just send her away.'"

"Mr. Grant answered back, 'Who says I can't kick her out? This is my home and I do what I want.'"

"Then young Grant say something stupid, 'Dad, she is someone special to me.'"

"The old guy explodes. He say, 'What do you mean special? Come with me. We are going to talk.'"

"Malama say that father and son went into the office of the ranch home while they waited in the kitchen."

"I remembered that," Robert interrupted. "My father demanded that I tell him if I had relations with Leinani. I denied it, but dad knew when I was lying. He shouted at me. Shook his fist. I was young, frightened. I admitted that we had made love many times. Then I said, 'I want to marry Leinani.'"

Sheila stopped her pacing. "Robert, you never told me this. Why didn't you?"

Grant ignored her protest and stared at Malia, "When I said those words. My father rushed out of the room locking the door. What did Malama tell you happened?"

Malia glanced at Leinani, huddling against Kingsley. "I don't know if you want to hear this. Maybe you should go outside?"

Leinani shook her head.

Malia rubbed her palms against her thighs. Kingsley offered her whiskey, but Malia said, "I'm a good Christian. Don't drink that stuff."

"This is all very melodramatic," Sheila scoffed. "I'm sure Eliza came outside and asked the women to leave the premises and they did. Nothing more happened."

"You think I'm making up a story? You think I lie? Where you think I got that medallion? You don't believe me, I'm going home." Malia pushed back on her chair and rose.

"No, mama," Leinani said. "Please stay and finish even if nobody else wants to hear what happened."

"We all need to know what occurred," Kingsley said. "No matter how difficult it is for you to tell it. Please go on."

Malia looked at Grant. Her stare sent shivers through his body as his thoughts raced back to that time long ago when he pounded against the locked door wondering what was happening outside. He needed to know about his Leinani and how the young girl across from him had gotten the medallion that he had given to the first love of his life.

"Please," he begged. "Tell me. I must know."

Sheila stomped outside. As she passed Seldon standing by the door, Grant heard her mutter, "I don't believe any of this." But he knew that so far every part of Malia's story was true. His eyes pleaded with Malia to continue.

"After your old man locked the door, he went to a hall closet taking from it several bamboo sticks. It was then that Malama and Leinani got scared. Mr. Grant comes to the kitchen door, his face ugly. He yelled at Leinani, 'You brown bitch. You whore!' He grabbed her by the hair, dragged her into the living room and beat her with the switches. All time he yelling, 'You sinner. Wicked woman. God will punish you. Filthy, dirty woman taking advantage of a young boy. Whore!' Each time he say a word, he whipped the girl. She shriek, cried, beg him to stop. Loud pounding come from locked door. Malama screaming, trying to stop him. Grant hit her too. Malama say everything was crazy."

Robert shook his head. "My father didn't tell me this. Those events happened almost two decades ago. How can you remember so well what Malama told you?"

Leinani's composure evaporated. Tears flowed from her eyes in streams. She reached to Malia for comfort, but the old woman had risen and with eyes ablaze stared directly at Robert Grant. "You doubt what I say?"

Kingsley reached his arm around Leinani's shoulders, drawing her body into his. Leinani sobbed against his chest. From the pocket of his coat he withdrew a handkerchief. "I'm so sorry. Let me wipe your tears."

"What you think? I lie?" challenged Malia, pointing an accusing finger at Grant. "What I say is what Malama tell me. Besides with my own eyes, I see the girl when she come to Lahaina. All bust up. Big welts on her body. Skin torn off her back. Whole body black. Hurt all over. Pain make her cry all the time. What's a matta you? Why you no take care of girl you play around with? You no believe me? I go home."

Miss Seldon gasped. "No, don't go. We need to know what happened."

Grant sank back onto the bench, his hands cupped over his eyes. In a shaking voice he said, "I apologize for doubting you. It's just hard for me to relive that nightmare. My father never told me what he did. Only that he sent the two women away. Please go on."

Malia grunted and sat down. "Leinani needs to know the truth so I finish the story. Everything is crazy, the women screaming, Grant yelling as he beat Leinani rolling on the floor. Malama grabbed his arm and Grant struck her across the chest with his bundle of sticks. With this last hit, Grant stopped beating people. He tell Malama to leave the house and said, 'take that slut with you.'"

"Malama ask for time to pack her things."

"Grant say, 'You have fifteen minutes to be out of here. I'll get a boy to take you into town, but don't stay in Wailuku and don't be anywhere near Grant property by the morning or I'll have you both thrown in jail.'"

"Malama help Leinani up and they pack. The orphan has very little. Malama throw everything into some sacks. They run out of the house in less than fifteen minutes they so scared. When they left there was still pounding at the door of the locked room. Wagon and Chinese driver take them to Wailuku. It took them two days to come to Lahaina.

"When I see Leinani first time, she is sore all over like I told you. We give them both great aloha for Malama is family. Pretty soon we can tell that the orphan is going to have baby. But even with this happy news, woman all time hurt. All time hide when man come near her.

"When her stomach big like ripe calabash, Leinani get sick. I think maybe beating cause damage inside. I don't know. When her time comes, she is very hot. This baby is her first one and she cannot handle. Baby no want come out, even though mother try shoving her out.

"After long time, Leinani say, 'I can't push any more. I'm going to die.'"

"'No, No,' I say. 'Don't die! Live for baby.' But I can tell she not going to make it. She took from her neck the ivory medallion over there." Malia pointed to the scrimshaw necklace that Leinani wore. "She says, 'Give to my baby. Tell baby, from father. Tell baby father will come someday.'"

"Then the dying girl sing, 'Robert *me ke aloha Leinani kuu ipo*.'"

"I know if I don't do something right away, baby going die too. So we cut the stomach and pull out baby girl. Mother had told us to name her Leinani after her.

"This girl here," Malia pointed, "is that child. "This," pointing to the medallion, "came from her mother."

Leinani was unable to control her tears. Kingsley held her close, soothing her. Seldon and Sheila remained silent, studying Malia who sat in her chair oblivious to their stares.

Robert Grant drummed his fingers on the table. "I loved her. She was beautiful. She needed someone to love her. I gave her that love. Whatever I gave, she returned tenfold. We had a glorious few weeks together until my father came. When he took me to his office, I tried to convince him that I loved her, that I wanted her to be part of my life forever and ever. I told him that we had made love with each other many times.

"My father grew furious. He said to me, 'She is a Jezebel, a seducer of an innocent boy.' He left the room and locked the door. I did not know what was going on outside. When my father released me from the room it was dark. I ran about the house. I ran all over the grounds. I called over and over for Leinani. When I returned to the home I threatened to search all of Maui, the world for her.

"My father said to me, 'You need to grow up. Become a man and learn to run the business. Marry a good Christian woman from America not some brown slut who only cares about making love to any man she might be near.'"

"I protested, 'Leinani is pure. She loves me.'"

"He stopped me, saying, 'You are young, immature, you have no knowledge of women. A Hawaiian sleeps with you today, and then chooses another tomorrow to bed with. I know these common wicked women well. They have no Christian morality. They will practice adultery, fornication with many, and be insincere to all. If you persist in your pursuit of this trollop, I will disinherit you.

Consider carefully what you will do. We've discussed going to college. I have made plans for your departure. A boat leaves for Panama next week. Travel from there to New England and go to Yale."

"I was young, weak-willed, and didn't know how my father had beaten Leinani. I thought she would find a home with Malama and make a new life. I did not know that she was pregnant with my baby.

"If I had known, I swear I would have defied my father and married her, giving my daughter a good name. Yet I did not know what happened, and my father's arguments were persuasive. I left for Yale and met and married a wonderful woman." He smiled at Sheila who looked away from his glance.

It was past midnight. The lanterns wavered, flaming high and then low. Grant and Kingsley returned Malia to her home and Miss Seldon to the school. She gave permission for Leinani to go home with her father.

The phaeton trundled into the driveway of the Grant residence followed by James Kingsley. At the house steps he leaped from his horse and offered his hand to Leinani. The couple stood together for a moment, their fingers touching.

"Thank you for all that you have done. You were wonderful this evening," Leinani whispered. She kissed Kingsley on the cheek.

"It is a pleasure to be of assistance to the Grant family."

The three Grants climbed the stairs of the mansion, watching the phaeton and its owner leave the property through its massive stone portals. As he exited Kingsley waved to his two friends and his new love.

Thirty-Seven

"**Y**ou want me to do what!" Joshua Kanakoa said.

John took a deep breath. "Act as Chin Sing's lawyer."

The attorney leaned back in his chair. "John, you know that Big Sugar runs the court system. If I help the Chinese it is bad for business, especially mine."

When John said nothing, he explained how it worked. For the sugar industry to be profitable, the companies needed to acquire land, workers, and equipment. Hiring cheap labor guaranteed a profit, and there was no cheaper labor than the Chinese.

"I understand that,"

"I'm sure you do. But there's another element that you might not know about. Labor contracts are written in English and plantation owners interpret them as they choose. The Chinese have to go on trust."

"And we know how far that goes," John said, with a shake of his head.

"It's even more complicated. If a Chinese laborer leaves his job to make a complaint to the Hawaiian courts, he's violated his contract."

"So we're talking about slavery,"

"From your viewpoint, yes. But countries that trade with us don't see it like that. To the world outside of Hawaii it is not slavery. Foreign nations do not bother interfering with domestic contracts."

John sat quietly and his mind drifted to his land. "So our law system cheats the Chinese and the Hawaiians."

The conversation that followed brought John to the edge of his seat. They discussed how land had once been divided by rulers among their supporters, but the boundaries were vague, sometimes a line of trees or the trajectory of a rolling stone.

"When Kamehameha the First conquered the islands, Russia, Britain, and France were colonizing the Pacific and grabbing native land. Missionaries arrived in Hawaii and found a nation without an organized government, so they convinced the king that further colonization could be avoided through a constitutional monarchy. It seemed to be the most effective way to pass laws, make treaties, and have courts to decide disputes between foreigners and Hawaiians." John studied Kanakoa for several moments. "So now you're going to tell me that the missionaries used our fear of foreigners for their own gain."

Joshua nodded. "And that resulted in control over the Hawaiian nation."

"How did this private property idea come about?"

"After the foreigners found Hawaii, sickness came, thousands of our people died. Add to this the devastation of King Kamehameha's wars and what were we left with?"

John understood this to be a rhetorical question, yet waited for the answer. There was little that he knew and so much to be learned.

Joshua answered, "Untended fields, dried up taro patches, and dead fishponds. Not exactly the elements that would keep a country alive. With a dying and largely homeless population, the king took his advisors' counsel and divided the land. It sounded like a good idea. The Hawaiian needed private ownership so he could build a home, have a plot of ground for a farm. His ownership would be permanent, not subject to redistribution every time a king died. A Board of Land Commissioners was created and the new owners only had to prove citizenship, be literate, pay to have the land surveyed, and then pay a fee to register the claim with the Board."

Sunlight filtered through the windowpanes and bounced off floating specks of dust. John sat silently, hands folded, as if praying. "If God helps those who help themselves," John said, his voice low and pensive, "I guess the missionaries knew how to ask for God's help. Do you have any idea how much land the common people actually received?"

Joshua shook his head. "My guess is: very little."

"So most of the land went to those who knew what to do?"

"I can't say that either, because much of the land is still held by the king-dom. But I do know that the white folk are smart and that they've made hun-dreds of land claims as compensation for services rendered to the nation, and that's without paying anything. Their claims have been filed with the Board of Commissioners and approved. If you add to this the land they received from the high chiefs through purchase, lease, or defaults on loans, you're talking many thousands of acres, and that's only to a few families."

Before John could jump in with his next question, Joshua rushed ahead. "Listen, you were moved off your property for the same reason plantations hire Chinese contract laborers: it was at very little cost. They'll use any excuse to justify their actions. Don't forget, Hawaiians have rights. We are citizens and our courts are supposed to protect us. So if you were kicked off your land, it's because a plantation owner was trying to circumvent any legal claim you had to the property. Mr. Grant was worried that if you stayed you might one day figure out how to make a claim."

"Can I make a claim?"

"I've been to the bureau of conveyances. Robert Grant has a surveyed patent to the Kahului property that may once have been yours."

"You're telling me I'm out of luck."

"One slim chance is left, there is no recorded court decree ending allodial rights."

"What's that mean?"

"It's residual rights that a former owner has to property. Establishing it can be complicated."

"And expensive, any money I have goes to hire a lawyer to defend Chin Sing. I know that a Chinese man without citizenship is considered no better than a dog, but would you help him?"

Joshua Kanakoa took several deep breaths before responding, and then he explained that no statutes existed that provided an excuse for murder. "The law aside," he added. "I have to think about the plantation owners and local mer-chants. If I take this case, will they boycott me and cost me my livelihood?"

John said nothing, simply closed his eyes and nodded slowly, as if suffering over the reality that too many people considered a Chinese life worthless.

"Fine," Joshua said. "Let them hate me. If you believe so strongly, I'll do it." He stood and moved toward the window. "My fee will be two-hundred-fifty dollars, plus expenses."

John leapt to his feet and dug into a pocket. "Thanks! Here's two hundred on account; I'll bring the rest tomorrow."

"Where did you get this money?" Joshua asked as he stared at the fistful of cash.

"It's the reward money. What better way to spend it than on Chin Sing's defense."

Thirty-Eight

"Hear ye, hear ye, the Circuit Court in and for the Island of Oahu, Kingdom of Hawaii, is now in session, the Honorable Isaiah Andrews presiding. All rise." Chairs and benches scraped the floor as a gallery of a hundred people stood as a wiry, middle-aged man, dapper in a dark suit, made his way into the courtroom, ascended a dais, and glowered at them.

"Be seated," the marshal said as the judge settled into a high-backed leather chair. After a few coughs, throat clearings, sneezes, and whispers, the room fell quiet.

Andrews sat between two *kahilis,* ancient Hawaiian symbols of royalty. "Call the case."

The clerk intoned, "Your honor, ladies and gentlemen, this is Number 1564, The King versus Chin Sing. Is the defendant, Chin Sing, present before this honorable court?"

"Yes," the marshal answered, gesturing for the manacled Chinese to stand.

"Who appears on behalf of the king?" the judge asked.

"I do," drawled a tall man rising from a table in front of the judge's elevated platform. "Attorney General Ambrose Wiseman."

"Clerk, read the charge," the judge said.

Before the clerk could begin, he was interrupted. "If you please, Your Honor, may I appear on behalf of Chin Sing? Attorney Joshua Kanakoa for the defendant."

With an incredulous expression, Andrews glared at the attorney. "Are you telling me that you are representing this Chinaman? Who's paying you to do this?"

Joshua glanced at John, who was seated in the front row. "That is a privileged matter, your Honor. I have properly been retained and I believe it is the duty of this court to ensure that every man brought before this honorable body has due process, legal representation, and a fair trial by a jury of twelve peers."

"Due process, fair trials, attorneys," the judge said with a dismissing gesture. "That's for citizens, not foreigners like this Chinaman,"

Joshua stood taller and adjusted his jacket. "I beg to disagree, Your Honor. This nation has many precedents of the right to jury trial and due process. They date back to 1825, when the British naval captain Lord Byron convinced the high chiefs that a jury trial in capital cases is mandatory. Since that time, we have had attorneys and jury trials for foreign seamen, traders, businessmen, and travelers."

The judge pondered the argument and turned to the Attorney General.

Wiseman said, "I am forced to agree with my colleague. A right to jury trial is fundamental. Furthermore, I can attest that the king will not object."

John watched Wiseman sit down and recognized the man's expression as a smirk. It struck him that the king's lawyer believed he couldn't lose. He sacrificed nothing by giving the impression of playing fair.

In a very loud voice, the clerk read: "Defendant Chin Sing, you are charged with murder. To wit, that on Tuesday, the twenty-fourth day of August, in the year of our Lord eighteen seventy, you did, with malice aforethought, kill Mister Roy Charles. How do you plead to this charge?"

"Not guilty, and not guilty by reason of insanity," Joshua Kanakoa said.

Wiseman shouted, "I object, Your Honor! The word of God as found in his Bible is the law of Hawaii. Insanity is not a defense to murder. The good Lord said, 'Thou shalt not kill.' He did not say, 'If insane, thou may kill!'"

The audience applauded, some saying *brilliant* and *Go tell him*, accompanied by acknowledgments that no insanity plea existed in Hawaii. As comments continued to ripple through the audience, the marshal pounded his gavel. "Order in the court. Order in the court."

Joshua immediately said, "Your Honor, allow me to—"

"Quiet!" the judge answered, his face flushed. "I've heard enough, Mr. Kanakoa. A plea of not guilty by reason of insanity is denied." Having delivered his decision, he added, "I will now send the marshal to collect twelve good men to try this case today."

Wiseman asked for a continuance to prepare his witnesses. Before Joshua could make his own request, the judge recessed the trial until nine o'clock the next morning.

At the end of the work day, after the marshal had arrived at the waterfront to subpoena him, John Tana ran into his friend Aaloa, the "Bone Breaker". As they spoke, a large double canoe with crab claw sails skimmed past Sand Island and pulled into the dock. John counted nine people seated inside. A burly Hawaiian lowered the sail and then called to them, "Aloha. I am Haku Alapai." The man clambered onto the wharf. "Can you tell me where to find Kalia?"

When Aaloa pointed toward Waikiki, the stranger scratched his head. "I'm not familiar with this area. Either of you know the Alapai family? Last I heard, they were living in Kalia."

"I know the family. I will show you where they live," John said as he climbed into the canoe.

It was during the short voyage to Kalia that John learned that everyone in the canoe constituted the last of the family from Kau. They had left their village and were looking for a better place to live. "Maybe we stay in Waikiki," Haku said. "Maybe we go on to Kaua'i."

After Haku beached the canoe at the mouth of a stream, John directed the family inland, toward a cluster of shacks. When they arrived, several men and women emerged from the compound. Haku invited John to stay overnight, but he declined. With many words of aloha, and an open invitation to return any time, John began his run back to town. A pair of eyes watched him disappear.

Thirty-Nine

Morning light spilled into the courtroom through great leaded windows. It cast a heavenly glow over a restive, expectant crowd. Selection of the jury was about to begin.

Joshua rose and announced, "Your Honor, I have looked at the jury pool and I object to the venire."

A murmur ran through the room, and the judge's face became red with anger.

"It does not contain any Chinese. With no Chinese on this panel, my client will not be tried by a jury of his peers."

Before Wiseman could respond, the judge said, "Overruled. Chinese are not citizens of Hawaii. Only citizens can serve on a jury. Counsel, no more of these frivolous motions or I will find you in contempt."

Joshua sat down, his expression passive. Next to him, Chin Sing said nothing. Behind them, John squirmed in his seat, his jaw tightening. He believed that everyone wanted his friend to hang.

By mid-morning, a jury of twelve men—nine Caucasians and three Hawaiians—were selected, and Wiseman called his first witness.

The local constable testified that he arrived at the residence at 4:30 p.m. and found Mr. Charles on his stomach, a pool of blood surrounding his body. He did not see any weapons, nor did he see a bamboo switch in the kitchen. There was no evidence of a struggle, either in the kitchen or on the ground floor of the house.

Wiseman's next witness, Dr. George Brown, testified that he was summoned to the residence that same afternoon, where he observed the dead victim in a pool of blood. At the morgue, he determined that the cause of death was a sharp object, the likely weapon being a long knife. Mr. Charles had bled to death by a stab wound to his abdomen; the time was approximately 4:00 p.m.

A black-handled knife was marked as exhibit number one. The doctor testified that the knife was certainly long enough to cause the mortal injury. On cross-examination, he added that, other than the single penetration into the stomach, there were no other cuts or injuries to the body. He also testified that Mr. Charles had been drinking before his death, indicated by the strong odor of alcohol about his person and clothes.

The next witness, a neighbor, said that she saw Chin Sing flee the Charles home at approximately 4:00 p.m.

Mrs. Rachel Charles testified that she and Mr. Charles had been married for twenty four years. She identified the knife as hers and was dismissed.

John noticed that Mrs. Charles hesitated before leaving the witness stand, as if she wanted to add something. Instead, she dabbed her eyes, gathered herself up, and walked tearfully from the courtroom. He watched her depart, and nearly missed his name being called.

John sat in the witness chair. He glanced at his friend, Chin Sing, and saw a man who looked confused and defeated. Even more, he saw someone who was living with the shame of having brought dishonor upon himself, his family, and his ancestors. Shaking off his thoughts, John focused on the questions directed toward him.

In response to Wiseman's inquiries, John testified that he met Chin Sing the night before the murder.

"Did the accused tell you that he would meet with Mr. Charles the following morning and demand money from him?"

"It wasn't like how you make it sound," John said.

"Just answer yes or no," the judge ordered.

"Yes."

Wiseman looked like an animal moving in for the kill. "When you learned that Mr. Charles had died and that Chin Sing was implicated in the death, you believed that Sing did not get what he wanted, is that correct?"

John stared at the man for a long beat, his brow furrowed. "What do you mean *implicated* or *believed*?"

Wiseman squared his shoulders. From John's vantage point, he seemed to be suppressing a smile. "Let's just say: when you found out that Chin Sing had run away, you believed he didn't get any money from Mr. Charles. Is this correct?"

"I don't know."

"You found this to be true when you captured Mr. Chin in the reed ponds near Mount Leahi, correct? That Chin did not get any money from Mr. Charles."

"Well, yes, this is true, but—"

"And when you found Mr. Sing was he not hiding in a shack located near the base of Mount Leahi?"

"Yes, he was."

"Let me show you King's exhibit one," Wiseman walked to the clerk's table and picked up the knife. "Mr. Tana, when you entered the shack, and saw the defendant, did he have this knife in his hand? And did he point this knife at you in a threatening manner?"

"Well, yes, what you ask so far is somewhat true, but—"

Wiseman stepped closer to the witness box, brandishing the knife. "You got this knife from Chin Sing, did you not?"

John nodded, and then said, "Yes, I did."

"And it was this knife that killed Mr. Charles."

John squirmed in his chair and looked to Joshua for guidance. The attorney merely nodded for John to continue. "The way you say it, I can only answer yes or no. So I have to say yes."

Wiseman replaced the knife and turned toward the judge. "Your Honor, this is the last witness in my case. The hour is late and I ask that we resume tomorrow morning. We can continue with Mr. Tana and then hear Mr. Chin's defense."

"A reasonable suggestion, Mr. Wiseman, court is recessed until nine o'clock tomorrow morning."

After the proceedings, John stayed to speak to Joshua. "Looks like your friend, Mr. Wiseman, thinks his case is won." He watched the jurors filing out of the room. "Just tell a bunch of citizens that a Chinese used a knife on a white man, and it's murder."

"You could be right about that," Joshua said, gathering a stack of papers from the table. "The majority of people in the room seem to be with him, but the case is not yet over."

The men moved toward the door, when John suddenly pulled on Joshua's arm. "Did you notice how Mrs. Charles started to cry when you mentioned her husband beating Chin Sing?"

When Joshua said nothing, John added, "When she was excused from the stand, she hesitated, like there was more she wanted to say."

Joshua chewed on this for a long beat, and John wondered if he would be taken seriously. "Interesting, I need to have a talk with her. Get some new clothes over to Chin Sing. I'll meet you at Ah Sam's in two hours."

Waiting at the restaurant for Joshua, John toyed with his food, pushing spicy pork across the plate and into a mound of white rice. He positioned the meat on the down slope of his dish and again thrust his missile into the sticky barrier.

Interesting, John thought. These small little seeds could puff up with water to create an impenetrable wall preventing his oily object from breaking through it. The rice barrier held it like a spider's web holds a fly.

That is just like the law. You take a kernel of truth. You take another kernel that may only be partially true. You take a third that might be false. You take a bunch of kernels like that. You puff them all up with fancy words and you get a sticky wall of justice. How could Chin Sing break through it? One thing he knew for sure, his friend would need to be very lucky to escape the web that held him.

"What are you doing, playing with your food?" Joshua teased. "Didn't your mother tell you to eat everything on your plate before it got cold?"

In one brief moment, the expression in John's face conveyed pain. "What is it?" Joshua asked.

John pushed another morsel of food into the rice. "My mother died when I was very young, so she never had a chance to teach me anything."

"Forgive me. Finish your dinner and let's go. We have work to do."

As they walked along Merchant Street, Joshua revealed what he had learned. "Mr. Charles had very predictable habits. He left home early in the morning for his mercantile business and arrived at the *Whaler's Bistro* around noon. There, he would drink his lunch, spend the afternoon, then leave for home drunk."

Dark shadows slanted onto the street as the light of kerosene lanterns pierced into the ink of evening through the opaque windows lining the roadway. "The *Bistro's* just ahead," John said, pointing to a sign.

Inside, a large iron wheel with a half-dozen oil lanterns provided sputtering light to the dingy space. A slender Hawaiian with a pock-marked face tended the bar. John recognized him as a member of the militia. "Daniel Noa, hello, this is Joshua Kanakoa."

The three men enjoyed a few words of small talk before Joshua asked, "Did you know Roy Charles?"

Daniel tucked clean glasses onto the shelf. "Yeah, I knew the guy, a steady customer. I hear he's dead, killed by some Chinaman." He moved closer to Joshua and John. In a lowered voice, he added, "I'm not surprised he's dead. The guy was a mean drunk."

Joshua pulled out a notebook. "I need information about Charles, his drinking habits, and if he was here the afternoon of August twenty-third."

Daniel took a step back. "Look here, Mr. Kanakoa, I don't want to get mixed up in some murder case."

John sensed that they might be losing an important witness. "I believe that Chin is innocent of murder," he interjected. "What happened was an accident caused by Charles being too drunk. If the truth isn't brought out, then—"

"Yeah, I see your point. I guess it can't hurt if I tell you guys what I know."

After a half hour of conversation, Joshua asked Daniel to come to the courthouse in the morning.

As John and Kanakoa were leaving the *Bistro*, two Caucasians walked in. One of them stopped in front of the attorney, blocking his path. "You're that slimy lawyer representing the damn chink. Your guy is going to hang," he said, pushing a finger into Joshua's chest. "Tell me," he went on, his voice challenging. "Why is a Hawaiian helping a lousy Chinaman? Don't you know that you're as good as dead in this town?"

Joshua shifted his stance and moved around the man, but his path was blocked. Before he could react, the belligerent haole swung an open palm toward his face. John stepped into the strike, grasped the man's little finger and bent it backward. A howl rang through the room. "We don't want trouble," John said, his voice low and menacing, "so how about leaving us alone before I break that finger, and maybe the wrist, too."

A bead of sweat formed on the aggressor's forehead and his eyes were significantly wider. He nodded and backed away, cradling one hand in the other.

John watched as distance was created between them. He noted that Joshua, who had stepped away, prepared to leave. They went outside, exchanged nods, and headed in opposite directions.

As he walked to Ah Sam's, John wondered how all of this would play out. He sensed the rising racial tensions caused by this trial and knew that they would only worsen as time went on. Would it mean serious trouble for Joshua, or the Chinese, or himself? Perhaps it foretold trouble for all of them.

Forty

Spectators filled the seats and stood elbow to elbow along three walls of the courtroom. A sunny day coupled with the mass of people produced a heat that made John wish that the walls would disappear and let the morning breezes flow in. Sitting in the witness chair with all this warmth it felt more like the precursor to his own execution. But, since Joshua would be questioning him, his sense of threat was lessened.

"Mr. Tana, the attorney general asked you about a money motive in this death. Would you explain to the court and jury how you learned of such a motive and what you learned?"

John thought through the question, as Joshua had instructed several times, shifted into a more comfortable position, then answered. "I met Chin Sing Monday night. He was hurt bad: his back raw with wounds. Chin told me that he was going to his employer, Mr. Charles, the next morning, ask for his pay, and quit."

Joshua crossed the room and stood closer to the jurors. "Mr. Tana, when you first observed Mr. Chin Sing in that shack, did he threaten you?"

"No."

"Was he cooperative?"

"Yes, I asked for the knife and he gave it to me."

The attorney nodded, a gesture John took as encouraging. "Did Chin Sing explain to you why he was at the Charles residence, and what happened?"

Attorney General Wiseman stood quickly. "I object your honor this is hearsay."

"Objection sustained."

"No further questions," Joshua said, taking his seat.

The bartender, Daniel Noa, took the stand and testified that Charles had come into the *Bistro* on the day of his death. He had arrived at noon and had begun drinking double shots of whiskey. "He kept talking about some Chinaman that worked for him."

"Do you recall what he said about Chin Sing?" Joshua asked.

The man glanced toward the jurors and then into the audience. "He said, 'The chink's a lazy son of a bitch,' and swore that he was going to beat him when he got home."

Joshua dismissed the bartender and asked Doctor Brown to resume the stand. He requested that Chin Sing come forward to help with an evidentiary demonstration.

"This is highly unusual," Wiseman challenged.

"Your Honor, we are going to show physical facts, which are certainly relevant evidence."

"Highly unusual," Judge Andrews said. "But you may proceed."

At Joshua's request, Chin Sing took off his shirt and walked to the witness box. Joshua asked him to show his back to the doctor and then to the jury. The patchwork of scars on his shoulders, back, and chest bore silent witness to repeated beatings.

With Brown's assistance, Joshua measured Chin Sing's height. "Five-feet-one inch tall," the doctor announced.

Joshua asked the clerk for exhibit one. The knife was handed over. "Chin Sing take the knife in both hands and hold it, as you did that night that Mr. Charles attacked you and then walked into the knife."

Wiseman leapt to his feet. "Objection, Your Honor. We can't have a knife-wielding murderer running amok in the courtroom!"

Joshua gave Wiseman a long look and then said, "Your Honor, the marshal has a gun. He can shoot the defendant if he threatens anyone. This demonstration is vital to the defense."

"Alright, alright, proceed with the demonstration," the Judge said. He turned to the marshal, "As for you, keep a close eye on the defendant."

Chin Sing took the knife and held it away from his chest.

"Dr. Brown, please assist me in measuring the distance from the floor to the position of the knife."

When the measurement was completed, the doctor announced, "The distance from floor to the position of the knife is four feet."

Joshua removed the knife from Chin Sing's hand and asked him to return to his seat. The doctor resumed his place on the witness stand.

"When you examined Mr. Charles in the morgue, did you measure his height?"

"He was six feet one."

"And did you note the distance from the sole of his feet to the entry wound? Is it, by chance, approximately four feet?"

The physician nodded for a moment. "I see what you're getting at. The entry wound was just above the victim's navel so, yes, four feet is a good approximation."

"You testified earlier that the wound is categorized as a thrust wound. Could this wound also be consistent with someone running into the knife?"

"I don't think Mr. Charles wanted to commit suicide," the witness said, frowning at the titter that ran through the courtroom.

"Please, Dr. Brown, answer my question. If the knife wound is at the four-feet level, and if the victim moved rapidly toward Mr. Sing while simultaneously striking him, could this wound be consistent with Mr. Charles impaling himself on the knife?"

The physician glanced toward Wiseman, then answered, "Yes, the death wound I observed is consistent with a thrust entry of a sharp pointed object. It is also consistent with an impaling entry."

"No more questions, Dr. Brown."

Attorney General Wiseman leapt from his chair, moving purposefully past the jury and close to the witness. "Doctor, you and the constable were the first persons to arrive at the crime scene. Did you or the constable see a long stick, a bamboo switch, or any type of weapon in the kitchen or entryway?"

The doctor shook his head. "No, I did not, nor did I see the officer find any such weapon."

"Did you see any evidence of Mr. Charles striding into the kitchen and impaling himself on exhibit one?"

"No, I did not."

"That is all. Thank you."

As the doctor crossed the aisle and resumed his seat, the judge said, "I assume Dr. Brown is your last witness."

John watched Joshua's expression and noted how his eyes seemed to dance.

"Your Honor, I have one more witness to call. However, it is nearly noon. Shall we continue testimony after lunch?"

The judge recessed the trial and the room emptied quickly. John caught up with Joshua on the courthouse steps. "You made some points this morning," admiration in his voice.

"Thanks. I was lucky. Wiseman made the wrong objection. Sorry, but I have to get my last witness. I'll see you when court resumes." With that, he strode north, leaving John perplexed as to who this mysterious witness might be and what he might say.

Forty-One

At one-thirty the audience rose on command of the marshal. The judge seated himself and instructed Joshua to call his next witness. Whispers filled the packed room. "Order in the court," the words and thunderous pounding of the marshal's gavel snapped the unruly crowd into silence.

Once the hush spread throughout the room, Joshua stood, adjusted his jacket, and cleared his throat. John felt tempted to call out something supportive, but knew to remain silent. He shared the curious expectations he sensed from everyone in the courtroom.

"Defendant Chin Sing calls as his next witness Mrs. Rachel Charles."

Noise rose dramatically, a combination of talking and coughing. The marshal pounded his gavel. The judge did also. In the throes of this drama the widow entered, her black garments a reminder of her loss. In her hands she clutched a long object wrapped in paper. The woman walked slowly to the witness chair, turned to face the room, and sat.

Joshua waited quietly for the crowd's noise to abate. Once satisfied, he asked, "Mrs. Charles, on the day in question, did you see the defendant, Chin Sing, at your home on Nuuanu Street?"

"Yes, I did," she answered with a decisive nod. "He came to the house and asked to be paid for the work he had performed for our family."

"What did you say to him?"

"I told him that he needed to wait for my husband to return in the afternoon. I didn't have the money to pay him, since it was Mr. Charles who controlled the household funds."

"What happened after you explained this?"

"Mr. Sing busied himself in the kitchen and I left for the day to do some visiting."

"At around three forty-five, where were you?"

"At my neighbor's, directly across the street from my home, Sarah and I had just finished quilting. We were having tea when Sarah said: 'Oh look, your husband is marching up the street.' I looked out the window. Saw him walking to the front gate and then striding toward our home."

"What did you do then?"

"I excused myself and went across the road. I approached the door, which was partially open."

"Did you see or hear anything?"

"I heard my husband yelling, 'You damn son of a bitch Chinaman! What do you mean pay? All you'll get from me is a thrashing.'"

"What happened next?"

"I looked in and saw Charles. He was holding a bamboo switch and staggering into the kitchen. I saw him swinging the switch. I saw it striking Chin Sing. He just stood there pleading, 'No hit, no hit.' I saw my husband stumble forward. I heard a gasp and other strange sounds. I rushed into the house, but fear made me hide in an alcove near the front door."

"And after you hid?"

"I was terrified, but I had to know, so I peeked out from the alcove. I saw Chin Sing passing through. He had blood on his clothes."

"Did you say anything to him or do anything?"

"No, I did not. I was afraid. He had a knife in his hand."

"What did you do after Chin Sing left the house?"

"I went into the kitchen. My husband lay on his stomach. Blood seeped from under his body and spread around the floor. I think I let out a shriek."

"What was Mr. Charles's condition?"

"He was not conscious, but he was breathing. I felt I had best get the doctor."

"Did you see a bamboo switch in the kitchen?"

"Yes, I did. It had fallen from his hand. It lay on the floor beside him."

"What did you do?"

"I picked up the switch and placed it in the hall closet where my husband kept it."

"Do you have the switch?"

"Yes, I do," Mrs. Charles handed over the wrapped item.

Joshua pulled the paper off and held it up. "Mrs. Charles, I have here a bamboo switch. Is this what Mr. Charles used to strike Chin Sing? Is this what you found on the floor of the kitchen?"

"Yes, yes it is."

"I notice that there is hair stuck on one end and what appears to be blood. Did you affix any of these items onto the stick?"

"No, the stick is as I found it on the kitchen floor."

"Why did you pick up the bamboo switch?"

"At the time, I was not thinking straight. I didn't want anyone to think badly of my husband. I didn't think it was important. I know now that I shouldn't have done it."

"What did you do after you placed the bamboo switch in the hall closet?"

"I ran to my neighbor across the street and she fetched Doctor Brown."

Joshua nodded to Mrs. Charles and offered her a slight smile. "Thank you, Mrs. Charles. Your witness."

Wiseman asked, "Mrs. Charles, you testified that you hid the switch to protect your husband's reputation. Why, Madam, are you coming here today and telling this story?"

The witness studied the attorney's face for a moment, as if trying to decide his motives for this line of questioning. Finally, she answered, "Mr. Wiseman, I'm a good Christian woman. When I sat in this courtroom yesterday, I realized that the man over there," pointing at Chin Sing, "might die for a crime he did not intend to commit. It is my duty to God and to my Christian beliefs to come forward and tell what I saw that day. My husband was often drunk. When he was drunk, he beat Chin Sing. It shames me to say this, but before Chin Sing worked for us, my husband would strike our children and me. My daughters left home because they could no longer tolerate his abuse. If you must know, we lived in terror of this man." Tears flowed from her eyes and she used an embroidered handkerchief to dry them. Several women in the audience wept with her, while others clucked in understanding, perhaps recalling their own painful encounters with drunken husbands.

Wiseman waited a good minute while she regained her composure. When he spoke, his voice was less accusatory. "Why did you not report these events between your husband and the accused to the constable, or to Dr. Brown?"

Mrs. Charles sat up straighter and locked eyes with Wiseman. "No one asked me. No one pays attention to a woman. We are the maids, the house cleaners, the cooks, laundresses and seamstresses. We are the comfort pillows, the givers of momentary joy, and the child bearers. Other than that, we are expected to be mindless, seen but not heard. We may tell God of our suffering. Otherwise, we must suffer in silence."

There were low murmurs within the audience. A raised gavel by the judge brought the room to silence. Wiseman thanked Mrs. Charles and dismissed her. With this examination ended, both sides rested and proceeded to closing arguments.

Wiseman began with a flourish. Bible in hand, he announced, "God's words: *Thou shalt not kill*. The most revered law in the holy book. It is a law that God writ in stone and gave to Moses. This Chinaman, Chin Sing, took a knife and killed a leading businessman of the Honolulu community. Mr. Charles was an upstanding man, a pillar of our society, a man made of fine New England stock. Are we going to let foreigners from some heathen country kill our people and get away with murder? There are more than nineteen hundred Chinese living among us. One-hundred-and-fifty Japanese recently landed here. Orientals out-number the American population in these Hawaiian Islands, the Islands we love and call our home. We cannot allow these opium smokers to run amok and kill. You must send a message to China, to the Orientals in Hawaii, and to the Orientals who will come here: *Thou shalt not kill*. I ask you for the only verdict you can render: guilty of murder."

Joshua sighed. Wiseman focused on race. He had made a blatant appeal to every man and woman's prejudice and fear. His face almost gaunt with fatigue, he walked slowly to the jury and looked at the twelve men. "We are all brothers together. Yes, gentlemen of the jury, brothers seeking the truth. In our everyday life we may want to avoid the truth, but in a court of law it is the truth that must prevail. We are here in God's temple of justice, where his holy words are *The truth must be found*. In His temple of justice, you may not decide this case based on prejudice, bias, hatred, or wicked beliefs, but on truth alone. To come to a decision of murder, you must determine that Chin Sing intentionally, and with malice aforethought, killed Mr. Roy Charles.

"Malice aforethought, what does that mean? It means that, for a substantial period of time before the killing Chin Sing had formulated the wicked intention to kill. Let us examine the evidence and see how it fits this law. My colleague suggests that money was the motive for homicide, that Mr. Sing intended to rob Mr. Charles. But Mrs. Charles told you that Chin Sing came to her home seeking his pay for work performed. She asked him to wait until her husband returned. As Mr. Charles entered his home, Mrs. Charles followed him. There is no evidence that Mr. Sing demanded money, or even made a request of money, from Mr. Charles. The only evidence is that Mr. Charles began beating Mr. Chin Sing. Remember what Mr. Charles announced earlier, that he was going to 'beat the lazy son of a bitch when he got home.' This is exactly what Mr. Charles did.

"Next, consider the physical evidence, the one penetrating wound. Clothes were not shredded by a savage knife attack. There are no multiple injuries or cuts to Mr. Charles's body. Just one single knife wound, the one that tragically caused a man's death.

"We agree that this wound was inflicted by the knife you've seen and that Mr. Sing held it. But… it was a knife held in self-defense, to fend off an intoxicated man who rushed into the defendant with a bamboo cane, flailing it and inflicting injury.

"Gentlemen, once you write your verdict in God's temple of justice, it is over, finished, and your decision cannot be erased. You must live for eternity with the decision you make: Chin Sing either lives or he dies. There is only one true verdict: Chin Sing is not guilty of murder."

John felt hopeful, cautiously so. He half-listened as the judge gave his final instructions to the jury. He felt a chill watching the twelve men file out to deliberate, not one glancing toward Chin Sing or Joshua. Several exchanged smiles with Wiseman.

Forty-Two

Outside the courthouse Maria came to him and seized his arm. "You are magnificent, John Tana, I adore you." Before he could draw away, she drew John into her. She placed her lips against his. Her tongue thrust between them expressing her passion.

"My, my, John Tana," Joshua said. "You do get around. Who is this pretty lady?"

Confused, John stammered through the introduction, adding, "Maria's father is Edward Francois, Minister of Foreign Affairs to King Kamehameha the Fifth."

Blushing, Maria gave a little curtsey.

"This is Joshua Kanakoa, the attorney who just finished the defense of a Chinese man accused of murder," John said.

"Oh, yes. I watched you in action, and I watched John testify. You were both magnificent, I hope you win."

Joshua nodded his appreciation and said, "We have high odds to overcome. How did it happen that you are here today?"

"I wanted to see John tell his story. There is nothing more interesting to do than to watch the most talked about trial in Honolulu? Besides, I don't know whether he has heard the news about Leinani."

She turned to John, "Leinani has found her father."

"Really, and which Hawaiian is it?"

"Not Hawaiian. It is Robert Grant, the plantation owner."

"What!"

Marie placed a hand on John's arm. "Mon *cheri*, you look distressed. Is there something that I have said that causes you pain?"

"It is Leinani's father who has caused me pain."

A voice called out, "*Hui.* John Tana." Two young Hawaiians trudged toward them, a tall man and a comely female barely in her teens. As the girl neared, she gave John a mischievous look and then placed a hand to her mouth to suppress a giggle.

"Who is she?" Maria demanded.

John laughed. "Don't worry, her name is Mahealani. She's just a child."

"Eh, Uncle John," the young man said. "Grandpa Alapai ask that you come to our house for a party tonight. He says, 'bring your friends.'"

John looked at Joshua.

"Go to the party. I'll keep an eye on what happens here. If there's a judgment, I'll get word to you."

"Can I come, too?" Maria begged, pulling John's arm.

John hesitated, wondering if she would be more of a responsibility than a pleasant companion. He saw her pleading, and did not have the heart to deny her. Besides, he reminded himself, it might be good for the Alapai family to have a friend in the white community. "Fine, but first you must get your father's permission."

"I'm eighteen I don't need his permission." Maria stomped her foot.

"I won't take you without it. Please go and ask him. We will be at the Hawaiian community in Kalia. I'll meet you at the courthouse steps in a couple of hours."

John watched her rush away. When she was out of sight, he headed for the waterfront to invite Aaloa and other stevedore friends.

Flames in coconut shells filled with kukui oil shone on mats of lauhala leaves covered with platters of fish, pork, yams, potatoes, chicken, fruits, and desserts. John dipped his fingers into one of the large bowls of poi, twirled the grey paste around his fingers, and sucked in the delicious starch.

Maria sat between him and the burly Aaloa who offered her a selection of Hawaiian delicacies: sour poi, raw fish garnished with seaweed, raw limpets. He laughed when Maria rejected the fish eyes.

A hand slapped a gourd, beating it in a rhythmic pattern as a chant began. Female dancers moved sensuously onto a cleared area of the mat. Their hands flitted along their bodies, hips swayed, feet treaded the ground keeping time to the sound of the beat.

John said, "In ancient times, Hawaiians combined movement of feet, hips, and hand gestures known as *hula* to the accompaniment of a chant. The chanter would recite poetic verses regarding the land, flowers, famous chiefs, or love. The dancers interpret the words with their arms and fingers."

"It's the most sensuous thing I've ever seen," Maria said, swaying her body as she mimicked the dancers.

As the beat intensified, John felt Maria's excitement grow.

"Can I try it?" Maria asked eagerness in her voice.

With a pleased look, John called over a young female and explained what Maria wanted. "Teach her a *hula* of love," he said.

An hour later, Maria returned wearing a white band of cloth covering her breasts, her hips bound tightly with strips of ti-leafs forming a skirt. A wreath of green maile leaves intertwined with small flowers, settled like a crown around her head.

Maria's light blonde hair flowed around her face, draping onto her shoulders. A dark brown kukui necklace rested against her chest, small red seeds woven between the nuts.

John grew excited. Maria is very pretty.

A young Alapai woman picked up an *ipu* and began to slap it. "A song of love: Why do you choose me?" she announced. Motioning for John to stand, the chanting woman beat upon her gourd. Maria stepped into a circle of firelight facing John who began to sway his hips as he said: "Why do you choose me?"

Maria did a treading motion with her feet causing her hips to sway emphatically from side to side. She stepped toward John reaching her hands out to him saying: "Why do I choose you?"

As John moved toward her Maria stepped away. Her eyes held his and then moved coyly down.

The slapping of the gourd increased in intensity. Soon bamboo sticks took up the beat. Excited musicians added music to the love song.

At one point in the dance John stood motionless as Maria danced around him swinging her hips in provocative motions. Then it was Maria's turn to be still as John stomped his feet as he circled her saying: "Let us come together if you have chosen me."

As the music peaked to a passionate crescendo, Maria swayed into John, kissed him, and dragged him into the darkness.

Forty-Three

The following morning, a stevedore asked John if he knew a *haole* from Maui. When John expressed confusion, the man said, "Some guy is asking around the harbor about you. He has a newspaper with your picture. Says he knows you from Maui. Nobody say anything."

John wondered if the whalers had caught up with him. Before he could act on the information a message came that the jury had asked to speak to the judge.

John got Mike's permission to leave and then stopped by the restaurant to tell Ah Sam. "Take Lehua," his friend said, explaining that the courthouse was no place for a Chinese man to be, and Lehua could return with any news.

By the time they arrived, the room was so packed that they could barely squeeze inside. Both attorneys were seated at the counsel table and Chin Sing looked aimlessly around the courtroom, his eyes vacant, as if oblivious to the hostility of the crowd.

The marshal called the room to order and announced the judge's arrival. Within minutes, everyone stood for the jury's decision.

"Bring them in," Judge Andrews ordered.

The marshal walked out of the room, unlocked a door and stood aside while a dozen tired men filed in. The marshal, assuming his position beside the jury, announced, "Your honor, all jurors are present and accounted for."

"Please be seated," the judge said. He faced the jury box and asked, "Will the foreman rise and present himself to the court?"

A well-to-do merchant with a business on King Street stood up. "I am the foreman your honor, John Kirkland."

"Has this jury reached its verdict?"

"Yes, your honor."

"Mr. Chin Sing, you will stand to receive the verdict of this jury."

Joshua helped Chin Sing to a standing position.

"Mr. Foreman, you will read your verdict to the defendant and the court."

In a loud voice, Kirkland said, "We the jury, in the case of the King versus Chin Sing, find the defendant guilty…"

A roar drowned out the remainder of the verdict and someone shouted, "Lynch him now!" The foreman remained standing as the judge and marshal pounded their gavels, demanding order in the court.

Lehua bawled, tears streaming down her cheeks. What would happen to Ah Sam and the Chinese community? Joshua sagged to his seat, the pain of defeat etched in his face. A usually stoic John Tana fought to control his emotions. His promise to Chin Sing of a fair trial had been destroyed by one word: guilty. Only the defendant seemed unperturbed by the jury's decision. Chin Sing looked about the room, as if unaware that this pandemonium had anything to do with him.

John noticed something unusual. Why was it that, throughout the shouting, John Kirkland remained standing in the jurors' box? Is he waiting for something? It was his sphinx-like demeanor that confused him, the same expression that brought calm to the room. As the hubbub subsided, others took note of the foreman's standing silence.

"Mr. Kirkland," the judge said. "I assume you have completed reciting the jury's verdict."

"No, Your Honor, I have not," he answered firmly.

A low buzz ran through the courtroom and faces changed from jubilation— surely the verdict was murder with the intent to kill, and with malice aforethought—to uncertainty.

The judge leaned toward the foreman. "Mr. Kirkland, please state the entire verdict."

Kirkland cleared his throat and lifted the paper. "We, the jury, in the case of the King versus Chin Sing, find the defendant guilty of manslaughter. We find him not guilty of murder with malice aforethought."

A startling silence permeated the high-ceilinged room. What only moments earlier had felt like the trough of injustice and despair had become, for John, a

200

giant wave of emotions that lifted him into the bright world of truth and fairness. Lehua stopped crying and Joshua beamed his thanks at Mr. Kirkland and the jury. Everyone in that room understood that the Chinese community had been spared a hanging.

The judge rapped his gavel just once. "Gentlemen of the jury, is this the verdict of all twelve of you?" When every member of the jury nodded in agreement, the judge added, "Let the record show that the jury is unanimous in its verdict of guilty of manslaughter. The defendant will be returned to prison, and I will set sentencing for the crime of manslaughter for one week from today."

Forty-Four

" **C**aptain, look at this picture. Isn't this the fellow that gave you a limp? I think he's the one that flattened Lazarus in the gut and put him out for a month."

Shaw stared at the front page of the *Pacific Gazette*. He seized the paper. Laying it on a table, mid-morning sun streamed onto a black and white picture of a smiling man. Stroking his chin, he studied the photo. "This fellow is bearded. The Hawaiian that attacked me was not."

"Captain, the man in the picture is big and broad shouldered like the kanaka that I fought in Lahaina. Not a mark on his face, just like the guy that did me in. The closer I look at 'em the surer I get, that this is the same man." Mattoon emphasized his opinion by pounding his fist on the cabin table.

"I think you could be right on that score. This could be him."

"Shall we make a complaint to the authorities?"

"I think not, Mattoon. Do you believe the Honolulu police would listen to a bunch of swabees like us? No, we will extract private revenge and make the kanaka suffer for what he did. Get into town and look around. Find out where he lives. When you locate him, I will make sure that he is properly dealt with," Shaw said, drawing a revolver from the center drawer of his desk.

"I've already asked around on the docks. I got a good idea where this kanaka lives."

The scene in the courtroom after the verdict could best be described as pandemonium. The silence resulting from the dignity of the foreman as he read the decision of the jury, and then the judge as he set a sentencing date, had been blown apart, like thunder claps during a pent up storm. Several deputies rushed into the court to quell the volatile crowd. Amid cries of *Lynch him now*! *Kill the Chinaman!* They struggled to clear the room.

John moved to protect Joshua and Chin from angry men shouting threats and waving clenched fists. When a sheriff pointed to the exit, Joshua yelled, "Meet me later," and rushed out. John found Lehua and they made their way from the building.

Outside the courthouse, John heard his name and turned to find Maria pushing her way through the crowd. "I've been looking for you everywhere," she said, out of breath. "I must talk with you, darling." With that, she kissed him long and hard.

John took a step back, removing Maria's hands twined around his neck. "What is it?"

"Oh John, darling, when I got home this morning there was a note from my father. We are to leave for France, his work here is ended. The sugar planters want a minister with ties to the United States, someone who can arrange some kind of treaty. You must speak to my father," she pleaded, her face filled with emotion. "It's the only way we can get permission to marry."

John delighted in her companionship, but marriage? Besides, he cared for Leinani more. "Maria, I must take Lehua home and then speak with Joshua about the trial."

Maria's expression of hope suddenly turned sullen. "But you must come to see my father as soon as possible. I'm going to tell Papa I want to marry—" Her voice trailed off and she stared behind John. Moving closer, she whispered, "There's an ugly man leering at us. I've never seen such an evil look."

John followed her stare, but saw no one. "Please go home," he told Maria. "I'll come as soon as I can."

Maria's face transformed itself yet again, this time to pure joy. "Oh, please hurry, I'm just bursting to share the wonderful news with my father."

John watched Maria rush off and began thinking of Leinani. With the trial over and the verdict in, he would deal with his feelings for her. She was not his cousin. Religious barriers had fallen. Maria's misinterpretation of his actions last night presented a problem, but he would deal with that. He would seek Leinani. Determine her interest in him. With this decision made, John headed for the Grant mansion.

Forty-Five

"Robert, you aren't seriously thinking of adopting this person?" Sheila Grant said a look of disgust upon her face.

"Since you express yourself that way, I am determined to do it," Robert Grant said his tone angry.

"Think for a moment of the social stigma that would attach to such a decision. You would be admitting that you had an illicit relationship with an under-aged brown woman. A woman you knew nothing about, and then abandoned to go to Yale. Besides, these Hawaiians think of nothing but fun and sex. For all you know this Leinani has had plenty of relationships before today."

"I have regretted all my life that I did not defy my father years ago. His dominance and avarice has visited upon me his worse traits. It's too late in the day to shed his power over me. But as God is my witness I will not abandon my only child."

Sheila sighed, "I regret we did not have children. Where the fault lies I do not know. But, where I grew up we never mixed with the dark folk. They lacked any of the social graces. They had no redeeming values. This Leinani may be no more than an unintelligent native girl who will embarrass us among our friends."

Grant withdrew a cigar, lit, and inhaled it. He blew out smoke away from his wife and said, "In Hawaii things are historically different from your home in New England. Early missionaries treated the Hawaiians with respect. Widowed or single missionaries married Hawaiian women and so did foreign traders."

Sheila smoothed her hands over her white dress seamed around its bodice with pearls. "These early missionaries dealt only with the high chiefs. They needed their help to make their work thrive. You well know that once a missionary married a chief's daughter, they could use this prestige to win Hawaiians to Christianity. With influence among the people they eventually controlled the government. This Leinani is not descended from Hawaiian nobility. She is of the lowest class. Good enough to be a servant or bear children, but nothing more."

Grant tugged deep at his cigar letting the warm smoke fill his lungs, soothe his nerves. "My experiences so far with my daughter are positive. I know she is intelligent. I will consult with headmistress Staley on this. I should tell you that the most important item for you to consider is James Kingsley. He is smitten with Leinani and wishes to court her. I could do great things in Hawaii with his wealth."

"Darling," Sheila smiled, "you should have said this earlier. Yes, make your investigation and be assured that I will find a way to tolerate your daughter."

"Good, make certain that none of the local riffraff get to her. I will inform the school to keep undesirables away from her. Once I am sure that my daughter is a virgin, I can promise Kingsley that he will be her first love."

Lost in thought, John was surprised to find himself at the gate of the Grant mansion. He followed the pathway to the door and knocked. When a servant answered, John mumbled, "I'd like to speak with Leinani."

"Wait," the man said, slamming the wooden portal into John's face.

After many minutes the servant reappeared. "Mistress Leinani is at her school. Mrs. Grant asked me to tell you that she doesn't want your lazy kind around here, and you should go back to your people. Do not return or you will be arrested as a trespasser."

With a supreme effort, John suppressed the bile rising in his stomach. "Tell Leinani that John Tana came to visit. I'll return tomorrow."

The stark white entryway closed in his face. He thought of breaking it down, but knew this would create trouble. Instead, he left and headed to the school.

At the entrance of St. Sebastian, a student directed him to the office of Miss Seldon. When he entered, he recognized her as one of the women he had seen leaving the Grant mansion. When she demanded to know why he wished to speak to Leinani, he explained that it was personal and very important.

"Are you a Makanani?" she asked.

"No, my name is John Tana."

She pursed her lips and then said. "I am sorry, but you must have permission from her father, Mr. Grant, before I can allow you to speak with her."

"But no one in the Grant home will talk to me."

"That is unfortunate, but without his permission I cannot permit you to visit with Mistress Grant. Her father was here an hour ago making inquiries about her. He left to see Malia Makanani. Please leave."

Thirty minutes later, John arrived at Malia's shack and learned that Grant had been there and just left. John kissed his aunt and asked, "I know that he's Leinani's father. Please tell me, what did he want to know about her?" John saw the way she looked at him, her eyes warm with affection.

Malia sighed before she spoke. "That guy, he tell me all kind of crazy stuff that he and his wife talk about." With that, she revealed Grant's desire to adopt Leinani and how his wife objected. "The guy, he beat around the bush long time, but finally he say that wife sure Leinani not virgin because Hawaiian women always sleep around."

John said nothing for a moment, struggling with his anger. "What did you tell him?" he finally asked.

"That Leinani is virgin, that every night I say prayer to God, asking him to save Leinani's maidenhood so her future husband will find that she is pure, and to please preserve her for a noble man of great power and wealth. I tell Grant that I protect her, and that you protect her, too. But when I tell him that Leinani might be royalty, he get excited, say, 'A virgin, royalty!'"

John shook his head a few times. "Wait, are you saying that Leinani might be a high chiefess?"

"I find out before her mother die, that she special kind person. Malama tell me to keep child safe for man of high rank because Leinani's mother and her baby are royalty." Before John could respond, Malia added, "You know what I think? That Leinani could be big money for this guy Grant because this other rich guy, Kingsley, is chasing after her."

Her words landed like a knife in John's heart. Everything suddenly added up: Mrs. Grant dismissing him and her husband's inquiries regarding Leinani.

She was being groomed for a wedding, but it was not a marriage that included John.

Dispirited, he returned to the restaurant and found Ah Sam cooking with abandon, clearly elated by the verdict.

When Ah Sam saw John, he said, "Tonight Chinese community celebrate with a big dinner, invite your friends and Joshua Kanakoa."

John felt devastated by what was happening between Leinani and him. Maria added terrible pressure onto his conscience. Why had he been so stupid? The last thing he wanted was a party. But he could not ruin the celebration proposed by the Chinese community.

Unhappy, John agreed to pass the word along. He went to the docks and told Aaloa to bring his friends, including men from the militia. His next stop was Joshua Kanakoa's office. He found the attorney listless, although his mood definitely lifted when he spotted his friend. John told him about the celebration and expected some enthusiasm. Instead, he saw only gloom. "What is it?" he asked.

Joshua sighed. "I just had a very unpleasant visit from Monsieur Francois."

John released a little groan. "What did he want?"

There was a lengthy silence before Joshua replied. "He wants your hide, John. He babbled on and on about your having violated his daughter, and that he must return to France. She refuses to go because she's in love with you, a Hawaiian." He leaned closer. "For God's sake, what did you do?"

John felt his world caving in around him, first, Grant; now, Maria's father. A pressure came onto his chest and he found it difficult to breathe. "I made a mistake with Maria, it was the dancing, the night, the moon, it was her——" His voice trailed off into confusion, his face a study in misery.

"Francois asked his daughter what she knew about you, but she said she didn't care. She wants to marry you and live here. He had no choice but to lock her in the house."

John's breathing became so shallow that he was dizzy and had to take several deep breaths. "So what did he want from you?"

"From me, I'm not sure, but it's a safe bet that he wants you dead. He mentioned challenging you to a duel. But then he suggested you be put in jail, or sent to where Maria can't find you. The man is at his wits' end, John. All I can tell you is that he doesn't want you anywhere near his daughter, ever again."

John nodded and pressed a palm against his forehead. "I can't leave until I finish some business. But tell him that I agree to stay far away from his daughter."

Joshua looked at his client, his friend. He thought of his own coming of age and he was thankful it had not been as painful as John's. "I'll do that," he said. "Now tell me about this party."

Forty-Six

A dozen vessels lay berthed in Honolulu Harbor. Within the main cabin of the *Jeremiah*, oil lanterns cast a pale orange glow on the sallow complexion of Captain Shaw and five seamen seated at a table.

"Mattoon, you've been in town. What did you learn about this man in the newspaper?" Shaw said.

"Captain, this John Tana is the poltroon that waylaid Will, Lazarus, and me in Lahaina. I got a good look at him when I was at the courthouse. Make no mistake, he be the one. For your information, people are mighty upset with the verdict in the Chinaman's case. Can you believe it, manslaughter?"

"Yeah, everybody in town wanted to see a hanging," Lazarus chimed in. "They wanted to enjoy watching the Chinaman kicking his heels in the wind. Now it will only be a prison sentence. The saloons in the harbor are full of men. They are talking about a lynching. With all the seamen in town plus the angry people in Honolulu there has to be a thousand men spoiling for trouble."

"Good, that fits into my plans," Shaw said. "Mattoon, do you know where he lives?"

"I am not too sure where, but I did have a seaman follow him from his work on the docks."

"Maybe we can waylay him right here and get him good," Lazarus interrupted.

"No," Shaw answered, "He probably has too many friends. There would be too many witnesses. We need a better plan than a daylight attack near our ship. We may need to return to Honolulu someday. I don't want any law boys laying for us. Besides, I intend to fix this scalawag permanently and I don't want any witnesses." Shaw put a pistol on the table. "Mattoon, you say that one of the boys followed him, where?"

"A Chinese restaurant, he went there several times yesterday and today. I'm sure that's where he hangs out."

"We need a diversion. Get everybody out of town. You, Peter, Daniel, Blade go to the bars. Take some of our boys with you. Get the men in town stirred up. Set them to thinking of marching on the prison and lynching that Chinaman. Bring torches. When it is dark, head everyone to the lockup.

"Mattoon and Lazarus, pick three of the toughest boys in our crew. Arm them with knives and belay pins and be prepared for action. Go to the saloons. Make sure everyone wants to get the Chink. Meet me on the dock once the march starts. We shall walk over to the Chinaman's restaurant and find Mr. Tana. If he is not there, we will wait for him. Tonight he will die and everybody in town will believe that he got killed for helping a Chinaman."

"Captain, what if there are witnesses to the murder?" Mattoon asked.

"There will be no witnesses," Shaw answered, loading his pistol.

John and Joshua worked their way through the mobs of ugly men crowding the streets of Honolulu. They did their best to keep within the darkness. "Nothing good can come of this," Joshua whispered.

John nodded. He found a gap between a building and a gaggle of yelling sailors and slid by the drunks, his attorney following him.

It was quieter when they got to Merchant Street, where the two men slipped into Ah Sam's restaurant, relieved that there had been no trouble. Aaloa and several other militia were eating, but there were no Chinese in the room.

"What's up?" John asked as he sidled up to his friend cooking at a stove filled with steaming pots.

"Big trouble outside. Sailors make humbug. Chinese friends no come. All scared. Maybe eat, then go home."

Flaming torches cast eerie shadows along the street as hooting men marched. They yelled as they passed, "Come join us, we're gonna lynch a Chinaman!"

As the stream of rowdies passed by, a man detached himself. Daniel Noa entered the restaurant. "Colonel Kalakaua wants the militia to meet at the prison. There's a big riot coming, some guys want to hang the Chinese, and the marshal needs our help."

"Let's go!" Joshua shouted. "We've got to save Chin Sing." The restaurant emptied, with the seven Hawaiians heading to the prison.

Pushing his way through the gathering mob, it was clear to John that liquor flamed their passions. He had his own problems to deal with as he shouldered through the press of angry men. The insults of Grant's servant, his inability to find Leinani, and his enemy's plan to marry her to a rich man frayed his emotions. He told himself to hold his temper, there was danger all around him and he needed to remain in control.

The Hawaiians arrived at the prison and found the marshal and a half-dozen deputies standing guard inside the gates. Facing them were rioters, including three sailors demanding, "Justice for white men. Surrender the prisoner or we will break down the gates and take him!"

Colonel Kalakaua stood at the side of the gate. John and his companions pushed through the crowd to him.

"Glad you're here. Between my men and yours, we are twenty-four, enough to handle this mob. Take these clubs and let's march, try not to hurt anyone, but it's time we put an end to this. John and Aaloa, you two stand on each side of me, the rest form a wedge behind us, and we'll march together."

In perfect formation, the Hawaiian wedge-shouldered aside the men assailing the gate. There the Hawaiians sealed the entranceway, leaving the three seamen standing alone against the marshal's authority. The colonel said, "It's time to leave, gentlemen."

One sailor eyed first the colonel then the mob. "Who's going to make us?" he said.

"We are," John and Aaloa answered. The men blinked when they saw Aaloa hulking over them. They vanished into the crowd.

Beyond the line of militia yelling rose and bodies pushed into them. The Hawaiians pushed back, repeating, "We don't want trouble, go home, go to your ships."

Suddenly, the prison gate opened and the marshal stepped through. "You got what you wanted. Chin Sing is dead, hanging in his cell."

The shouting subsided as word spread though the mob that "the Chinaman committed suicide."

Someone yelled, "Show us the body."

"He's dead," the marshal answered. "I swear to God he is."

There were grumbles and hoots from men cheated of a lynching, but, like a deflating balloon, the rioters melted away.

Kalakaua watched them go. He turned to the militia, "Our job is done. Go home."

John spied Joshua leaning against the prison gates his chest heaving. He came to his friend and placed a hand on his shoulder. His eyes blinking away tears, Joshua sighed, "Go home. There is nothing more you can do. I'm going in, find out what happened. I'll stop by Ah Sam's on my way back."

Forty-Seven

"What have you men been doing? Streets are empty. I had to come find you. Stop your drinking and let's get to the restaurant and deal with the scallywag," Shaw ordered.

"Just one more drink Captain before we go," Lazarus said, standing by the saloon bar. His three companions nodded their agreement. He called for another round of rum and water.

"It is only one man that we have to deal with. Let's be off."

"I hear," Rufus said, swigging his grog, "that this Tana guy is one tough hombre. Put Scarface and Mattoon into sick bay."

"Watch your name calling," Lazarus said, aiming a punch at Rufus. The whaler danced away swirling rum and water over the bar and onto another who snarled, "You clumsy bastard."

"Damnation," Shaw stepped between the scuffling sailors. "Stop this. We have work to do. Mattoon, show us to the Chinaman."

The cutthroats grumbled, finished their drinks, and shuffled out of the saloon. The streets were empty, though in the distance you could hear the roaring of men. Mattoon led them to the restaurant. Inside, a Chinese busied himself by a stove.

The captain stalked up to him. "You own this place?"

"Yes," a startled Ah Sam said.

"Where is John Tana?"

Ah Sam looked at the Captain, a blank expression on his face. Shaw's men aligned themselves about the restaurant, knives and belaying pins ready.

"I said where is John Tana?" Shaw asked again, whipping his pistol across Ah Sam's head.

213

The Chinese crumpled to the floor, dazed by the blow. Shaw grabbed an iron bar used to stoke the cooking fire. He thrust it into the burning stove. "Look Chinaman, we want Tana. Talk or get branded."

Ah Sam stopped moaning and skittered away from the Captain. He yelled wildly in Chinese as he squirmed alongside the back wall.

Shaw watched him scramble away. "Scared Chinaman? Don't want your face burnt? Talk or cooked meat."

Ah Sam crouched against the wall, facing Shaw, jabbering in Chinese.

"Shut up, damn you or I'll whip you good,"

Ah Sam kept muttering. The volume in his voice subsided.

"Just about hot enough to fry you," Shaw said as he pulled the burning iron from the fire.

Approaching Ah Sam with the glowing metal, Shaw placed its bright orange point near Ah Sam's left cheek. His drooping moustache shriveled up, filling the air with the smell of burnt hair and skin.

"He go prison. Stop angry men," Ah Sam said, pressing into the wall trying to escape the red hot rod.

"Damn it all," Shaw swore. "Look here, Chinaman. Is he coming back? Does he live here?" He waved the brand in Ah Sam's face singing his cheek.

"Yes, he live here," Ah Sam confessed speaking in a loud voice.

"Where in this place does he live?" Shaw demanded.

His eyes darting, Ah Sam began to blubber holding his hand to his face, and wailing in Chinese.

"I said, where does he live?" Shaw jabbed the hot poker into Ah Sam's arm. The sizzling of fried meat sounded and smelled like steak being cooked in a frying pan. Ah Sam howled. He jerked his arm away. Tears rushed from his eyes down his cheeks, splattering onto the wooden floor.

"Where?" Shaw said his voice ominous. He thrust the iron bar so near the tortured man's face that it steamed the tears trickling down his cheek, burnt his eye lashes, and singed his flesh.

Ah Sam pointed to a door leading to the back of the premises.

"Mattoon, take two men, check it out."

The three opened the rear door, knives in hand. Shaw ordered Ah Sam to return to the cooking stove. He instructed Lazarus and Rufus to dim the lanterns. He returned the iron to the fire and sat in a chair, waiting.

After a time, Mattoon returned, "No one is in the back. But somebody lives there."

Before Shaw could determine what to do next, a young woman charged into the restaurant saying, "John! John! Where are you?" She stopped when she saw the whalers. Lazarus, a leer on his face, spread his arms to embrace her.

Forty-Eight

A subdued John Tana and five of his militia friends, Noa, Aaloa, Kimo, Kawika, and Keoki, threaded their way through a crowd of sailors. Some of the tars gave them surly looks, but those that did shied away from a fight, cowed by the size of Aaloa and his companions. Flaming torches brightened the night and the pungent smell of oil smoke masked the street odors of offal and garbage. Except for the firebrands, there were no lights from the homes. Doors and windows were shuttered tight.

The group took a short cut through an alley. Jimmy Noa swore, "Jesus Christ, its dark in here. We could be stabbed and not even see who hit us."

"Don't use the name of the Lord in vain," Kawika said, his voice semi-serious, "or else I must wash your mouth with soap."

"Ha," Keoki laughed. "You should criticize. Your mother scrubbed your teeth white for all the times you used the almighty's name in curses instead of in prayers."

"Damn," Kimo said. "I just stepped in a pile of goop. Do we have to use this dark alley?"

"It gets us away from the mob of sailors marching back to the saloons and leads onto the street by Ah Sam's," John answered. "I think you guys could use some time in church."

"Prayers won't help this scum," Aaloa laughed.

The narrow road led into a wider street. Some distance ahead hung a sign with a red painted dragon belching fire. Above the beast were the words "Ah Sam." Below his belly were Chinese symbols. There was no one in sight. Faint light from the restaurant made flickering shadows in the darkness. When John stepped into the roadway, he heard a tiny voice say, "Uncle, momma like see you."

"What the hell is that little kid doing here?" Aaloa asked, sidling up to John. The other men clumped around them staring at little Choi. He sucked his thumb and held onto his shorts as they slipped below his knees.

"Where's momma?" John asked.

With the thumb in his mouth and a hand on his pants, Choi waddled to a white wooden fence. John followed and found Lehua standing in the shadows, cradling her baby.

"What's going on?" he asked.

"Ah Sam in big trouble. Sailor men in restaurant they hurt him. They come to kill you. Ah Sam tell me, find you. Tell you not to come back to the restaurant."

"I won't leave Ah Sam to be killed," John whispered. "I'm going in there."

"Eh, brother," Aaloa said. "Whoever they are, those guys know you. Maybe we go in the front and you come from the back and we get 'em."

"This is not your fight. These men want me."

"Eh, bra, what you think? We scared of some no good haole? You think we let you fight alone? No way. We going bust them up, the dirty buggers."

The other men nodded.

A female shrieked, her cry deciding him. "That's Maria! You guys get weapons. Go to the front. I will come in from the back."

"Lazarus, shut that woman up," Shaw ordered.

The scar-faced seaman struggled with Maria. He slapped her across the face. "Stop screaming," he snarled.

Maria whimpered and went slack.

Lazarus pushed his unshaven cheek against hers. He laughed as she wiggled. He thrust his nose against hers, gnawing at her cheek and mouth. His hand groped down her side, grasped her buttocks, and shoved her pelvis into his, saying, "You'll love what I give you."

Five Hawaiians came to the open front of the restaurant with fence sticks in their hands. "Hold it right there," Shaw yelled, waving his pistol and moving past Ah Sam's stove. "You fellows are interrupting a little fun. Now why don't you just be on your way?" Shaw emphasized his demand by pointing his weapon at the men.

Ranged around the restaurant, Shaw's sailors taunted the Hawaiians. "Come on and fight us you dirty kanaka, or are you too chicken?" Lazarus moved his kissing to Maria's throat while fumbling with the belt at her waist. She moaned again as he pulled her skirt away. Shaw cocked his pistol, ready to fire.

John entered the back door of the home, the living area brightened by light filtering through cracks in the thin wooden walls separating the living area from the restaurant. He picked up a knife and retrieved a short club. He crept to the entryway and turned the handle, pushing the door slowly. He heard a moan and the sound of a pistol cocking.

Through the cracked opening, John saw Shaw a few feet from him aiming a pistol. Just beyond the captain Lazarus attempted a rape of Maria. John yelled, charged through the door, and hurled his knife.

Shaw swung his pistol. The knife cut into his side. The gun discharged. The Captain sagged to his knees, his hand clutching the blade protruding from his body. Maria screamed. Lazarus cuffed her. Aaloa, and the four others charged into the restaurant, sticks held high, overturning chairs and tables in their rush to combat.

Before John could reach the girl, two whalers challenged him with knives and belaying pins. He grabbed a stick of wood from a storage box and held it and his short club in front of him, fencing with his opponents.

Lazarus dropped an unconscious Maria and moved to join Mattoon and Carl fighting the four Hawaiians. Before he reached them, a chair smashed into him.

One of John's attackers flung his belaying pin, striking the side of his head. Stunned, he staggered. The second man stepped in thrusting his knife. Clumsily John slid to the side barely escaping a goring as the blade ripped his shirt, drawing blood. His move placed his back against the kitchen wall, and his attacker drew back to impale him.

John glimpsed Aaloa lifting a dazed Lazarus by his neck and crotch then hurling him into his opponent. Both men smashed into the wall with a resounding splintering of wood. A knife clattered to the floor.

The remaining attacker swung a belaying pin. John pivoted and drove his foot into the sailor's belly. The wooden bar, used primarily to hold the rigging of a sailing ship, smashed into the muscles of his neck. A numbing pain shot down John's arm. His opponent sagged and John chopped his open palm onto the whaler's neck, finishing him. A voice nearby said, "One more dead kanaka."

Shaw stood by the stove, the knife no longer in his side. Blood smeared his shirt. One hand rested against the cooking counter. The other held a wavering pistol. The gun cocked as the captain squeezed the trigger.

"Oh," Shaw gasped. A red-hot poker struck his arm. The gun dropped to the floor. The smell of burnt flesh filled the room.

"It hurts," Shaw screamed.

Ah Sam stuck a hot iron into Shaw's shoulder. His shirt flamed.

Yelling, the captain tore at his blouse, his neatly combed hair crackling as it burned. "Put it out, put it out," he pleaded.

Warm dish water splashed onto Shaw's body. Ah Sam stood with an empty pan by the burnt whaler who fell to his knees and then rolled over onto his back moaning.

The battle ended. Lazarus and two sailors were unconscious. Mattoon and Rufus huddled in a corner guarded by four Hawaiians. John leaned against the kitchen wall, one arm limp at his side, his white shirt soaked with blood. He staggered toward Maria crumpled on the ground, a crimson welt slowly blooming on her face.

Joshua walked in. "Oh my God!" he said.

Forty-Nine

Rain pelted the streets of Honolulu. People scurried about seeking shelter from the squall. Robert Grant cantered to a hitching post, slid from his horse, tied the animal to it, and hurried across the street to his office. A carriage nearly ran him down, and he shook his fist at the driver whose conveyance disappeared in the deluge.

Muttering invectives, Grant mounted a sidewalk searching for the key to his office. An unshaven man came from the shadows and said, "Sir, I have something important to show you."

"Oh, it's you Gonzalez. Have you found John Tana?" Grant asked as he unlocked the door.

"Not yet, but I have information. I just need a little more money to hire some help."

"I gave you a hundred in silver," Grant answered, stepping into the room and striding toward his inner office.

"I'm obliged to you sir for your generosity," Gonzalez said as he followed him, sarcasm in his voice.

Grant ignored the disrespect as he walked into his inner chamber. Lighting a lantern, he went to his desk, fumbled in a humidor for a cigar, lit it, and settled into a red leather chair. He motioned Gonzalez to sit across from him, but the field supervisor moved to the desk and laid out a newspaper. Pointing to a picture he said. "Sir, look at him. This is the guy who burnt your property in Kahului."

Grant stared at the front page of the *Pacific Gazette* studying the photograph. "I've seen this man. He was in church before my dinner party. Did you follow up on the attorney information I gave you?"

Gonzalez leaned across the desk. "A false lead. This is the kanaka-boy who defied us in Kahului and jumped me in Lahaina."

Studying the photograph Grant mused, "The caption identifies him as John Tana. You must be right."

"When I saw this picture and read his name, I knew it was him."

"This Tana person has pestered my wife and gone to my daughter's school. We must teach him a lesson he will not forget."

"Damn it sir, for all the grief he has given us, he should be drawn and quartered."

Grant paused for a long moment. "I can see that you want him to suffer before he dies. But when you get rid of the body make sure it is never found. Here is a purse of coins and a key to an unused warehouse. Hire some bully boys to help you. Be sure they can't trace anything to me. How you revenge yourself on the Hawaiian is your choice, not mine."

Grant drummed his fingers on his desk, smoke pushing through his lips. Tana will die. The boy's claims would disappear and his interference with his marriage plans for Leinani ended.

Gonzalez fingered the purse, "Plenty of gold here, enough to buy a small army."

"What you don't spend on hired help is for you, and the good work that you will do for me."

Gonzalez left.

Rain poured onto the roof in a rapid staccato of drumming. The noise roused John. It was late in the day and his head throbbed. Awake, he felt a sharp pain jolt from his neck into his shoulder and down his arm. When he breathed his chest hurt but the cut along his ribs and stomach was healing. He glanced into Ah Sam's room and saw him sleeping, his face and arm bandaged.

John walked into the restaurant. Lehua piled up broken furniture in a corner. Her baby girl slept in a box near the cold stove. Choi played with blocks on the floor. "I'm sorry about your place being smashed up. I didn't think the publicity of the trial would lead Shaw to seek revenge."

Lehua sighed, "He wrecked the place. Wall busted. Tables, chairs need replacing. Ah Sam hurt. Don't know if we can open again."

Before John could answer her, Aaloa came in. "Eh, sheriff wants to talk to you. I told him everything when we brought the sailor guys in, but he wants to talk to you about the girl."

"What about Maria?"

"We took her to the hospital. She be okay."

"Has her father made a complaint against me?"

"Don't know. You ask him."

John mumbled to Lehua about the damage and left with the bone-breaker. He still had reward money. But he wanted to use it for his pursuit of Leinani, and finish paying Joshua. Then there was Maria. What would that cost to solve? He hustled to the barracks with Aaloa worrying about what to do.

"Honolulu's big harbor now with all these wharves," Aaloa said as the two men walked along the waterfront. "Better place than San Francisco for the ships. They don't rub together."

"Oh, yeah?" John answered then fell silent. He let Aaloa prattle on as he mulled over the problems he faced. Did the sheriff want him for sleeping with Maria? It wasn't rape. She consented. She enjoyed their love making. But she was white and he was brown, and who would believe a Hawaiian? One thing he knew for certain, the reward money wouldn't solve the problem.

"Hey, we're here. Room over there," Aaloa pointed to a door with a kingdom insignia on it.

John opened it and entered. There was a large cabinet against a wall, boxes in corners, two desks and some chairs. A heavy-set Caucasian with full whiskers and bald head sat at a desk reading some papers. He looked up as the two men came in and growled, "Don't you savages know to knock? Who are you?"

"Name is John Tana. You wanted to talk to me about the fight last night. At least that's what my friend said."

The sheriff squinted past John and saw the bone-breaker. "Yes, I did tell him to fetch you. Sit. You, wait outside." The sheriff pointed John to a chair and motioned Aaloa out the door.

John felt uncomfortable as the sheriff stared at him. He took a seat in a hard wood chair, the back of it nudging into his spine. He dropped his face to avoid eye contact. He had seen the man once before. Through the trees as he shot his teacher.

There came a pounding against the back wall. The battering shook the room. "Don't pay any attention to that. Just a prisoner wanting supper. I'm Deputy Sheriff McCoy. About last night, you know this Maria?"

John swallowed. There it was, the first accusatory question. What to answer? "Yes." "Lazarus?"

John scowled. "In a way."

"What do you mean, in a way? He says you were the reason the whalers were at the restaurant. That you had beat him up in Lahaina. Did you?"

John didn't like the way the question was asked, as if he had done something wrong. With as much restraint as he could muster, he briefly explained what happened.

"So you say it was a kidnap try. But Lazarus and one of his mates say you cold-cocked him outside a bar."

"That's a lie It was a shanghai and I fought to save myself and my cousin. What's this got to do with Maria?"

"Shut up. I ask the questions. Yesterday evening, the Foreign Minister reported his daughter kidnapped. Was it you who did it?"

"No!" John's answer exploded like a musket shot. At the same moment the pounding on the wall resumed, making the room shake again.

The sheriff yelled, "Lazarus, cut that shit out or I'll come in and whip you good."

"His other friends in there?" John said pointing to the wall.

"Don't weasel away from my questions. Did you put the mark on her face, rip her dress?"

"Is that what that damned Lazarus and his pals told you? He's the one who hit her, grabbed her, ripped her clothes. Not me."

"Yeah, you got any proof?"

"It was a good thing that you stayed around," John said as he and Aaloa walked toward the water front. "You saved me from being tossed into jail. As it is, the sheriff told me not to leave town. He has to talk to Maria."

Aaloa frowned, "I hope she likes you."

"You were there. You saw what happened."

"Brother, those sailors will lie. Blame you for everything. If this Maria doesn't back you up, you're dead. Come, let's eat."

John followed his friend to the waterfront where they joined other stevedores for a fish and poi dinner. Stories of sexual escapades and waterfront brawls punctuated the mealtime conversation. John didn't participate in the ribald talk. He dreamed of Leinani. What could he do? He was denied access to the Grant home and to her school. The only friend that he knew of was Maria and he couldn't ask her to help. Then there was that rich man that was after her. His worry mounted as he mumbled goodbye and left.

He passed black hulks of ships berthed in the harbor, dim lights on their forecastles marking their presence. He wondered if one of them belonged to Shaw. That was another worry. The sheriff had said that everybody but Lazarus had been released. He didn't explain why and John didn't ask. But would the captain try again?

A breeze whipped up, sweeping through the yardarms of the vessels creating eerie rattling sounds that pulsed through the port. The noise jarred John's emotions, frayed by two days of victory and defeat. The new marine light cast a dim glow over the water sluicing through the channels around Sand Island and brushing against the seawall. He turned away from the docks, his face hardened as he retreated into deep thought.

"I got you now, you damn kanaka." A harsh voice cut through the darkness and an object rapped his skull. Rough hands grabbed him and a rope settled over his body.

It's Shaw come to finish me, John thought. Damn the sheriff. He tried to fight back, but another blow ended his struggles.

Fifty

Water sloshed over his face, dripped down his body. His arms and shoulders ached from being stretched. His head pounded with pain. John tried to focus, but his surroundings were a misshapen blur.

"Get up, damn you," a voice snarled as more seawater cascaded over him.

John's eyes stung from the salt. He couldn't clear them. He hung with his arms spread and his wrists tied to a rafter above him. A weight, bound to his feet, pulled his body taut, the tightness creating a growing soreness in his hips, back, and groin. The stretching had parted the scabs along his chest. The seawater seeping into the wounds made them flame.

His head exploding, his body a mass of hurts, John willed his eyes to see, but they refused to focus. His body convulsed. Searing pain ran through him as the weight jerked. Someone laughed. His thoughts wandered to a figure in Father De Veuster's church. A man in a loincloth stretched out like he was. He concentrated his thoughts on the image, trying to recall why the holy man had been splayed on a cross. His sight cleared, and he recognized the face of the Grant supervisor. He had a whip in his hand.

"You're finally up, you sneaky bastard. Tonight, I get even for all the trouble in Kahului and Lahaina. You are going to die slow. When the sharks get you, you'll be nothing but raw meat."

The whip crackled, it stung John's flesh below his waist. The rawhide whipped across his groin, raising a welt. Gonzalez retreated behind him. John felt the sting of the lash scoring his back. A trickle flowed down his skin and he knew he bled. The lash smashed into him with a numbing ferocity. He wanted to howl, but clamped his mouth tight refusing to give Gonzalez the pleasure of knowing that he suffered. If he must die, he would die in silence. The man would work for his death. Someone had once told him that after the first thirty lashes the pain was all the same.

Salt water washed over his back, seeping into the torn flesh, stinging like thousands of bees. "Scream, damn you. I want you to scream," Gonzales yelled as the lash struck John's back, snaking over his shoulder and onto his chest. "If you aren't going to yell then maybe a little bleeding will make you beg for mercy."

"You must know that it is important to this household that you have a suitable relationship with a gentleman," Robert Grant said, swigging his brandy. He stared at Leinani, her exquisite face framed by dark hair aristocratically coiffured around her head. She wore rich clothes that he had purchased. A personal maid had applied eye shadow, powder to her cheeks, and a light touch of lipstick. But her true beauty lay in her hazel eyes. Eyes like his. They enhanced her exquisite face, and he understood why James Kingsley fell in love with her.

Not receiving a response, Grant continued, "I am told by the servants and the school that a young Hawaiian is seeking you. Is this someone from your past?"

Leinani paused for a moment before answering, "No one told me of inquiries being made. Could it have been John, the man I thought was my cousin?" She kept her tone inquisitive hiding the excitement building within her.

Grant studied her closely, suspicious that there may be more than a casual interest in this visitor. He sipped his brandy, then said, "Yes, I think it could be that man. John Tana is his name."

Grant saw Leinani's eyes flicker, her face soften, and a slight tremor of her hand made the teacup she held jiggle. There was something to this relationship he thought. But Malia had assured him that Leinani is a virgin. But was she? He must have her examined to assure Kingsley of her purity. One thing was certain, Gonzalez would finish Tana, and the filthy Hawaiian would no longer exist to spoil his plans. But if his henchman failed, he had a trump card to play.

Grant broke the silence. His voice placid, his tone neutral, "I am led to understand that this Tana fellow has angered Monsieur Francois."

"How so?" Leinani asked, her voice quivering.

"He claims that Mr. Tana raped his daughter!"

"He is a liar!" Leinani shouted, then burst into tears and ran from the room.

John tensed as he waited for the next round of torture. Gonzalez rubbed a blade across his thigh and mumbled about sharpening his knife. He heard a thud and another. The room went silent. The quiet became more unnerving than the torture. Something was being dragged along the dirt floor of the room. A ladder slid along the rafters. His eyes blinded with sweat and aching from salt water, he vaguely saw a knife reaching toward his hand.

"I'll cut you down," a voice said.

"Cut the weight from my feet first."

The man slid from the ladder and sawed the stone off. Then he looped a rope around John's armpits and over the rafter, before freeing John's arms of their bindings. Lowered to the floor, he staggered like a drunken sailor. His eyes cleared and he saw his sparring partner from the lua temple. In the dirt lay Gonzalez, a wooden club by his side.

Come," his friend said, helping John to remain upright. "We go."

Fifty-One

Hens clucking roused him at mid-day. His head ached. His back flamed. His groin felt numb, and he wondered if he was still a man. Thirsty, he found a jug by his blanket, and poured the warm water down his throat. John vaguely remembered being helped along the street, and led into the chicken yard by his lua friend.

He dropped to the blanket exhausted by the effort of drinking, only to squirm in pain as raw flesh protested his sudden movement. John saw a platter of food and a note. "Not safe outside. Stay here. See you tonight." He managed a wry smile. He hurt too much to go anywhere.

A door creaked, the scratchy noise brought John awake. The sky had darkened. He could hardly see in the dimness of the hut. He searched for a weapon. Found nothing. He rose to a crouch, waited, and prepared to fight.

His lua mate peered into the hovel. John relaxed. During the next hour, his friend Lukela, explained that the Portuguese had come into the bar where he worked seeking men who asked no questions. He offered gold. Lukela and two others were hired.

The group waited in darkness near a Chinese restaurant. Late in the night, the Portuguese nudged them awake and they attacked John. While Lukela carried him, he recognized his sparring partner from the temple. After leaving the warehouse, he split from the other two, doubled back and found his employer whipping John. "I hit him with the same club that he used on you, and then helped you here."

"Thanks."

"It's the least I could do for saving us from the revenuers with your warning."

"How long can I stay?"

Lukela's eyes dropped. "There are others living in the main house. We share it. I snuck you here last night while they were asleep, but today is different. I don't think they would talk, but you never know."

Silence fell between the two men, broken only by the scratching of chickens and the sounds of a nose flute wailing from the house. John considered his options: stay in the hut and risk capture, head for Ah Sam's and put the family in jeopardy, or——. "Can you help me to the Waikiki Road?"

"Sure. I'll go to work for a few hours. Leave when its midnight. Come back for you then."

John didn't like the idea of waiting, but he realized that late at night, people would be asleep and he could make his journey without detection. He nodded his agreement. Lukela left.

The night wore on. Laughter, ribald shouts, came from the house next to the chicken coop. Hens who had skittered away when he moved, went to sleep. Even the resident rooster who had clucked and scratched during the day, making it clear that he ruled the hen house, had settled down. John dozed, then came awake from a pounding on a door nearby.

John worried that it might be police, but nothing came of it. He settled back to an uneasy sleep, every part of his body aching.

Rusty hinges protested. John opened his eyes. He tensed. He searched the darkness.

"Easy," Lukela said. "It's time to go." He held out a staff and offered his arm.

John grasped his shoulder and they stumbled out of the yard and onto the street. As they hobbled on the packed dirt roadway John heard the drumming of hooves. His eyes darted about for a place to hide as two horsemen cantered around a bend in the roadway. The riders would be upon them in moments.

Lukela pulled him into a ditch where they huddled as the men passed. Darkness made it impossible to see who they were. Once the riders were gone, they headed for Waikiki Road.

Fifty-Two

Weak light filtered in through the thin cracks of the grass-covered shack and a fresh breeze cooled his face. John wrinkled his nose as he inhaled the fragrance of flowers. He rose from his blanket and sensed someone inside. His quick movement caused a throbbing in his back. Through the threshold he saw a mass of dark clouds blotting out the sun. Rain fell like the tentacles of drifting jellyfish. Kane, the thunder god, blasted the heavens with rolling cracks that rattled the thin thatch-covered frame of the hut, and bright light flashed in the sky.

John's head throbbed as he searched the dim interior of his shelter for an intruder. In a corner he saw a slender figure, the brown color of the young girl's skin blending into the dried thatch of the hut. The teen-ager giggled when John's search met her eyes. She stepped from the shadows, a bouquet of flowers in her arms. A plain sack covered her, belted tight at the waist. John admired her contoured shape, flowing brown hair that framed a pretty face enhanced by high cheekbones, pert nose, and heart shaped lips.

Two steps from him the young woman stopped. "I...I love you," she flung the flowers, clapped a hand to her mouth, shrieked, and ran from the shack.

What a pest, he thought, an infatuated fourteen-year old who hovered near him ever since he stumbled into the Alapai compound. Too young, he thought, but eager for plucking. He knew that the Alapai family wanted him to couple with Mahealani, and have John become part of the clan. But he had a more pressing problem to solve and involvement with another woman would only add to his woes. Many days had passed since Chin Sing's death, and he needed to see Joshua.

John dressed, wrapped a *tapa* cape around his shoulders, and hobbled into Honolulu. He hoped that the rain and his broad-brimmed hat were sufficient to hide his face. Fortunately, the streets were empty, the downpour keeping people indoors. Near the office he paused in an alley, searching the area for an enemy. Satisfied, he slipped through a doorway, walked down a hallway, and knocked on the attorney's door.

Joshua was upset that John had gone missing for five days, but apologized for his ire when he learned of the beating by Gonzales. After John finished his story, he asked, "Why did the Portuguese want to kill me?"

Joshua frowned, thought for some moments before answering, "It could be revenge for the past, or maybe Grant wanted to eliminate the only legitimate claimant to the Kahului property that he stole. You know I made inquiries at the patent office. Grant has many spies."

"He would commit murder to be rid of me? Why do that? Reverend Zachariah told me, 'Grant owned the property and I'd go to jail if I didn't leave.' Did the Reverend lie?" John asked, his voice rising, anger welling up inside.

Joshua pushed back from his desk and walked to a window. "I'm not saying the Reverend lied, he only told you what the legal papers said, but I do know from experience that the sugar planters have taken advantage of ignorance and made land claims that are questionable or even false. I also told you about allo-dial rights."

"Can I get my land back?"

Joshua shook his head, "I don't know. There is an 1850 kuleana law that lets Hawaiians convert gifts from the king into private property. But Grant got the patent to the Kahului land and you didn't assert your kuleana rights when you got the eviction notice. You could be out of luck. It would take a lot of money to undo the failures of your family. There is a slim hope. The court hasn't ruled on any residual rights you may have."

"You're telling me that I could spend a lot of money trying to prove my case, and yet still lose in the end, because I didn't fight the eviction notice? This law stuff is not fair."

"John, the present legal system we have is a lot better than the old *kapu* rules that the chiefs forced on the common people. In the old days what your chief ordered, no matter how ridiculous, you had to obey or die. At least you saw in a court of law that Chin Sing could prove his innocence of murder and not be hanged."

"Yeah, well all I know is that Kamehameha gave my grandfather the Kahului land and now it belongs to Grant."

"The king's dead. We are living in a new world, a capitalistic world where making money is more important than people. The smart get rich because they know how to use the current law system. You've got to educate yourself, not fight the legal process.

"I want to talk to you about something personal, you've walked into forbidden ground and crossed an invisible line. Minister Francois is angry with you."

When John tried to interrupt, Joshua cut him off. "And don't protest that Maria wanted you. There are things that brown men do not do with white women." He took a few steps closer. "Watch yourself. I'm quite sure that serious trouble is coming your way."

"How come I'm in trouble for doing something people do every day and Shaw and his men get out of jail for attempted murder?" John said his tone belligerent.

"It's capitalism."

"What does capitalism have to do with it?"

"Simply this: whaling companies invest money in ships and equipment to hunt whales. The sailors they use are cheap labor. At sea they work twenty-four hours a day. They are bullied, disciplined, fed bad food and little of it. There is no fun on a whaling ship. It is all work, and for what? Maybe a small lay, profit money if the whaling season is good. Merchants in Honolulu or Lahaina want to attract the ships to have them buy supplies, spend money on women and alcohol. So long as all crimes are committed at the waterfront the law doesn't care. Return the wrongdoers to their ships and send them on their way."

John's brow furrowed, then he relaxed, the thoughts that troubled him smoothed away. "I get it. The waterfront beatings and killings only hurt people. But if you enforce the law and put a sailor in prison or hang him the whaling company loses its cheap labor. The investors will lose money. A whaling captain will only go to a port and do business where the law looks the other way when a sailor does something wrong."

"You got it. It is bad for merchant business if you put sailors into jail for going wild when in a port. Wrongdoing by whalers on the waterfront is permitted except…"

"But what about when you hurt someone like Maria?"

"That is the exception. Lazarus crossed the line. He hurt someone from the white community. He is going to spend time in prison for his attack on Maria. It doesn't pay to mess with high class folk. What will happen to Lazarus is a warning to you. You also have crossed an invisible line."

John sat quietly for a long beat, absorbing this warning from a respected friend. As the rain subsided and sunlight shot through the window, he asked "What happened to Chin Sing? And how much more do I owe you for defending him?"

"You've paid me enough. Chin Sing's final story is tragic. Abused for so many years, by the time he got to trial, his sanity was gone. From what I learned, one of the guards gave him a rope and played so dramatically on his fears that the poor man hanged himself."

Joshua paused for some moments, and John sensed he had more to say. He wondered what added trouble he might be in beside an angry father, a rapacious sugar planter, and a vengeful sea captain. The silence lengthened between the two men, until John could stand it no longer, "Out with it. What further bad news do you have for me?"

"Leinani Grant has been seen in the company of James Kingsley, the richest, most eligible bachelor in Honolulu. The rumor is that they will be engaged soon."

"What…" John stuttered, Joshua's words hurting more than the wounds from the beatings. "It cannot be…" His voice trailed off, his hands cupped his head, trying to still its throbbing, as his heart pulsed hard against his chest.

By the time he left Kanakoa's office the streets were bustling with people. He debated going to Grant's home and seeking out Leinani, confronting her, asking for the truth, but he realized that if Grant wanted him dead, he would be walking into a death trap. He decided to go to Leinani's school and leave a note seeking a meeting.

After he did, he returned to the Alapai compound, brusquely brushed away an eager Mahealani, and dove into the sea. The ocean rolled with great swells from the storm that had just passed, but despite the pain in his shoulders, back, and hips, John fought through the crashing waves.

Finally, with darkness all around him, he turned for shore, keying on a burning bonfire, its flames shooting high into the sky. The ocean swells had moderated, and he found it easier to swim in than to go out. He was near exhaustion when he floundered onto the beach and staggered into his shack. He fell asleep mumbling, "It cannot be."

Before dawn he awoke and exercised away the aches in his body. What would he do, if Leinani chose Kingsley? "It cannot be," he said, practicing a flip that he had seen Chinese acrobats perform.

"It can be," Mahealani giggled, a broad smile arching over a set of perfect white teeth. "You can have me," she said, her voice suggestive.

"Beat it kid," John said, irritated that the girl continued to pester him.

"Hey, you good looking guy," Mahealani teased, refusing to leave. "How about you and me work out together?" she asked, a promise implicit in her voice.

John ignored the pretty dark-eyed girl's suggestive teasing, thinking it the kind of small talk enjoyed by young women. His focus was on his lua moves, building his strength, and trying to forget the pain of Leinani.

"Why you doing that?"

"Go play with the other kids," John replied, but the girl refused to budge, smiling every time John looked at her. He resigned himself to having her as a companion and exercised until the sun stood high, then quit and trooped off with Mahealani to eat and visit with her family.

Aaloa came to the Alapai compound in the afternoon, bringing a summons from Colonel Kalakaua. "Do you know what's being asked of me? I'm waiting to hear from Leinani. I want to stop her from getting married."

"Eh, bra, I don't like to make it tough on you, but the Colonel says he needs all the militia guys to help him. There's big trouble in Ewa."

John weighed disobedience to the order, but he knew that duty had to come before passion. He would not fail the Colonel. Grudgingly, he followed Aaloa out of the compound, consoling himself with the belief that whatever the trouble, it would be over quickly and he could return and pursue Leinani.

Thirty men reported to the barracks on Palace Walk. Prominent among them were ten Hawaiian Zouaves, dressed in the fashion of the famous French soldiers of Morocco. They were dashing in bright red kepi, dark blue coats, crimson pantaloons, and white spats.

In sharp contrast, the rest of the militia wore ill-fitting blue coats that identified them as soldiers of the crown. Their pants were of various colors, chosen by what fit best. Most of the militiamen were barefooted, and their hatless appearance made them seem ragged. But they stood at attention, ramrod straight, waiting for orders.

Colonel Kalakaua rode up in the lead wagon and directed John, Aaloa, and seven militia to "climb aboard." The rest of the men piled into the remaining transport. "Wagons forward," Kalakaua ordered. He led his troops away from the barracks and onto King Street, heading toward Pearl Harbor. The colonel was handsome in his light grey uniform with its braided gold buttonholes, brass buttons, and gold piping on the sleeves. Bright yellow tassels dangled from dark blue sideboards, which were fixed onto the shoulders of his jacket, and jiggled as the wagon bumped along the rutted roadway.

The colonel spoke to John in a hushed voice. "I understand you may be in a bit of trouble. It's been reported to me that you've dallied with a certain young lady whose father is a highly placed man in our kingdom."

When John did not answer, Kalakaua said, "I understand that Monsieur Francois wants to challenge you to a duel for dishonoring his daughter's reputation."

John sighed, "I'm a fool, Colonel. I can only blame myself for what happened. What should I do to make amends?"

"Don't visit this girl. Keep yourself hidden, perhaps disappear to another island for a time. The Frenchman will be leaving Hawaii soon. After he goes, your troubles will be over."

John listened as Kalakaua explained that they were about to confront a man passing himself off as a religious leader. "His name is Jonah, and he's lured people into his fold. Jonah is preaching the second coming of Christ."

John had heard of this cult, but didn't understand why they had to travel to the other side of the island with armed men to suppress it.

The wagon lurched as they rolled over a large stone, jostling the militia against each other. Complaints were called out. The driver spat a stream of tobacco.

Several minutes passed before Kalakaua answered John's question. "We've had volcanoes and earthquakes these past weeks. Jonah claims they're signals from God, a warning about the second coming. His flock's been going a little crazy, disturbing people all over the west side of Oahu, telling folks to sell all they have and join them in preparations for the end of the world."

Before John could speak, Kalakaua rushed on. "Jonah and his people have taken over a church and are threatening to kill anyone who doesn't join them. Yesterday evening, when a deputy sheriff tried to get them to vacate, they cut him down with stones and knives."

"So we're going to arrest them?"

Kalakaua nodded.

"Why do we need thirty men?" John thought he could find a way to leave, and visit Leinani. He felt Kalakaua's eyes on him and wondered if he'd gone too far.

"I don't know how many people we'll find there, perhaps a hundred, maybe more? How well armed are they? I don't know. But since they killed a sheriff, we must arrest them and take all of them to prison." He glanced behind him, as if confirming that a full contingency still rode with him. "We need everyone with us tonight."

John sighed, knowing that his ploy to escape his duty had failed, and prayed to every god he knew that Leinani would wait for him and not rush into an engagement with Kingsley.

It was not yet nine o'clock when the militia pulled up to the Ewa church. There were candles inside the building and bonfires outside lit up the white walls of the holy place and the grounds around it. John heard ragged singing coming from inside, along with fervent cries of "The end is near. Jesus our Lord save us. Enter us through the gates of heaven."

Kalakaua ordered the men to unload the wagons. "We do not want unnecessary bloodshed," he instructed his soldiers. As he spoke, the singing in the church softened.

"On my order, we'll march to the front of the church. Your weapons are not to be loaded. You, Aaloa and John, will accompany me ahead of the others. We'll try to talk some sense into these folks."

With parade-ground precision, the soldiers moved forward, led by their colonel. Dogs barked as they approached, then scurried frantically about, howling. Inside the church, singing and shouting ceased. Several people outside approached the militia armed with stones. Others, curious about these intruders, thrust their faces through open windows to see for themselves what riled the dogs.

"Halt." Kalakaua commanded. "Order arms. Parade rest." He instructed John and Aaloa to approach with open palms, as a sign of peace. The three men moved toward the cultists, who called out warnings of doom.

"Volcanoes no blow up," Aaloa called back. "Pele no angry. She stopped her anger a long time ago."

A slender Hawaiian pushed to the forefront. "Is that you, cousin? What you mean volcanoes no blow up? Jonah tell us big fires, big shakes. He dreams Christ is coming."

"Hey, cousin, no big fires, no big shakes, Pele all quiet. She go sleep. Everything on the island is sleeping. You guys are making a big thing out of nothing. Where is *tutu* man, *tutu wahine*?" The man pointed to the church. Aaloa asked him to bring them out.

Kalakaua said to those still milling about. "He's right, Pele is no longer angry. She has stopped her explosions, she has stopped her fire, and she has stopped the shaking of the ground. Everything is quiet. *Mililani I akua*, praise be to God. Give thanks that *keola o aina*, life on earth, continues."

Those in front of the church, and the members standing at the windows, took up the chant, singing *Mililani I akua keola o aina*. As the sound swelled, they began to walk to Kalakaua and the waiting soldiers. Before they got far, a booming voice came from within the building. "Stop this heresy, this abomination in the eyes of God."

A huge, bearded Hawaiian appeared at the entrance, hands raised heavenward. "Verily, I say unto you, I have seen Jesus in my dreams and He is coming in all His glory to judge the living and the dead."

John watched in amazement as this six-foot-four apparition thundered his predictions.

"He has promised eternal life for he that believeth in Him, and eternal damnation for he who does not. The mountains fling forth their burning rocks; the earth shakes, signaling His coming. Those that deny these signs commit blasphemy and will be damned to hell."

The exodus of followers came to a halt and they clung together, as if unsure what to do.

Kalakaua called to the man, "Jonah, you have misread the signs. Pele has stilled her fury. It is not God who created these warnings, but Pele. Why has her fury stopped? Because God has suppressed her anger and now all of Hawaii is at peace. Sing forth all of you, *Mililani I akua keola o aina.*" With that, the exodus began anew.

Jonah rushed forward, brandishing a sword, eyes wild. "You shall taste of death and never see the coming of the Son of Man." With his weapon high, he ran at Kalakaua.

John scooped up dirt and flung it into the crazed man's face. "My eyes," Jonah screamed. His blade crunched the earth, inches from the Colonel.

Scabs split, sending jolts of pain through John's body as he did an acrobatic flip, driving his feet into the prophet's stomach. Jonah howled and crumpled to the ground, his sword clattering beside him. Aaloa smashed a fist into his face, and the cult leader wilted into an unconscious heap.

With Jonah out, the remaining cultists surrendered. "Gather them up and begin processing," Kalakaua ordered.

John pushed himself from the dirt, his brain screaming that he had abused his body beyond the normal. He stumbled to the Colonel thinking of the time he had lost in his pursuit of Leinani. "Permission to leave sir."

"I need you here. Request denied."

Fifty-Three

Grant paced his office, sucking his ever-present cigar, its end bright red. Smoke fumed from his lips. Gonzalez propped himself against a wall, a bandage like a skewered white crown plastered to his skull. His hands curled and uncurled the brim of his Stetson.

Leinani's father flicked ashes onto his desk, grey from the soot that had not been swept away for hours. "He slipped through your hands again," Grant said his voice rising in volume. "How did you let him escape?"

"He had help."

"That's how you got the knot on your head?"

Gonzalez nodded.

"I pay and pay and get no results," Grant squashed his smoking weed into a tray, its dried leaves crackling. To do a good job sometimes you had to do it yourself, he thought. That's how I've been successful. But manipulating human beings is different than destroying them. That kind of dirty work is for men like Gonzales. He made up his mind.

"It's time to give up revenge." Walking to a rack, Grant took the Winchester from it. "Hire some men to watch over the haunts where Tana visits. On my desk are newspapers with his picture. Visit his attorney, the man's address is also in the news. When you spot the kid kill him with this." Grant handed over the rifle.

Two days after the end of the religious rebellion, John rode with the wagons hauling cultists to the county jail. After processing the herd of people into the lockup, his guilt over abandoning his Chinese friends overwhelmed him. He set aside his desire to seek out Leinani and, disregarding danger, walked to the restaurant.

Outside it still showed damage, shards of broken wood around its doors. Inside, the bare room attested to the mindless destruction by the whalers. Only the stove stood intact. The wooden bin that John filled each day, empty.

"Ah Sam, Lehua," John called striding toward the rear residences.

"What want?"

John heard a rapping. With extreme caution he opened the door that he had burst through many times before. He re-lived that evening eight days ago when he came into a scene of chaos with Shaw holding a gun. What would he find inside? What did that persistent noise mean?

He pushed in. The family residence stood clean and neat, furnished as in the past. In a chair Lehua nursed the baby. Choi sat in a corner pounding a wooden hammer on the floor. John sighed with relief.

"Everybody okay?"

"Oh, John, it's good to see you."

"Where is Ah Sam?"

"Looking for money, we have nothing to fix the place," Lehua sighed as her baby gurgled contentedly after her meal. She placed the child against her shoulder, patting her until she burped.

A mixture of thoughts raced through John's mind. He made a decision. "Are all my things still in my room?"

"Of course."

Lehua's words struck his heart. He knew what he must do. He entered his sleeping chamber and rummaged through his belongings to find a heavy purse. Next to it lay his weapons bag from which he took a short club, strangling cord, and sling. Placing round stones in his pocket he returned to the inner residence.

Making small talk with Lehua, he waited for Ah Sam to return. Within the hour his Chinese friend came in, his face wreathing in a smile when he saw John. "How you? Where you been?"

"Long story, any luck with money?"

"No. Credit bad. Muk Fat maybe help, but…" Ah Sam's voice trailed off.

"Here's a purse of silver, two hundred dollars in it."

Ah Sam smiled, then his face turned serious. "You need money. Keep. Use for you."

"No. We will use it together, and with the help of my friends we will rebuild this place."

"John, no can. You need the money," Lehua protested.

"You need it more. Ah Sam take the silver. Buy lumber, furniture whatever is necessary to put this place back in business. My friends and I will supply the labor. We will have it open in no time."

Ah Sam laughed, then cried, "Thank you, thank you. Two hundred dollah plenty fix place."

John left. He strode toward the docks committed to helping his friend. He noticed a man with a foot against a wall reading a paper. The stranger looked up, stared for a moment, then returned to the news. Nothing unusual, John thought as he continued to the seaport in search of Aaloa.

Fifty-Four

Door construction requires experience and precision. John had neither. All his life he had lived in shacks without doors. To ensure safety from intruders the threshold opening would be built low so that anyone who wanted to enter must bend or crawl. This gave the person inside a slight advantage in case an enemy tried to come in.

Puzzled by the complexities of building an entryway and a door to close it in, John left the street and entered Ah Sam's. Inside, the freshly painted white walls gave the once dingy restaurant an antiseptic look. Framed pictures of scenes from the 'China Trade' of flat-bottomed junks, sailboats, clipper ships, and dockside work hung evenly spaced. Brass lanterns for light were fixed symmetrically on all four walls. They created elegance unusual for the waterfront of Honolulu.

Aaloa worked at setting up bamboo furniture whose color matched the oil lamps. Jimmy Noa and a stevedore friend were adding ivory molding bordering the top of the walls. A storage box next to a new stove brimmed full with evenly cut, rectangular pieces of wood.

Ah Sam trundled through the threshold with a cart filled with groceries. "Lookee, Peking duck," he pointed to a pair of red, dressed fowl dangling from a hook. "Cha sui pork, duck eggs."

John pinched his nose. Aaloa said, "Only *Pake* like the smell of that stuff soaked in salt water."

"You Hawaiian no like try pork hash, egg on top? Very good."

"Just looking at those white balls soaking in green water makes me sick," John said with a laugh. "But if Chinese like it, eat all you want, won't bother me."

Ah Sam's face wreathed in a smile, "It's okay. Big party tonight. You see what we eat."

"That's what you like," John said. "Cooking good food and having people enjoy it. When they give you praise for your special talent it makes you happy."

Ah Sam nodded.

"But good cooking aside, do you know how to make a door?"

"Takes talent," Aaloa said.

"Which I don't have."

"Let's take a look."

The two men walked to the entrance examining the threshold. Wood shattered above John's head and a whining sound pierced the air.

"Down," Aaloa yelled.

Another bullet struck the frame for the new door, driving a tiny splinter into John's side. Another shot followed, plunging into the street, scattering pebbles where it hit.

Squirming behind a wall John looked around him. "Everybody okay?"

"Yeah, we okay, the guy, he shooting at you," Aaloa said. "Good thing he lousy shot."

"Did you see anybody with a musket in the street?"

"That's not a musket. Shoots too fast."

"Yeah," Jimmy Noa interrupted. "That's some kind of rifle. Takes a minute or more for a shooter to load ball and powder into a muzzle and tamp it down. What is firing at you loads from the back with metal cartridges."

"Three shots in seconds and we can't see who's shooting," John said.

"I heard talk at the bar that there's some new kind of guns. 'Repeaters' they're called. Crank 'em, a bullet loads in a chamber in back, fire, crank, fire, crank, fire. Those kind of guns have longer range than muskets," Noa answered.

"We got to do something, can't just hide here all day," Aaloa said.

John thought for a moment. "Whoever it is wants me. I'll go to the door. You guys watch from the windows. When he shoots locate him."

"Too dangerous," Aaloa said.

"I go empty lot next door. I have spyglass. Look around," Ah Sam said.

"You could get killed. It's me he wants."

"No, no, I small, can hide in bushes. You see outside big clouds. Getting dark. Rain."

"Yeah, maybe we can create a diversion," Jimmy Noa said. "John, you're always wearing a hat when you go outside. Put a stick in it and show it at the door."

"Okay. Ah Sam go next door. Be careful. When it starts raining I'll stick the hat out."

Ah Sam nodded and scurried into the back rooms. The four men in the restaurant waited. John fingered the pebbles in his pocket. These are useless, he thought. If you can't see what's shooting at you, what good are stones? Aaloa picked up sticks from the wood box and handed them around.

A few passersby hurried along the street, scurrying for shelter from the coming storm. One man came to the threshold. "Why are you guys on the ground?"

"Somebody's shooting at us," Aaloa answered.

The stranger scurried from the doorway.

"Why doesn't the rain come? I can't breathe in here," Noa said.

John noticed the tension building in the room. The stevedore huddled behind an overturned table, the bartender lay flattened against a wall. Aaloa squeezed the makeshift club, relaxed, and squeezed again.

"You guys can leave," John said his hand sweeping around the room. "The shooter wants me."

"Not smart," Aaloa answered. "In this darkness the minute one of us steps outside we'll get shot."

"He didn't shoot the man at the door."

"He was coming from outside. We would be coming from inside."

Gusts of wind whipped against the building. Rain began to fall, at first slow, then increasing in intensity. John slid along the floor holding a stick with a hat on top. A bullet struck the back wall, another clipped the top of the decoy making it wobble. John flung it down.

In moments Ah Sam scurried in. "I see gun flash, smoke. Man standing long way away. On second floor red building."

"That's two hundred yards away. Man's shooting over a bunch of shanties," Noa said.

"Yeah, but the shacks are low. From where he's at, the guy's got a clear field of fire," John said.

"What goin' do?" Aaloa asked.

"Ah Sam, that red building's near Muk Fat's store. A mom and pop business, sell downstairs, live upstairs. Right?"

Sam nodded.

"I'll go into the side yard, circle around the alley and head to the other street."

"We're coming with you," Aaloa and Jimmy chorused.

"No. It's my fight."

"It's ours too."

Without arguing further, John headed to the side yard, running low to the alley. The other two men followed. He wondered why there weren't any more shots. Maybe the pelting rain hid their movements or maybe the shooter thought the last shot killed him. He fingered his small club. Whatever the reason, he would find the man and finish him.

Coming around to Muk Fat's street, the three Hawaiians took shelter under the awnings of buildings as they moved, stopped, and moved again. The rain had kept the roads clear of people. Shops they passed contained customers who were not leaving.

Near the red building, John halted, sheltering behind boxes crowding the walkway and spilling into the street. The two other men knelt beside him. "Can't see anybody," Aaloa said.

"Somebody's got to get across the street. A better angle to look," Noa added.

"I'll go," John said, leaping from his hiding place and zigzagging across the road. Fear of this new weapon constricted his breath. He prayed God to let the rain hide him or at least blind the shooter.

Except for the pelting water, there was nothing. No sounds. No bullets striking around him. He reached the other side and slid behind a cart. Boxes lay on its top. John slowed his breathing, controlled his anxiety, he sought that Zen state where worry disappears.

"See anything?" Aaloa called.

John did not answer. He peered around the side of the cart. Where is the Chinese couple that minded the store? No one moved inside the business. The second floor appeared clear. Could Ah Sam be wrong? This is not the right building?

John signaled with his hand pointing to the red building. He headed across the street gaining shelter under the roof. "Nobody inside," Aaloa said.

"No one up top when I looked," John said. "Stairs are to the right. Rain has stopped. I'll head up."

Aaloa grabbed John's arm, saying, "No sense we all go up in a bunch. You have a sling, maybe go out in the street and watch. Somebody peep out, throw the stone."

"No. It's my fight."

"No. It's our fight. Get out there."

John shrugged, un-wrapped his corded weapon from his forehead, and inserted a small rock in the leather pouch. He stepped beyond the roof, his slippered feet sinking into a flowing stream of water heading to the sea. His missile clutched in one hand, the other tensed the cord. He trusted his weapon. He knew he could hurl it accurately a hundred feet, far enough to reach a shooter on the second floor.

John looked up. There was nothing. "Go up slow." Aaloa climbed the stairs followed by Noa. John watched them step along the second floor porch and disappear through a door. Noa came out. "Two people tied up. They're beaten bad."

John raced upstairs to the sleeping quarters. He saw two trussed Chinese being freed by Aaloa. "What happened?"

"These people are still kind of out of it. From what I see and the little they say, someone with a golden stick clubbed them. Guy must have tied them and..."

"Started shooting at us," Jimmy Noa said holding up a shiny metal cylinder. "Found this on the porch outside. It's made in America. Smell it. Still has powder burns. I've never seen anything like it in Hawai'i."

John felt a chill stab into his body. A new weapon, long ranged, able to fire multiple bullets in seconds. Muzzle loaders couldn't compete. What chance did he have? His club, cord, and sling were useless against this weapon. He understood what the early Hawaiians must have felt when cannon fire raked into them.

His troubles with Shaw and the whalers had been easy, mostly hand-to-hand stuff. But today he could be sniped at and never know where the bullet came from.

After helping the two battered Chinese, the three men returned to Ah Sam's. A weeping Lehua comforted a worried Ah Sam. When she saw the men, she said, "You boys okay?"

John nodded, "Did you get to see Leinani?"

"Yes, I went to the school with the children. I asked to see their godmother. The woman kind of give me hard time, but I beg 'Children want to see god-mother.' Lady feel sorry, get Leinani."

"What did she say?" John asked, eagerness in his voice, his heart tripping faster.

"She say, 'Father wants me to marry a rich man. I don't know.'"

"Anything else?" John interrupted, unable to contain his desire.

"Yes, she asks me to tell you to meet her tomorrow at the Makanani place. Even though watched she will try to slip away from school and meet you about four o'clock."

"I'll be there."

Fifty-Five

Rapping at a window roused Grant. Heavy rain that pelted the panes moderated as wind blew the water-filled clouds into the hills. Lanterns barely brushed away the darkness in his office. In this dim light, Grant peered through the opaque glass seeking to discover this nocturnal intruder. "Why not go to the front door," he groused, then remembered it was locked.

Grant went to the sash and pushed the window open. Leaves outside dripped water, and rain on the window frame soaked his coat sleeves. "Damn it man, why are you standing outside?" he asked, spotting the Portuguese huddled against the wall. "Did you get the boy?"

"I had to see you, but I didn't want to come to the front," Gonzalez said, fumbling with the Winchester.

"Give me that gun. How dare you get it wet?" Grant seized the rifle, took a cloth from the shelf and wiped the stock, barrel, and firing chamber.

"You've been shooting. I can smell it. Did you get the boy?"

"Maybe, I'm not sure. I know I hit something, but it was a long ways away. I couldn't find out. Too many people at the Chinaman's place."

"The kid went back to the restaurant?"

"Yeah, one of my spies tipped me off. I had him in my sights, but this gun is new…"

"You missed him. I told you squeeze the trigger slow. Aim low, the gun kicks up when it fires."

"Not enough ammunition to practice with. You only gave me five bullets. I need more to finish the job."

"You used them all! Missed five times? Ammunition is hard to come by, can't find it in Hawaii. Got ten rounds when I bought the gun. That's all. You get somebody back to the restaurant. Find out if the kid is dead. I'll check around. Get back here by noon tomorrow."

Grant watched the Portuguese leave. "Stupid fool." But what choice did he have? His henchman already knew too much. Besides, he argued silently with himself, he's the only one that would commit murder for me.

"I told him I would get rid of him if he failed," Grant said to an empty room. He shrugged knowing he had no one else to turn to. He decided to head home and speak to Sheila. He would send her to the school to make sure Leinani did not have unwanted visitors.

The next morning Grant sucked on his cheroot, blowing smoke out in a wide cloud that swirled about his head and filled his inner office with a pungent aroma. The tobacco calmed his nerves. He needed his wits sharp to engage in the most delicate negotiation of his career.

"Mr. Kingsley, may I offer you a cigar? It's made of the finest tobacco from the southern states of America."

Sitting across from Grant, the young factor said, "It would please me immensely. Please call me James or Jim. Let's have less formality between us since I trust we may soon be family."

Not wanting to appear overly eager, Grant asked, "You've made your money through lending to businesses?"

"Yes. My father garnered a fortune in San Francisco helping miners finance their gold operations. He taught me the business. I wanted to make my own way in life. He gave me a stake. I saw opportunity in Hawai'i with all these start-up plantations so I came here," Kingsley said, inhaling as he studied the street outside. "Honolulu has changed. It's a thriving little metropolis and mark my words, we will both get rich in sugar."

Grant sighed, watching that he did not place his burning cigar on the beautiful red leather armrest of his chair. "I don't know about that. Sugar profits were up during the American Civil War, made a lot of money. The war's over and the southern states are producing sugar again. Things are looking bleak for the industry. The two-and-a-half cent duty tax charged by the United States is eating up our profits. I'm having some trouble meeting my obligations to creditors like you. But let's not dwell on my problems. You wanted to speak to me about Leinani."

A broad smile spread over Kingsley's face. "Yes. With your permission I propose to ask for her hand in marriage. It would make me the happiest of men if she accepted."

"She is not yet eighteen and will not finish her schooling until the end of this semester."

"I want to ask her now and secure her acceptance. We can be married in the late summer when she has reached her eighteenth year."

"You are moving rather quickly."

"Your daughter is the most beautiful woman I have ever seen. Every time I am with her I am hypnotized. Those eyes, delicate features, and slender figure are enough to drive men wild. I want to be the first to love her."

Grant joined in Kingsley's smile. He realized that the man had taken the hook, now he would set it so there could be no escape. "I agree she is a special person. I already know of other suitors. But I could be persuaded to use my influence with her to bend her in your direction."

"I would be most grateful if you did. You say there are others. Can you assure me that if we married, I would be her first love?"

Aha, Grant thought, here is the clincher to making a deal. "I have made certain that she is a virgin. She will wear white at her wedding and on her honeymoon night you will find her as clean as new drawn milk. You will be the first and only man to ever love her."

"Then I have your consent?"

Grant paused, savoring the conquest. He thought over how he should play his request. As the moments passed he saw the eagerness fading in Kingsley's face. "My dear sir, we owe you so much for your past assistance. But as a father with an only daughter I must be certain that she is well cared for."

"I assure you that I will love her and care for her with all I have."

"That is very noble of you. Of course you may have my consent, and I will do all in my power to persuade my daughter to accept your proposal. I do have a small trifle to ask of you."

"Sir, you have made me the happiest of men. How may I be of service to you?"

"I do have a small loan with your company..."

"I see. You are squeezed for money. I will be pleased to partner with you in your ventures and let me add that you need not worry about what you owe me."

"I didn't expect such generosity, but since we will soon be related by marriage I accept your offers. Give some thought to the new sugar plantation in Kilauea, Kauai. It may be a good investment."

Robert Grant blew out a thick cloud of smoke, then filled his lungs with more. He watched Kingsley leave, contented with what he had achieved. By brokering a marriage he saved himself from financial ruin.

Elated by his success he kept busy in his office waiting for his wife to return from the school. He counted his money over and over again, realizing that Kingsley's forgiveness of his loan and the promise of a partnership would aid him in his grand schemes. His Kahului enterprise proceeded well, but Wahiawa Sugar lagged in production and profits.

Deep in thought he did not hear Sheila entering his office. He learned of her presence when she announced, "Do you know what that trollop daughter of yours is doing? She is making an assignation with a Hawaiian boy today."

"What!" Grant said the vehemence in his voice reflecting the anger he felt for this disruption of his plans.

"Leinani had a visitor yesterday, a fat lady with two children. Mistress Staley allowed your daughter to speak with them. To be on the safe side she eavesdropped on the conversation. Leinani is meeting with this John, whatever his name is, at the Makanani compound today at four o'clock."

"Did she find out the reason for the meeting?" Grant said, desperation evident in his voice.

"To talk about marriage and what she should do. Staley thinks that Leinani may be in love with this John. She is not certain on this, but their meeting today could be decisive on whether she accepts Kingsley or not."

"Staley said the meeting is at four o'clock at the Makanani compound, correct?"

"Yes."

"Then I will deal with it. She must marry Kingsley or we will be financially ruined."

Grant watched his wife leave. He played with his moustache, retrieved some wax from a drawer, lubricating both ends of the hair crossing over his lips. Sheila's information had been devastating. Where is that damn Portuguese?

In a few moments his clerk opened the inner door announcing, "Mr. Gonzalez to see you."

"Let him in." Grant reached into the case on his desk, lit a cigar, sucked in, and watched it glow. Gonzalez entered freshly shaven. His usually unruly hair, cut and slicked down. The sides along the skull were short with the sideburns long and thin. A black moustache, like a smudge of coal tar, hid the dip below his nose.

"You seem happy."

"A glorious day, no rain."

"It is not happy for me. I learned that a battering of two people occurred in Chinatown. They are in the hospital, beaten by a club or a rifle by a bearded Caucasian with a mound of unruly hair on his head. The word on the street is that the man used a yellowish gun," Grant said, watching for Gonzalez's reaction.

The Portuguese dropped his eyes. He shuffled his feet. "In doing a job there is sometimes collateral damage."

"Oh, yes, and there is a lawyer in the hospital beaten by a Caucasian fitting the same description."

"You told me to check the papers, find the kid's lawyer. He wouldn't talk friendly-like. I hit him a few times. He wouldn't talk. I meant to put him away, but some people interfered and drove me out."

Blowing smoke like a steam engine pulling a heavy load, Grant said, "And I know you are going to tell me that the kid is not dead."

Gonzalez paused, his eyes glancing around the room, finally resting on the floor. "He's still alive."

Grant flung his cigar into a trash can. "Tarnation, you failed again. But you have one last chance to redeem yourself. My daughter's made a date with that kid at the Makanani home. He's to be there at four o'clock. Only way to go is by the Waikiki Road. You get out there and finish him. Here are three bullets. I'll delay the girl. I won't stop her from getting there otherwise she will get suspicious. Bushwhack him on the roadway. Where, is your choice. Get rid of the body. Make sure no one can find it."

Grant placed the Winchester into a brown box. "I don't want people to see you leaving my office with this gun. Keep it undercover until you need it. This is your last chance to rid me of that boy. When you do, the reward money will be yours."

Fifty-Six

John used a devious route of back alleys and trash-filled pathways to work his way to the hospital. He needed to visit his beaten attorney, but somewhere in Honolulu a sniper lay hidden, seeking to shoot him. The man was invisible. His mystery weapon could kill from unbelievable distances. Avoid the open areas, John thought. Use all the cover you can find.

At a street bordering the medical treatment center John paused. He must cross a long stretch of open ground. He searched the area, seeking vantage points where a killer might hide and get a clear shot. How far must he look? Militia training had taught him that beyond a hundred feet muzzle loaders were ineffective. But this new gun had put a hole in his hat from hundreds of yards away.

Hyperventilating, he left his shelter racing zigzag across the road. Startled pedestrians stared at his odd movements. For their safety, John did his best to keep away from them. With a burst of speed he raced into the portico of the hospital and sheltered behind one of the Grecian columns that kept the roof upright.

Guy can't shoot through walls, John thought as he burst through the doors of the hospital, his entry making a loud clatter. A startled receptionist whispered, "Sir, we expect visitors to come in quietly and respect our patients' need for peaceful solicitude."

"Sorry, sorry," John said. "Some guy's trying to sho…" He stopped realizing his loud voice frightened the woman in front of him. With an effort he calmed his gasping and asked, "Where is Joshua Kanakoa?"

"Down the hallway, third door to your right. In the future please be respectful of our need for quiet."

John apologized once again, noting that people waiting in the reception area stared at him as if he had brought a disease through the door. One person put a finger to his lips. John thought to mimic a gun to his head, but decided better of it and walked carefully down the hallway.

When he found Joshua he saw his friend lying on a white-sheeted bed with a splint keeping his arm rigid and a wide bandage circling his head. One eye was shut, the other ringed with black.

"You fall out of bed," John quipped.

"No, a friend of yours thought I needed a makeover."

"I'm sorry. Just thought I'd share some humor with you. What happened?"

"A man with mounds of hair on his face and head wanted to know where you lived…"

"So that's how he found me."

Joshua grimaced, "I told him nothing."

Too late John realized his error. He saw the pain in his attorney's face, his one good eye moving away from him. "I'm an ignorant child. A friend would not betray a friend. Forgive me."

Joshua shifted. He winced when he turned his face to stare directly at John. "It is said that from the mouth of babes come foolish words. I'm sure there's a reason for your sudden outburst. Tell me what happened."

Taking a chair and speaking low, for there were others in the room, John related the events of the previous day. Once finished, he waited.

Joshua had his good eye closed. He appeared to be asleep. I talked too long, John thought. He rose from his chair preparing to leave.

"Don't go yet," his injured friend said. "I'm thinking. I didn't tell the man who attacked me two days ago anything. Before he could do more damage my neighbors came to the rescue and he ran away. Why attack me? Because I've been checking in the patent office regarding your Kahului property, Grant learned of it. He sent his hired goon to beat me to find you. But this bullyboy got nothing from me. He located you through spies."

"Spies? Like people peeping through keyholes or peering through a window? That's crazy."

"Please understand John, you are a dangerous person who is in the middle of the biggest growing economy in Hawaii. Men like Grant are rich because of it, and you are trying to keep a piece of his cake. He's worried. He wants you dead."

"What can I do? Go to the sheriff?"

"Police won't help. He's probably paid them off anyway. Besides, we have no evidence against him just speculation. Be careful. Maybe go to another island."

"That's Kalakaua's advice. I don't like running, but that weapon the man's got scares me. I never saw the shooter. He fired three shots in a few seconds. I can't fight somebody who is invisible and throws bullets at you like darts."

"Lay low or get out of town," Joshua's voice trailed off. "Let me rest."

John said goodbye and went to the portico. He searched the area outside for sniper spots hundreds of yards away. Unsure of what to look for, he ran zigzag from the building, across the street, and into an alley.

Hidden in the dimness of the small side road, John checked his pouch. It contained six round stones and a sling. He loosened his strangling cord from his waist, snapping it several times to test its strength. Rubbing a hand over the small club that hung by his side he felt satisfied there were no cracks. He didn't have a clock. Time was measured by the position of the sun. Better move on, he thought, it will take me more than an hour to get to the Makanani compound.

Running through Honolulu John made his way to the Waikiki Road. He sped onto the hard-packed earth moving right, left or left to right in a pattern he hoped would fool a shooter. He avoided people, and they avoided him. His gait appeared erratic like a man drunk with alcohol.

Passing Punchbowl Crater the terrain changed to country rural. Large bushes of weeds grew along the roadway and up to the low, round hill. Shacks of grass were scattered in haphazard fashion along where he ran. Hawaiians toiling in the soil or preparing food looked at him with vacant eyes, some raising a hand in half-hearted waves. Soon he came to stands of trees and ponds of water. Behind him the sun spun toward its descent. Worn by his long run John thought that a shooter in front of him would be blinded by the bright rays. He slowed to a walk.

At a slight bend in the road, he saw a familiar copse of coco trees. To his right lay the taro patches of Moiliili. He would soon see what had once been his home.

A place where he lived with Leinani. He felt sudden warmth as he thought of her, a woman like no other that he had ever known. Excitement rose within him as he anticipated their meeting. He would ask her to marry. She wouldn't say no. Why else had she sought this tryst?

In the distance, rising majestic above the trees, towered Diamond Head. Its peak, shaped like the fin of the tuna, spearing into the sky. His heart pounded faster as he recalled that moment when they had stood alone at the top of the volcano, the wind forcing their bodies together.

Fifty-Seven

Hot metal plowed into John's side, twisting his body, staggering him. The whine of the bullet clapped his ears. Instinctively he went to the ground, rolled, and slid over the embankment into a muddy field of green leaves. His hat lay on the roadway too far for him to reach. John peered above the berm's edge, searching.

Yards away, in the copse, he saw a figure running to a horse. What a fool he had been. It was an ideal place for a sniper to hide. Why hadn't he seen the horse? His carelessness cost him the sharp pain that pulsed near his stomach.

With his fingers he found the wound. Blood flowed freely from it. How stop it? He did not know. The man mounted. If he stayed in the mud he would die.

John rose to a crouch. He plodded into the goo of wet earth heading for a causeway that separated fields. Mud clung to his legs. A cry came from afar, "I'm going to get you kanaka-boy." He heard the click clack of shod hooves striking stone.

"Move," he said willing his feet to pull his body through the mud. John felt he was in a nightmare being chased by the dead, unable to go forward. Sounds like the sucking of a child on a nearly empty glass of milk came from the water-filled earth, as his feet, calves, thighs strained to pull him through the soft dirt. The jangling of harness, the snorting of a straining animal, forced the realization that his enemy would be on him before he could free himself from the field.

John hurled himself forward into the water, using legs and hands to claw through the mud. A farmer working his hoeing stick in the soft dirt yelled, "Out, out."

Behind him a horse stopped its gallop. He dared not pause to look. Was a man rising in his saddle, aiming his gun, and taking one last deadly shot?

The sharp crack of a bullet did not come to his ears, only the sounds of stomping, snorting, and the neighing of an animal. John did not look, concentrating on his escape from the slime.

He reached a causeway, crawled onto it, glanced back. A man leaped from his balking animal and pulled something from the saddle. Sliding into another taro field, bending low, John plodded along the narrow earth divider heading for another bank. He heard someone call, "Damn you. I'm going to get you."

"Gonzalez," John said. Joshua's words rang in his ears, "Grant wants you killed." He needed to find a way to fight back, but his few weapons were useless against a gun that could shoot far and fire forever. All around him lay fields of water, slender green stalks sprouting from the mud. He had nowhere to hide. He needed to find shelter, tend to his wound, and plan.

He reached the far bank of a third field. John draped over its edge, plunging into a pond. He took some moments to wash away the mud that clung to him, his hand movements creating pain at his side. Blood still seeped from the wound, but its flow had slowed. He wondered how much he could lose before he went to sleep forever.

He kicked and stroked through the still water. He glimpsed Gonzalez trotting along the edge of the fields. John knew that he would find the path, the bridge, and soon be upon him.

His hands touched oily green stalks. He grasped them, pulling himself into the reeds. He searched for the hidden bank where ducks lay their eggs. An animal hissed. The sound drew him deeper into the slender grass. Hooves pounded on hard earth. Gonzalez was coming.

Rock brushed his hand. He reached into the softness of a shallow bank and pulled himself from the water. Ducks scrambled away, complaining of his intrusion. He spoke soothingly to quiet their hissing but without success. Would their noise draw the Portuguese to him? He knew if they flew he would be found. The reeds prevent their flight. But as I crawl through them they sway, marking my path. Should I just stop and hide?

He broke free of the tall grass. Ahead lay a grove of kiawe trees, the ground beneath them littered with branches and twigs. He stopped to tear his shirt to bind the wound at his side. He wrapped his strangling cord around his makeshift bandage. The throbbing of the cut flesh lessened. From his right he heard the jabbering of a Chinese, "What you do here? Come steal duck? I fix you." He came at John with a rake.

"Not a thief. Bad man is trying to kill me. Help me."

"You go away. I hit you."

Sounds of a pursuit grew nearer. It made no sense to struggle with an innocent man. John hobbled toward the kiawes. A whip cracked. A howl.

"You see the kanaka-boy," Gonzalez yelled.

Gibbering Chinese words answered him.

John smiled as he hurried toward the low growing thorn forest. He knew the farmer was saying, "I know nothing you white shit."

He had very little time to find cover. He hobbled over rock-strewn ground scurrying into a sparse kiawe grove. Pain stabbed his side. Low-growing trees with branches of sharp thorns cut into his skin. The ground sloped up. John realized he ran at the base of Diamond Head, the once black sides of the five-hundred-thousand-year old volcano worn dirty brown by wind and rain.

He recalled instructions from his militia officer, "In combat, always seek the high ground." He remembered his battle with Shaw at Waianae beach. Rocks thrown from low hills had forced the whalers to flee. John searched for the trail up the volcano. Behind him he heard curses. He hoped the low-growing kiawe slowed his enemy. Maybe force him from his horse. Though the twigs and branches caused pain as they whipped his body, they hid him.

John broke through the grove and spotted the trail. He stumbled to it and climbed. Every piece of ground around him was barren. He was exposed with nowhere to hide.

Something monstrous came through the trees. John's eyes caught movement. Fifty yards below Gonzalez raised his rifle. This is it, he thought. He dropped, squirming into a shallow trough in the trail. A bullet struck rock above him, showering pebbles onto his back. He waited for the killing shot.

Silence except for the scrambling of the Portuguese. John looked. He saw the man with a golden rifle in his hand climbing. His horse wandered away into the forest. Why Gonzalez did not shoot again puzzled him. But he dared not wait to ask. Though exposed, he rose and kept going up. His eyes searched for loose stones.

At the mountain's crest, John found rocks and lobbed them at his enemy straining to climb the hill. A missile struck Gonzalez. He yelled, "I'm going to kill you." He raised his rifle.

John fled from the edge taunting, "You're a fat piece of shit, only brave enough to beat old Chinese. When I get you, I'll roast you in the ground like the pig you are." He picked up rocks and hurled them, then followed the ridge to higher ground.

His side pain eased. Blood no longer dripped from his wound. Moving fast along the path he looked for a place to hide for an ambush. He paused behind a large rock. Gonzalez struggled along the trail below, watching where he climbed. John could see his chest heaving and his pauses to breathe. Clearly the burly man was accustomed to riding a horse while using a whip and club to enforce his orders.

John undid his sling. He selected three stones. Inserting one into a pouch, he whirled the weapon's cords and let fly. It hit the Portuguese. The man staggered but did not fall. He raised his rifle. John dropped a stone into the sling's cradle. For a moment man and youth faced each other.

"Just like that evening in Kahului," John thought. He flung his rock. A sharp report echoed around the bowl of the dead volcano. Searing pain spread through his head. Darkness came.

Fifty-Eight

Blood flooded down the side of John's face. He woke with his head a mass of hurts. Warmth bathed his eyes. He tried to wipe the red liquid from them, his hand slimy from the wound along his skull. Through a curtain of red liquid he barely saw Gonzalez stumble toward him, a hand to his stomach, the other holding a lash and gun. Within a few feet he stopped, raised the rawhide weapon, and whipped it. The strike landed on John's shoulder. It did not sting as that night in the warehouse where he hung by his wrists.

The next blow flicked onto his back, weak and slow. John realized Gonzalez had been hurt by his stones. He wobbled upright. He searched for shelter. A low cave opened into the mountain. He stumbled into it, fumbling for his club.

For a moment he crouched safe within the refuge from the downward striking of the whip. How long could he hide from death in this hole? He had crawled into a trap, cornered like a caged animal. His only hope the darkness within the cave. The muzzle of a rifle poked in.

John went down, pressing into the furthest part of the crevice in the rock. Even if bullets missed they would shatter. The resulting shrapnel or chipped stone could kill him. He squeezed his body into the rock and waited for the weapon to fire.

The gun kept poking. Its barrel glanced off the stone walls.

"I'm coming," Gonzalez said.

A body blocked the dim light at the entrance. Rays from a dying sun glinted from a knife thrusting into the gloom. John moved away from the back wall, his head brushing the roof of the cave. He paused and waited in the darkness, his short club in his hand. Bleeding from his skull hadn't stopped, drops slid down his cheek. Weakness spread over him. He grew dizzy. "Stay awake or die," he muttered.

Again, a knife thrust into the cave. John swung his club. Gonzalez howled, "My hand." The Portuguese backed out. John followed.

Cool breezes swept across the ancient volcano. John filled his lungs with clean air forcing himself to remain awake. Gonzalez stood unsteady a few feet away. He rubbed one hand against the other, his knife on the ground. He picked it up and lurched forward.

John shuffled back, his wounded side protesting his movement. He needed to lie down to sleep. This fight must end soon. "You are a coward, only able to beat old men and children," he taunted.

Gonzalez lunged, his movement slow. John stepped back, his foot finding the edge of the mountain. He had nowhere else to go. The Portuguese smiled. John sucked in air pumping oxygen into his heart, forcing his mind to be clear, his body ready. "You are a pig, an eater of offal. An ugly carrion that feeds only on the weak," John baited his enemy as he watched his feet.

"Dirty swine," Gonzalez said, rushing forward, thrusting his knife hand out.

John stepped to the side and into his enemy. He twisted his hips, seized Gonzalez's arm, pulling him across his turning body. The Portuguese sprawled to the ridge line, his face and shoulders over its edge.

"Help me, help me," Gonzalez screamed as he tried to stem his slide over the hill. His knife bounced down along the side of the mountain, a shower of stones chasing it. His hands grasped for anything that would keep him from plunging to his death.

Despite his hatred, John felt he could not let the man die in this way. He grasped a leg and pulled. His effort slowed the Portuguese's slide. He attempted to seize Gonzalez's belt. His enemy grabbed his foot seeking to yank John over the edge. He hit the man's fingers with his club. Bones cracked. Gonzales tried to rise. His clumsy movements slid him over the edge. Down the side of the crater he cartwheeled, his body, back, and head striking the dead volcano's western side several times.

John staggered to the path, worked his way over the ridge, and slid downward to level ground. His steps slowed as he plodded to the home of Hawaiians whom he knew. John collapsed near their threshold.

Fifty-Nine

Storm clouds blew past Nuuanu onto the mountains of Waianae. Rain which had deluged the valley during the night moderated to a drizzle. In his mansion, Robert Grant sat at the breakfast table studying his daughter. Leinani held her hands folded in her lap, her eyes cast down as if fascinated by the elegant scrolling of the silver service set before her. From an exquisite porcelain pot a maid poured tea into delicate demitasse cups.

"It is settled then. You will marry James Kingsley," Grant said casting a look of triumph toward his wife. The sun, obscured by the heavy rain clouds, flashed over the ridgeline, lighting the alcove where the family took their breakfast. Seated in a wicker chair, Leinani avoided the stare of her father. A tear came to her eye. Inwardly, she cried that John had failed to meet her. She kept her face lowered, fidgeting with the dainty French half-cup ringed along its rim with gold. "The kitchen didn't strain this tea before it was served," she answered.

"Nonsense, the staff knows their duties. There is nothing wrong with the tea," Sheila said, her voice cold and disapproving. Then she moderated her tone, "James Kingsley is quite handsome and very rich. We would welcome him to this household."

"Sheila, don't push the issue. A marriage is not a simple thing. You know that when a choice is finally made it is forever. Leinani has given me her word that she has accepted Kingsley's offer. That is true isn't it?" Grant said, drumming his fingers on the breakfast table.

Leinani raised her face, a small tear trickled down her cheek. "Yes," she whispered.

"Good, then all we need to do is settle on a date. Sheila will plan the wedding. It will be the finest ever in Honolulu. Malia may come, but we will not invite the other Makananis."

"Why not?" Leinani interjected suddenly, thinking of John.

"They are not family. I'm investigating your blood line. You may be related to King Kamehameha. It is not proven yet, but likely. I do not wish your royalty to be tarnished by those who are not."

"My dear young lady," Sheila added her tone sarcastic. "We must make suitable explanations for your parentage. Kingsley knows your story and brushes it aside, but others will gossip. We will make your past intriguing, majestic, and dripping with kings and queens."

Grant gave his wife a quizzical look. "You sound very dramatic. Don't make the tale such a fairy story that none will believe it."

"Trust me Robert, I will keep it modest, but I do not want shame to be visited upon this wedding. It must be without blemish."

"Since we are all agreed on what will be done, it is time for school. I will have a man-servant escort you to Saint Sebastian. Sheila, come to the den where we may talk."

In the coolness of his opulent smoking room, Robert Grant motioned his wife to a comfortable red leather chair and sat opposite her. He paused for several moments considering what to say, then on an impulse stood and began pacing the room.

"Robert whatever is the matter?"

"That kid who has bedeviled us is somewhere at large in Honolulu."

"What are you saying?"

"You recall the young Hawaiian who came to our door looking for my daughter? He even went to her school to find her. He is the one called John that Leinani promised to meet three days ago. I tried to get rid of him but failed."

"I don't understand. Did you attempt to kill him?"

"You know I would not do anything of the sort. But one of my employees, thinking to ingratiate himself with me, took it into his head to eliminate the boy."

"And he didn't do so. Why is that a problem for you?"

"The employee is dead. He was found at the base of Diamond Head bruised and broken, probably from the fall."

"So, he was hiking, failed to mind where he walked, and went over the edge."

"A rifle was found on the rim of the crater. My gun, it had been fired."

Sheila paused for some moments, her eyes flickering over the design of the rug in the room. When she spoke her words were terse. "Your man shot the boy. He fought him. He fell. The boy is alive and will make a complaint. Is that your concern?"

"That sums up the problem. An inquiry before the wedding is embarrassing enough. Worse would be an accusation from this boy, especially if he appeared at the ceremony."

"I see why you did not want the Makanani family at the wedding. We must think of what to do. Are there any reliable men in your employ?"

"Only the one who died."

"There must be others who can help us. I will talk to our house boy. You check with your employees in Waipahu, see who can help find him. Do you have a picture?"

"From the newspaper."

"That will do. You're close to the sheriff, start a rumor that this boy may be a person of interest in the death of your man. Maybe offer a reward. I also have heard that the French Minister is seeking this lad for violating his daughter. Suggest to him swearing out a warrant for rape of a white woman. Once he is caught we will find a way to permanently stop this Hawaiian from interfering."

Astonished by his wife's vehemence, Grant paused in his pacing. He looked at her in a new light. He knew she hated Hawaiians, barely tolerating Leinani because of Kingsley and the money he could provide the family by the marriage. "You are willing to eliminate this boy?"

"If the choice is preserving our wealth or the life of this Hawaiian then for me preservation is paramount."

Sixty

He woke with a fever, his head stitched and bandaged, his side tender from the probing that had drawn out the bullet. He barely remembered the journey to Kalia and the medical care.

Mahelani sat by his side placing wet cloth on his forehead. When his eyes came open she shrieked, "John is up," and ran outside.

Haku Alapai came in with his wife. "Water," John asked. Mahealani poured some into a cup and fed him.

"Why isn't she in school?" John asked, embarrassed by her attention.

Tears welled in the teenager's eyes, and John realized that he had hurt her.

"Once you were brought in by the family living below Diamond Head, she would not leave your side," Haku said.

"I'm sorry."

The girl smiled, nuzzling her face into his chest.

Haku Alapai said, "A letter came for you delivered by your Chinese friend. He said to tell you sheriff asking for you. John, our family has decided to leave for Kaua'i. Join us."

Mahealani seized the letter. "Please come."

His heart tripping like a hammer pounding onto an anvil, John tried to get his letter, but the girl refused to release her hold upon it.

"Mahealani, let the man have his mail," Haku scolded his voice harsh.

Reluctantly, she let it go and stepped away.

John knew the letter came from Leinani. He asked for privacy. Mahealani would not move, but Haku took her hand, and led her away.

An annoying fly flew into the shack, its buzzing sounds making his head throb. John waved it away. He unfolded Leinani's letter.

Dear John,

I waited for you at Malia's. You did not come. I thought you might contact me the next day. But I did not hear from you. You have been like a brother to me. Your wisdom and opinion I treasure very much. I needed your help and advice on a matter of great importance. Only you could have made a difference in my decision. I consulted with Malia. She told me my mother would have approved of what I have been offered. My father has urged upon me a favorable answer to this offer.

Today, I have conveyed my acceptance of James Kingsley's proposal of marriage. He is a handsome gentleman and is generous and kind, especially to Malia. He has given her his cottage to live in.

Let me mention that Maria has been quite ill and begs to see you. You should not visit her. Her father threatens to do you harm. I can only speculate what may have caused such trouble for the poor girl.

With fondness, I wish you all the best in your future life.

Leinani

Anguish pierced him. It took all his strength to control the tears that threatened to flow. It could not be. Leinani would marry another. If only she knew what prevented him from seeing her. Couldn't she have waited? John crumpled the note and tore it to shreds.

While he pondered what to do, a messenger came with a summons from Colonel Kalakaua to come to his home at once. "What now?" John wondered. He felt certain that a black cloud hovered over him. He hobbled outside and found Haku Alapai. "How long have I been in bed?" he asked.

"Three, four days."

"Kakakaua wants to see me. Your cart with the donkey, may I borrow it?"

Haku thought for some moments then said, "Our family is packing for Kauai. I didn't say it earlier, but our *ohana* lost the lease for growing taro. Chinese farmers outbid us, so that's that. We sold everything we can't take. The buyer of the donkey and cart will be here this evening."

"Can I use it until then?"

"You're sick."

"I can manage."

Haku scratched his head, cracked his knuckles. "Kauai has very few people living on the north end, and there's plenty of rich land and water. It's good for growing taro. John, come with us. We need a strong man like you to work with the family. Besides, my daughter loves you."

John ran both palms over his hair, his mouth dry, his thoughts swirling with conflicts and the ache from his head. Was Leinani gone forever? Would Maria's father charge him with rape? Gonzales is dead, but would Grant find a way to blame him for his death? Would he continue to pursue him until he also died? With Haku Alapai and his family he might find a happy life. What should he do?

"After I see the colonel, I'll give you an answer. May I use it?"

Haku sighed. His bid for John to commit had failed. "Yes," he answered.

John left for Waikiki, the donkey a slow but sure walker. He thought of his troubles and what he could do. Is running away his only option? With a multitude of issues swirling in his head, he arrived at the Colonel's home.

Kalakaua opened the door his smile of welcome fading when he saw John. "What happened?"

"May I sit? I'm worn from the ride."

"Yes. Come and rest. Tell me your story."

John pondered his answer for many moments before saying, "A rich sugar planter wants me dead. He sent his hired man to ambush me. I got shot twice. We had a fight and that's it."

"I won't pry further into your affairs. First, I want to thank you for saving my life from crazy Jonah. How on earth did you learn that flip?"

John smiled. "I taught it to myself after watching Chinese acrobats perform a backward somersault. It takes a lot of practice. I spent hours perfecting the maneuver."

"Well, you kicked the hell out of that preacher," the colonel said, pouring two glasses of guava juice and handing one to John. "I never had a chance to tell you how sorry I was about Chin Sing. Poor fellow, he did not have a decent life."

John nodded, lost for a moment in reminiscence about the Chinese man that he had known for a short time. Instead of coming to a paradise he found hell in Hawaii. Death was salvation for him.

"Let's get to the reason you're here. You made an enemy of Monsieur Francois. It's far worse than I thought. He's sworn out a warrant for your arrest, for raping his daughter."

John felt his innards spasm. He remained silent fearing that if spoke he would erupt.

"I know you would never do such a thing. But this charge is serious. You could hang for raping a white woman. To be honest, a Hawaiian doesn't stand a chance against a white man's word. There is, however, some hope. His daughter is very much in love with you. I am told that she will not cooperate with her father. Nevertheless, I think it best that you leave Honolulu, at least until they return to France."

John studied the Colonel's face, saw in his eyes sincerity and concern for his welfare. With a shrug, he confessed, "He has cause to be angry with me. Should I seek him out, apologize, even offer to marry his daughter?" John said this with mixed emotions. He loved Leinani, but he thought the Christian thing to do was to make amends for his indiscretion.

"You are an honorable young man, but I will tell you that Francois will never accept you. With your dark skin, native blood, and no means to care for his daughter he will reject your offer and want you dead. Let him return to France with Maria. There he can make a suitable marriage for her. French men love women who have had a little indiscretion while they are young. At least this is what I am told. Get away from here. It is the wisest thing to do."

John thanked the colonel and left. Despite his weariness, he decided to visit Malia.

"Aloha John, you big guy now, no more boy," Malia laughed as she offered a cheek to be kissed. Stepping back, she said, "What happened, you all bust up."

"I had a fight with someone who didn't like me. That's why I never made it to your house to see Leinani."

"Too bad. Come sit over here," Malia, pointed to a kitchen table. "What you think of this place? Nice huh? No more dirt floors, no more fleas, flies, mosquitoes, no more. I have screens on windows." She pointed proudly to the latest home innovation in Hawaii. "This guy Kingsley, good to me, good for Leinani."

John sucked in his breath, Malia's words pounding into his heart. She had touched on a subject that he dreaded, yet he knew the reason he came was to find out why Malia wanted Leinani to marry that man. His jaw tense, he muttered, "What do you mean?"

Malia looked into his eyes and the humor in her face slipped away. "It's hard to talk about this thing. For long time, I know you care for Leinani. But you are a good man. You think she is your cousin, and you know that missionary people say no to that kind of love, so you protect her, not damage her." Malia paused in her praise, as if hoping that John would understand what she was about to say. "John, I make promise to Leinani's mother to take care of baby. I make promise to mother to keep Leinani away from bad men who only like fool around. I promise to keep her for man of great power."

John sat straight in his chair, the sudden movement sending pain through him. "Auntie, I'm a special man. I have strength in my arms, legs, and body."

"You have special gifts. But think, you strong, but what else you got? Hawaiian man got no land, he no can make money, he only work like slave, and for what? What he got? Nothing." She examined her hands, as if unwilling to look John in the eye. "I don't like say this, but the white guy got the money, the land, and the power."

What could he answer? That he was a good worker, a good fisherman. That he could grow taro and build canoes. But there was the other side as well. He had no job, no house, and was a hunted man. Malia is right, he had nothing. He wanted to explain how the work he had on the docks was lost due to the trial, that he could get another job, and he still had his canoe. John knew that none of these explanations were convincing.

"I know you try hard. But you no can give Leinani what she gets from Mr. Grant, or Kingsley. Nephew, love is wonderful today, but tomorrow all worthless, all nothing."

A hard reality seeped into him, damping his burning emotions. "You're saying money talks, not love."

"No, I say love dies if there is no future for the family's children."

"Where is Leinani?"

"I tell her keep away. I tell her I will talk to you."

John felt a terrible weight pressing against his heart. "Give her my aloha. Tell her I will always be her cousin. Here is the last of the reward money. Would you give it to the Catholic priest at the Church of the Sacred Heart?" John bent down and kissed Malia's brow. He saw tears in her eyes. He turned and fled from her cottage.

He arrived at Kalia to find a very nervous friend. "The sheriff is coming for you," Haku said. "I got someone watching the road. Your canoe is packed, ready to go. You come with the family?"

It was spoken as a question, but John knew that his friend was begging. "Sure, I'll come. Who's coming with me?"

"I am," Mahealani screamed. "And my brother, sisters, cousin and Momma, they're coming too."

John thought that having Mahealani around might not be so bad. He hobbled to his double canoe, bobbing on the ocean swells of Waikiki Beach. A quick check told him that all his earthly belongings were on board. Seizing his paddle, he took the steersman's position.

Mahealani pulled herself out of the water into the canoe and moved her body against his. Six members of the Alapai family joined them.

"Paddle," John called, and six shafts hit the sea. The vessel surged through the low waves, cutting a trough in its wake. Soon the canoe and its crew were over the fringing white foam of the barrier reef and into deeper water.

A good distance from shore, John looked back. On the beach, a man on horseback spoke to Haku Alapai. Gestures passed between them, with Haku shaking his head and pointing inland, beyond Diamond Head.

They were well out to sea, with the world darkening about them, when John finally went to the center pole and raised the red, crab claw sail. Wind flapped the fiber for some time until it finally became taut, puffing up as it caught the power of a rising breeze. John returned to his seat behind Mahealani and folded her into his arms. "I think there will be a full moon tonight."

She turned, her lovely face lifted toward his. Their breath washed together.

About the Author

Bill Fernandez, half Native Hawaiian, was born and raised on the small island of Kauai in the Hawaiian Islands. An alumnus of Kamehameha Schools, Stanford University, and Stanford Law School, he practiced law in Sunnyvale, CA, home to the future Silicon Valley, and served on the Sunnyvale City Council and as mayor. Bill served twenty years as judge of the Santa Clara County Courts. Retired, he and his wife, Judith, live on Kauai where he writes memoirs and novels, and gives author talks. He served as president and member of the board of the Kauai Historical Society, on the board of a social service agency, Hale Opio, and is a member of the State of Hawaii Juvenile Justice State Advisory Commission.

Bill and his wife Judith enjoy the ocean breezes sitting on the lanai of the old plantation cottage Bill inherited from his mother. They are avid travelers and opera lovers.

Judge William J. Fernandez,
Santa Clara County Court, California

www.kauaibillfernandez.com   fcb: Bill Fernandez Hawaiian Author